the
DRAGON'S
LEGACY

DEBORAH A. WOLF

the
DRAGON'S
LEGACY

TITAN BOOKS

THE DRAGON'S LEGACY
Paperback edition ISBN: 9781785651083
Electronic edition ISBN: 9781785651090

Published by Titan Books
A division of Titan Publishing Group Ltd
144 Southwark St, London SE1 0UP

First paperback edition: March 2018
2 4 6 8 10 9 7 5 3 1

A CIP catalogue record for this title is available from the British Library.

Printed and bound in the United States

This book is dedicated, with great love, to my children—

P E T E ,   R O W A N ,   E L I S S A ,   A N D   K E I R A

—who made me a better person.

THE PEOPLE

From the Notes of Loremaster Rathfaust

Aadl (Istaz Aadl): Zeerani youthmaster

Aaraf (Loreman Aaraf): Zeerani storyteller and bard

Aasah (Aasah sud Layl): priest of Illindra, shadowmancer and advisor to Ka Atu

Adalia: Warrior of the Mah'zula

Ani (Istaza Ani): Youthmistress of the Zeerai prides; also the last known Dzirani

Annila (Annila Ja'Akari): young Zeerani warrior, peer to Sulema and Hannei

Annubasta (*see* Hafsa Azeina)

Ashta: journeyman mantist studying under Loremaster Rothfaust

Askander (Askander Ja'Akarinu'i): First Warden of the Zeeranim

Bardu: Daechen prince

Bashaba: former concubine of Ka Atu; mother to Pythos (deceased), Mattu, and Matteira

Basta (cat): kima'a to Hafsa Azeina

Bellanca (Matreon Bellanca): Matreon of Atualon

Belzaleel the Liar: an ancient, wicked spirit, currently trapped in a dragonglass blade

Boraz (Boraz Ja'Sajani): Zeerani warder

Bretan Mer (Bretan Mer ne Ninianne il Mer): salt merchant and liaison from Salar Merraj to Atualon; son of Ninianne il Mer

Brygus: member of the Draiksguard

Char (Charon): Guardian of Eid Kalmut

Daeshen Baichen Pao: the first Daemon Emperor, ruler of Sindan

Daeshen Tiachu: the current Daemon Emperor, ruler of Sindan

Daru (Cub-in-Shadows): a young Zeerani orphan; apprenticed to Hafsa Azeina

Davidian: Imperator General of Atualon

Davvus: a legendary king of Men

Dennet: a daughter of Nurati

Devranae: legendary daughter of Zula Din; abducted by Davvus, king of Men

Deyenna: a young woman who seeks to escape Atualon

Douwa: bathhouse attendant in Atualon

Duadl (Duadl Ja'Sajani): Zeerani warden and churra-master

Eleni: attendant at the Grinning Mymyc in Bayyid Eidtein

Ezio: Atualonian Master of Coin

Fairussa (Fairussa Ja'Akari): warrior of the Zeeranim

Gai Khan: Daechen prince

Gavria (Gavria Ja'Akari): Zeerani warrior

Ginna: Atualonian maidservant

Hadid (Mastersmith Hadid): Zeerani mastersmith

Hafsa Azeina: foremost dreamshifter of Zeeranim; mother of Sulema, and the queen consort of Atualon. Rarely: Annubasta.

Hannei: a young Ja'Akari warrior; best friend to Sulema

Hapuata (Istaza Hapuata): Zeerani mentor to Theotara Ja'Akari

Hekates: Draiksguard of Atualon

Hyang: village boy from Bizhan

Ippos: Stablemaster of Atualon

Isara (Isara Ja'Akari): Zeerani warrior

Ishtaset: Mah'zula warrior

Ismai: younger son of Nurati, First Mother among the Zeeranim

Istaza Ani (*see* Ani)

Jamandae: (deceased) youngest concubine of Serpentus, deposed Dragon King of Atualon

Jasin (Ja'Atanili'I Jasin): Zeerani youth and would-be warden

Jian (Daechen Jian, Tsun-ju Jian): young Daechen prince; a Sindanese daeborn youth

Jinchua (fennec): kima'a to Sulema

Jorah: Zeerani craftsman

Kabila (Kabila Ja'Akari): Zeerani warrior

Kalani: Zeerani maiden

Karkash Dhwani: powerful Daechen prince, advisor to the emperor

Lavanya: Zeerani warrior and peer of Sulema

Leviathus: son of Ka Atu, the Dragon King; born surdus, deaf to the magic of Atualon

Makil: Zeerani warden

Mardoni: Daechen prince

Marisa: maidservant in Atualon

Mariza: Renegade Ja'Akari. Once banished and declared Kha'Akari, she now rides with the Mah'zula.

Matteira: daughter of Bashaba, a former concubine of Ka Atu. Twin sister to Mattu, and sister to Pythos (deceased).

Mattu (Mattu Halfmask): son of Bashaba, a former concubine of Ka Atu. Twin brother to Matteira, and brother to Pythos.

Naruteo (Daechen Naruteo): Sindanese youth. Daeborn and yearmate to Jian.

Neptara (Umm Neptara): daughter of Nurati

Ninianne il Mer: Lady of the Lake, matriarch of the clans of Salar Merraj, city of the salt merchants; mother of Bretan Mer, Soutan Mer.

Nurati (Umm Nurati): First Mother of the Zeeranim; mother of Tammas, Neptara, Ismai, Dennet, Rudya, and an as-yet unnamed infant daughter

Perri: Sindanese youth; daeborn and yearmate to Jian

Pythos: (deceased) son of Serpentus, deposed Dragon King of
Atualon

Rama (Rama Ja'Sajani): Zeerani warden and horsemaster from
Aish Arak

Rheodus: young Atualonian man, member of Leviathus's
Draiksguard

Rothfaust (Loremaster Rothfaust): loremaster of Atualon, keeper
of tomes and tales

Rudya: daughter of Nurati

Sammai: Zeerani child

Santorus (Master Healer Santorus): Atualonian patreon and
master healer

Sareta (Sareta Ja'Akarinu'i): ranking warrior of the Zeeranim

Saskia (Saskia Ja'Akari): Zeerani warrior and peer of Sulema

Soutan Mer (Soutan Mer ne Ninianne il Mer): son of Ninianne il
Mer

Sulema (Sulema Ja'Akari, Sulema Firehair): Zeerani warrior,
daughter of the dreamshifter Hafsa Azeina and Wyvernus

Sunzi: Daechen prince

Tadeah: (deceased) daughter of Bashaba and Ka Atu

Talilla (Ja'Akari): Zeerani warrior

Talleh: young Zeerani boy

Tammas (Tammas Ja'Sajani): Zeerani warden, eldest son of Nurati

Teppei: Daechen prince

Theotara (Theotara Ja'Akari): honored Ja'Akari

Tiungpei (Tsun-ju Tiungpei): a Sindanese pearl diver who took a
lover from among the Issuq; mother of Jian

Tsa-len: yendaeshi to Naruteo

Umm Nurati (*see* Nurati)

Valri: warrior of the Mah'zula

Wyvernus: Ka Atu, the Dragon King of Atualon
Xienpei: yendaeshi to Jian

Yaela: apprentice to Aasah
Yeshu: Atualonian weaver

Zula Din: trickster/warrior of legend, daughter of the First People

THE LANDS OF THE PEOPLE

From the Notes of Loremaster Rathfaust

ATUALON

The mightiest kingdom in the Near West, Atualon is the seat of Ka Atu, the Dragon King. Fabled to be built on the back of a sleeping dragon, Atualon is the wellspring of a deep and ancient magic.

This magic is known as atulfah, and is comprised of sa and ka, female and male, heart and spirit, the Song of Life. Only those born echovete—able to hear the magical song of creation—have the potential to manipulate this magic, and only an echovete child born and raised to the throne may be trained to wield it.

SINDAN

The Sindanese empire stretches from the pearl-choked waters of Nar Kabdaan in the Middle East, over the ice-tombed peaks of Mutai Gon-yu, to Nar Intihaan in the Far East: End of the Bitter Lands, End of the Great Salt Road, End of the Known World. The story of Sindan stretches far beyond written memory and into the misted memories of the First Men, before the thickening of the Veil. The Daemon Emperor of Sindan rules absolutely from his throne in Khanbul, the Forbidden City, though his thoughts turn ever westward. He is covetous of atulfah, for its power is the only thing greater than his own.

QUARABALA

Once a place of beauty and art, high learning and gentle culture, the Quarabala was scorched clean of life and hope during the Sundering. Few now survive in the dead lands west of the Dibris. Occasionally a story will turn up in the slave-trading town of

Min Yaarif, rumors of wicked beasts and wickeder men driven to desperate acts as they struggle to survive on the Edge of the Quarabala. Even more rarely an Illindrist, a shadowshifting sorcerer, will emerge from the smoking ruins, night-skinned and demon-eyed, leading a trader or three with packs full of the precious red salt and eyes full of waking nightmares.

THE ZEERA

A land of silk and honey, great warriors and greater predators, the Zeera is a vast golden desert and home to the desert prides. Once a proud and prosperous nation, the Zeeranim are now a remnant of their former glory. The Mothers live in mostly empty cities along the banks of the Dibris, the Ja'Sajani take census and record the final days of a dying people, and the Ja'Akari guard the people against enemies within and without the prides. Too few are born, too few survive, and too few are chosen to become Zeeravashani, bonded to the great saber-tusked cats with whom they are allied. The wardens write, the warriors fight, and the Mothers sing lullabies against the coming darkness, but their struggles are like the notes of a flute, lost and forgotten in the coming storm.

TERMS AND PHRASES
OF INTEREST

From the Notes of Loremaster Rathfaust

Aish Kalumm (the City of Mothers): Zeerani river fortress

Akari (Akari Sun Dragon): according to legend, Akari is a draik (a male dragon) who flies across the sky bringing life and light to the world as he seeks to rouse his sleeping mate, Sajani the Earth Dragon

aklashi: a game played while on horseback; it involves a sheep's head and quite a lot of noise

Arachnist: a human mage, who worships and does the bidding of the Araids

Araid: massive, intelligent spiders that live deep in the abandoned cities of Quarabala

Atualon: a western kingdom founded upon the shores of Nar Bedayyan; home to the Dragon Kings

Atukos (City of Dreams, City of the Sleeping Dragon): dragonglass fortress of the Dragon King, named for the living mountain into which it is built

atulfah: sa and ka combined to create the song of creation

Ayyam Binat: a period of time in the spring during which young Zeerani women vie with one another for the sexual favors of men

Baidun Daiel (also known as the Sleepless, or Voiceless): warrior mages who serve Ka Atu

Baizhu: a religious order of Sindanese monks

Bayyid Eidtein: trading town near the mouth of the Dibris, a known den of miscreants and rogues; the southernmost trading post along Atualonian-maintained roads

Beit Usqut: the Youths' Quarter in Aish Kalumm

bintshi: an intelligent flying animal with some natural affinity for psionic manipulation; carnivorous; considered kith

Bohica: patroness divine of soldiers

Bonelord: one of the greater predators, bonelords are massive carnivorous creatures that rely on camouflage, speed, and mind-magic to capture prey

bonesinger: Dzirani medicine man

Bones of Eth: an ill-reputed ruin or monument in the Zeera, formed of a rough circle of tall, twisted pillars of red and black stone

churra (pl. churrim): a hardy desert omnivore prized by the Zeerani as a pack animal, and seen as a suitable mount for outlanders

craftmistress/master: Zeerani women and men who have been trained in and work at their particular craft—blacksmithing, painting, building, weaving, etc.

Dae: a race of magically gifted people who reside in the Twilight Lands

daeborn: of dae descent

daemon: commonly used to describe any wicked thing (also daespawn)

Daechen: half-Dae, half-human Sindanese warrior caste (male)

Daeshen: half-Dae, half-human, member of the Sindanese imperial family

Daezhu: half-Dae, half-human Sindanese ruling class (female)

Delpha (Big Sister): one of two moons; has a twenty-eight-day cycle

Dibris: a river that runs through the Zeera, supporting a wide range of life

Didi (Little Sister): one of two moons; has a fourteen-day cycle

Dragon King: Ka Atu, the monarch of Atualon (currently Wyvernus)

Draiksguard: elite military unit assigned to guard members of the Atualonian royal family

Dreaming Lands: *see* Shehannam

dreamshifter: Zeerani shaman who can move through and manipulate Shehannam

Dzirani: wandering storytellers, healers, and merchants

Dziranim: a member of the Dzirani clan

echovete: one who can hear atulfah

ehuani: Zeerani word meaning "beauty in truth"

Eid Kalish: trading town, a stop on the Great Salt Road, known for its thriving black market and slave trade

Eth: Quarabalese destruction deity, he whose breath creates the darkness between stars

Great Salt Road: trade route that stretches from the Edge of the Quarabala in the west to the easternmost cities of Sindan

Hajra-Khai: Zeerani spring festival

hayatani: a Zeerani girl's first consort

hayyanah: Zeerani couples who are pledged to one another and remain more or less monogamous

herdmistress/master: responsible for the health and well-being of a pride's horses and churrim

Illindra: Quarabalese creation deity, an enormous female spider who hangs the stars in her web of life

Issuq: Twilight Lords and Ladies who have a clan affinity for the sea and can shapeshift into sea-bears

istaza/istaz: youthmistress/master of the Zeerani prides

Ja'Akari: Zeerani warrior, responsible for keeping all the pridelands safe from outside threats

Ja Akari: Zeerani phrase meaning "under the sun"; loosely translates to being completely open and honest, hiding nothing

Ja'Sajani: Zeerani warden, responsible for maintaining order and security within his local territory

Ja Sajani: Zeerani phrase meaning "upon the earth"; loosely translates to being present in the moment

Jehannim: a mythical hellish place of fire and brimstone; also the name of a mountain range west of the river Dibris and east of Quarabala

jiinberry: a water-loving berry that grows along the banks of the Dibris during the flooding season

ka: the male half of atulfah, known as the breath of spirit; it manifests to most as an expanded awareness of one's surroundings

Ka Atu: the Dragon King of Atualon (currently Wyvernus)

Kaapua: a river in Sindan

Kha'Akari: Zeerani warrior who has been exiled from the sight of Akari

Khanbul (the Forbidden City): home of the Sindanese emperor

khutlani: Zeerani word meaning "forbidden"

kima'a: avatar spirit-beast in Shehannam

kin: intelligent creatures descended from the first races and considered relatives of dragons—vash'ai, wyverns, and mymyc are numbered among the kin

kith: term used to describe creatures that are more intelligent than beasts, but lack the awareness of kin or humans

kithren: Zeerani person bound to a vash'ai, and vice versa

Ladies/Lords of Twilight: Dae lords

lashai: modified half-human servants that wait upon the Daechen and yendaeshi

lionsnake: an enormous, venomous, two-legged plumed serpent that lives in the Zeera

the Lonely Road: in Zeerani mythology, the road traveled by the dead

Madraj: an arena and gathering place of the Zeeranim

Mah'zula: a society of Zeeranim who live a purely nomadic life and abide by the ancient ways of the desert

Min Yaarif: trading and slavers' port on the western bank of the Dibris

Mutai Gon-yu (The Mountains that Tamed the Rains): mountain range in Sindan

Mymyc: one of the kin, mymyc live and hunt in packs. From a distance, mymyc strongly resemble black horses.

Nar Bedayyan: a sea to the west of Atualon

Nar Intihaan: a sea to the east of Sindan

Nar Kabdaan: a sea east of the Zeera and west of Sindan

ne Atu: member of the royal family of Atualon

Nian-da: a ten-day-long festival in Sindan. Any child born during this time is assumed to be fathered by a Dae man during Moonstide, and without exception is taken to Khanbul at the age of sixteen.

Nisfi: Zeerani pride

outlanders: term used by the Zeerani to describe people not of the Zeera

parens: heads of the ruling families in Atualon

pride: Zeerani clan. Also used to describe all prides as a single entity.

Quarabala (also known as the Seared Lands): a region so hot that humans live in cities far underground

Quarabalese: of Quarabala

reavers: insectoid humans that have been modified by the Araids; their bite is envenomed

Riharr: Zeerani pride

russet ridgebacks: large (five-pound) spiders that live in underground colonies. Harmless unless they are disturbed. Their eggs are considered a delicacy in the Zeera.

sa: heart of the soul. An expanded sense of empathy and harmony.

Sajani (Sajani Earth Dragon, the Sleeping Dragon): according to legend, Sajani is a diva (a female dragon) who sleeps beneath the crust of the world, waiting for the song of her mate Akari to wake her

Salarians: citizens of the salt-mining city Salar Merraj

Salar Merraj: city of the salt miners built upon the shores of a dead salt lake; the Mer family stronghold

sand-dae: shapes made of wind-driven sand

Shahad: Zeerani pride

Shehannam (the Dreaming Lands): the otherworld, a place of dreams and strange beings

shenu: a board game popular in the Zeera

shofar (pl. shofarot): wind instrument made from the horn of an animal

shofar akibra: a magical instrument fashioned from the horn of the golden ram

shongwei: an intelligent, carnivorous sea creature

Sindan: empire that stretches from Nar Kabdaan in the west to Nar Intihaan in the east

Sindanese: of Sindan

Snafu: patron divine of fuckups

Sundering: cataclysm that took place roughly one thousand years before the events of this story

surdus: deaf to atulfah

Tai Bardan (Mountains of Ice): mountain range in Sindan, east of Khanbul

Tai Damat (Mountains of Blood): mountain range in Sindan on the Great Salt Road, north of Khanbul

tarbok: goat-sized herd animal, plentiful near rivers and oases

touar: head-to-toe outfit worn by the Zeerani wardens: head wrap and veils, calf-length robe, loose trousers, all blue

Twilight Lands: a land at once part of and separated from the world of Men; home of the Dae

usca: a strong alcoholic beverage popular in the Zeera

Uthrak: Zeerani pride

vash'ai: large, intelligent saber-tusked cats. Vash'ai are kin, descended from the first races.

Wild Hunt (also the Hunt): deadly game played by the Huntress, a powerful being who enforces the rules of Shehannam

wyvern: intelligent flying kin

yendaeshi: trainer, mentor, and master to the Daechen and Daezhu

Yosh: name of the wicked spirit or deity that rules Jehannim

youthmistress/master (istaza/istaz): Zeerani adults in charge of guiding and teaching the pride's young people

Zeera: a desert south of the Great Salt Road, known for its singing dunes, hostile environment, and remote barbarian prides

Zeeranim: people of the desert

Zeeravashani: a Zeerani person who has bonded with a vash'ai

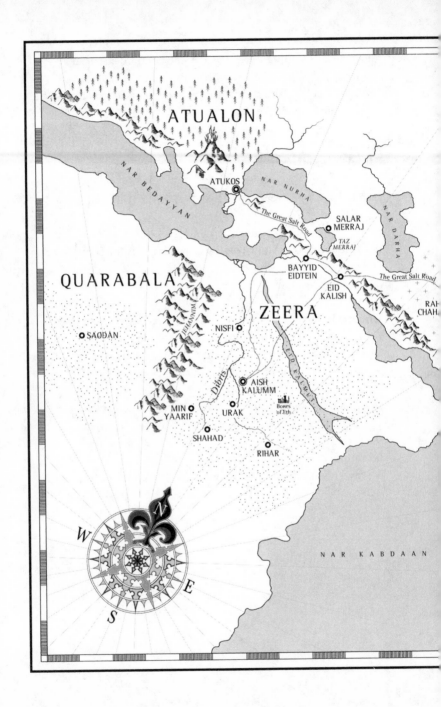

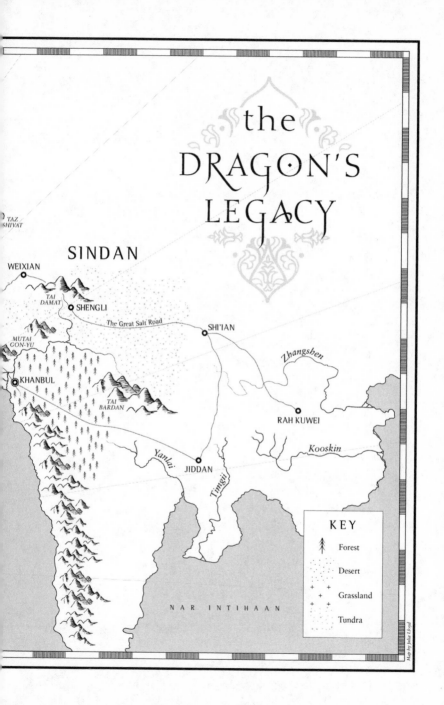

A LONELY ROAD

The wind was born of a shepherd-girl playing her lonely flute. Nimble fingers that had once danced across smooth bone were lost to memory now, sweet young breath was long gone to dust and war and the tattered cloth of memory. But the sunlight was still the same, pouring across the Zeera sweet and rich as mead poured from a pitcher of gold.

Born of song and longing and the magic of young girls, it swept across the soft yellow dunes, rousing them to song, raising an army of wistful little sand-dae that would die before they could become anything. They danced away what time was given to them, and died without regret.

Gusts rattled and knacked through the desiccated branches of a blackthorn, startling a hare so that she dashed from cover and fell to a hawk's talons. The story of their battle was painted in blood, and the hawk rose from her masterpiece, screaming in triumph.

The morning was rank with night's dying, and hare's breath, and the song of silenced girls. Though Theotara was past caring about omens, and though it did not matter this day whether she rode toward the shadows or toward the light or down the throat of a dragon, she caught her breath at the sound of the hawk's scream. This in turn caused her oft-mended left leg to twitch so that her faithful old mare shuffled and stumbled a bit to the east. The old woman shrugged and changed her course.

When all roads lead to death, she supposed, *one might as well ride toward morning.*

As their path changed, so did the wind. It sang to her of death, a song of blood and fire. Zakkia tossed her fine head, sucked in a lungful of air, and let it out again in a long and thoughtful snort. Years past, the war-bred mare would have pranced and danced

3

and fought for her head at the scent of death. Years past, the woman would have laughed and roared a challenge and plunged them both into the heart of whatever trouble lay ahead. It was a wonder either of them had lived so long.

They had drawn close to the Bones of Eth, a place of murder and ambush. Raiders had been known to pass this way, bent on taking captives for the slave markets. Perhaps she might find a few of them nearby, and rid the world of their filth. One last battle under the sun, and then she could fade away like the sand-dae. Theotara smiled, and turned to her true companion, her one love, her breath-and-blood.

Shall we join the dance, my Saffra'ai?

But Saffra'ai was dead. He had gone ahead down the Lonely Road and left her all alone. The grief came crashing down once more, and its weight was staggering. Her soul reached out in vain, like a warrior groping for a severed limb.

Zakkia wandered a bit, head nodding low. The dream-milk tea they had shared would give them three days of false life, and a gentle passage into sleep. This was the second day of their three-day journey… soon they would rest. Theotara and Zakkia had served pride and kin and herd, and none living would breathe a word of reproach if they turned aside from whatever peril lay ahead.

After a hard life, did they not deserve an easy death?

Theotara laughed at the thought and urged her mare on. One might as well bid the stars in the night sky to cease their shining, as well bid the hawk not take the hare, as ask an old warrior to turn her back on danger. Even on the last day of her life.

Especially on the last day of her life.

Mutaani, she thought. *There is beauty in death.* Every warrior mouthed these words, but Theotara had finally come to understand them.

As they drew closer to the Bones, Theotara was not surprised to see carrion birds. She should have seen them earlier, damn her dim eyes. Damn the weakness that trembled in her hand. And damn whatever danger lay ahead if it thought to feed on her stringy carcass. She still had enough teeth to chew her own meat, enough strength to draw a bow and wield her sword. The sands of the Zeera would lie cold and silent before Theotara Ja'Akari was frightened off by a pile of rocks.

Even *this* pile of rocks.

The Bones of Eth was a lonely place, a shadow-stone set in gold. Nestled in the burning sands, it seemed to offer relief from the sun, a place to rest one's weary bones. The traveler might look at the spires of rock and wonder whether there had once been a city here, before the Sundering, perhaps, when this land was cool and verdant. They might wonder why, when the road was so long and respite so fervently desired, travel-weary animals would balk and scream and bolt at the sight of the twisted stone columns. A wise traveler would heed the warnings of her four-legged companions and avoid the Bones altogether.

Yet wise travelers, like old warriors, were rare as rain. The wise stayed home and grew old, while the foolish became travelers, or warriors, and died young.

She drew her sword. Perhaps Saffra'ai was waiting for her beside the Lonely Road. *Soon*, she promised her heart's companion. *Soon*.

The air between the Bones was not simply cool, it was *aware*. The rocks shimmered and danced like a mirage on the horizon, and the ground shuddered at their touch. Theotara urged her unhappy mare between the red-and-black banded pillars of stone that thrust up from the flesh of the world like the tormented legs of a monstrous spider. A chill caressed her spine as she passed through the scant shade. This earth, these rocks, had drunk deep of rage and blood and they were thirsty for more. She could feel death, smell it in the air, hear it in the desert's hot breath as it hissed through the Bones.

Her heart skipped as she heard something besides the *pock-pock-pock* of Zakkia's hooves on stone. A hopeless sound, weak and lost, faint as the last wisp of smoke from a dead man's campfire. The cry of a human child.

Theotara resisted the urge to rush in. More than one of the greater predators could mimic that sound. She closed her eyes and allowed her *ka*, the breath of her spirit, to roll out from her body, prodding and poking at the land around her. She felt the chill regard of the Bones, and the small, warm lives of the carrion birds. She sensed no other humans, no greater predators, nothing that might be a threat to herself.

She opened her eyes again and frowned. Something had happened here, perhaps very recently, but whatever danger there had been had passed them by. Zakkia seemed to agree. Her ears swiveled this way, and that way, and then she reached back to nip at her rider's foot.

Theotara nudged her horse's teeth away and scowled, shading her eyes against the sun as it rose above the Bones of Eth. There, in the farthest and darkest corner of the clearing, was a huddle of painted wagons of the type used by merchants along the Great Salt Road to the north. She brought Zakkia down to a slow walk and as they drew nearer she could see, scattered among the broken wagons, the still and bloated forms of pack animals. One of the carrion birds lit, wings outstretched and screaming with glee. Theotara sheathed her sword. She could hardly do battle with rocks and buzzards.

They had missed the battle, but she could still hear the piteous wails of a human child. There was work to be done. *"If you cannot slay the enemy,"* she had often told the younger warriors, *"then save the living. If you cannot save the living, soothe the dying. Send their spirits off with a drink, a song, and fragrant smoke.*

"And never forget to loot the bodies."

Theotara sighed, lifted a stiff old leg over the back of her stiff old horse, and slid to the ground, grunting at the hot little needles in her knees. She could have done anything she wished with her last three days. She could have ridden down the road to Nar Kabdaan, and let the red petals of a dying sun blossom before them as they shared the last cup of tea. She had always wanted to stand before the sea, to smell the salt air and listen to the waves. She had heard that the sea sang a lovely song. That the water stretched farther than your eyes could see.

It would have been glorious.

The old warrior left her mare to doze in the sunlight and flapped her bony arms at the fat red buzzard that hissed at her and spread his wings. She sucked her teeth and sighed. The buzzard's meal had, until recently, been a brace of churrim, spotted and sleek and fit. Stronger, hardier, and ornerier than horses, churrim were valuable animals. These were no more than so much spoiled meat, their graceful limbs and delicate ears broken and torn. They were not long dead, either. If she had ridden a breath faster, if she had arrived an hour earlier...

If she had wings, she might fly to the sea.

She turned from the slaughtered beasts and studied the broken wagons. Small, bright houses they were, all of wood and with little doors and oiled-hide windows, red lacquered roofs that reminded her of the jiinberry farmers' broad, pointed hats. The wagons' narrow wooden wheels were made for hard-packed roads, not for the soft singing and ever-changing sands of the Zeera. The wandering Dziranim were gone, long gone, to dust and sung bones... and yet here were their heavy wooden wagons, as if they had dropped out of the sky.

How had they come here? Where were the people that had driven them? The smell of fresh death was heavy, and she could see a thick splattering of blood and hair and other bits. By the looks of it, someone had had his head smashed open on the side of the nearest wagon. She could all but hear the wailing spirits of the newly slain, but there were no bodies. Even a dreamshifter left bodies behind.

There it was, then. Magic.

Theotara felt the hair at her nape prickle. She crept closer, wishing with every step for the sharp wisdom and sharper teeth of her Saffra'ai. As she drew near, she could see what damage had been done to the beautiful wagons. Gashes and gouges such as a lionsnake's claws might leave, or those of a larger wyvern. One of the wagons had had its roof smashed in, and the slender wooden wheels had been crushed to bits. There was an odd metal-and-sulfur smell that reminded her of the Uthraki hot springs, and the least damaged of the wagons was burning. A thin trickle of smoke breathed forth from the smashed door, and from this wagon came the sound of a crying child—if it was a child, and not some bit of fell sorcery.

The old woman did not fear death, but she had never liked magic.

Theotara stilled herself body and mind, closed her eyes, dug her toes into the sand through the worn, soft leather of her favorite sandals. Again she allowed her ka to unfurl like the petals of a blackthorn rose, like the supple stretch of a waking cat, like the kiss of dawn on the last long day. She opened herself to the feel of things: the buzzards filling their bellies with dead meat. Beloved Zakkia, her familiar spirit now flaring with brief, false life, now spluttering like a campfire burned down to its last embers. Her own spirit, crippled and broken, bleeding from a wound that would never heal. Half a soul weeping in the dark.

Saffra'ai, my love, I cannot do this alone...

She tore herself away from the truth of her own grief. There was work to be done.

She reached her ka into the sky above, and felt nothing. In the sands about her, nothing. In and around the three crushed wagons, she discovered half a score of new ghosts, angry but impotent. In the fourth wagon...

A small and bright life. Human. Wounded.

No, there were two lives.

No... one. One small candle, burning against the dark.

Then again, two. One bright flame, and one falling into shadow. A living child, a dying adult.

Theotara opened her eyes and grimaced as the vertigo hit, staggered a short step before shaking it off and walking toward the smoking wagon, where a child lay weeping in terror and grief because her mama would not wake up. Outlanders, no doubt, thin of blood and unlikely to survive a single day in the desert. Here they were, three days' ride from Shahad, she with but a day to live. Theotara had no hope for herself, and less to offer another. A scant mouthful of water, the dubious honor of her company along the Lonely Road.

And here I thought you a warrior. The thought was old and hollow, as if it had traveled a long way to reach her.

She jerked to a stop, heart stuttering in her chest. *Saffra'ai?*

Where there is life, there is hope. Did you not teach me that? Foolish human.

Saffra'ai, beloved...

I will wait for you, Kithren. A cat's laugh, more felt than heard. *For a while, at least. We will face the Lonely Road together... but first you must save the child.*

Then he was gone.

Theotara crossed to the burning wagon and wrenched open the broken door. A small face peered up at her, pale and streaked with soot and tears. A child with hair as red as sunset, and next to her an unconscious woman with hair of moonsilk, both of them looking as if they had been dragged through a slaughter pit. Soft-skinned outlanders, and though that woman was not dead yet she looked to be well on her way.

Where there is life, there is hope. She looked at the child, and thought of the long road to Shahad. The woman might be dying, but the child was alive... and so, come to think of it, was she.

Where there is hope, there is room for foolishness. Her heart, still beating, urged her to folly.

A FALSE HOPE

"We should go no further," Hamran said, pulling up his sleek dun stallion. "These lands are outside our borders." Indeed, they had ridden so far from the river that Kemmet imagined he could feel the hot breath of Jehannim upon his face.

"Are you afraid of a few slavers?" Duna Ja'Sajani asked, pulling the veils of his blue *touar* down from his face and grinning at the dreamshifter. "They invade our lands every day. It is time we invade theirs."

Hamran met the warden's grin with a cool stare. He had been the dreamshifter of Nisfi for a score of years, and the scorn of Duna Ja'Sajani held no fear for him. "We have lost their trail," he pointed out, "and Ja'Sajani duty ends at the pride's borders. We should turn back and let the Ja'Akari take up the chase, if they will."

"Lost the trail?" Duna leaned from his saddle and spat. "How do we know you have not simply lost your courage, old man?"

"Kemmet says they are gone, and he can track a hawk on a cloudy day. His ka is that strong."

Kemmet shrank into his saddle, pinned by the stares of two powerful men. "They are gone," he agreed.

"Gone how? Gone away? Gone to ground? Gone fishing? Men do not simply disappear." Duna shot a sideways look at Hamran. "Or are these slavers all dreamshifters, able to slip into Shehannam?"

Kemmet shrugged. "They are gone, is all. I do not feel them on the wind." He felt something, or thought he did, but did not give voice to his uncertainties and fears. This was his first time accompanying the dreamshifter on such an important task, and he did not want his master or the Ja'Sajani to decide he was too young for such responsibility.

"It grows late," Hamran noted. "Akari turns his face from us."

Duna made a show of looking up at the sky. "So he does. I find it pleasant to ride by the light of the moons. Surely you do not fear the dark, Dreamshifter? Are shadows not your companions of choice? Surely you have faced worse than slavers in the Dreaming Lands."

Kemmet shrank farther into his saddle at the look on Hamran's face. It was dangerous to anger a dreamshifter, everyone knew that. Worse than the anger, though, was fear. Kemmet saw it in the way the old man gripped his reins, could see it in the way his mare played with her bit. If the dreamshifter was afraid, Kemmet figured the rest of them should be terrified.

Fear nibbled at the edges of his mind, as well. Kemmet had been apprenticed to the dreamshifter for six years now. He had grown up on tales of Shehannam fit to make the blood run cold, but nothing he had seen or experienced in that green world had been much cause for alarm. Until now, Kemmet had begun to think that neither this world nor the other was as dangerous as he had been led to believe.

As this day breathed its last, however, the old tales of war and wickedness seemed more real. The air grew cold, and still, and stale, and not just because Akari Sun Dragon had flown beyond the horizon. There was a smell on the wind that was unfamiliar to him, and which caused the chillflesh to rise on the backs of his arms. All day they had been riding hard, hunting a pair of slavers who had crept into their territory. They had passed the bloodstone spires that marked the foothills of Jehannim just before midsun, and ever since then Kemmet had felt a prickling at the back of his neck, as if he were a rabbit watched by a circling hawk. He had not wanted to say anything to the dreamshifter, or to the warden, lest he appear less than a man among men. Now he wished he had— and he wished harder that he could turn and ride for home, even if the warden mocked him for it and called him coward.

Duna Ja'Sajani was a champion among the people and a terror to outlanders. The boundary-stones around Nisfi were ringed with stakes set with the heads of their enemies, laughingly called

Duna's Wall, and their pride had not lost a child to the slavers since before Kemmet was born. Duna was the very picture of what a warden should be—tall, strong, and fearless, his skin baked dark by the sun despite the indigo touar which covered him from hair to ankles, his arms big around as a maiden's waist. Duna rode the stallion Rudyo Fleet-foot, and he was Zeeravashani. His *vash'ai* queen, Tallakhar, was back in the village nursing a litter of fine new cubs. There was no reason to feel fear, if such a man as Duna was in charge.

Yet the fear was there just the same, and it would not be banished.

"The duty of a warden is to keep the pride's territories clear, and you have done that," Hamran pointed out. "They are well out of our lands and still running. If the boy cannot feel them, they are long gone. Our duty now is to return to the pride and tell the Ja'Akari what we have seen."

Duna paid no heed. "Tell me, boy, do you feel anything? Anything at all?"

Kemmet glanced toward the dreamshifter, but his master's face was a mask of stone. "There is something…" he hesitated.

"Yes?"

"Not human, but… something. Just past that tangle." He pointed to a tangle of brush and debris, a dark smear against the coming night.

"Not human? What then? Is it a greater predator? Kin? A herd of *tarbok*?"

Kemmet wished he could follow Akari over the horizon. "I do not think it is kin. It is like nothing I have felt before."

Duna snorted and pulled his veils back over his face. "You are as useless to me as the old man. Well, let us go see what this feeling is. I wager we will find a pair of pale-assed slavers, and I will have two more heads on my wall before morning. *Het!*" He kicked his stallion into a brisk trot.

Kemmet looked to Hamran, who scowled and gestured for him to follow the Ja'Sajani. The old man brought up the rear, cussing under his breath. When he heard his master utter the phrase "titless idiot," he picked up the pace. Whatever was ahead, it could not be more frightening than a dreamshifter in a fell mood.

The night took hold. The moons Didi and Delpha graced them with plenty of light by which to ride, and the stars danced bright overhead. The land on this side of the spires was dark and unfriendly, and the dunes lay mute in the bitter wind. Kemmet thought longingly of a bright fire, and warm food, and a game of *shenu* after the evening's chores. Why had he ever thought he would like to be an adventurer?

Somewhere off in the distance, a *bintshi* screamed.

Rudyo stopped, and Kemmet urged his silver mare alongside, giving her a little kick when she reached over to bite the stallion's rump. As Hamran joined them, Duna shouldered his bow, kicked a leg over his stallion's back, and slid to the ground.

"What are you doing?" Hamran asked.

"Just past this tangle, right? Better to go round it on foot."

The bintshi screamed again, farther away this time. Duna's eyes crinkled over his touar at them. "You old men stay here, if you wish. I am going to kill some slavers." Then he slipped away into the night.

"That man's mouth is going to get him killed some day soon," muttered the dreamshifter, but he dismounted. "Well, come on, boy!" With that, Hamran was off after the warden. There was nothing for it, then—Kemmet hopped off his mare and followed them, though every bone in his body told him it was the wrong thing to do.

He heard the men before he could see them.

"There is something here," Hamran whispered. "Something…" and then as if to himself, "I have never felt *that* before."

"Surely even you have not felt everything there is to feel in the world, or seen it either," Duna replied in a low voice. "Look, there, I see something." He moved forward at a quick half-crouch, bringing his bow to the fore and reaching for an arrow. "Men!"

Not men, Kemmet wanted to tell him. *Whatever those are, they are not men.*

But it was too late for a warning.

The figures they found, seated round a dead campfire, certainly looked like men. Two of them looked like the pair of slavers they had chased from the pride's territory, and the other three were dressed as slavers as well, all in sand-colored linen with bits of leather armor, the better to remain unseen. They shone oddly against the dark, as if they had been draped in moonslight. They did not stir at the man's approach.

"Dead!" the warden shouted, when he reached the cold fire. "I thought you said your apprentice could tell the dead from the living, Dreamshifter."

The hairs rose all along Kemmet's arms, his legs, up his back and the nape of his neck. He felt a sudden urge to piss.

"These are… they are not…" and he began to back away. These had been men, but now…now they were something else, something wrong.

They were not men, and nor were they dead.

"Boy!" Duna called to him. "Feel about with your magic, see if we are alone besides our friends, here. What do you suppose killed them? Poison, maybe?" He gave one of the still forms a shove with his foot, so that it toppled over sideways and slid to the ground. "*Auck*, these are covered in… what is this?"

Hands shaking, Kemmet prepared to unfurl his ka as he had been taught, but his master gripped his arm, hard enough to hurt.

"No," the dreamshifter whispered, his voice urgent. "No. Those are *reavers*." Louder, he said, "Warden, we must leave this place. Now!"

But it was too late to leave.

The glistening man-shape that had slid to the ground shuddered and writhed like a beast that had been shot in the head. It struggled to its feet as the moons peered down, and as it did Kemmet could see that the thing was shrouded tip-to-toe in some white, filmy substance.

It looks like corpse linens, the boy thought, gorge rising. *Like spiders' webs.*

A man's hands tore through the bindings, peeled them aside.

A man's face emerged, and a man's shoulders and body, but its skin looked pale and hard as a scorpion's chitin, and the eyes that glared at them from burned and bloodied pits glittered in the thin light like an insect's. As it freed itself, the thing cast about with its hands like a blind man feeling his way in the light… and then it turned toward them, and *hissed*.

Not a man, Kemmet thought, his mind gibbering with fear. *Not a man, not a man.*

Duna nocked an arrow, drew and released in a single movement. His shot was true, and took the not-man dead between its fell eyes.

Or should have.

There was a sound like metal on stone and Duna's arrow skittered along the slaver's face before falling away into the dark. It left a deep score from eyebrow to temple, and a pale ichor oozed out to drip down into the glittering eye. The thing that had once been a man opened its mouth wide, too wide, and a hissing laugh crackled forth. Then it *moved*. It scuttled sideways and leapt, crossing the distance between itself and the warden in two great leaps, and as it hit it wrapped its legs and arms around him so that they went down in a tangle. It opened that mouth wide, wide, and Kemmet saw a mouth full of needle teeth and a writhing black tongue. It sank those teeth into the side of Duna's neck, and he shrieked.

Behind them, one of the horses screamed in answer, and then Kemmet heard the heavy *thud thud* of hooves striking flesh, followed by the sound of hoofbeats fading away. Their horses were gone.

He jumped when a heavy hand closed upon his shoulder, and a hand across his mouth muffled his scream. He blinked and shuddered. There was a sharp smell in the air, and his trousers were warm and heavy. Kemmet had pissed himself, and he did not even care. One of the other pale shapes began to move, and the warden's shrieks had been replaced by a wet sucking noise worse than anything he could have dreamed.

"Come, boy," the dreamshifter whispered. "It is time for us to go."

Kemmet pushed the hand away from his mouth. "But the horses…" he whispered.

The second man-shape turned its pale face toward them and hissed even as a third began to struggle against its bonds.

"I am going to take you through Shehannam." The old man firmed his grip on Kemmet's shoulder, and raised his fox-head staff trembling into the air. Kemmet grabbed onto the old man's tunic, daring to hope as the air before them brightened and shimmered with the false light of the Dreaming Lands.

The man-shape laughed at them, and crouched, and leapt.

It was too late for hope.

ONE

"It is only trouble if you get caught."

Akari Sun Dragon had long since flown beyond the horizon in search of his lost love, and the night unfurled velvet-soft. A hundred girls and half again as many women had left Shahad at daybreak and traveled to the Madraj, the meeting-place of all the prides.

Sulema stood tall among her yearmates, surrounded by Ja'Akari, warriors stern-faced and proud. When next the sun rose, she would be one of them. It was the first day of spring in her seventeenth year, and the last day of her childhood.

The Madraj lay cradled in the bosom of Aish Kalumm, the City of Mothers. Larger than any three villages together, built as a semicircle of stone seats curled like the Sleeping Dragon above a raised stage and the red-stained grounds beneath, the great arena was where babies were named, where *hayyanah* couples were pledged and leaders elected, and where criminals came to die. Most importantly, this was where Zeerani girls were selected to become healers, or Mothers, or blacksmiths. Where a favored few would become Ja'Akari, beautiful and fierce and beloved of Akari Sun Dragon.

In the days of their glory, hordes of mounted Ja'Akari had rolled across the Zeera like thunder and the songs of the Mothers fell like gentle rain. But war, and slavers, and the failure of the Mothers to bear live young had left the people a shadow of a remnant. The voices of their ancestors echoed in the halls beneath the seats of the Madraj. As she looked upon the small crowd of girls that had gathered this year, Sulema shivered to think of the Madraj staring with empty eyes across an empty desert.

Conspicuous in their absence were the girls from Nisfi. Sulema had overheard talk that the northernmost pride had been hit hard by slavers this year.

Her sword-sister Hannei thought that the people would never be able to regain their former glory. Too few children were born, and each year fewer warriors found favor with the vash'ai, the great saber-tusked cats that lived among them. The world had simply become too hostile for a return to the long ago of war and plenty.

Ehuani, she would say, meaning *there is beauty in truth.*

Saghaani, Sulema would argue. *There is beauty in youth.* They were young, they were strong and unconstrained by the failures of their elders. They would find a way to secure a future for the people. If there was no way to be found, she would make one.

First Mother insisted that the pride's best hope lay in moving more of the people into stone houses along the Dibris, like those of the outlanders to the north. For most of a generation the craftspeople had been hard at work building and fortifying Aish Kalumm. Sulema privately thought that First Warrior had the right of it, and that their future was rooted in the past, in seeking out and joining with those Zeeranim who still lived a purely nomadic life. But such thoughts, as she had been told repeatedly, were too big to fill the mouth of a mere girl.

She found a place not far from Hannei and sat upon the ground, beneath the rising moons. Even as she settled herself, the girls from Nisfi filed in and took their places. The sky faded from dove to lavender, and then from indigo to deep, silent black. She could hear the breath of her yearmates in the wind, feel their combined heartbeats through the ground, smell the sweat of anticipation and fear. As the wind shifted she breathed in the cat-musk of the vash'ai, and her bones sang at the touch of their rumbling voices. They were out there, in the dark, watching.

See me here, she thought to them. *Find me worthy.*

A great fire roared to life, shattering the night. Sulema's heart leapt like a startled hare, and one of the girls shamed herself by crying out. Far away as she was, Sulema could feel the heat of it on her face, and blinked back tears.

The pride's most powerful dreamshifter stood before them, above them, wreathed in flame. Her skin, dappled from long bonding with her vash'ai, had been rubbed in precious oil and gold until she gleamed. She was naked but for the golden armbands of Zeeravashani bondage.

Hafsa Azeina held her cat's-skull staff of charred blackthorn in her hands and all the heat of the sun in her pitiless golden gaze. As the dreamshifter raised the staff above her head, Khurra'an, First Sire of the vash'ai, threw back his massive head and roared. His gold-cuffed tusks had never seemed so deadly, nor the dreamshifter so terrible, as in that moment.

Sulema felt her ka, the breath of her spirit, quiver like a trapped bird.

Show no fear, she reminded herself. The woman was her mother, after all.

"*Yeh Atu,*" she whispered. "You would think she might have tried to do *something* with her hair."

"*Hssst!*" Hannei elbowed her ribs. "Already you get us in trouble."

"It is only trouble if you get caught." But she fell back into silence as those bright eyes found her, sought to burn her into submission. Sulema raised her chin and met that golden stare with her own. *Saghaani,* she thought. *There is beauty in youth. This is our world now, Mother.*

Her mother's spell had not been broken, but its hold on Sulema had been tempered. As torches were lit all round the Madraj she felt anticipation begin to win its battle against dread. This was the night she had dreamed of, fought for, lived for. No longer would she be a child, with a child's voice lost in the howling wind. No longer would she be that freckled outlander girl, daughter of a great and terrible dreamshifter. She would be Sulema Ja'Akari, a warrior under the sun, free to choose her own path.

The wind picked up, and the Zeera sang.

Three Ja'Akari stepped into the light. One held a dagger, the second a bowl, and the third held nothing at all. They were naked, oiled and dusted in gold just as the dreamshifter, for on this night all women were equal under the moons. They had painted their faces with streaks and whorls of black and white and gold, transforming themselves into snarling creatures half-human, half-vash'ai. Their dappled skin glowed with feral health, and elaborate headdresses framed their faces like many-colored manes.

Wordless, they stalked the young women, catlike in grace and intent, and as they pulled the first girl from the crowd Sulema's breath caught in her ribs. The girl, a short Nisfi, trembled like a hare as the empty-handed woman stripped her plain garb away, as the woman with the bowl painted her face in deft strokes, and as the woman with the knife shaved the hair from her temples, all in the space of time it took Sulema to find her breath again. The girl's clothes—and her hair—were handed to her and she was shoved toward the dreamshifter, even as the three women turned to their next victim.

Three craftmistresses stepped into the light. One held a stylus, the second a bowl, and the third held nothing at all. Their skin glowed in the firelight, their eyes flashed with pride, for on this night every woman was a pillar of her community. Their hands had been painted with whorls and swirls of henna, it stained their skin with beauty and proclaimed their place in the world. Wordless, they advanced upon the young women, sure in themselves and their choice as they drew a stout girl from Uthrak to her feet.

The woman with a stylus dipped it into the bowl of henna paste and then drew it across the skin of the girl's outstretched hand, a few simple lines that would stain the skin for a short while, but mark her forever as a blacksmith. The empty-handed woman stripped the girl of her linen tunic and then gave it back. The clothes of childhood would be fed to the flames as the pride's newest apprentice took her turn before the dreamshifter.

Three herdmistresses stepped into the light. One held an awl, the second a bowl, and the third held nothing at all...

Daru, the dreamshifter's apprentice, came into the light alone. Sulema's heart skipped into a trot, and then to a canter, as his dark eyes wandered wide and dreaming among the girl-children of the pride. She held her breath as his gaze found hers and held, as he took a step forward…

…no, please Atu, no…

…and then the little shit winked at her before turning away. The dreamshifter would take no new novitiate this year.

By the time the Ja'Akari came for her, Sulema had taken hold of her fear and throttled it into submission. She stood proud as they tore away the plain tunic that marked her as a child of the Shahadrim, as they painted her face to invoke the protection and ferocity of the great cats, and—finally!—as they cut away her sunset braids. Gladly she took her clothes and cast-off hair, and smiled as she fed them to the fire. The stink of charred hair was an offering to the pride, and sweet. She would have stayed to watch it blacken and burn, but a hand gripped her shoulder and turned her away.

Beaten-gold eyes peered out at her from beneath a pale crown of tangled locks, like a wild thing staring into the world from another place. They burned, with or without the fire they burned, and though they peeled back the layers of her soul, somehow never seemed to see her. The words, when they came, were as empty and cold as unsung bones.

"Sulema Shahadri."

"There are no Shahadrim here."

"Sulema Ali'i."

"There are no children here."

"Umm Sulema."

"There are no Mothers here." She lifted her eyes to that fiery stare, willing her heart to courage. "No mothers at all."

The dreamshifter's eyes flickered, in pain or fury or through a simple trick of the firelight. She heard Khurra'an growl as the dreamshifter raised her cat's-skull staff and touched Sulema's forehead. It felt, oddly enough, like a kiss.

"Who stands before me?"

Sulema straightened her shoulders. She was taller than her mother, now, if only by a hairsbreadth.

"I am Sulema," she answered. "Sulema Ja'Akari warrior of the

Zeeranim." Then she held her breath, because the dreamshifter had the power, in that moment, to deny her heart's desire. One word, and Sulema might be sent, not to the warriors, but to the dreamshifters. Those rare individuals who could hear the songs of *sa* and ka were rarely allowed to choose any other path in life, and Sulema knew herself to be gifted.

Or cursed, depending on how you looked at it.

Hafsa Azeina gave the tiniest shrug, as if it were of no matter to her at all. Her eyes were already on the girl behind Sulema.

"I see you, Sulema," she intoned, "I see you, Ja'Akari. I see you, warrior of the Zeeranim." She raised her staff high, and brought the end of it down upon the ground. Khurra'an threw his head back and roared, a sound that made the bones of her feet tingle where they met the earth, and several of the vash'ai added their great voices to his. She had been found worthy. Sulema's heart sang in her breast. Almost, it seemed, the heart of the world sang out an answer, a rumbling song of welcome from the very ground beneath her feet.

She felt a faint tickling at the back of her mind. A voice, at once unfamiliar and beloved.

I come, Kithren, he said to her. *I come!*

The vash'ai roared again, and the moons bathed the desert in silver light, and all was right in the world.

It was done.

"What happened?" Hannei asked. "I heard the vash'ai roaring. They hardly ever do that when a warrior is raised. I do not know whether I should hug you, or hate you. They say when that happens, a warrior is always chosen Zeeravashani."

"It was nothing," Sulema replied, and then ruined it by grinning. Humility had never been her strength. "Is there mead? I am so thirsty I could drink moonslight."

"There is mead, and *usca*, and food. The fast is over." Hannei's brown eyes sparkled in the firelight. "The fast is over, Sulema, it is all over. We are women now. Warriors!"

Sulema reached a tentative hand to the bare skin at her temple, shorn even as Hannei's was shorn. Tomorrow they would oil the skin with *sisli*, and braid their remaining hair into warriors' plaits. Tomorrow they would don the traditional garb of Ja'Akari, and fight for honor before the eyes of the First Warrior. Tonight, though…

"Tonight, we are women." The words were strange in her mouth, bitter as red salt, sweet as jiinberry wine. "Tonight, we are warriors!"

"Ja'Akari!" Hannei laughed, and drew back her arm, and slapped Sulema with her open palm so hard it set the stars in the sky to dancing.

"Ja'Akari!" She hit back, a solid blow, so that Hannei made a face and spat a thin stream of blood.

The girls shared a grin. It was the last time either of them would allow herself to be struck and not answer with death.

"Come, Sister, let us get to the feast before the food is all gone." Hannei held out her hand.

Sulema met her friend's grasp, and they twined their fingers together. "To Yosh with the food. What I need now is…"

"Mead!" They finished together and set off toward the fires at a half-run, hand in hand, an entire lifetime before them.

Saghaani.

There is beauty in youth.

TWO

"It is a good day to die. It is an even better day to live."

Ani loved the Zeera, but it had never loved her back.

She had taken in sand with every breath, every mouthful of food or drink, sucked the grit in through her very skin. By now she was doubtless more sand than woman. But no matter how much of her blood she might pour into the desert, it had never welcomed her home. She was a dark stranger, lost in a golden land under a golden sky.

She had been born into a Dzirani caravan, one of the clans that used to wander along the Great Salt Road. In better days—if those dispossessed by Iftallan can be said to have had better days—the Dzirani had been known as far south as Min Yaarif, as far north as Atualon, and to the east beyond myth-lands of the Daemon Emperor.

Though her mother's brother had named her "Beauty," her face would never have caught at the heart-strings of a king, or even the purse-strings of a fat salt merchant. Rather than feed another worthless mouth, her father had sold her to the desert barbarians for two bags of salt, one red and one white. A fair price for a plain face. She did not remember much of her father's people beyond the pretty painted wagons and the great blunt-horned *ghella* that pulled them, the smell and taste of fish from the mountain streams, and her mother's cries on the day she was sent away. Young Ani had sworn on the stars, a different one each night, that one day she would find her mother again and they would be made whole.

Young Ani had run out of wishing-stars long ago. Istaza Ani, youthmistress to the pride, had no time to spare for foolish dreams.

Though the Zeera had never welcomed her, the Zeeranim had.

She loved them, loved her life and her place in it. She was valued despite her barren womb and her failure to bond with a vash'ai. In many ways she was less of an outsider than the woman she sought now, the most powerful dreamshifter in the Zeera, who had once been as close to her as a sister. That friendship, much as her youthful passions, had faded with the years. One could love the fire, but never come too close. Never embrace it.

Ani was a woman of muscle and blood and bone. Her strength and comfort lay in things of the physical realm—horses to ride and tarbok to hunt, enemies to conquer and men to love, men to conquer and enemies to love. She loved her big red stallion, her worn bow, the whisper of finely woven linen against her legs as she walked. Spiced mead and smoked meats. Things she could touch, and taste, and smell. The world was dangerous enough, to her thinking, without adding to the mess by meddling in the affairs of dreamshifters and dragons.

As she turned from the hurry and bustle and laughter of Hajra-Khai, the spring festival, the wind slapped her face. She wiped grit from her eyes and walked toward the river Dibris, swollen and sluggish from the first spring rains. Whenever the people gathered in numbers greater than three, Hafsa Azeina would pack her tent and seek solitude. After that incident with the snakes Ani had given up lecturing her friend about the dangers of being alone.

For appearances' sake, Hafsa Azeina kept a tent of her own. She wore the robes of a respected woman, and gems upon her fingers, and treated any guest to fragrant teas and sweetmeats. Ordinary things, as if she were an ordinary woman, but Hafsa Azeina was no ordinary woman. She waded through the people's dreams like a jiinberry farmer in shallow waters, plucking the ripe fruit of fertile dreamings. Some of this harvest was hoarded for later, some was sold at market, and some—Ani was certain of this last, though she had never asked outright—some of the dreams were eaten fresh, staining the lips and fingertips and the soul of the woman who ate them with their dark, sweet juices.

Overlooking the muddy banks of the river was an area left dark and bare by last year's cooking pits. Still rank with the smells of old fat and charred flesh, likely to attract scavengers and predators when the winds blew out of the south, it was the least desirable site one could imagine wanting to claim. In this place Hafsa Azeina had made her camp.

The breeze had died in the rising heat, yet the dreamshifter's tent still shivered like a dreaming beast, its painted hide twitching and glinting as it napped in the sunlight. The indigo spidersilk tent, smaller than most, was embroidered in thread-of-gold and thread-of-blood with fantastical creatures and scenes. Kraken and *kirin*, wildling and wyvern crowded together chaotic as the script on a bonesinger's skin. Above them all, coiled round and about the roof of the tent and watching her with eyes of lapis, the gold-and-green scaled form of Akari Sun Dragon searched for his lost love.

As always, Ani made a small sign against ill fortune as she neared the tent. Hafsa Azeina had been a friend to her these many years, but the youthmistress would sooner wrestle a lionsnake than sleep beneath those disturbing images. Her sleep was fitful enough of late without wyrms and wyverns clawing their way into her dreams.

Ignoring all the glittering eyes, she gave the visitor's bell a shake and ducked through the doorflap. The dreamshifter's tent was surprisingly roomy inside, though much of the space was occupied by the black-maned and massive hulk of a vash'ai. He was an older cat, his black-and-silver dappled coat faded to a pale gold, and heavily scarred.

"Khurra'an." She bowed respectfully. "Hafsa Azeina."

The sire curled his black-tufted tail at her dismissively, and the white eye spots on the back of his round ears did not so much as twitch. Khurra'an had perfected the art of arrogance.

Hafsa Azeina sat cross-legged and cloaked in shadows on the far side of the tent, a scattering of wood and blades and small pots all around her. Her head was bowed over some project, masses of pale locks hiding her figure and face. When the dreamshifter finally looked up at her, Ani could scarce repress a shiver. The woman's hands were stained with blood, and the great golden eyes were fierce.

"Istaza Ani." She had the faraway voice of a person who sings in their sleep.

"Dreamshifter." Ani forced a smile. "You are not dressed for Hajra-Khai."

A strange expression played about the other woman's mouth, like sunlight on cold water. "I need to restring my lyre."

"Ah," Ani said, and for the first time noted the loops of fresh intestine in a basket of water, gray and gleaming, ready to be scraped clean. Well, that explained the smell. "Nobody I know, I hope."

That smile again. "I think not."

"Sulema was very brave at her ceremony."

"Sulema is always brave."

"I hear that Hannei and Saskia were made warriors, as well. Not that there was ever any doubt. Nurati's girl, Neptara, was claimed by the artists' guild. I did not see that coming—I hope she is not too disappointed. And I hope Sulema can learn to control that hot temper of hers before it gets her into too much trouble."

The dreamshifter bent over her work again. "It is past time Sulema learns control. She is a grown woman now, not a child, and the dragon is waking."

"Children's tales," Ani replied, watching the woman work. Her cat's-skull lyre was propped in a corner next to the blackened staff, tools of the dreamshifter's trade. Deadly as swords, in their own way, and as beautiful. "Sajani will sleep till the end of time."

Hafsa Azeina glanced up at her. "You should listen to children's tales more often. They hold more truth than you know. There is a restlessness in the land, you have said as much yourself. The people's dreams are darker, and tempers run hotter. We lose warriors and wardens with every ranging. Not three moons past, the Nisfim lost Hamran and his apprentice, and their strongest warden as well. They rode out in pursuit of slavers and never returned."

"The slavers grow bolder because Atualon and Sindan eye one

another and think of war. The kin grow bolder as the spring brings less rain each year, and there is less prey for them to hunt. These are natural things, surely."

"And the dragon is not?" The dreamshifter reached into the water, brought forth a coil of intestine, fixed it to the board in front of her. "She would have woken completely during the Sundering, but for the magic of the Atualonian queens and kings. Her dreams are as restless as your own, Youthmistress. We have only three dreamshifters now to protect all the prides, though a score would scarce be sufficient if the Dragon's dreamings rouse the kin. I do not believe for a moment that a handful of slavers could have bested Hamran. No… dark dreams gather in the shadows of Jehannim. Things are only going to get worse."

"Things always grow worse, when kings and emperors join the dance." Ani frowned. "The Sindanese emperor will not rest until he holds the world in his hands, and the moons in the sky as well. And the drums of war have ever been the heartbeat of Atualon. Ka Atu would see us all burn before he ever bends knee to Tiachu. But what has that to do with the dragon? We are to Sajani as ants in the shadow of a warrior, you have told me so yourself."

"Yet ants may sting, and draw unwanted attention to themselves. *Ehuani*, old friend, we should turn our minds from such things lest we do the same. Leave the war to warriors, and the dragon to her dreams." Hafsa Azeina smiled and stretched her back. "Why have you come here today? Surely not for tea and gossip. Or did you come to help me string my lyre?"

Ani glanced toward Khurra'an, whose eyes upon her had grown suddenly sharp. Knowing that the vash'ai could smell fear did nothing to soothe her nerves.

Ah well, she told herself. *It is a good day to die.*

"Umm Nurati called a secret meeting of the Mothers last night, and the Mothers just informed the Ja'Sajani and Ja'Akari. If I had known earlier, I would have told you."

"Told me what?"

There was no way but to say it straight. "Do you remember last year, when those Atualonian men came down the river seeking news of a white-haired woman and a red-haired girl? Then they… disappeared?"

The dreamshifter's eyes went flat and hot. "I remember." She squeezed a handful of gut.

"Nurati sent an envoy to the Dragon King, in secret. Hafsa Azeina, he knows about you. He knows about Sulema."

Ani had been a hotheaded young warrior when old Theotara had returned from the Lonely Road, carrying a woman over her shoulders and a child in her arms. That young outland mother, though untrained in dreamshifting, had somehow killed an entire gang of slavers with magic and transported herself, her daughter, and their wagons deep into the desert. But Ani knew, because they had shared a room in Beit Usqut, how Hafsa Azeina had cried herself to sleep for love of the man whose wrath she had fled.

The first bounty hunters had arrived before that year was out. Men from Eid Kalish in bright silk cloaks, wearing knives at their hips and handing out coins and sweets to the children. "*Tell us what you know,*" they had coaxed, to no avail. "*A moon-haired woman, a flame-haired girl. The Dragon King is very generous to his friends.*"

The men from Eid Kalish had disappeared, too. Nor had Ani to wonder what became of them. She had, in fact, helped her friend feed their corpses to the river-beasts.

Ah, to be young again.

"She sent an envoy. To *Ka Atu*. How long ago was this?"

"Moons ago, I suppose. Too late to do anything about it, certainly."

"We shall see about that. And about this… treachery." Hafsa Azeina pushed away the bowl of guts, and stood. "Are the Mothers still at the Madraj?"

"Dreamshifter, it is too late for that. I believe she only told the Mothers when it became apparent that her envoy had been received, and now we know there has been a reply."

The dreamshifter bared her teeth. "I will stop her."

"Would that you could. I tell you, it is too late. A runner has come from Nisfi. Ships have been sighted on the Dibris."

Hafsa Azeina went still as dead water. "Ships. What kind of ships?"

"Dragon-keeled ships with striped sails. Half a score, by scout's report."

The dreamshifter's eyes glittered, cold and hard as a viper considering her next strike. When she moved it was so quick and unexpected that Ani stumbled half a step backward, but the other woman simply stooped to pick up the basket full of guts. When she straightened again, her face was a frozen mask.

"So. Ka Atu would stir from his throne. He would reclaim what he sees as his." She brushed past Ani and paused at the mouth of her twilight tent, silhouetted against the bright bite of the sun. "How long until they are upon us?"

"The runner was swift. We have a few days, at most."

"I will speak with Umm Nurati, and then I will speak with the Mothers. The people must make ready to greet the king of dragons." As she slipped out into the day, Ani let out the breath she had been holding.

It was a good day to die, of course. But it was a better day to live.

Khurra'an padded past her, a mountain's rumbling whisper, bone-and-shadows bulk reaching almost to her shoulder, silent as death in the night.

Somewhere in the distance, a vash'ai roared.

The fist in her gut unclenched. Slowly. Ani peered around the tent, at the worn cushions and discarded clothes, the usual bits and pieces of another woman's life. Ordinary things… but there was the cat's-head lyre propped in its corner, waiting to be restrung. The cat's-skull staff, blackened and dead. And the tent's eyes, the stares of the embroidered beasts so heavy on her they made her skin crawl. She fled the tent at a walk and did not look back.

Ani was startled to find the sun still bright, and the air still merry with the sounds and smells of the people enjoying Hajra-Khai. She raised her face to the sky and stared up at Akari Sun

Dragon until tears slipped from the corners of her eyes.

"I am not sure which is worse," she told him, "an Atualonian invasion, or an angry dreamshifter."

THREE

"I will remember."

His mother handed him a package wrapped in yellow rice paper, and tied with cords of red silk. "Open this. It is yours." Her eyes were bright. "I made this for you."

Jian pulled the tasseled end of one cord and the massive knot slid apart smoothly. He unfolded the expensive wrapping with great care, ashamed at the rasp of his rough skin against the soft paper, and sucked in a breath at the bright garments within, yellow silk hot as the sun and heavily embroidered with thread-of-blood. "I cannot wear this!"

"It is your right, my son." She blinked, pressed her lips together, and drew in a deep breath. "It is your right, and it is your duty. You represent the whole of Bizhan, now. You are Daechen tonight, and it is most important that you look like a prince, not some sort of... peasant." Her hands fluttered to the silk like small birds, and then she held the robe up to his shoulder, and smiled the small, secret smile of a mother. "Besides, you will look so handsome. My son, the Daechen prince."

Tonight was the Feast of Flowering Moons, and Jian's sixteenth nameday. Tomorrow he would walk through the wide gates and become Daechen Jian, a prince of the Forbidden City.

A prince, Jian thought No longer a pearl-diver's son, a boy who was at home in the water and ill at ease on land, a boy who was better with the flute than with words. A prince. Though he had been preparing for this day his whole life, the words were still a punch in the gut. He took the heavy robe from his mother and held it away from his body as if the embroidered serpents would bite him. The yellow cloth would have cost as much as a new roof, he knew, the pearls spent on thread-of-blood might have fed them for a year.

And when had she the time to make this? His mother was often up late, bent over her sea-charts or account ledger, trying to find one more bed of oysters, one more trade route, trying to pay their way for one more day. Every stitch, every thread was one more moment he had stolen from her life.

"Mother, I cannot…" *I cannot take this*, he might have said. Or perhaps, *I cannot leave you*, but they both knew that there was no choice. As long as the false king in Atualon threatened their lands, the emperor needed the daeborn for his armies.

"Hush," she warned him, and held up her hand. Her hands were so small, frail little bird-bones, skin as thin as golden parchment. "It is the emperor's right to demand your service. It is your right to wear this, and it is my right to give it to you." A single tear defied her iron will. Jian caught it with a finger before she could wipe it away, and brought it to his lips. Then he crushed her to him as if he were still a child and could not bear to be parted from her.

For a long moment she clung to him, thin arms still surprising him with their strength, and then she laughed a little, and pushed him away. "Ai! Look at me, I am a mess. I will have to start all over again." She smoothed her silvering hair with her hands, wiped at her face.

Jian's heart ached to see her brave smile. "I would not leave you."

"I would not have you go. But the world is woven of wind and tide, my son, and neither of us has the power to sway it. You are bound to the Forbidden City, as I am bound to the sea, and I would not change one single thing about you, not even this. I am proud to be your mother."

In other lands, he had heard, the daeborn were free to do as they wished with their lives, with every right given to a fullborn human. It was even said that in Atualon, a man might belong to himself, and not to an emperor. Jian dreamed, sometimes, that the Dragon King might burn Sindan to the ground and free them all. That he might some day ride south and hear the long, slow songs of the golden sands, or west toward the Sea of Beginnings, and watch the sun set behind the dragonglass fortress Atukos.

In truth, the Dragon King was no likelier to spare his hide than was the emperor. The Daechen were born to kill, and to die, and that was all. If they rode to a foreign land, it was not for the pretty sunsets.

"You are proud that I am... cursed?"

"Cursed." She snorted. "That is village-talk. No more of that for you, now. Are the blessed cursed? Is the emperor cursed? No more than you."

"And my... father? Will you speak of him to me, now?" Jian looked away so that he would not see if his words hurt her.

She smoothed the hair back from his face, and leaned in to press her lips against his forehead as she had when he was a small boy with a hurt. "I cannot."

Those words, from her, were a blade of obsidian plunged into his breast. Jian turned his face from his mother. "You will not do this thing for me, even on this day."

"I cannot grow wings and fly. I cannot bend the wind to my will, not turn the tide, nor bid the moons to set ere their time. And I cannot speak to you of this thing."

"Hyang told me that I was... that you were." He swallowed. "That I was born of rape." That had been the kindest thing Hyang had said about his father. *Daeborn* they called him, Daemon seed, an ill-luck child that should have been exposed to the elements at birth.

"Hyang has picked most of his brains out through his nose." She snorted again. "I can tell you this much... you were not born of rape. By the sea, you were not."

A weight Jian had not known he carried was lifted from his chest, and he took a deep breath. Not a child of rape... Hyang had seemed so sure. Then again, Hyang *was* a nose-picker.

"This room is too small." His mother frowned. "You should have better." She walked to the small window, tripping a little on the foot of his bed as she passed. "You cannot see the water."

"I can smell the sea, if the wind blows just so. I can hear the ocean calling me." *I can feel her calling me home,* he thought, but did not say the words. He feared that the calling, calling, calling of the sea would break his heart to pieces, like waves upon the rock.

She pressed her hands hard against her eyes, and then her mouth, and then her heart, before turning to face him. She was still so beautiful, he thought, the salt and the wind had scoured away what was soft and weak in her, and left a warrior-woman in their wake. Her eyes were creased from squinting out across the sunstruck waves, and her long hair was shot through with sea-foam, but men's heads still turned as she whispered past, a gentle breeze with the promise of storms to come.

In her youth, her beauty had inspired the poet Jiao Jian to write about the maid who loved the sea, and Jian was proof that hers had not been a one-sided love.

"You will wear the silk."

Jian went to his mother, and enfolded her in his arms, and he held her like that until she relented and hugged him back. When had she gotten so small?

"I will wear the silk," he agreed. "I will make you proud."

She fought her way loose and smacked him in the shoulder. "I would be proud of you if you went to the feast wearing nothing but a smile and a necklace of old clam-shells." Her eyes laughed as he blushed, remembering a time when he was little and had showed up at a village feast wearing just that. "I would not recommend it, though."

"Mother!" he protested. "I was only five years old... how long will you tell that story?"

"If wind and tide will, I would tell that story to your children, and to their children." She kissed her fingertips formally.

He repeated the gesture. "If wind and tide will."

"Now—" she firmed her mouth "—I will leave you to get ready. I trust you do not need my help? No? We do not wish to give these city dwellers another story to tell, do we?"

He waved her out, laughing. "Goodbye, Mother. I can dress myself. I will see you at the feast tonight."

37

"You will be the handsomest man in the city. You will have to beat the girls away with an oar."

"Mother!"

"Have courage, my son. And hang up your clothes!" She slipped from the room, sliding the screen behind her with scarcely a whisper.

Jian touched his fingertips to his lips again, and pressed them against the screen. "Until we meet again," he promised. "*Jai-hao.*"

When he could no longer hear the faint patter-patter of her feet on the bamboo floor, Jian went to the window. He looked out over the shining walls and palaces of Khanbul to the distant slopes of Mutai Gon-yu, the mountains that tamed the rains. If he craned his neck he could just see a glint of sunlight upon the Kaapua, whose wide blue waters danced their way from the foothills of Tai Damat and Tai Bardan all the way to Nar Kabdaan... and home. Beyond that lay the bright sands and brazen warriors of the Zeera, and the Araid-infested ruins of Quarabala far beneath the scorched earth. Hovering to the north of those fabled places, like the crown on an undeserving head, stretched the salt-rich lands of Atualon, home to the Dragon Kings who had ruined them all. He wondered idly if any of those people celebrated the first rains of spring. Did it even rain in the desert?

The air was heavy with the sweet-and-spice perfumes of many kitchens making ready for tonight's feast. Jian heard children laughing, and the *hum-thrum* music of prayer bells spinning in the wind, and the occasional *ratta-tat-tat* as white-robed Baizhu monks twirled through the streets, tossing firecrackers at the feet of unwary lovers. For a moment he wished that he was a child among them, running wild with the pack of younglings, begging a treat from the sweet-seller's cart or trying to snatch a rope of firecrackers to toss at the young girls, confident that tomorrow would be the same as today, every day as lustrous and alike as pearls in a bowl.

As a child, he had loved stories and songs, riddles, and poetry, and the tales he loved best were of the Dae. He smiled a bit, remembering the firelight and the sea-song, and his mother's voice rising and falling with the waves as she read to him from the Book of Moons:

> *"Somewhere in the far away, past Kaapua's flowered skirts, beyond the wind-scoured rocky shores, past singing cave and towering wave and the jaws of the great striped shongwei, rose a chain of islands shrouded in magic thick as fog. There, antlered kings and queens white-skinned raised conch-shells to their ruby lips, where daeborn creature fair and foul held endless feasts and games of death, and Daelords in their golden halls wove dream-sung spells into the wind..."*

The worlds of men and Dae had been rent asunder by the corrupt magic of the Atualonian kings nearly a thousand years ago, and year by year the veil between the two worlds thickened. The Lords of Twilight came rarely now to the shores of men. Some said they feared whatever had frayed the weft and warp of land and magic. Others suggested that the Dae had caused the Sundering, but Jian refused to believe that the Dae would deliberately loose magic that would harm the great sea-beasts, their kin. He, himself, had seen the carcass of a *shongwei*, its hulk rent with gashes and bites so monstrous the mind shied away from wondering what might have caused them.

Jian had thought to scavenge the shongwei. Its massive tusks, longer than two tall men laid foot-to-head, gleamed pale and smooth in the morning light. That ivory would have been wealth enough to buy his mother freedom from her deadly work. Wealth enough to purchase a young man's release from destiny. But the wind shifted as he approached, and the stench of the rotting corpse drove him to his knees.

He told no one of his find, and when he returned the next morning the shongwei was gone. It had been dragged back out to sea, leaving behind a trench in the sand deeper than his house was tall and one small tooth hardly as long as his forearm. Fear of whatever had taken the shongwei kept him from venturing into deeper waters for weeks, and now that tooth lay among the few treasures and wadded-up clothing of his childhood.

Sea-beasts or no, Jian had dreamed, deep in the undercurrents of his heart, that he might escape from the world of men. He would sail across Nar Kabdaan of a Moonstide night, when the waters were still as glass. On such a night it seemed all a boy had to do was stretch forth his hand and pluck the low-hanging stars from the sky, and taste the nectar of freedom. Sometimes Jian imagined that he would steal one of the Western barbarians' dragon-faced ships and sail to the Twilight Lands. He would step onto the far shores just as his ragged craft fell apart, and surely such a brave and arrogant act would win him a place among his father's folk, a place in his father's heart.

No matter how far his dreams took him, Jian would always return to harsh reality. No boat in Bizhan was more than a mouthful to the shongwei, and no ship in the empire could get past the greater creatures of the deep. Though ships full of men had ventured out upon the blue waters of Nar Kabdaan in search of the Twilight Lands, none had ever returned. If the emperor's ships were no match for the sea, what chance had a daeborn boy?

Some among the Sindanese blessed the Dae and begged their favor through small rituals and burnt offerings. Others cursed them as the spawn of Yosh, called them daemons or worse. Some few mortals might take a Dae lover on the one night of the year that their two worlds met, when the blood ran wild and nothing was forbidden under the stars. Any child born during the festival of Nian-da, the Two Moon Dawn, was said to be born of such a union.

A child of the Two Moon Dawn was said to be a citizen of two worlds, and welcome in either. Legend held that the youths were sent to Khanbul lest their Dae parents try to steal them away to the Twilight Lands. Jian's whole life had been haunted by the vision of those islands rising blue and green and wild from the mists, the horn calling him to the Wild Hunt, and Issuq laughing in the waves.

He had studied his own face bit by bit in his mother's small mirror. The high curve of his cheek, eyes so large and round, brown and deep as a seal's, teeth that were just a little too sharp, a little too white. His heart had taken his wishes, his dreams, and his dread, and with those had formed a small, secret, perfect pearl of its own. His father, he felt sure, laughed and lived and loved among the Issuq. A tall man, like himself, sleek and dark and quick. A man who even now might wonder whether he had sired a child, years past on a Moonstide night, when the veil between worlds had thinned.

Jian had been born on the very morn of Nian-da, midwifed by the moons and the sea. His mother had claimed that she had not felt the pangs of birth before the time was upon her and she had gone to the sea to make prayers, but Jian had always believed that she had felt his true nature in her womb, and had honored that by giving birth in the foaming embrace of a two-moon tide. His first breath of air had held the tang of the great salt winds, and his mother gave him a fingerful of brine to suck before ever he tasted milk.

If the circumstances surrounding his birth had not been enough to name him daeborn, his appearance would have erased all doubt. Jian was born with the large, round, near-black eyes of his sea-kin father—never cloudy like those of other newborn infants, but bright and alert and merry as sunlight on the water. Tiungpei was filled to overflowing with joy in her son. When he was but a tiny infant she had a painting commissioned of him sitting on her lap, and this she hung in a place of honor on the wall behind her chair. When he was small he would sit at his mother's feet as she worked at some bit of mending or needlework, and she would let him play with handfuls of imperfect pearls as she told him stories about his infancy. How he hung in his cradle-board wide-eyed and silent, never crying like the other babies. How he was first to walk, to talk, how he learned his numbers with such ease the monks feared to teach him more, how he would toddle away down the moons-lit path, when he was scarce as tall as the salt-grass, and make singing prayers to the sea.

This last bit, he could remember. Pebbles smooth against the soles of his soft little feet. The cries of the sea-birds, calling him away, away. The warm waters that welcomed him home, on those rare occasions when he made it to the beach before his mother could snatch him up and carry him to bed. For he had swum in the water before he had walked on the land, and ever he longed for the sea.

He also remembered the heavy, jagged words of the man his mother had been married to, the hard looks thrown his way dangerous as stones. Little Jian had learned to walk quiet and wary around the house, always ready to duck aside. The man had been shorter than Jian's mother and broad, with a square face and large, square teeth, and he had left the discarded shells of boiled peanuts on every flat surface. Jian could remember his mother complaining about them, and could remember that the empty, slightly soggy shells made excellent little toy boats.

One night the man had raised his voice, demanding that the boy be sent to live with the monks of Baizhu. Jian had huddled under the soft cotton quilt his mother had stitched together from her old dresses, and he fell asleep with the salt of tears upon his lips.

The next morning, he woke to the sound of his mother's singing and the smell of cinnamon bread. The man was gone, and there were two goats tethered in their little yard, yellow-eyed milk does with striped faces and soft ears. It was many days before Jian could work up the courage to ask his mother whether she had traded her husband for goats, and when he did, she laughed until tears rolled down her beautiful round face. But she never did answer the question.

It had been just the two of them that day, and every day since. Though theirs was not a particularly quiet life—Tiungpei was as noisy as the sea, always singing like the waves, or laughing like the wind, or scolding her son like an irritated sea-bird—still, it was peaceful between the storms.

Tiungpei sold her family's house in town to the fish merchant's son, and commissioned an elegant home to be dug into the cliffs near the water. Their new rooms were much smaller but very beautiful, with tiled walls and floors of polished wood. Jian had a room all to himself, with a bed deep and soft as an albatross's nest carved into the wall and a little stone oven to keep him warm on a winter night. Three great arched entries of bamboo and precious sea-glass overlooked a sunken courtyard, and high stone walls, painted red and yellow, kept the sea from his mother's garden. There were mango trees in the garden, and a little stone fountain where tiny bright fishes begged for crumbs. They kept black chickens, and orange ducks, and of course the goats. Jian grew particularly fond of those goats.

He knew from an early age that, aside from the scolding, his mother was not like other mothers. She was a beautiful woman with a face round as a harvest moon and the long, sensitive hands of an artist, and she took great pride in dressing well. Even her plainest clothes had a bit of embroidery, a scrap of silk, a flash of color. Her hair, when it was unbound, rippled down her back and almost to her knees like a dark and perfumed waterfall. Yet she never painted her face, or modulated her voice into a soft and breathy little song, or walked with the mincing steps of a *oulo*-dancer. Tiungpei strode through life as if she were going to battle in her finest silks, and the enemy had best beware. The only pearl diver in Bizhan, Tiungpei brought honor and the emperor's favor to the village. Her otherness was tolerated, and her daeborn son as well, but the common people of Bizhan were only too happy to keep them both at a distance.

A child, after all, was only a child, and even a strangeling child was more of an oddity than a threat. Daechen children, without exception, disappeared behind the great walls of the Forbidden City on the very dawn of adulthood and were never seen again. The boy Jian with his seal eyes and otherworldly ways might be ignored, for Daechen Jian would never return to the village. He would never walk past the fruit-seller's cart and the herbwoman's garden, never set foot upon the grassy pebbled path to his mother's house. He would never again walk through the tall red gates of their little courtyard and see his mother's face light from within at the sight of him.

❖

There came a *tap, tap, TAP!* Upon the bamboo screen.

Jian jumped, his reflections shattered.

"I am here," he called, unsure of the protocol in this strange place. He turned from the window as a troop of servants marched in and proceeded to ignore him completely as they set his room to rights. The servants of the lesser palaces unnerved him. Clad all in dark gray silk, with their faces powdered white and long braids hanging with severe precision down their backs, the *lashai*, as they were called, were slender and alike as the silvered trunks of bamboo in a long-dead forest. Jian could not tell, from the peeks he had stolen, whether they were male, or female, or both. He wondered if they were all related, but thought perhaps it was rude to ask.

They rummaged through his belongings much as his mother had done, shook out his clothes and hung them straight and neat, cleansed the air with a bundle of burning sage, and tossed salt into the four corners of the room. All the while he stood there clenching and unclenching his fists, feeling both violated and invisible.

A second mob blew into the room on the breeze of their departing, and this group carried buckets of steaming water. They filled the big copper tub, stripped him of his clothing, herded him into his bath, and proceeded to bathe him as efficiently as he would have washed a kid bound for the market. An oil was ladled into the water and scrubbed briskly into his hair and skin. It smelled of lemons and mint and burned his eyes. The servants ignored his coughing and muttered indignations.

So much for being an honored prince of the Forbidden City.

Jian tried to banish thoughts of a sparkling white kid led merrily down the path to slaughter.

When he had been sufficiently cleaned, herbed, and marinated, the servants dragged him from the cooling water and scrubbed him dry with rough linen cloths till his skin gleamed like burnished wood. His face glowed especially warm. He had been cleaned in places he had not known were meant for scrubbing. The gray servants combed more of the fragrant oil into his hair with a wooden comb, brushed it with a boar's-bristle brush till it gleamed like wet black silk, and then twisted it atop his head in a knot so severe he could hardly blink. This they tied off with a length of yellow cloth. They dressed Jian in the silks his mother had given him, and his feet were clad in golden slippers soft as a baby's skin and utterly unsuitable for what he had in mind, which was climbing out the window and running all the way home.

One of the servants pulled a plug from the bottom of the tub. The water swirled and gurgled and drained away down a drain too small to be used as an escape route.

The screen door slid open with a bang, and a short person with the air of authority and robes the color of deep twilight blew into the room like an early summer storm.

"Excellent, you are almost ready. Excellent." She smiled, and her small, bright eyes all but disappeared into the folds of flesh. She glided closer—this woman had quite perfected the manner of walking like an oulo-dancer—and Jian was enveloped in a cloud of jasmine. It was not subtle, but neither was it unpleasant. She had a kind face, he thought. Kind and formidable. She was probably a mother.

"Come here," she said. "Here. No, not there... here. Turn around, let me see you." She tugged at the cloth wrapping his hair, poked his shoulder, and pinched his cheek, hard. "Still a bit of the baby fat, but it will do. It will do. Let me see your teeth... *aaaah*." She pried open his mouth, and flashed a smile of her own. Jian startled to see a dragon's hoard of gems and gold in her mouth. "And those *eyes*. Oh yes, you will do just fine.

"Some children born during the Two Moon Dawn are simply human children whose fathers had bad timing. But you, my boy, are the real thing. Give you a few years to grow into those eyes, and you could pass for pure Issuq. I can smell the sea on you." She took a deep breath, as if she really was smelling him, and let it out in a satisfied sigh. "Would that I had a thousand of you, we would march upon Atualon this day and return with the false king in a cage. Azham, Ninianne il Mer, even that she-cat Sareta

45

would strew our path with flower-petals to be out from under his shadow. I will make such a gift of you to the emperor, young prince." She patted his bruised cheek, smiling like a cat that had gotten in the morning's catch. "One empire stretching from Nar Bedayyan to the shores of Nar Intihaan. A glorious future, do you not agree?"

The names meant no more to Jian than did her vision of a glorious future. He really just wanted to return to his home by the sea.

"I am confused, ah, *Gianpei*." He was not sure how he should address this woman. "Do I not already belong to the emperor?"

"Hush you. Do not cast your fishing net at a dragon. And I am *Xienpei* to you." She dug into the deep pocket of her robe. "One more thing, and then we are finished with you. Here. Jade for luck." She stood on the tips of her toes and looped a heavy strand of beads about his neck. "Amber for courage. Finally, pearls... pearls of wisdom." The last necklace was the most magnificent Jian had ever seen, and he had seen a lot of pearls. Black pearls, almost purple in the sunlight, big as the last joint of a man's thumb. A prince's ransom.

"From your mother." Those small, bright eyes watched him, weighing his reaction.

Jian's eyes stung, and he tried to blink the tears back.

"She does me much honor."

"You honor her with your tears, boy. Remember that." She pinched his cheek again, hard enough that he winced. "Remember her. Remember who loved you first, and you will never forget who you are."

"Forget who I am?" Jian resisted the urge to rub his cheek. "I do not understand."

"Of course not, foolish boy. You are a yellow-road princeling with the taste of mother's milk still sweet on your tongue. You know nothing. Accept that, remember where you come from, and you may survive."

Jian looked at her, and then at the pearls hung about his neck, dark as the last breath of twilight. He thought of his mother, of the way she tossed the wet hair back from her face and laughed when she broke the ocean's surface with a basket of fat oysters. He closed his heart around the memory, and he closed his fist about the pearls, and he stood up straight as if she was there to scold him for slouching.

"Yes," he promised. "I will remember."

FOUR

"Life is pain. Only death comes easy."

The invaders came as a dark stain upon the moon-blue water, bladed keels of the great vessels hacking through the soft tourmaline skin of the great Dibris, sails like halberds stabbing into the sky.

Every one of the Atualonian ships was an artist's life's work. Carven dragon and kirin and roc glared across the water, offended that the peoples at water's edge did not yet bend knee to Ka Atu, the Dragon King of Atualon. Each had oars bristling along its sides like the spikes on a quillfish, and colored lanterns hung fore and aft. Massive drums labored and throbbed with the urgency of a thousand frightened hearts, and one could smell the incense even from this distance.

In the very midst of this fleet was a massive war-craft, a king among serfs, his prow and sides fashioned into the likeness of a great wyvern. His black face was twisted in a silent roar, and he plunged and reared in the water like an angry river-beast. Dark sails snapped and bellowed in the wind, and his decks were so crowded with the gold-masked Baidun Daiel that a glittering slick of pure magic rippled in his wake.

Hafsa Azeina was not impressed.

At her signal, shofarot began to wail up and down the beach as women raised them to their lips and sounded the ancient calls of welcome and warning: two short blasts followed by a drawn-out bellow, the ululations lapping up and down the river's edge until ears rang and teeth rattled. The sounds faded away, leaving an odd tingling sensation on the skin. As the last call rolled across the water, it was answered by a long, thin shriek. Some large serpent

48

had found in their song an echo of its own pain and loneliness.

She smiled. *That should get them out of their boats quick enough.*

In her hands Hafsa Azeina held the shofar akibra, a heavy, curled instrument she had fashioned from the horn of a golden ram. It was a thing of beauty, translucent and shining as a river pearl, delicate and deadly and sweet. The spirit within whispered to her, as it always did.

Use me, it urged. *Release me.* With this instrument she could open a door between worlds and summon the Wild Hunt, and rid the world of the Dragon King. That the Huntress would kill her summoner first was a matter of little importance. What was a king's life, against the fate of all the people? What was her own life, when she had taken so many?

Of course, if Ka Atu died without an heir, there would be no one left who could control *atulfah*, no one to hold the Dragon fast to her slumbering state, and the world would be cracked open like an egg in her struggles to break free. It was something to consider.

She lifted the shofar to her mouth, and pursed her lips, and blew. All movement on the beach stopped for long heartbeats as the song of the golden ram drifted upon the air, stilling the wind, beautiful and terrible and lost. The river-beast bawled in terror—it had swum closer in those few heartbeats—and bellowed farewell from a greater distance as it took its leave. Even the beasts knew that voice.

Hafsa Azeina lowered the shofar and wiped at the mouthpiece with the hem of her tunic, ignoring the throbbing malice of the horn's frustrated spirit. She had chosen not to summon the Huntress after all. Perhaps she was not as ready to die as she had thought.

That was interesting.

Outland men and women poured from the dragon-faced ships in a riot of color and noise—crimson silk and white linen, armor of leather studded with brass, and cold steel bright in the sun. Soldiers and fancy boys, matreons and patreons and slaves… the City of the Sleeping Dragon had descended upon the Zeera.

I would not go to Atualon, she thought to herself, *so Atualon came to me.*

Hafsa Azeina knew many of the Atualonians, some from her youth, others from encounters in Shehannam. Her eyes were drawn first to the king's shadowmancer, a Quarabalese man who stood head and shoulders taller than the rest. His skin was black, not merely dark but true-black and studded all over with gems so that he glittered like a starlit night. Cat-slit eyes the color of a summer sky blinked languidly against the noonday sun. He was accompanied by a lush young woman half his height, swathed neck-to-ankle in pale green silks. His daughter, perhaps, and surely a shadowmancer in her own right. Only a dark mage could hope to survive the journey from the Seared Lands.

Mattu Halfmask had come, as well. The younger son of Bashaba wore his usual leather half-mask, this one fashioned into the face of a bull. Matreon Bellanca, in her heavy robes of state, trailed a clutch of dour-faced patreons like a mother hen with her brood. There were servants and slaves, soldiers and guards—the royal family's Draiksguard with their wyvern-headed helms, the king's Imperators in their studded leather armor, and a startling number of white-robed Salarians, private troops trained and maintained by the salt merchants of Salar Merraj.

Hafsa Azeina frowned when she saw them, and her frown deepened when she caught sight of a half-dozen Baidun Daiel, the blood-cloaked, gold-masked warrior mages who answered only to Ka Atu.

Then she saw Leviathus.

The tall youth who raced laughing down the gangplank, arms spread wide, hair whipping about his face like dark flames, could only be the surviving son of Ka Atu, grown to manhood in her absence. His gaze raked across the crowd, caught on hers, and his grin widened even further. He jumped into the water and strode through the river toward her as if the two of them were all alone in the world, and then he caught her up in a spine-crushing hug, laughing and twirling her about as she had once done with him.

50

Hafsa Azeina squeezed her eyes tight and her heart even tighter. *Of course you would send your son,* she thought, *you dirty bastard.* He had told her, and more than once, that only a foolish king would play by the rules.

"Zeina! Zeina! I knew I would find you." Leviathus dropped her to the sand and grinned, and she could see the little boy she remembered peering out from behind the mask of a man. "Ah, Zeina, you are more beautiful than I remember, and I remember you as the most beautiful woman in the world. But you seem to have gotten shorter... and your skin, spotted like a cat's! I had thought those stories were rumors."

Hafsa Azeina tilted her head back to look up into the face of the boy who had chased at her heels all those years past, and who she had loved as her own. He had been a sad and quiet toddler when she had come into his life, and a vibrant, noisy youth when she had fled the city. She could see both of them in this beautiful young giant standing before her, the shadow of hurt curled behind his laughing eyes.

Though he stood before her soaking wet and smelling of the river, and though her heart would see him always as a boy, Leviathus was a man grown. He wore upon his brow a circlet of gold and sparkling gems, cunningly wrought into the shape of the Sleeping Dragon of Atualon. He wore the blue-and-gold kilt of the ne Atu, royal family of Atualon, and the sword at his hip was plain and well used. And so Hafsa Azeina did not cling to him, or smile, or tell him any of the things her heart wished he could know.

"You are welcome to this shore, Leviathus ne Atu, son of Wyvernus," she said.

"Welcome to this shore, and no other, hm?" He gave her a measuring look. "Have things between us changed so much, Zeina? I think not. I would have you..." His eyes fell on her ram's horn, and kindled with enthusiasm so familiar she ached with it. "Is that a shofar akibra?" He made as if to reach for the instrument, but drew back at the last moment. "It is, is it not? Did you slay a golden ram?"

He had defeated her before the game was even begun. Hafsa

Azeina held up the horn so that he could see, and smiled. "I see you have only grown on the outside. Go on, take it."

He hesitated. "Is it safe?"

"Of course it is not *safe*. You may touch, but do not try to play it." She smiled again at the expression on his face, an eager puppy that has been given a bone much too big for him to chew. Then there was nothing for it but that she should tell him of her hunt for the golden ram, how she had tracked the beast for six days along the cliffs above Eid Kalish, and how as it died it plunged into a chasm filled with blackthorn so that she almost lost her prize. She did not tell him what had driven her to the desperate kill, or show him the terrible scar high on her leg where it had gored her. As she told him the happier version of her story, he turned the instrument over in his hands, ran a reverent finger along its length, peered down its fluted throat.

He handed it back without meeting her eyes.

"I wish I could have been there," he said.

She touched his arm, and let her hand drop away. "So do I."

Sending Leviathus to her had been a very dirty trick.

Ani approached with the Mothers, a heavily pregnant Umm Nurati in their midst. Introductions were made and honorifics given. Leviathus went down upon one knee and kissed Nurati's sunblade as if she were a queen. The Quarabalese man was presented as Aasah sud Layl, shadowmancer and advisor to the king, and the girl Yaela as his apprentice. Hafsa Azeina wondered if the pale and cat-slit eyes were usual among their people, or if it was the mark of a sorcerer.

Mattu Halfmask winked at her, and kissed Umm Nurati on the cheek, an offense for which he might have been gelded on the spot had Nurati not signaled an angry young Ja'Akari to back down.

Leviathus shifted from foot to foot all through the formalities, and finally gave in to impatience. "Take me to her, Zeina… please. I wish to see my sister."

Not "my half sister," Hafsa Azeina thought, *not "the girl," not even "the daughter of Ka Atu." He wishes to meet his sister.* If she still had tears, she would have wept. And how would Sulema react? Not well, she feared. Too late, she wished that she had prepared the girl for this moment.

The Quarabalese girl, Yaela, began to protest. They had been on the river for days, they needed quarters and baths and food, in that order. Surely the prince would care to refresh himself first. Introductions could wait.

Leviathus glanced at her, and Aasah touched her shoulder, and she retreated into a stony and cat-eyed silence.

Nurati and the Mothers swept the shadowmancer, his apprentice, and the rest of their guests toward Aish Kalumm in a storm of grim hospitality that would not be denied. Hafsa Azeina turned to Leviathus.

"This way," she said. "She is in the Youths' Quarter."

Leviathus surprised her by waving the Draiksguard off, and they surprised her by leaving without protest.

Bold, she thought. *Bold and foolish.*

Where did he learn that, I wonder? came the voice of Khurra'an.

Hush, she replied. *You did not stay in the tent, did you?* The vash'ai, wary and unpredictable around strangers, had been asked by their kithren to remain in the city while the two-leggeds attended to human things. But Khurra'an was a king, and a cat besides, and he did not play by the rules.

I am hunting, he told her, and she could feel his vast amusement.

Hunting what? she dared ask.

He did not answer.

They walked along the river's edge together, Hafsa Azeina and the boy grown to manhood. The steps to Beit Usqut, the Youths' Quarter, were so rocky and steep that one had to be young and foolhardy—or part goat—to attempt them. Hafsa Azeina went first, feeling Leviathus's eyes boring into her back with a thousand unasked questions.

"I was starting to wonder whether we would make it this far upriver," was all he said. "We lost two of our ships and a handful of boats to the river beasts."

"I am surprised you did not lose more than that. The kin are angry. You will not be able to return by river, you know. Your boats and your magic will have the serpents in a frenzy for at least a moons' turn. You will have to travel overland." Hafsa Azeina turned her head, grimacing as the scab along her new wound stretched and tore. "Did you have trouble with wyverns?"

Leviathus shook his head. "Serpents, mostly, I think. We lost a few during the night, so it is hard to say for certain. We heard a bintshi on the third night, and some of our men went overboard before we could get them to plug their ears. You say the kin are angry? Is that why we saw so few barbarians?"

"Barbarians? Mind your tongue, boy, these are my people now."

"Your people." She heard him chuckle—he did not realize she was serious. "All right, then, your people. Still, I had expected to see more of them. Until we reached this place, we had seen only a few stragglers and fisher folk along the river."

"The Zeeranim have never recovered from the Sundering, Leviathus. The people you see here are all that remains. A remnant."

"The Sundering? But that was so long ago... surely the effects would have faded with time?"

"What did you think happens when empires collide? When the world burns, what happens to the people?" She shook her head. "For what? So this man or that man can sit in a golden chair, and wear a golden mask, and hope that one of his children might live long enough to watch atulfah kill him. The people will never recover, not in a thousand years, not in ten thousand. Now the Dragon King turns his thoughts toward the Zeera once more. How many will die this time, do you think?"

"This land has made you bitter."

"The world has made me bitter. This land suits me well."

"Come back to Atualon," he said, as if she had not spoken. "The orange trees are just starting to blossom, and the ginger as well. Do you remember how we used to walk together, before the city was awake? You would pluck down the ginger blossoms for me to taste, and tuck the flowers into your hair until you looked like a Twilight Lady from the pages of a story-book. You would hack off a bamboo shoot and we would roast it with soft-shelled crabs, right there on the beach, and you would give me a taste of wine." He looked at her with the same wide eyes that had gotten him out of so much trouble when he was a boy.

"Our vineyards have grown, Zeina," he continued. "We have a new master gardener from the northern isles, and with his modern techniques... I have been helping him with this new variety, we call it Purple Rain, the grapes are big as plums and so sweet they explode with sugar if you harvest them an hour late. We will be tasting the first wine from these grapes this year. Wait till you try the brandies!" His grin was infectious. "And the cheeses! We had so much pomace it was coming out our ears, so we got desperate and started feeding it to the goats. Now the city smells like a winery, and in the morning when the smell of wine and fresh-baked bread mix with the breath of the sea... the air in Atualon is as good as a feast anywhere else."

She stopped at that, and turned to face him. Best to put an end to such thoughts before they could take hold.

"What of your neighbors? Do they feast as well in Eid Kalish, in Salar Merraj? Or does the Lady of the Lake look upon your laden tables with hungry eyes? Greed, lust, envy: these things are wont to stir the heart of the dragon to waking. Any child knows this."

"Ah me, Issa, has your heart grown as dry as the desert? It is good that I am here. You need to lay down that staff and have some fun before that frown cracks your face. We could pack a loaf and a skin of wine and sneak off to spend the whole day fishing. And... my sister, Sulema... she could come too. Any sister of mine must love to fish." He looked like a boy of six again, and Hafsa Azeina wavered. Sensing victory, he pressed harder. "Come home with me, both of you. Learn to smile again. You would be safe in Atualon, Zeina. She would be safe."

"Safe, in Atualon? Have those responsible for the deaths of the ne Atu been found, then? Have their heads been soaked in honey and set upon a shelf? I had not heard. There is also the minor matter of a price on my own head. A thousand bricks of red salt, last I heard. I am hardly inspired to confidence."

Leviathus grinned with delight as he shrugged a satchel from his shoulder and handed it to her.

"Ka Atu offers amnesty to Hafsa Azeina, Queen Consort of Atualon, and to her daughter Sulema an Wyvernus ne Atu. On one condition only: that they return home to him. To us."

She took the satchel and opened it. Inside was a pair of heavy scrolls sealed with wax and the king's signet. The long-forgotten smell of him curled out of the bag and caressed her cheek. Home. Hafsa Azeina closed her eyes, and turned away lest the longing burn her to a cinder.

"Zeina." He spoke the words she had dreaded for sixteen years. "Why did you leave?"

"I had no choice." It was a lie. There was always a choice.

His voice was so soft. "You left me behind."

Just like that the years melted away and she was a young concubine, a young mother, abandoning the child of her heart in a desperate bid to save the child of her flesh. She had made a choice, and he had paid the price.

Silly humans. Khurra'an rumbled in her head. *Life is pain.*

Life is pain, she agreed. *Only death comes easy.* Nothing good ever came of opening a sealed tomb.

"Come," she told the young prince, and turned away. "We are nearly there."

The last twisting passage of the path was nigh vertical, and narrow enough that Hafsa Azeina's shoulders brushed against bare gray stone. Mosses and fungi had been allowed to grow on and about the rocks. The footing was slow and treacherous, a natural defense against enemies. She stepped quickly across the smooth stones set into the very top of the cliff, and then turned to watch him. Leviathus clambered to the top, a bit slimed with moss and rock mold but not in the least out of breath.

He looked down at his ruined clothes with a bemused smile, and then glanced at her.

"Satisfied?"

A smile slipped through her resolve. "You will do."

Akari Sun Dragon filled his wings with the desert wind and soared high and brilliant above the glittering white buildings of Aish Kalumm. Hafsa Azeina led Leviathus along a path under the trees so carefully planted and tended by the Mothers: sycamore and mulberry, lotus fruit and sandalwood and sant. The trees were a valuable source of fruit and shade, and this time of year the ground beneath was littered with fallen blossoms. The vash'ai loved them, loved to rub against the bark and doze in the shade, and were liable to attack any human who thought to fell a tree for its wood.

Many a beloved friend had been interred in this place and remembered in marble and granite, carvings so skillfully wrought and so tenderly cared for it seemed a pride of vash'ai dozed in the dappled shade. Here a great black-maned sire stretched out full on his side, there a queen lifted her head to stare across the water, perhaps thinking to rouse her pride to the hunt. A younger male, ruddy mane spare and disheveled, lay curled in deep sleep. A wreath of palm leaves and flowers had been laid at his head, and the ground there was scorched. Someone had recently made a burnt offering, someone who mourned their heart's friend.

Hafsa Azeina averted her eyes from the proof of another person's grief.

"Beautiful," Leviathus whispered. "I would never have imagined this place would be so beautiful."

As she led him deeper into the Mothers' Grove, the stone vash'ai they passed became older, worn with wind and time and grief. More of them depicted aged companions with battered tusks and an air of deep wisdom about them. The great cats, like their human companions, had lived longer lives in ages past. Many of these older statues wore wreaths about their necks, though the humans who loved them were also long dead. Some, in the olden style, sat or crouched or reclined upon slabs of white marble.

They passed one sire in his prime, all white gold and bronze dapples, his black mane and striped legs so exquisitely detailed it seemed he would lift his head and roar at them.

The statue lifted its head and roared at them.

Leviathus yelled and scrambled backward, tripped over a stone tail and landed hard on his backside in a pile of flowers. Hafsa Azeina put her hands on her hips and turned to glare at Khurra'an, now sitting upright and letting his mouth hang open, displaying his tusks in a cat's-grin of victory.

"Was that really necessary?" she asked aloud for the boy's benefit.

No. But it was entertaining. Khurra'an grunted, pleased with himself, and shook his mane out before padding over to watch Leviathus pick himself up. *Whose cub? He smells like your she-cub.*

Same sire, different queen. Aloud she said, "Khurra'an, sire of the Leith-Shahad, under the sun you see Leviathus ap Wyvernus ne Atu, cub of Ka Atu, Dragon King of Atualon."

Leviathus bowed deeply to the sire of the Shahadri pride. "My kill is yours," he intoned, and Hafsa Azeina could feel him pushing his thoughts outward in a clumsy attempt at *shaaiera*. She shot him a sharp look, and he smothered a grin.

So, she thought, *the young cub has been reading old books.* That was interesting.

Khurra'an took his time in stretching, and then padded over to her, butting his enormous head under her throat in an affectionate display of possession. *This one is arrogant,* he thought, *a good strong cub for the pride. I approve.*

Leviathus's eyes were as big and round as mangoes. He had gone very still at the big cat's approach. "Magnificent," he breathed. Then he quoted, *"O golden king of the Zeera, how I tremble at your might."*

Khurra'an purred. *I like him.*

Hafsa Azeina shook her head. "You quote poetry as well? I am not familiar with that line. Whose words are those... Kibran's?"

Leviathus flushed red from his neck to his hairline.

"Yours? I would not let the girls here know that you are a poet, *ehuani.* You would not survive three days."

"'*Ehuani*'?"

"It means 'beauty in truth.' The Zeeranim are not fond of lies. Or of liars."

"I will keep that in mind." Leviathus was still transfixed by the vash'ai, who had begun sniffing and rubbing against the trees. "Where did you get him?"

Khurra'an stopped in his rubbing, and shot the boy a look of contempt.

"We found each other." Hafsa Azeina smiled at the affronted cat. "On a dark and bloody day, he saved me."

We saved each other. The voice was soft with remembered grief.

"But that is a story for another day, perhaps." They had come to the edge of the grove, and were walking now through a miniature forest of calf-high saplings fussed over by a tree-nurse. Hannei stood guard at the gate, eyes heavy-lidded. Hafsa Azeina knew that the girl's attitude of boredom was an artful sham.

"Ja'Akari!" she snapped. "*Het het!*"

Hannei jerked to attention. "*Aho!*"

"Sulema *itehuna?*"

"*Aho!*" Hannei affirmed.

"*Maashukri, ya* Hannei." She turned to Leviathus. "She is here. Stay close. The streets of Beit Usqut are no place for a man to walk alone, especially during Ayyam Binat."

"I would be pleased to guard his backside," Hannei murmured. Leviathus turned to her, mouth hanging open. The young woman stood guard still and proper as if she had not said a word, though her eyes shone and dimples played at the corners of her mouth.

Hafsa Azeina snorted. "As I said… not safe. Now, stay close."

Khurra'an rumbled as they passed the guard, and she nodded to him. "Sire."

The streets of Beit Usqut were indeed treacherous. They had been laid out as a labyrinth, intended to draw invaders into the heart of the quarter and their death. Young women strode about in the manner of young vash'ai, assured of their place in the pride and definitely on the hunt. The second time one of them had laid a hand on him, Leviathus turned to Hafsa Azeina with such an expression of horrified confusion that she burst out laughing.

"Did I not warn you of Ayyam Binat?" she chuckled. "You had best take care. These girls are fresh from seclusion and deep into the hunt."

"Do I want to know what they are hunting?" He edged closer, and Khurra'an gave an amused grunt.

Young females in heat can be dangerous, he suggested helpfully. *It is best to simply give in to their demands before the claws are unsheathed.*

A short and busty young warrior stopped dead in her tracks and raked the boy up and down with her eyes, hands fiddling with the laces at the front of her vest. He scooted by nervously, and her grin would have done a vash'ai queen proud.

Hafsa Azeina swallowed her laughter. "All I will say is this… if one of these girls offers to cross swords with you, run. Run away as fast as you can."

Khurra'an turned his sunset eyes toward her, great forehead wrinkling. *If he runs, they will give chase.*

I know. She grinned. *Shahad will be rolling in red-headed cubs this time next year.*

Leviathus could not have heard the exchange, but he glared at them both.

"Ah! Here we are." She paused at an arched entrance. "Are you ready?"

Leviathus took a deep breath and nodded.

They stepped through the wide arch and into an open courtyard, and Leviathus blushed at the sight of several young women bathing in the central pool. As one, they turned toward the newcomers. An image came to her mind of a fat tarbok parading before a pride of young queens, and Hafsa Azeina smiled.

The tarbok stands a greater chance of survival, Khurra'an purred. *This one does not even know he is being hunted.*

They crossed the courtyard and climbed the narrow stairs to the third level, where the rooms were smallest and least open. They stopped midway down the hall and Hafsa Azeina raised her hand to knock.

Khurra'an roared.

He used his indoor voice, a very small roar, but it was still loud enough that she covered her ears and glared at him in reproach. Leviathus staggered three steps back, arms cartwheeling, and almost ran into the opposite wall before clapping his own hands over his ears. His eyes were enormous.

"Do that again!" he yelled.

Hafsa Azeina glared at the vash'ai. *Was that necessary?*

Khurra'an let his jaw drop open and huffed a cat's laugh between his tusks.

Doors all along the hallway banged open, and young women in various stages of undress spilled into the hallway. Perhaps a third of them were armed, and every one of them was dangerous. Leviathus lowered his hands slowly and his eyes darted about, seeking escape, but there was no escape to be had. Finally he settled for standing very still, eyes straight ahead and staring at nothing—especially not at the shapely and very naked Lavanya standing so close she could have reached out and touched him with her knife.

Lavanya smiled at him, opened her mouth, and then noticed Hafsa Azeina at his side.

"Dreamshifter." Her bow was deep, her voice set to carry. "*Ina aasati, ehuani.*" Still bowing, she backed into her room and closed the door with a faint *snick*.

And *snick, snick, snick, bang, snick*… the hallway was empty.

Leviathus glanced at her and raised his brows.

Yes, she wanted to tell him, *they fear me. As should you. As should every living creature, save one.*

Khurra'an twitched his tail.

My apologies, she amended, *save two.*

The door before her opened slowly. Sulema stood framed in sunlight, though its golden glow could not match her for radiance. Her braided hair was flame, her eyes beaten gold, she was lean and tawny and strong. She wore a pair of loose linen trousers, and her muscled torso was slick with sweat. Her eyes flashed as they lit upon the tall youth, and away again, dismissing him as a threat.

In one hand she held a heavy quarterstaff, bound at each end with cold iron and battered from long use.

Those eyes, so like her mother's, revealed nothing at all. Not anger for the interruption, and certainly not pleasure. Sulema shifted her grip on the staff and executed a bow so correct it was just short of insulting.

"Khurra'an," she said, and then, after a short pause, "Mother."

When no invitation was forthcoming, Hafsa Azeina made an effort to swallow her irritation. "Sulema Ja'Akari. May we come in?"

Sulema shrugged and stepped back from the door, then turned and walked back into the room. As Hafsa Azeina followed, she saw that what few furnishings there were had been pushed up against the walls, and a *hoti* had been drawn in red chalk on the floor. The girl walked to the center of this, bowed to an invisible opponent, and drew herself up into Crane Watches the Sun.

"Sulema. I need to speak with you."

Crane Watches the Sun became Lotus Morning, and then a flurry of high kicks and a spinning short-strike with the staff brought Sulema to the very edge of the hoti. She met her mother's eyes with an insolent stare, and then whirled away.

"So. Speak."

Hafsa Azeina's mouth tightened. She drew a breath deep, stepped forward and erased a hand's width of chalk. Then she stepped into the circle and banged her cat's-head staff down thrice.

"*Het het het!*"

Sulema was a warrior now, and no warrior could refuse a challenge.

Cat Stalking the Moon flowed into Halving the Wind. Sulema's braids whipped about as she whirled, front kick flying and staff slicing downward so quickly that the air whistled as it passed. But her opponent was not there.

Hafsa Azeina grasped her sa effortlessly and floated between one heartbeat and the next as a feather between gusts of wind. Holding the moment, she extended her staff and struck lightly, contemptuously, at the side of Sulema's head.

Time released her and she stood facing the girl, leaning easily against her staff. Sulema was sprawled on the other side of the room. She raised a hand to her temple, lowered it again to stare first at the blood, and then open-mouthed at her mother.

Hafsa Azeina hardened her heart against the look on Sulema's face, and the shock on Leviathus's. *She must learn, or she will die... the time for childhood has passed. The dragon is waking.*

"You forget yourself, girl," she said. "You may hold your mother in contempt, but never turn your back on a dreamshifter."

Khurra'an rumbled approvingly, and sat with his back to the door. One look over his shoulder dispersed the audience their scuffle had drawn.

Hafsa Azeina stood and lowered the end of her staff to the floor. Blood splattered Sulema's new trousers, but she resisted an urge to comfort the girl. *Life is pain,* she reminded herself harshly. *Only death comes easy.* The girl was no longer a child, and a child's tantrums could get her killed.

She watched Sulema's mouth harden. Those round eyes, so strange, so like her own, blazed with fury.

I have taken this bright child, Hafsa Azeina thought, *and I have forged her into a weapon.*

Better a weapon than a corpse.

Sulema sat up, folded her legs lotus-style, and clasped her hands loosely in her lap. "Sit," she invited Leviathus. She ignored her mother, as she ignored the blood that dripped from a shallow cut by her eye. "Would you like tea?" She rapped at the wall beside her. Thin wood and linen were no barrier to snooping.

"Tea... would be welcome." Leviathus sat, and crossed his legs somewhat less gracefully. He was trying to watch Sulema without looking at her chest.

Hafsa Azeina snatched up a pale blue tunic that had been

discarded on the floor, and tossed it to the girl. Sulema wiped her face with the linen and moved as if to set it aside, but at her mother's glare pulled it over her head. She looked at the rumpled linen, now smeared with blood, and then at her mother, as if adding one more bead to the string of hurts. Khurra'an grunted and moved away from the door as a young boy entered and bowed.

Sulema smiled at the boy, and her face was transformed. When she smiled, she was the very image of her father. Hafsa Azeina heard Leviathus's sharp intake of breath.

"Tea, Talleh. And coffee. *Maashukri*. Oh, and something to eat." She was still smiling when she turned to address Leviathus. "We just broke fast this morning, and I am starving. *Yeh Atu*, forgive my manners! I am Sulema."

Hafsa Azeina sat upon the floor as well, so that the three of them formed a rough triangle. Khurra'an curled at her back and she leaned into his warmth, grateful for his support. Her daughter's disdain did not hurt any less for being deserved.

"Leviathus ap Wyvernus ne Atu," he replied. Now that Sulema was clothed, Leviathus watched her closely, waiting for a flicker of recognition. When he saw none, he turned to Hafsa Azeina, a look of puzzlement and accusation on his face.

"You are with the outlander delegation?" Sulema asked.

"I am…"

"The son of an old friend," Hafsa Azeina interrupted.

Sulema looked from one to the other. "An old friend, hm." Her eyes flashed. But the laws of hospitality were as old as the Zeera, and Sulema was Zeerani to the marrow of her stubborn bones, outland-born or not. She would not pry until they had shared bread and salt, meat and drink.

These came soon enough. Nobody went hungry in the Youths' Quarter during Ayyam Binat. Talleh returned with a handful of brown and barefoot youngsters, most of whom Hafsa Azeina did not recognize. A simple meal was laid out before them. Loaves of heavy flat bread sprinkled with precious red salt, goat's cheese and dried figs, still fat and sweet with last year's summer. And, of course, there was tea. Sulema laughed openly at the look on Leviathus's face.

"We Zeeranim may be savages," she teased, "but we are well-fed savages."

Hafsa Azeina poked at the food without much enthusiasm. She was not eager to speak the words which would bring nothing but pain to her daughter.

When the food had been pushed aside, they sipped at their tea. It was Riih Atu, Breath of the Dragon, grown by the Mothers along the banks of the Dibris. Leviathus inhaled the fragrant steam, took a small sip, and sighed appreciatively.

"Wonderful," he said.

Then Sulema asked the question that broke a fragile peace.

"Why are you here?" she asked. "Surely you did not come all this way just to have tea with your father's old… friend."

Leviathus turned the horn cup round in his hands.

"Leviathus ap Wyvernus," Hafsa Azeina prodded gently, "son of Ka Atu, tell her why you have come."

Sulema choked. "Son of Ka Atu? The Dragon King? Then you are a… prince?"

Leviathus stared at her, and then turned to Hafsa Azeina, brows drawn together in a thunderous expression that reminded her painfully of his father.

"You have not told her? Zeina, how could you not tell her?"

"Son of Ka Atu?" Sulema repeated, and then, "Tell me what?"

Leviathus folded his arms across his chest and they both glared at her.

Hafsa Azeina folded her hands in her lap, took a deep breath, and closed her eyes.

"He is your father."

"My father?" Sulema stared at Leviathus, puzzlement writ across her face plain as sacred script. "My… what… but you are so young."

"Not I." Leviathus leaned forward to take one of her hands in both of his. The girl, in shock, did not resist. "My father. Our father. I am your brother, Sulema." He laughed, a little breathless, waiting for her to react.

"My brother…?" She turned to Hafsa Azeina at last.

"Half brother," she explained. "You share a father."

"Ka Atu is my father." Sulema repeated. The years seemed to melt from her face. She was a little girl again, eyes and mouth round with shock. "My *father*."

Leviathus gathered her other hand and brought them both to his mouth. He kissed her fingertips tenderly, formally, and looked into her eyes. Sulema came back to herself and tugged away from his grip. She reached a tentative hand to his face, his cheekbones, and then his hair, red as her own.

"I have a father," she whispered, and burst into tears.

Life is pain. Only death comes easy.

FIVE

"Love is a dream worth chasing."

Ismai had been born under a red sky two moons too early, and six years too late. The awkward younger son in a family of strong women, it often seemed that the only time he was noticed was when one of his female relations tripped over him.

The art and curse of being invisible often worked in his favor. When a tray of sweets was left unattended, for instance, or when heavier chores were being assigned to the younglings. As he walked along a low arched tunnel that led into the lower balconies overlooking the Madraj, laden with a pilfered cask of beer and a whole roast fish stuffed with rice and wrapped in fig leaves, it occurred to him that this might be one of those times.

The air was so ripe with wine and beer, spiced meats and fish stew that a boy could just about open his mouth and lick it. The hearthmothers and hearthmasters had been preparing for this feast as ardently as the Ja'Akari prepared for battle.

As if they could feed us back to the glory days, he thought. *They think if they can fill our bellies, they will fill the Madraj once more with life.* He was willing to eat his share, though, if it would make them feel better.

Although so few of the seats were occupied, what the people lacked in numbers they made up for in color. The modest sky-blue touar of the Ja'Sajani complimented the bright silks of the Mothers, and the Ja'Akari watched over them all, proud headdresses proclaiming their deeds for the world to see. Ismai shook his head at the impractical clothing worn by the outlanders. Their heavy layered robes dragged in the sand and made their faces drip with sweat. These unwanted visitors sat huddled together at the far end of the Madraj, disdaining the company and even the food of the people.

Their rudeness seemed to know no bounds. Ismai saw one man in striped robes leer at a passing warrior and reach out a grasping hand. Fortunately for him, the man's gold-masked companion grabbed his arm and the girl passed without insult. Apparently they had no warriors in the outlands.

Or perhaps the man had no need of his hand.

The mask glittered as it turned toward Ismai, and he stepped deeper into the shadows with a shiver. Bound neck-to-ankle in strips of black leather, faces hidden from the sun under smooth gold, those men made him feel as if spiders were crawling over his skin. If the man was suffering from the heat, he did not show it. None of them did. They stood in the sun with their blood-red cloaks gathered about them, staring out at the world through their heavy masks, strangers in a strange land. They never spoke, from what Ismai had heard, they never ate. And they were never far from the side of the outlander king's son.

The tall red-haired man whose arrival had caused such a stir sat at Sulema's side, laughing when she spoke, touching her shoulder with his. He wore a short, straight, brutal-looking sword at his waist, a heavy torc of enameled gold at his throat and a fancy golden circlet upon his brow. It was gross, the way he flexed and twitched a new set of muscles with every breath, but Sulema did not seem to mind. She touched the gilded stranger on his arm and laughed as if they had been friends forever.

Ismai had known Sulema his entire life, and she had never once looked at him like that.

Sometimes, being invisible was as much fun as having sand in your pants.

Ismai sighed and settled down cross-legged to enjoy his stolen feast. He was skinnier than a tarbok, as his mother reminded him constantly, and fish was good for building muscle. He would eat a whole river serpent, if that would help him gain favor in Sulema's eyes.

It was the second day of Hajra-Khai, and the youngest would-be Ja'Akari were playing a perilously disorganized game of *aklashi*. The game was near its end. Several riders had lost their mounts, one was screaming at the top of her five-year-old lungs with outrage, and the sheep's head was starting to fall apart. The horses were having as much fun as their small riders, snorting and blowing and flagging their tails like a bunch of silly yearlings.

If he craned his neck Ismai could just see the First Warden and First Warrior, a few elders, and the mistresses and masters of craft. They stood with the Mothers in grim-faced splendor beneath the feasting-tents. Above them, silk tassels danced in a breeze that did not reach Ismai, a thousand little hands waving gaily to their favorite contestants.

His own mother, Nurati, sat on high, draped in the many-colored silks of the First Mother of the Zeeranim. Glossy black curls were piled atop her head, braided and belled, with a few long ringlets left to curl disingenuously along her slender neck. Her formidable laugh rang out across the stones like a war-horn. He smiled to see her reclining like a queen upon a low divan, surrounded by a flock of little girls all trying to tempt her palate with fruits and sweets and horns of water sweetened with juice.

Umm Nurati was heavy with her sixth child, when so few women bore even one, and she was venerated by the people. She looked tired and thin, aside from her gourd-round belly. Paraja, the sleek vash'ai who called her kithren, stretched along the front of the divan and fixed her yellow eyes on any who ventured too near. No other vash'ai were in evidence on the high dais. Paraja was a jealous queen.

One of those who drew Paraja's hot yellow glare was the cat-eyed girl from Atualon. She had the smoothest, darkest skin Ismai had ever seen, true-black like the night sky. She wore her hair in locks like Hafsa Azeina, but where the sorceress stared out from beneath an eagle's nest of white-gold tangles, this girl had even, oiled locks drawn back from her exotic face and fastened with bands of hammered gold wide enough to circle his forearm. She wore gold at her wrists and ankles, and kept her fascinating curves swathed in jade silk the same color as her strange and beautiful eyes.

Those cat-slit eyes had looked straight through him earlier, as he stood near the mango vendor's tent with juice dripping from his chin, feeling like a six-year-old child faced with a real Dae princess. She was not as flashy as Sulema, he decided, nor as beautiful as his mother, but it was hard to keep his eyes from her. He stared, the people stared—though they tried to do so discreetly—and Paraja stared, but the night-skinned girl ate figs from a clay bowl in tidy, neat bites, and ignored them all.

If the girl with jade eyes was a moons-lit night, the man at her side was the shadows between stars. A mountain of a man, bald and shiny as if he had been carved of a single piece of obsidian and set with gemstones. His oiled skin was bound from scalp to waist with a symmetrical pattern of delicate scars, as if a spider's web had been draped over him and had burned itself into his skin. This web was studded with tiny gemstones, so that the man glittered like a starlit night every time he moved. Eyes like a pale blue morning, cat-slit like the girl's, curved into half-moons as he bared his big white teeth and laughed at the children playing aklashi. He was clad in a brief garment of bright red, and his broad feet were bare. He wore no jewels besides his skin, bore no weapons that Ismai could see.

Several steps higher and not far from Sulema sat Ismai's elder brother, Tammas. He was, as usual, surrounded by a colorful flock of women and girls. Tammas was the one who had inherited their father's dimpled face and powerful build. Worse, he was bouncing their youngest sister, four-year-old Rudya, on his knees. The females in his immediate vicinity were all mentally braiding stud-right beads into his hair. Many of them had petitioned Nurati for the chance to bear his child, and none of them bothered to hide it.

Ismai sighed to the soles of his feet, wondering whether there were enough fish in the river to pack that kind of muscle onto his light frame. He had gotten their mother's fine-boned and delicate looks, and that paired awkwardly with Father's enormous hands and feet. When he was a small boy, he had thought it a fine thing to be fussed over by all the Mothers for his thick lashes and pretty looks.

At fifteen, it was nearly unbearable.

Their far-cousin Hannei, sword-sister to Sulema, was one of Tammas's admirers. Her shorn scalp was still paler than the skin of her face and shone with sisli oil. She wore a warrior's vest hung with small brass bells, and trousers rolled up almost to her knees. Bells flashed at her wrists and bare ankles as well, and upon the dainty chain that dangled from nose-ring to earring, caressing her soft cheek. She was a poet's vision of saghaani, pure desert beauty on the hunt for her first lover. It seemed to Ismai that, although his brother handed out smiles to the women like flowers, his eyes loved her best. It was known that Tammas Ja'Sajani had never surrendered his dignity to a girl during Ayyam Binat. Perhaps this would be the year.

Ismai sighed again, and ate a mouthful of fish. The skin was perfectly crisp, lemony and salty and spicy all at once. He told himself that he was not envious of his brother's horde of admirers. In truth, he would be content with one.

The sheep's head split in two and both halves went sailing into the stands, much to the delight of everyone who was not sprayed with gore.

First Warrior Sareta was up on the high dais near Ismai's mother, smiling as if the two of them had never been rivals. She stood beside the dreamshifter and Istaza Ani, and the three of them watched the younglings' game. The pride's highest-ranking warrior stood head-and-shoulders taller than the sorceress and was more finely muscled than the youthmistress. Her temples were smooth as old leather, and a hundred braids fell behind her magnificent lionsnake-plume headdress in a black-and-gray waterfall nearly to her knees. She wore the traditional trousers and bead-and-bone vest of the warrior, and a graceful golden *shamsi*, prized sunblade of the desert, gleamed at her side.

She was old, older even than Istaza Ani, and her face had been tempered by time and sun, by blade and wind. Her laughing hawk's eyes were fixed upon the field. Judging the prospects, he was sure, tallying every strength and weakness of tomorrow's little warriors.

See me, he urged her with all his might. *Find me worthy.* Ismai dreamed not of tallying herds and taking census and keeping the borders secure, but of riding a proud war mare across the golden sands with his face bared to the glory of Akari Sun Dragon. In the old stories, Iftallan had ridden at the side of Zula Din, a warrior in his own right. *He* had not covered his head with the blue touar and stayed home to father babies and tend sheep.

Every spring, girls who would be warriors dropped little clay tablets inscribed with their names into a clay pot set before the First Warrior's tent. This year, his had been among them. It was a foolish dream. But as Theotara herself had said, "*Where there is life, there is room for foolishness.*" His heart, young and strong, urged him to folly.

The dreamshifter turned her face and peered directly at him through the thornbush tangle of her pale locked hair. She stared at him, golden eyes hot on his face even across the distance, weighing and measuring him as if he was a fish she might bring home from the market.

The mouthful of food he had just chewed stuck in his throat. He took a long swallow of beer, but sputtered and choked as it went down the wrong way.

Hafsa Azeina smiled slightly and turned to her odd young apprentice, Daru, who was tugging at her hem. Ismai stared down at his tunic in dismay, wondering which was more foolish— spitting beer down his front under the eyes of the sorceress, or falling in love with her daughter.

Sulema laughed. Ismai looked up just in time to see her kiss the flame-haired stranger on his cheek. They were holding hands. She had found her *hayatani*, then. She had chosen a man to be her first lover. Ismai stood to leave, swallowed the last bitter dregs of beer, tore off his best tunic—ruined now—and threw it on the ground, beside the remains of his meal.

Four Ja'Sajani stepped into the arena, brought the shofarot to their lips, and blew, signaling that the game was over.

A stinging slap of wind filled his eyes with sand and tears. Ismai turned and ran from the arena, too full of fish and noise and bright things he could not have for his own. His shoulder scraped against rock and he stumbled, then tripped over his stiff new sandals and fell headlong into the hard-packed sand. He slid a short way, leaving a considerable bit of face behind, and when he came to a stop he simply lay there, childish tears dripping down his skinned nose and turning the dirt to reddish mud. His knees hurt, the palms of his hands stung, and his face burned, but none of that could eclipse the agony of his heart.

Something in the tunnel growled, a low rumbling song that turned his innards to water and chased away all thought of pain. The scrape of claw on stone, the hush of hot air as a greater predator passed. He held his breath, straining to listen around the drumming of blood in his ears, every muscle strung tight as he tried to blend into the ground. The older tunnels were known to be haunted by all manner of kith and kin, and though the Ja'Sajani cleared them out as best they could before Hajra-Khai, they had been known to miss a beast or two.

There it was again—a low grunt, a heavy breath, a heavy mind pressing against his, hungry and sharp and bright as a new-forged sunblade. One of the greater predators, then, and a boy like him would be not much more than a snack before the midsun meal. Ismai supposed he would taste of fish and beer.

He wondered whether Sulema would notice his absence.

Hello.

He froze from the inside out. The sounds and smells of Hajra-Khai faded until there was nothing left but him, the gritty dirt of the tunnel floor, and an amused presence in his mind. He lifted his head, slowly, and watched open-mouthed as the shadows danced themselves into a recognizable shape. She was smoke and bronze mirrors, midnight moons and found gold. Her eyes were the bright blue-green of gemstones in the river, and her short tusks flashed ivory in an open-mouthed grin.

I said hello. He had not imagined it. She was *laughing* at him.

Ismai drew himself up into a crouch, and then sat heavily back on his haunches. His mind groped for hers, and it was every bit as awkward as the first kiss he had shared with Kalani, a month past when they had both drunk too much jiinberry wine.

Much as Kalani had, she reached out and showed him what to do.

Like this.

It was beautiful. She was beautiful. She was…

Ruh'ayya. The name came to him, though it was less a name than the idea of the end of a song in the hour just before midnight, when one moon hangs golden in the sky and the other is hidden in darkness. *I am Ruh'ayya. You are mine.* She sat half-in and half-out of the shadows, he could see her clearly now. She was nearly black, very young, and obviously pleased with herself.

"We are…" …*too young to bond,* he protested, and *you are beautiful,* and *I am Ismai,* though his name came across as *laughter in the morning sunlight just before the spring rains.* "I love you."

"Rrrrrrr," she disagreed, mocking his voice. She detached herself from the shadows and he could see how very young she was, and how lean. It had been a hard winter with nothing bigger than tarbok to eat and one plumed serpent washed up on the beach, rank and good to roll in, and she had smelled the fish he was eating and had wanted a share but decided she would have him instead, but not to eat. He was scrawnier than a tarbok but they would grow together and the pride would simply have to accept it and Khurra'an was her sire and she loved him, too.

I am in love, he said.

Foolish cub. Love is a dream, she chided.

Yes. But it is a dream worth chasing.

She rumbled, a purr, a growl, and knocked him over with her huge head so that she could scrape the rest of his face off with her rough tongue. Ismai laughed, twined his hands in the sparse mane of his Ruh'ayya, and let go of everything he had imagined himself to be.

S I X

Hafsa Azeina's young apprentice, Daru, hustled up to where she stood with the First Warrior and Istaza Ani enjoying a spectacularly messy game of aklashi. He stopped to catch his breath—born early, the child was regrettably weak and always panted as if he had run miles beneath the hot sun—and bowed so deeply he seemed to fold in half.

"Dreamshifter... Youthmistress." He gasped. "I was sent to tell you... Ismai..."

Ani hoped that the child was not about to expire in front of them. "Ismai? He is one of Nurati's youngest, is he not?"

"Third youngest, I think." Sareta corrected. "Or fourth, perhaps. Dreamshifter?"

"Third, soon to be fourth." Hafsa Azeina raised both eyebrows at Daru. "Is there trouble?"

Sareta snorted. "There is always trouble around that one. I caught him kissing Kalani behind the stallions' pasture, not a moon hence. Although I do not doubt he was wishing it was... ah—" she glanced at Hafsa Azeina "—some other girl. Do you know, he asked to be trained as a warrior?"

Ani blinked. "That is... different. Perhaps he means to become a warden, like his brother?"

"Oh, no. He argued—*argued*, mind you—that a boy should be able to travel the world if that is what he wants. As if we need our males riding across the sands, spending so much time on horseback that they kill their seed."

Ani grinned. "I can see how a young man might find the idea attractive. Spending his days surrounded by warriors, bareheaded and free from responsibility. I will go see what the problem is."

"Ah, I will go." Sareta laughed. "I wanted to speak to some of the new Ja'Akari before the dances, in any case." She nodded to Hafsa Azeina, who did not seem to notice. "Dreamshifter. If I might borrow your apprentice…?"

Hafsa Azeina waved one hand, distracted.

Daru snapped to attention, and his face lit with delight at the honor. *He really is a beautiful child,* Ani thought. *A pity he is so weak.* As they left, she turned her attention back to the day, and the game, and anticipation of the night's activities.

Of all the days in the turning of a year, Ani loved Hajra-Khai best. This was the time that the people shone brightest. The prides came together to play and hunt and compete and, of course, they came to eat. They came to race horses and show off babies and make a few more of each. Small things, ordinary things, but enough of these slim reeds gathered into a bundle might just be strong enough to ensure the people's survival.

Ani would sing tonight. She always sang at Hajra-Khai, added her rough voice and her music to the noise and mayhem. This was the heartbeat of the pride, the drumming, thrumming, foot-stomping music was the blood that flowed through their dreams. The smoke and sweat and animal smell of so many drawn together rose up and into the sky as a prayer, a wish that life would continue as it had always been—birthing and loving, feuding and bleeding, all sewn together by the singing desert and the great deep dreams of the river Dibris.

In this, as in much else, she and Hafsa Azeina were opposite sides of a sword. As much as Ani enjoyed the gaming and the noise, the smells and sounds of so many brought together under the sun, her old friend only barely tolerated such chaos. The same woman who would wade bareheaded into the steaming belly of a disemboweled lionsnake could hardly stand the sight of a dozen people seated together for a meal. Gather a few thousand of the people together for a springtime feast, throw in a few outlanders, and Hafsa Azeina would start getting restless.

Ani came to Hajra-Khai in hopes of getting drunk, watching the games, and wrestling with an old friend. The last thing she needed was a twitchy dreamshifter ruining her holiday with chaos and bloodshed.

So it was that as they stood together on the high dais, Ani took a handful of dried figs with honey and nuts from a tray borne by a smiling boy, but Hafsa Azeina made a face and waved him away. The dreamshifter had eaten earlier—dried strips of flesh of a peculiar dark color streaked with yellow fat—but there was a difference, Ani felt, between sustaining the body and feeding the spirit. She was tempted to press the sweets upon her friend, to point out the pleasing strains of a bard's song and the well-shaped backside of her old friend Askander. First Warden or no, gray hairs or no, that man was as tasty a dish as any laid out at Hajra-Khai.

But the dreamshifter insisted on drinking only from the bitter well, and never the sweet. Such things did not speak to her. Ani caught Askander's bold eye, and they shared a grin before he turned away. Later, if he was fortunate, they might share more.

"I will not let her go."

Ani followed her friend's gaze, and watched as the new Ja'Akari filed out onto the red sands of the arena. Sulema glowed among the young women, an ember in the coals, shorn and oiled and braided as if she had been born under the sun. She brought her fingers to her mouth and whistled, and the red-haired youth in the stands stood and waved to her. After all these years of believing herself abandoned, unwanted, the girl finally had a family. A doting brother, a powerful father. As for her mother...

"Not let her go?" Ani swallowed a mouthful of sharp words. It was never a wise thing to anger a woman who ate the hearts of her enemies, old friend or no. "The sun is setting on her childhood, Zeina, and it will rise on her life. I fail to see how the choice is yours, now."

Hafsa Azeina raised her eyebrows. "Zeina? You have not called me that in years. Do not soothe me with soft words, Youthmistress. Say what you would say... you are angry with me."

"She thought herself unwanted, by you or anyone else. And now she finds that she has a brother. A father. How do you think you will prevent her from going to meet him?"

"The past is behind us. Nothing good ever comes from opening a tomb, once that tomb has been sealed."

"Ka Atu is *your* past, my friend. Not hers. How do you think to stop her from going off on her own, now that she knows the truth? If you do stop her, what of us? The Zeeranim cannot stand against the wrath of Ka Atu."

"You think I should take his offer of amnesty."

"I do. I accepted years ago that you did not wish to raise your own child. I never understood, but I accepted it. But this I can neither understand nor accept. My father sold me like a goat. Hers has torn the world apart to find her. How can you think to deny her this? It is her birthright."

She was all but shouting. Several of those surrounding Nurati glanced in their direction, and quickly diverted their attention elsewhere. The tempo of the drums increased—*ra-dum ra-ra-dum*—until they echoed the beating of her angry heart.

Down in the arena, the first of the young warriors leapt into dance.

Hafsa Azeina never moved, but her eyes clouded like the sky before a storm. "You speak of her birthright. You know nothing. You understand nothing. You imagine her father will sweep her up into his arms as if she were a lost child, and shower her with wealth and love, and every hurt I have ever caused her will be healed in the golden glow of his regard. You know *nothing*.

"You think I do not love Sulema?" the dreamshifter continued. "I died for her, Ani, I died for my child, and then I lived again for her sake. You think you have bled for her? I have killed a hundred men for my daughter, killed them and eaten their living hearts, all to keep her safe from the past. You would do what? Put her on a boat. Pat her on the head, kiss her cheek, and feed her to the dragon with your own hands. Tell me again how I do not love my daughter… old friend."

Ani struggled to rein in her temper, but a steady head had never been her strength.

"I know nothing? Fine, then. Explain it to me. Use small words… I am only the woman who raised your daughter. You owe me this much."

The dreamshifter's eyes flashed. "I? I owe *you*? You have no idea what I have done for you. For the people. How every waking hour, I… no." She bit the word short, as if biting off a piece of gut string. "*Khutlani*, Ani, your mouth is too small to speak of these things."

Ani took a step back, fists clenched at her sides. She did not know this woman, this fell-eyed sorceress with the blood of enemies upon her lips.

"My mouth is too small to speak of such things? *Mine?* Well I remember the day, Hafsa Azeina. I was there when Theotara Ja'Akari dragged your sorry dead ass into camp. Do you have any idea what she was to me, what she gave up in order to save you and your child? She had… she was…" Ani choked on the words. "She gave you her death, Zeina, her *death*. Do not say the people have not earned your protection a thousand times over. Whose blood called you back from the Valley of Death, there in the Bones of Eth? Whose flesh sustained you? Whose child dances, even now, whole and healthy upon the sands of the Madraj? You tell me, Dreamshifter, tell me where the debt lies."

Ani felt the hairs on the back of her neck rise as Hafsa Azeina stared at her. Through her. Surely those eyes looked again upon the hot yellow sands, and the Bones of Eth, and the day a good woman gave up her death in order to save two lives.

Ah, well, it may be a very good day to die, but it was an even better day to live. As it was not in her nature to wound a friend, Ani softened her voice. "The past is past, Zeina, that lonely wind is long gone to dust. Surely the girl's wish to meet her father is not as dangerous as all that. Ka Atu may be a powerful man, but he is only a man, Zeina, and he is her father."

"Truly, you do not know." Hafsa Azeina's voice had shrunk to a whisper.

"There are many things I do not know. If you tell me, there will be one less."

The drums faded, and a flute picked up the song—a breeze, the cry of a lonely spirit, a shepherd-girl lost in the hills. Young Hannei whirled about, limbs akimbo, and executed a spinning kick so high and so perfect that the crowd gasped in delight.

"I can do things..." The dreamshifter's smile was strange. Sad and strange. "Monstrous things. I can reach through worlds, Ani, right through the curtains that separate us, I can reach out my hand like this, and pluck a man's heart from his chest as he sleeps. I can eat *dreams*, Ani. Man, woman, beast, child. No one is safe from me."

"Zeina..."

"I am powerful, Ani, more powerful than you know. No one should have this much, to be able to sneak into a person's soul while they are sleeping, and change things. End things. Easy as lighting a candle... it is not right. It does bad things to you, inside. If it were not for Khurra'an..." Her voice trailed off.

"You could stop."

"You are not listening to me. *Listen* to me. I can do these things, and if I am a child lighting a candle... he is a flame, Ani, a great roaring flame, and I am all that stands between him and my daughter. He will not have her. If I have to die again, he will not have her."

"Why would Sulema's father wish to harm her? Is she not precious to him?"

"She is precious to him, and not just because she is his daughter. Sulema is *echovete*. She will be able to hear atulfah, the magic of Atualon. She will be able to wield the reins of sa and ka, and control the direction of the world."

"Sulema, control the world?" Ani chuckled, her earlier anger melting away. "I cannot imagine. She can scarcely muck the *churra* pens without getting into trouble. How can you be certain she is one of these... echovete?"

The dreamshifter's eyes were far away. "You can hear it, if you know what to listen for. Atulfah is a song, Ani, the Song of Dragons. A song greater than our little minds can hold, a song mightier than our little mouths can sing. The song of being. Before this song, there was nothing. Nothing." She opened her arms wide, and a smile such as Ani had never seen spread across her features. "Then the dragons were singing, and it *was*."

"You can change this song with your music?"

"*Khutlani*." The rough voice was so soft. "A dreamshifter, change the song… no. If atulfah is an ocean, I am a child skipping along the beach, collecting broken sea-shells to make a pretty necklace. But Ka Atu has waded far out to sea. He is in the song, he is of the song, and it listens to him."

"You say Sulema could do this thing?"

"Oh, yes. She is strong. Stronger than her father. If she goes to Atualon…

"I have seen it," she went on. "If Sulema goes to Atualon, Wyvernus will make her his heir. He will fill her eyes with wonder and her heart with music, and she will shine so brightly that Akari Sun Dragon himself will fall under her spell. She will be Sa Atu, the Heart of the Dragon. Mountains will bow to kiss her feet. An emperor will die of love for her. Her song will be the most beautiful thing this world has ever known…

"…and then it will kill her, just as it is killing her father."

Before Ani could so much as open her mouth, they were interrupted by her long-time friend and sometime lover, Askander. The least excitable man she knew was nearly running, and his eyes showed white at the edges like a spooked stallion's.

"Dreamshifter," he huffed. "Youthmistress. There has been some trouble…"

Ani laughed. "The year is new, and blood runs hot, First Warden. When is there not trouble at Hajra-Khai? It is what I like best about—"

Shouting erupted from the tents whence Askander had come, and someone screamed in fury. Then there was a sound—such a sound, a deafening crack like thunder that had them all clapping their hands to their heads. The vash'ai roared.

Askander spun about and sprinted toward the tents like a bee-stung horse.

"Baidun Daiel," Hafsa Azeina called back over her shoulder. She, too, was running.

It occurred to Ani much later that if a dreamshifter is running, perhaps the wisest course of action is to run the other way.

SEVEN

The feast-day revelers scattered before the dreamshifter as tarbok before a hunting cat, and well they might. Echoes of her unease shivered through this world and the Other, growing stronger as the crowd parted and Hafsa Azeina saw the tableau before her.

A young Ja'Akari, vest torn and angry red marks livid against her bare flesh, was being held back from a green-robed Atualonian man by a pair of stone-faced wardens. The girl radiated fury. Her young vash'ai, a coal-and-gold male, was lashing his tail and singing as he tried to find a way past green-eyed Paraja.

The Atualonian man seemed to have fared poorly against his opponent. He was face-down in the sand, with two warriors sitting on his back and another binding a tourniquet around the bloody stump where his right hand had been.

She nudged Khurra'an. *Kithren, get that cub out of here before he makes matters worse.*

Khurra'an flattened his ears.

Please.

His girl was attacked. This kill is his.

Please, she repeated. *Bloodshed between the vash'ai and the outlanders at this point would be like walking into an oilsnake's den with a lit torch.*

He twitched the very tip of his tail, and his voice was very soft. *I will lose face because of you. Again. There is a debt of blood between us if I do this thing.*

Agreed.

Khurra'an roared, and the young sire yowled back, fury bristling from every hair of his lean body. The older sire let his lower jaw drop, displaying massive gold-cuffed tusks in a blatant threat, and the smaller male slunk away, snarling and looking back over his shoulder.

Barekh says you owe him blood debt as well, the great cat said.

The two of you can fight over my stringy carcass later, she snapped back. *Now let me get to the bottom of this…*

Goatfuckery?

She snorted. *Best I get this sorted before Nurati…*

The crowds parted again. This time reverence, not fear, shuffled their feet as the First Mother swayed gracefully through their midst. Her feet were bare. She wore bells upon her wrists and ankles, and bells in her hair. A translucent linen shift parted as she walked, displaying her moon-round belly and swollen breasts to their best advantage. Umm Nurati, the most fecund First Mother in living memory, was the living embodiment of the river Dibris— beauty and fertility in a harsh and barren world.

"She does not even waddle," Ani whispered close to her ear. "It really is not fair."

Hafsa Azeina did not reply. She had learned long ago that "fair" was an empty word devoid of truth, and it certainly did not apply to people such as Nurati or Ka Atu.

Or to a dreamshifter, for that matter.

A fist of older Ja'Akari, faces hard as flint, came to surround the First Mother. Each of them had the dappled skin and fierce eyes of those long-bonded. As their vash'ai padded out to stand with Paraja one of the larger sires, a scarred old tusker, butted the vash'ai queen affectionately under her jaw and shot an insolent side-eyed look toward Khurra'an.

What was that *all about?* Hafsa Azeina asked him.

It is of no concern to a human. He would say no more.

Interesting. But she thought it very quietly.

Umm Nurati stopped, and the warriors stopped with her, and when she raised one hand the crowd went silent but for the wailing of an infant and the hoarse cries of pain coming from the one-handed man.

"Tell us, Gitella," she said to the Ja'Akari with the torn vest, "what happened here?"

"That fucking cunt! She cut my hand off!" screamed the outlander.

Nurati did not so much as look at the man. Her eyes lit upon the First Warrior, standing near her warrior with a face of stone and anger. "Sareta?"

Sareta nodded to one of the warriors who was sitting on the man's back. The girl, grinning widely, took off her tunic and stuffed it into the man's mouth, muffling his shrieks.

"Now then." The First Mother held out her hand to Gitella, and gave the girl an encouraging smile. "What happened?"

"This… this maggot-crotched outlander came at me with his filthy mouth and his filthy eyes, and he grabbed my tit. *Hard*," the warrior said. Her hands shook as she pulled the ragged edge of her vest back and exposed an ugly row of angry red rake-marks. "So I cut off his hand. My Barekh would have finished him, but Paraja would not allow it."

"Paraja was right," Nurati said. "Both sides must be heard before death is handed out. I would hear the outlander's words. Oh, and First Warden, if you would bring the… yes, thank you."

Askander had slipped away and returned with a heavy woven basket of river-grass with an iron chain and collar attached. The Atualonian man's eyes bulged even further when he saw this, and he renewed his struggles.

Save your energy, Hafsa Azeina thought. *You will need it for the chase.*

Not that it will make much difference. Khurra'an yawned a laugh.

Ehuani.

The warriors stood, dragging the bloodied man to his feet between them. His eyes darted about the crowd, desperate and wild. They lit with hope when Leviathus stepped into the ring of angry pridespeople.

"What is this?" Leviathus frowned.

"Your man is accused of assaulting one of our warriors, ne Atu,"

Nurati explained. Her voice, usually strident, had softened to a honeyed contralto. "We were just about to ask for his side of the story."

"Just about to... but the man has already lost a hand!"

"He *touched* me!" Gitella cried, and spat upon the sand. "He is fortunate I only took a hand." Her vash'ai emerged, clearly subdued and accompanied by Khurra'an, and took his place at the girl's side.

Leviathus looked at the girl, taking in her torn vest and the look on her face, and then to his own countryman, sagging handless and white-faced between two furious warriors. He looked then to Umm Nurati and bowed deeply.

"*Meissati,*" he said, "if I may...?"

She nodded her assent.

Leviathus closed the distance between himself and the accused, and reached for the cloth gag, but a gasp from the audience stayed his hand.

Several Baidun Daiel—a dozen, maybe more—had appeared in their midst as if risen from the sands like dark ghosts. One of them, a slight, lithe figure, strode without hesitation to stand beside Leviathus. It gestured gracefully to the doomed man, tilted its gold-masked face in inquiry.

"Very well," Leviathus said, stepping aside. "If it is my father's will."

"What is this?" Umm Nurati demanded. She would have stepped forward but for the knot of warriors who closed about her like a protective fist, naked blades flashing in the midsun glare.

Hafsa Azeina stepped forward, joining the game with a reluctant sigh. "The Baidun Daiel are... connected to the Dragon King. They can see for him—"

"*And speak for him.*"

The crowd went silent, the singing dunes went silent, the world went silent at the sound of that voice. It was the voice of a young woman, light and sweet—and it was also the voice of a man, a voice as dark and rich and dangerous as blackthorn honey. That more powerful voice rode the first as a man might ride a horse, and it came from the blood-robed mage. Even as it spoke, the smooth and featureless mask shifted as if a man's face pressed out from behind a curtain of gold. Golden eyes fixed upon her, and golden lips formed the ghost of a smile.

"There you are, little one," it rasped. "Did you really think you could hide from me forever?"

Hafsa Azeina did not answer. A shudder took her from head to toe, and the words stuck in her throat like crow's meat.

"Father," Leviathus murmured, and dropped to his knees. The rest of the Atualonians, to a soul, fell to the ground like so many sheaves of wheat under the reaper's blade.

"What goes here?" The face of the Dragon King grew more distinct upon the mask, and as it did so the girl's voice was lost. "Why am I called? I was at song." He asked the question of Leviathus, but those hard bright eyes never left Hafsa Azeina's.

"There has been a bit of a… situation. One of our men may have assaulted a young woman of the Zeeranim…"

"'May have?'"

"Your Arrogance," Nurati interrupted as she stepped forward, "we have heard the girl's words, but we have not yet questioned the man." The Ja'Akari murmured angrily at this, and the girl with a torn vest flushed with rage.

"Ah, so it is truth you want, is it?" Golden lips curled into a sardonic smile. "I have heard that your people value truth above their own lives."

"*Ehuani*," murmured the warriors.

"*Ehuani* indeed. If it is truth you want…" The Baidun Daiel turned abruptly toward the accused and tore the cloth from his mouth.

"My king," rasped the man. He would have fallen to his face had he not been held. "My king…" He looked up, beseeching, and then froze. A look of horror such as Hafsa Azeina had never seen rippled across his face. The lips pulled back from his teeth, his eyes went wide and wild, and the cords in his neck stood out as if he would shriek till his heart burst. But there was no sound, and the silence was terrible.

Then there was sound, and that was more terrible still. The sound and smell of bloody meat hissing over a fire, the hiss and pop and crackle of a man being seared from the inside out. Stinking, oily smoke poured from his mouth, and as the warriors dropped the man in horror, he thrashed and twitched upon the sand. At the very last a long grayish wisp of smoke rose from his nostrils, and a face like smudges of coal opened its mouth in a silent scream.

The desert wind, capricious and merciless, tore his burnt-out soul to shreds.

The Baidun Daiel turned back to the stunned crowd. The face of Ka Atu smiled once more, as a magician might smile at the reaction of very small children to his simplest tricks.

"Your warrior was telling the truth," he said. "This man did, indeed, assault and accost the young woman. I assure you he will not do so again. Are you satisfied?"

Askander cleared his throat.

"No?"

"Actually," the First Warden said, though his voice was not as steady as usual, "as the warrior is ours, and the grievance is hers, justice was ours to mete out. That life was not yours to take."

Ani, behind her, made a worried sound in her throat. *Ware, Askander,* Hafsa Azeina thought. *You do not know this man as I do.*

The expression on the golden mask did not change. "Very well, Pridesman. I owe you a life. You may have… this one." The Baidun Daiel went stiff all over. Waves rippled across the golden face from the center and out toward the edges as the mask became blank once more, a smooth and polished oval without the slightest hint of a human face save the eye-holes.

The Baidun Daiel fell to the ground like a rag doll dropped by a careless child. The Zeeranim, the Atualonians, even the other Baidun Daiel stepped back from the bodies that lay prone upon the sand.

Not Daru, of course. Hafsa Azeina had not seen her apprentice until that moment, had not even known he was there, but nodded her approval as he stood his ground.

And not Hafsa Azeina, foremost dreamshifter of all the prides. She shook herself like a wet cat and stalked forward, not bothering to wrinkle her nose at the smell of burnt flesh. She had smelled worse.

She had done worse.

The Atualonian man was dead—past dead, the soul burnt out of his body—and she paid him no mind, kneeling instead beside the night-bound form of the Baidun Daiel. She rolled the body face-up, surprised at how light it was, how slight, how easily it turned toward her. A small gasp escaped the crowd as the golden mask fell away...

...The years fell away, and Hafsa Azeina was again a young mother, clinging desperately to the side of a fortress wall, peering through an arrow-slit window and into a chamber of horrors. She knew this face, this girl. Had watched her die at the hands of Ka Atu, so very long ago.

"Tadeah," she whispered. She could hear her other self, her dream-self, screaming in rage and horror. She gathered the girl up into her arms, ignoring the mutters and curses and shouts, ignoring the sun and the sand and the wind and her own tears. "Oh, Tadeah."

A shadow fell upon them, but she did not care. For Sulema's older half-sister, whom she had loved as her own, opened those wide blue eyes and smiled.

"Zeina," she said. "You have come. I knew you would save me."

"Of course I came," Hafsa Azeina choked on the lie. Tears dropped fat and hot from her eyes to fall upon the girl's face, even as tears of blood welled and spilled from those wide blue eyes. "How could you think I would not come for you?"

"How could you think to escape the Dragon King?" the girl rasped. Her lips were flecked with bloody spittle, her skin fading to a deathly white. "No one may defy the will of Ka Atu. Not even his... his own... daughter." Her eyelids fluttered, and she closed her eyes with a rattling sigh. "I am so tired. So tired, Zeina."

Hafsa Azeina leaned close, so close her lips brushed the girl's ear. Already she could smell death upon the girl. "Stay with me," she pleaded. "Tadeah, please stay."

The girl barely breathed, and her lips scarcely moved, but her words rang in Hafsa Azeina's soul like stones dropped into an empty well.

"You left," she whispered. "You left me to die."

EIGHT

"I am stronger than they know."

D aru's legs were trembling again.

He tried to take a deep breath, to fill his lungs all the way down to the bottom of his belly, as the dreamshifter had taught him. He looked over to where the First Warrior was speaking with the newest Ja'Akari, Hannei foremost among them. Hannei had been his minder when he was tiny and nobody expected him to remember that, but he did, just as nobody had expected him to survive when his mother had died of last-laugh fever and he had been born early and weak.

Daru especially remembered a night when his lungs had been bad again, and he was moved into a little room by himself. The healers had filled the room with fragrant steams and herbs, and told him it was for his own good, but he had believed—and still believed—that he had been hidden away so that he could die without upsetting the other children. He had heard one of the boys say as much, and Hannei's sharp words were forever etched upon his heart.

"He will live," she had insisted. "He is stronger than you know."

Now he stood motionless, silencing the tremble in his legs, worried that the First Warrior would notice that he was still there and send him away. He was not supposed to be overhearing the words she spoke to these girls. This was a secret and sacred time for them and he was just a boy. But he could hardly be expected to play aklashi with the other boys, to race horses or parade himself in front of the vash'ai in the hope that they might consider him as a companion for one of their cubs.

He did not wish to draw the attention of the vash'ai, at all. Daru could feel the great cats watching him, always watching, and he knew what they thought of allowing a weakling to live. Khurra'an was bad enough—the huge sire ignored him as if that alone would cause him to cease to exist—but Paraja was a million times worse. She had looked at him once, when he was very young, and she had gotten into his head, and told him to die. That was when his lungs had gotten sick and they had hidden him away.

But he was stronger than they knew.

He pretended to be studying his fingers, and peeked at Hannei out of the corner of his eye. She was tall, and proud, and beautiful like a hero in the old stories. Not a trickster like Zula Din, but a real hero, living a life of truth *ja Akari*—under the sun—in service to her people. Some day, he knew, Hannei would be the First Warrior, foremost warrior of the pride. She would wear a cloak of serpent's hide and lionsnake feathers in her hair. He, Daru, would be First Warden and kneel at her feet during the Feast of Daylight Moons. Never mind that this was an impossible dream for a weakling boy, the child who was born to die. He was stronger than they knew. And he had seen it.

Hannei saw that he was watching them, and gave him a wink and half a smile.

One of the other girls noticed him standing there, and elbowed her, smirking. Hannei pretended not to notice, but when the girl attempted to jostle her again, she stepped back so that the other lost her balance and nearly fell.

The First Warrior stopped midsentence and turned her head to the girls. "Is there a problem here, Annila?

Annila, a pretty curly-haired girl, turned red as a sunset. "Apologies, First Warrior. I was… there was… this boy should not be here." She jerked her chin in his direction.

The First Warrior did not turn. Daru realized that she had known full well that he was standing there. "Does the presence of one small boy interfere with your concentration, then? Perhaps you would like to join the dance next year instead."

"No, First Warrior." The words tripped over themselves in their haste to get out. "I am sorry. I just... ah." She bowed low, face still aflame. "These are not words for a boy to hear."

The First Warrior regarded Annila for a long, heavy moment. The girl remained bent as she was, obviously wishing that the warrior's attention might be directed elsewhere. After a few heartbeats' time, she turned her face so that he could just see one cheek and the corner of a dark eye. Her face did not move, but Daru thought she was laughing on the inside.

Laughing at him.

"Annila has no manners, but she does have a point. Unless you have also decided to become Ja'Akari?"

Daru started. What was she talking about? A boy, become a warrior? He shook his head, and saw her mouth twitch. She *was* laughing at him.

"Good. I do not have time for more than one troublemaker today. Go on, Daru, see if your mistress has something for you to do. Or go find something to eat before a strong wind carries you away to the Edge."

Annila, straightening, did not bother to hide her mocking smile. Hannei gave him a look of sympathy, but one of the other girls laughed out loud. Daru turned and fled, tears welling in his eyes and threatening to spill over.

He had no intention of seeking out his mistress, who had hardly spoken to him at all since those outlander ships had come to Aish Kalumm, except to send him running for the root of this herb or the stomach of that lizard, and some of the things she had asked for gave him a bad feeling in the pit of his stomach. Umm Nurati would be there, and with her Paraja. The vash'ai queen would stare at him with her yellow eyes, thinking he ought to be dead. Worst of all, Tammas Ja'Sajani would be sitting in the stands watching Hannei, and she would watch him back.

Hannei would choose him, everyone could see that. They said that Tammas Ja'Sajani would never allow himself to be hayatani, but Hannei was no ordinary girl, and the warden was just the sort of man she should choose. Strong, and handsome, and whole. The vash'ai did not see *him* as a weakling cub unworthy of the food on his plate or the breath in his lungs.

I am stronger than they know, he thought, dashing the tears from his face with the side of his hand, hard enough to hurt. *I will be stronger than him, some day. I have seen it.*

He had come to a place he knew, close enough to watch the doings in the Madraj, but hidden from view. A low growl stopped him in his tracks and he looked up, wary. If the vash'ai ever caught him alone…

He stumbled as his weak legs turned to water. It was a vash'ai, all right, a young female the color of moonslight on black water. She was close enough that a half-hearted leap would bring her within killing distance, and she was sitting on her haunches, laughing at him.

"Ruh'ayya, do not scare him. Hello, Daru."

"Ismai?" His voice was a breathless squeak. "Ismai? You have… you are…"

The older boy walked to where the vash'ai sat, and scratched behind one huge ear. She rumbled low in her throat, a sound that never failed to turn Daru's insides to water, and knocked her head against his shoulder. Ismai laughed and stared at the cat with big eyes and a lopsided smile.

"We are Zeeravashani," he said. "Yes. Ruh'ayya chose me. Is she not lovely? Is she not the most beautiful thing you have ever seen?"

Daru eyed the vash'ai warily. She was certainly one of the largest he had ever seen. Half-grown, she was still nearly as big as Paraja. "She is very pretty, Ismai. But you are…"

Ismai stroked the cat as if he could not resist touching her. "Too young. I know. Nobody has ever heard of Zeeravashani this young. But," he shrugged, blushing a little, "Ruh'ayya is different." His voice trailed off. He smiled. "Would you like to touch her?"

His heart tripped. *Touch a vash'ai?*

"She says you may. She says…" He tipped his head to one side, eyes unfocused as he spoke with his companion. "She says you are stronger than you seem. She likes you."

Daru could hardly refuse such an invitation. He shuffled forward until he was so close he could feel heat radiating from the vash'ai, smell her breath, see the fine lashes that ringed her moonsilver eyes. She huffed a breath, impatient, and tipped her head so that he might stroke along her jaw. Daru stretched forth his trembling hand and touched life itself. She was, oh, she was hot to the touch, he could hear the breath purring and rumbling in her throat, it sang it in his bones. Her fur was thicker and coarser than he had imagined, and bristled under his hand as if each hair was alive and aware of his touch.

"Oh, Ismai," he breathed. "She is wonderful."

Ruh'ayya swung her huge head around so that she was staring straight into his eyes. He thought he might lose himself in their pale depths, if she let him. She blinked, and showed her tusks in a little cat-laugh, and padded a short distance away. Then she flopped to the ground and began washing her enormous paws, as if she were a small-cat and nothing out of the ordinary had just happened.

"She is, is she not?" Ismai agreed.

"Is this why you are in trouble? The First Warrior is coming to find you, when she is done with the girls."

"I do not know. Probably." Then he grinned, the same Ismai Daru had always known. "But it is worth it."

Daru had to agree. For a moment he let himself imagine…

Not for you.

He jumped like a startled horse, and met Ruh'ayya's bright stare. "What?"

"She spoke to you?" Ismai glanced at the vash'ai. "I did not know she could do that. What did she say?"

Ruh'ayya mocked them both with her eyes.

Daru shrugged and stared at his feet. *Not for me,* he thought. *Of course such a one as she could never be mine.* "*Khutlani,*" he suggested in his quietest voice. For surely his mouth was too small to voice such a large wish.

Ismai grinned and ruffled his hair, just like a grown-up. "She is rather imposing, *ehuani*. Perhaps you might come hunting with us one of these days. It will take a lot of meat to feed her, she is still growing."

"Hunting." Daru schooled his face to stillness, a taste like bitter medicine filling his heart.

"Yes. Hunting. You are old enough, and—" Ismai eyed him critically "—I think you are strong enough. You could keep up with us if you ride."

"I… I… I never…"

Ismai shrugged dismissively. He had left his childhood behind in the blink of Ruh'ayya's silvery eyes, and Daru struggled to catch up. "Never sat a horse before, I know. I will teach you. It is not that difficult, Daru, truly it is not. You are Zeerani. It is not fitting that you should not learn to ride. You are Zeerani," he repeated, as if that was important.

A roar from the crowd drew them both to an arch overlooking the arena. Tammas Ja'Sajani sat astride Azouq, not a stitch of tack between them, and they were performing the Dance of Kiadra. The near-legendary blue roan stallion moved like magesilver, like shadows in the pale moonlight, and his hide shone like a silver bell. Tammas's vash'ai Dairuz sat near the dais, head thrown back and soot-and-ash mane drinking the sunlight. His eyes were half-closed and his mouth half-open as he roared and purred and crooned.

Azouq leapt high into the air, kicking out with his hind legs. Tammas threw his arms wide, ululating a challenge, and Dairuz roared with such force that Daru's feet tingled. The crowd answered Dairuz. Shrieking, stomping, clapping, blowing the shofarot, the people sang the Song of the Zeera.

Longing burned in the marrow of his bones, and filled his mouth with bitterness.

I am Zeerani, his heart insisted, and, *This,* and, *Yes.* His spirit cried out for the life that his body denied him.

"Now imagine that Tammas is your brother."

Daru jumped, startled, and turned to Ismai. The older boy shook his head, lips twisted in a wry smile. "Imagine that the old stories wrapped themselves in the painting of a hero and came to life, and that is your older brother." He sighed. "You are lucky."

"Lucky?" Daru's laugh was ugly to his own ears. "Lucky. Under the sun, I am so fortunate I envy myself."

"But you are lucky," Ismai insisted. "You are the strongest dreamshifter's apprentice in a hundred years. You get to live with her… train with her."

"The strongest apprentice in a hundred years? Who says this?"

"My mother, for one, and you know that whatever she says, comes to be. The dreamshifter may see the future, but the Mothers make it so. They say you have already walked the paths of dreams. What is it like?"

"Shehannam?"

Ismai nodded. "Is it like the dreams you have when you are asleep?"

Daru looked out across the arena, but his mind's eye was focused on the lush green paths of Shehannam. The strange trees, silver and gold and straight as river reeds, and the shadows… It was not the same as being asleep, not the same at all. You could not die in a sleep-dream. You could not kill. He remembered the making of his bird-skull flute, and shuddered.

"I am sorry." Ismai looked embarrassed. "I should not have asked."

Daru shrugged. "That is okay. It is just… Shehannam is hard to describe. Dreamshifter does not like me to speak of it."

Ismai nodded. "Hafsa Azeina casts a long shadow." He jerked his chin toward the Madraj. "Just as my brother does."

Your brother does not kill people in their sleep, Daru thought.

Ruh'ayya stared at him as if she could read his mind.

Ismai glanced toward the arena and then froze.

"*Au'e. Ai yah.*"

Daru followed Ismai's gaze. A pair of naked combatants had

entered the Madraj. He grinned. "Sulema looks fine today, does she not?"

Not as beautiful as Hannei, his heart whispered. He urged it to silence.

Air hissed between the older boy's teeth. "Is it that obvious?"

"I am small, Ismai, not blind." He was happy for the change in subject. "Everyone knows you favor Sulema. The *dead* know you favor her."

Something cold chuckled in his ear at that, and a chill hand scraped down his spine. Daru bit his lip and wished, for the thousandth time, that he would learn not to say such things.

But Ismai was not listening. His eyes followed the dreamshifter's daughter. "She is like a poem given breath."

"Do you think she will beat Hannei?" Daru pressed close to the low stone barrier, wishing his eyes were sharp like a hawk's. The two Ja'Akari bowed to the audience, then to each other, and then they both sank down into a fighting stance. They were the best of this year's new warriors, and would fight for the right to be named champion.

"Of course," Ismai said. "Well... *I* think she will. But they are both very strong."

Ruh'ayya grumbled a laugh at this.

"Strong by human standards," agreed Ismai. "Shush! Listen!"

The drummers had taken up their positions, and the *thrum-thrum-throb-shuuuushhhh* of fingers against hide drew an echo from Daru's heart. From every heart in the Madraj, he imagined. *Thrum-thrum-shushhhhhh* and the girls spun into motion.

Hannei moved first, stooping to grab a handful of sand, and then she flipped completely over, twirling and spinning, braids whipping about her face. Sulema bent back, and her feet too came up and over. Their bodies, oiled and muscled and scarred, glowed with fierce beauty. One girl would attack and the other would counter, back and forth like the play of fire and shadow. It was a kind of music—battle-cries and the grunt that followed a well-placed blow, the beating of the drums, the pounding of his heart.

Sulema screamed and leapt into the air, legs churning as if she walked on the wind. Hannei spun to the side like a sand-dae, and the red-haired girl's kick found only air. Flame and water, wind and sand, the two girls told the story of the Zeera with their strong young bodies and the fire in their hearts.

Then it happened.

The girls spun face-to-back-to-face, trading blows and kicks and blocking each with such speed the movements blurred into one. Sulema snapped a kick up and to the side just as Hannei dropped low. Sulema's foot connected with the other girl's chest, there was a sharp crack, and Hannei crumpled to the ground.

Silence fell upon the Madraj. Not the silence of a summer's hunt, or the silence of a winter morn, but the silence that stalks a sick child in the night. Daru knew this silence. Ignoring Ismai's hand that tried to clutch at his tunic, Daru leapt from the low balcony. He landed badly, in a heap, teeth snapping shut and splinters of fire shooting up both legs, and then picked himself up and took off at a hobbling run across the arena.

Hafsa Azeina got there first.

Sulema was crouched at her friend's side. Hannei lay limp, eyes rolled back in her head and the skin around her mouth a hideous shade of purple-gray. Her mouth parted and a trickle of bright, bright blood rolled down her cheek to stain the skin at her temple.

It is not right, Daru thought wildly, not right that she should die before the sun had turned her skin brown, before she had a chance to prove herself. It was not right that those bright eyes should ever grow dim, ever.

Sulema screamed, and her scream made the shadows hum with pleasure.

Daru could feel the danger pressing close. The Madraj was home to many ancient and malicious beings, things that were not fond of humans and their meddling ways. Fell spirits that liked to still the heart, shadows that hungered after the breath of a young boy. Or a girl just becoming a woman. He limped to a halt near the girls and closed his waking eyes so that he could see better, as he had learned to do when he was very small and very sick and had been shut away to die. The world grew dark, and then flashed into bright relief as his dreaming eyes came to life.

He saw them. Shapes like ill-formed children, less substantial than smoke, clawing at Hannei's mouth with long, greedy fingers, leaning close to sip at her breath. One of them saw Daru watching and turned the hot red glare of its eyes upon him. It shrieked, a long, thin wail of hate and despair from beyond the ends of the earth, a piercing sound that hurt his ears and made him feel as if he would wet his pants, right there in front of the whole pride.

"I know you," Daru whispered to the shadows. His breath rasped in his throat, and it hurt to draw breath. "I know you, *ja Akari* I know you, under the sun I see you, felldae."

Someone laid a hand on his shoulder, and Hafsa Azeina spoke nearby. Her voice was loud and slow, and he did not understand the words she said. He shook the hand off and faced the shadows. The first spirit hissed at him, teeth and tongue flickering like dark flames in the wide hole of its mouth. The other felldae looked up from their feast and hissed as well, a sound like tea-kettles and chattering urns, but he would not listen to them. Their song was death, and he had heard it all before.

Without taking his eyes from the creatures, Daru reached into the left sleeve of his tunic and drew forth a bird's skull, as oddly formed and wrong as the felldae. This he raised to his mouth. He pressed his lips to a small, precise hole that he had drilled into the paper-thin bone, and blew.

This time, the shadows fled.

NINE

"A mother plants trees so that her
children may have shade."

Nurati hurried down to the arena as quickly as she could,
but the stairs were steep and the moon of her belly had
eclipsed her feet some time ago. Thus it was that by the
time she stepped onto the hot sands of the arena, the girl Hannei
was already being helped to her feet.

She will live, all thanks to Atu she will live. The prides could ill
afford to lose one so young and strong, especially one whose blood
traced back to Zula Din. A faint relation, perhaps, but enough that
she had already been written into the Book of Blood along with
the best possible mates for her. The very best of possible mates,
indeed—Nurati intended that this young woman should bear
children by none other than her own son, Tammas.

But only if Sulema, that little red-haired cub of a she-daemon,
did not mess things up. Nurati was First Mother, mother to all the
prides, and she would not allow the line of Zula Din to be fouled
with outlander blood.

She stopped short of the scene, leaning heavily against an arched
doorway. From this vantage point, she could watch the game play
itself out, moves and counters on the board of life.

The dreamshifter and her daughter helped Hannei Ja'Akari to
her feet. Istaza Ani was there, and the dreamshifter's weakling
apprentice as well. He had been playing that moons-cursed flute
of his, unnatural little thing that he was, and as a small crowd
of the concerned gathered around Hannei he scrambled to his
feet, swaying like a reed in the wind. He was shoved aside and
disregarded... but Nurati saw.

She saw how his eyes darted about, following things that could not be seen by ordinary humans. She saw him kiss the bird's skull and tuck it away again. That one was only half in the land of the living—so she had always thought—and needed but a gentle push to the other side.

He is just a cub. Why do you hate him so?

He is weak. Weak and strange since birth, and stranger every day he spends in her *presence.* Nurati watched as the dream-shifter thumbed Hannei's eyes open and peered into them. She shuddered. To have those golden eyes staring into one's own soul was the stuff of nightmares. *You should have killed him when you had the chance.*

Paraja's voice in her head rolled with laughter. *He is stronger than he looks, Kithren. I encouraged him to die. He chose to live.*

Are those teeth of yours for show, then? Are your claws dull?

She could feel Paraja's presence as the great cat came to sit silently at her side. *Have a care with your words, human.*

Forgive me, O Queen, I speak only out of concern for my people.

There was no answer. Well, let her sulk.

Through her link with Paraja, she felt another approach before a hand touched her shoulder. "The girl will live."

"Of course. She is of good stock." She turned her head slightly and nodded to Sareta, now and for the rest of their lives First Warrior. "Is the girl Sulema our champion, then?"

"So long have you known me, and still you do not grasp the way of the Ja'Akari." Sareta shook her head, a faint smile deepening the creases in her face. "Watch."

Even as they watched, Hannei Ja'Akari shook off those who would help her, support her, take her from the field of battle. Her voice carried to the far corners of the Madraj.

"No. I do not yield. No." Though she could not stand straight, though she barely stood at all and her skin was a ghastly shade, she swayed into a painful approximation of a fighting stance. "I do not yield."

The noncombatants pulled back as the girls faced off. Sulema

Ja'Akari was slow to take a stance, and reluctance screamed from every line of her body. Nurati wondered: did she want this thing so badly that she would risk further injury to her own sword-sister? The girls were close, everyone knew this.

Hannei swayed forward, and landed a weak and awkward blow to Sulema's upper arm. The red-haired girl dropped to her knees and held up both hands, palms-out.

"I yield," she cried out. "I yield!"

The day went silent, so silent Nurati fancied she could hear the golden scales of Akari Sun Dragon sighing as they caressed the soft blue sky.

Then Sulema stood, and the girls embraced, and the crowd roared its approval.

"Well played, Ja'Akari. Well played." Sareta, the hardest woman Nurati knew, watched with tears in her eyes. "Young Sulema will be First Warrior after me, mark my words. She and Tammas are the future of the pride."

Nurati looked from her, to the red-haired cub of the she-daemon, and to the crowd, whose screams and ululations grated in her ears. She watched the dreamshifter and her apprentice slip away into the shadows.

The child in her belly kicked as if she, too, sensed the danger.

That red-haired she-daemon, become First Warrior? The dreamshifter's daughter, mated to her own son? *Not on my watch.*

Umm Kalthea, First Mother before her, had spoken these words: "*A mother plants trees so that her children may have shade.*"

And if those trees are threatened by a vine, Nurati thought, *she must tear it out by the roots.*

TEN

The moons rolled over in their sleep. Sounds of merriment ebbed like the tides of the Zeera, flowing away into yesterday as the new Ja'Akari tucked their tents and belongings into the churra packs, making ready to ride out into the desert.

The wind carried away the last bits of song and smoke, and girls who hoped to become warriors poured sand into the cooking-pits, just as she and Hannei had done this time last year. As she watched them from Ismai's old hiding place beneath the arena, Sulema's heart was heavy. She had waited for this, bled for this, wished for this her entire life. And now—in the last hours of the last days of her captivity—her mother's past threatened to snatch it all away.

It was not very warrior-like to cry about life being unfair, so she clenched her jaw and said nothing.

She wore a warrior's vest and trousers, and a proper shamsi hung at her hip. The sunblade had been a gift from Istaza Ani, and was one of a great many gifts given to her after she ceded the championship to Hannei. Had she continued the fight against a weakened opponent, she would have claimed an honor as empty and useless as a waterskin full of holes. As it was, even Umm Nurati had come to pay respect.

After the fight Sulema's mother had clasped her shoulder. Just a brief touch, no words, but she had given Sulema a look and a nod of approval, and those were worth more than all the water in the Dibris.

She hated herself for that, for being so easily bought. A look. A touch. Pathetic.

"Sulema Ja'Akari."

She jumped half out of her skin at the voice, spun so hard the shamsi banged against her thigh, and snapped a smart bow to the First Warrior. Sareta laughed, and held out one of a pair of drinking horns.

"I thought I might find you here. I used to hide in these tunnels, myself, back when I was young. Would you share a drink with an old warrior?"

"You are not old." She took the horn gladly—to share usca with the First Warrior was an honor.

"Do not argue with me, brat." She raised her cup high in salute. "The way is long!"

"Life is short!"

"Drink!" They knocked back the usca together, and a warm glow settled around Sulema's heart, loosing the grip of her disquiet.

The First Warrior thumped her chest and grinned.

"That never gets old, unlike us warriors. So, child, have you decided what you will do now?"

Sulema cleared her throat and blinked back tears. The cheap usca available to younger warriors did not have the kick this stuff did. "Do?"

"Istaza Ani assures me that you are not stupid, so do not pretend with me. Will you remain among your cousins?" The warrior gestured with her empty cup. "Or will you travel outland to sit at the feet of the Dragon King?"

The usca had begun to burn. "He is not *my* king."

"No, but he is your father."

"So *she* says."

"*She* is your mother." The First Warrior's voice had a bite to it. "She would know." She sighed, and took a step closer. "It is hard, I know. I understand how you must feel."

"You do?"

"Of course. You are trapped." The older woman shook her head, and the morning sunlight kissed her silvered braids. "You wish to meet with this man, with your father, but you do not wish to be seen as an outlander among your own people. Above all else, you crave acceptance—and you fear being seen as disloyal."

"I would never betray the people!"

"I know this, child. I have seen you struggle with this your whole life, with the thought that you are not one of us."

Ehuani, she thought, but the word stuck in her throat.

"You are one of us, Sulema, you are Ja'Akari to your bones. It is true that you do not have a warrior's hair," and here she reached to tug at Sulema's copper-red braids, "nor a warrior's eyes. There is too much cream in your coffee. You are spotted like a churra."

Sulema felt her freckled skin heat with shame.

"But you see nothing, Ja'Akari. You fight this battle with your own shadow. Everyone else can see that your sa burns with the light of a true warrior. I name you Ja'Akari, under the sun I see you, Sulema. Warrior of the Shahadrim. True daughter of the pride." Her brown eyes burned fierce.

Sulema bowed her head. "Thank you, First Warrior."

"Ha, brat, do not thank me yet. I have a task for you, and a gift, and I am not sure which is worse."

Sulema looked up, wiped the tears from her face with the back of one hand, and waited.

"The task will not be to your liking. I would have you go to Atualon with this red-headed stud of a brother of yours, and meet your father."

It was the last thing she had expected to hear. "I do not understand."

"You heard me right. Meet your father—Ka Atu, the king of Atualon, the man who wields the power of atulfah. The man who sings to the Sleeping Dragon. It is time for you to open your blind eyes and see what lies before you, Sulema. The dreamshifter says you are this man's daughter, and I believe her. They say you can learn to wield this power... that you could become his heir. Sa Atu, the Heart of Atualon."

"I do not wish to become this, this Sa Atu."

"Do you think I care what you wish?" The older woman's smile belied her words. "Think, child. You would be Sa Atu... and what else?" She reached up and tugged at one of her own braids.

Sulema blinked. *Oh.* "I would be Sa Atu... but I will also be Ja'Akari."

"Just so. Yes." The First Warrior nodded, pleased. "You could learn how to use atulfah, the most powerful magic this world has ever known..."

"Learn this magic... and bring it home to the people."

"A fine gift, would you not agree? A gift to the people, worthy of a great warrior." Her voice fell to a near whisper. "As great a warrior as Zula Din. Greater, perhaps."

"You think I could do this thing?" A new dream, an impossible dream, gripped her. Sulema could hardly bear to breathe, she wanted it so.

"I know you can. I have been watching you, remember? I know you, Sulema, better than the youthmistress knows you, better than your cousins or that boy Tammas. I know you better by far than your mother does."

"Is this the gift, then? Or the task?" Her head spun. *What was in that usca?*

The First Warrior laughed. "This is your task, Ja'Akari, though I am pleased to find you willing. As for your gift, it is this: three days to yourself, and a word of advice. No warrior is complete until she is Zeeravashani. Go now, and find your kithren."

"Find my... but the vash'ai chooses the warrior, never the other way around."

The First Warrior winked. "That is the common belief, yes. But like many common beliefs, it is not... quite... the truth. The vash'ai are always close to the Madraj this time of year, seeking the best, the boldest of our warriors for their young. You are already in the best place, at the best time... now, you have only to prove yourself worthy."

"Hannei is champion. Should she not be accepted first?"

"Human titles mean nothing to the vash'ai."

"I do not understand what you expect me to do, First Warrior. We are leaving with the moons, and if the vash'ai are not impressed by fighting..." Her voice trailed off at the other woman's slow smile. "What would you have me do?"

"Seek out the Bones of Eth."

Sulema blinked. "The Bones of Eth?"

"Umm Nurati tells me that the Bones of Eth have become infested by a lionsnake. A very young, very small lionsnake. The wardens have been complaining that it poses a threat to the eastern herds, and that the Ja'Akari have not yet killed it. It would only take a small party, they say. Two warriors... three, at most. One, if she were bold and foolish enough. But of course, I will not send a single warrior to this task. Only an exceptional warrior could hope to kill a lionsnake by herself. Such a warrior would surely find favor with the vash'ai."

"They say you killed a lionsnake by yourself, once. When you were young."

"Do they? I do not listen to gossip. It is almost always wrong." The First Warrior touched the plumed headdress upon her brow and grinned, and Sulema caught a glimpse of the young scoundrel she must have been. "It was *two* lionsnakes. This is one of the reasons I was named First Warrior."

Sulema's heart danced at the possibilities.

"The gift I give you is this, Ja'Akari, as a reward for an honorable fight. Three days to yourself as the people prepare to return to the villages. Your horse is in the easternmost pasture, and there you will find weapons and supplies enough for a short journey. Ride to the Dibris and go fishing, if that is your pleasure, ride south and do a little tarbok hunting if you prefer. Or you could ride to the nearest oasis and take your ease.

"These three days are your gift. I will not tell you what to do with them... and for once, I will not tell you not to do anything stupid."

The First Warrior put her hands on Sulema's shoulders and kissed her on both cheeks, as warriors had done for years beyond count. "Akari be with you, warrior."

"And with you," Sulema replied.

She could hardly believe her luck.

＊

Sulema knew the Zeera as she knew her own body, the rise and swell of it, every mood and season and scar. She understood the desert as she could never quite understand people. When she was riding her mare across the golden sands she felt in place and at peace as she never did when she sat near the fire with her peers, telling stories and matching wits and eyeing the eligible young men. When she was younger, she had liked to pretend that the Zeera was her mother, that Akari Sun Dragon was her father, and that she was beloved of them both.

She and Hannei had ridden to the Bones of Eth and back many times in the past—as a dare when they were younger, out of boredom or the need to escape Istaza Ani and her endless lists of chores when they were older. The path was so familiar they could have found their way on a moonless night, were it not for the threat of greater predators.

Today, *she* was the predator. Today she left the games of childhood behind and became a woman, no matter what her mother might say.

The shrill cry of a raptor snatched at her attention. She looked upward, shading her eyes against the midsun, but it was only a bird after all, a large hawk of some kind with the sunlight filtering through his tail feathers. They were close, then.

Sulema whooped as Atemi surged up the dark side of a particularly steep dune, her mare's hindquarters bunching and flexing as she surged upward. As they came again into the sunlight, she could see, off in the distance, the dark and dangerous wound in the world that marked the Bones of Eth. The small specks that floated so lazily above the stone columns would be buzzards, but that larger speck might well be a wyvern. She had best keep an eye on that one, then, because if she could see a wyvern it had surely been watching her for some time.

The Zeera shimmered in the late heat. As she drew nearer to the Bones she could make out the twisted and ugly shapes of the columns rising from the ground like the legs of a dead spider. There were a lot of buzzards—something big must have died recently—and, yes, the larger shape was a wyvern. A small one, half-grown but deadly enough. The wyvern trumpeted, a high and pretty note nowhere near the deep bass rumble of a fully grown greater predator, and plummeted out of sight.

Atemi tensed from neck to tail and protested with a little buck. But the presence of so many scavengers was a good sign. It meant the lionsnake had killed recently, and a lionsnake that had gorged would be easier to kill. Sulema gripped her bow tight, clenched her jaw, and drove them both on.

The wind shifted, and the air burned with the thick stink of a lionsnake. Atemi bucked to a halt, nostrils flaring, eyes rolling, sides heaving slick with sweat. Sulema slid free of her trembling mare and gathered up her weapons. Atemi roared a little through her nostrils but stood still as she had been trained. She would not bolt.

Maybe.

Then again, Sulema had been better trained than to hunt a lionsnake alone, and yet here she was, fitting a trembling arrow to a trembling bow, with an unblooded sword at her hip. Killing a lionsnake or two by herself had seemed like a good idea when her belly was full of usca.

The First Warrior has done this, she reminded herself. *Twice. This is what I must do if I wish to become Zeeravashani. I am a warrior.*

It is a good day to die.

Another, treacherous thought tickled the back of her mind.

I should have gone fishing instead.

Sulema stepped gingerly and winced, wishing she had worn boots instead of sandals. Her feet were tough as old leather, but *za fik* the sand was hot out here. She stepped into the shadows, hoping the ground would be cooler underfoot. It was not, though a shudder of cold air sliced through her, raising chillflesh along her arms and tightening the skin at the back of her neck. As she walked between the black-and-red striped rocks, the air thickened and cooled. It stank of old death, and new.

The wind picked up, twirling the sand-dae into a mocking little dance around her feet, daring her just one step closer to death. There was a strange quality to the air, the breath of a scent or the faint note of a song she could almost remember, or the ghost of an old warning. She moved deeper into the shadow of the Bones, lifting her head as a tarbok might as it scented danger. There was something here beyond even the threat of greater predators. Something wrong.

This was a very bad idea. For a moment, her mind cleared and she shivered. *I should go. I should go now.* She shifted her weight, intending to turn and leave, and forget whatever madness had driven her to such a place.

A vash'ai roared nearby.

Help me!

The voice in her mind, weak and full of fear, was the same voice she had heard at the ceremony. Sulema quit thinking and ran toward its source. The air snapped shut behind her as she passed through the Bones and she stumbled, blinking, into the thin sunlight. There, in the far and darkest corner of the clearing, huddled a young vash'ai, black and gold as a statue passed through fire. The straggling wisps of a mane and bright tusks marked him as less than half-grown. His throat and chest were splattered and stained with bright blood, as was the sand all around. One foreleg canted outward at an awkward angle, and he snarled in defiance at a pile of tumbled rocks, old bones, and debris.

He looked at her, *into* her, and his thoughts were the last sweet notes of a lost song.

Help me, Warrior. Kithren. You are mine. Mine. Help me...

Ah, she could feel his heart pushing the blood through her veins, a stout heart and true. Warrior-poet, true friend, a song of tooth and claw. He was her light in the dark, she was his, they were...

Ware, Kithren. Ware the lionsnake!

No sooner had the thought touched her mind than the pile of debris shifted and the broad, plumed head of a lionsnake reared high in the air, blocking out the sun. Its mouth gaped wide, showing row upon row of inward-pointing teeth, glistening as venom welled from their needle tips to hang in long, viscous strands. The beast scrabbled at the mouth of its lair, claws like black scythes scraping against bone and rock as the beast hauled itself into the clearing on two long, muscled limbs.

Sulema gaped in shock.

This was no small hatchling, but a red-wattled old bitch of a grandmother snake. The tattered and faded crest of plumes stiffened and shook, and venom-sacs along her jaw swelled. She drew breath in a long, rattling hiss, and shrieked.

The young warrior cried out, nearly dropping her bow as she clapped her hands over her ears and remembered, belatedly, that the lionsnake was related to the bintshi. Its cry might not be deadly, but it *hurt*. The vash'ai snarled, but it was a weak sound, a dying sound. He flattened himself against the rocks as the lionsnake kneaded the sand beneath her claws, head weaving to and fro and eyes narrowed as she hissed in pleasure, anticipating the kill.

Istaza Ani is right, she thought. *It is a good day to die…*

Silently she stepped from the shadows, nocked an arrow and drew in a single, smooth movement, and shot the old bitch in the face.

…but it is an even better day to live.

Her hand was steady, and her aim true. Sulema's arrow shot straight through one vulnerable eye—tip, shaft, and fletching—and put out that fell and ancient light.

The lionsnake screamed, jaws gaping and snapping shut as her head whipped about, seeking the enemy who had dared to wound her. The ruined eye dripped ichor as she screamed again, clawing at it, snaking her head back and rubbing the wound along her armored hide.

Then her good eye found the small warrior standing alone upon the sand. She froze, and let a long, slow *hissssss*. Sulema saw the pupil snap shut like a cat's, saw a protective membrane slide over the eye. There would be no second lucky shot.

But Ja'Akari are not trained to rely on luck.

Sulema stepped back into the shadows of the Bones of Eth.

Between the ringing in her ears and the trapped-bird pounding of her heart she was near deaf, but she schooled herself to stillness as the lionsnake thrashed and wailed, half-blind and maddened with pain.

It might be enough. She felt the fluttering in her soul as she felt the young vash'ai—*Azra'hael,* she thought, *his name is Azra'hael*—take a step toward the Lonely Road without her. *It will have to be enough. I cannot lose him.*

She watched as the lionsnake's shoulders bunched and flexed, claws gutting the sand as the wounded beast dragged herself forward, propelling her bulk with agonizing slowness. In her youth the beast would have moved swiftly over short distances, but a lionsnake this massive would need the meat to come to her. Likely this had not posed a problem until this day, as there were always creatures that needed shade and shelter more than they feared ambush.

The Bones of Eth were cold and hard against Sulema's back. The vash'ai lay tumbled to one side, limp and broken but still breathing. She could hear Atemi whinnying in fear, and smell the hot sand, and the stink of venom and blood and carrion. She realized that within the hour—perhaps within minutes—either she or the lionsnake would be dead.

She drew a deep breath and nocked another arrow.

The broad plumed head wove back and forth, foul breath wheezing and hissing as the lionsnake sought her prey. Her head was tipped so that Sulema could see the dim light of her good eye flickering and moving behind the protective lid.

Ha, you old bitch, Sulema thought. *I am Ja'Akari, and I am no easy meat.*

She drew the arrow back to her cheek, slowly, slowly... and let fly, shot high and wide, so that the steel tip of her arrow skittered along the Bones, drawing a thin line of blue sparks. The lionsnake whipped her head toward the sound and shrieked, plumes bristling and rattling, venom pumping as she prepared to strike.

Sulema loosed a third arrow, and watched in satisfaction as this one sank deep into the unprotected folds of the lionsnake's engorged venom sac. She reached for another, ready to make an end of this.

Easier than I thought.

The lionsnake bellowed and reared, clawing at the sky and thrashing wildly from side to side. Sulema was hit by a wave of malice so strong that she reeled, stumbling and falling to her knees. Stupid luck saved her hide. The creature's claws swiped so close that she went tumbling ass-over-end across the dirt. Hot agony blossomed in her shoulder and Sulema screamed with the realization that the claws had not missed her, after all. She screamed again as the massive tail whipped sideways, catching her in the thigh and sending her rolling like a sheep's head in a game of aklashi.

She staggered upright, spitting sand and blood, unable to stand fully upright or raise her left arm. As the lionsnake reared to its full height, bellowing in injured outrage and planning to crush the small intruder who dared bring the fight to her very lair, Sulema realized three things in quick succession.

She had lost her bow.

She still had her sword.

And this had been a very, very bad idea.

Sulema drew her sword and threw herself to the ground, face-down, sword point up, and hoped that Atemi would make it back to the pride unhurt.

The cool shadow of the lionsnake washed over her, and then the full weight of the beast crashed down upon her like the end of everything, a massive weight that blocked out sun and sound and hope, smashing, crushing, suffocating her. The lionsnake's flesh was slick, corpse-cold, and soft.

Soft...

Sulema felt the bones of her lower arm snap as the thing fell upon her, sword sinking deep, deep into the soft flesh of its throat. She screamed as the beast came down, screamed again as it thrashed upon her in a lifetime's worth of dying, and a third time as it rolled off her, crushing her shoulder as it went. It writhed and humped along the sand in its extremity, shrieking, moaning, spraying hot blood and venom that smoked and burned where it hit rock and sand and flesh.

As she crashed down upon the shattered rocks, the lionsnake released a musky stink so vile that Sulema gagged and heaved, rolling over onto her side so that she would not choke on her own vomit.

Her shoulder and arm were on fire, an exquisite chorus of agony. Every bit of exposed skin itched and stung as droplets of the lionsnake's venom burned her skin.

She rolled to a sitting position, cradling her broken arm, and then struggled to her feet—prepared for the worst—but the lionsnake was dead. Nothing could stink like that and not be dead. The lionsnake was dead, and she had survived.

Eventually she would be glad of it. At the moment, however, she concentrated on standing upright and not passing out from the pain.

The creature gave a final, bubbling hiss. Sulema jerked away, and cried out in pain as the bones in her arm ground together, but the creature seemed to deflate as sa and ka left its massive, stinking body.

I need to clean my blade, she thought. But her arm would not respond. *Might as well skin the lionsnake while I am at it.* Sulema giggled, a bit drunkenly. She would skin it and collect the plumes— just as soon as she could coax Atemi to enter a lionsnake's lair, carry her wounded vash'ai to safety, and perhaps bind her wounds as well.

Za fik, everything hurt.

"That was the stupidest thing I have ever seen."

Sulema nodded—there was no arguing with that. Then she stiffened, new agony screaming up her arm, and turned slowly toward the far, dark corner of the Bones. A figure stepped from the shadows. She held her breath, wondering if the Guardian of Eid Kalmut had come to snatch her breath away, for surely such a thing could only have come from the Valley of Death.

He might have been a tall man, bent in upon himself to conceal his true size, or he might have been twisted like an old tree left too long in bitter winds. It was hard to tell, enshrouded as he was in layer upon layer of shadowy robes. A mask of beaten metal and leather strips revealed more of twisted ruin of his face than it concealed, and he leaned easily against a massive war hammer that reeked of old blood and new murder.

"Brave, though." Another voice, softer and higher than the first. Sulema searched the edges of her vision for the source of it, not willing to let this man slip from her sight, certain that if she looked away—even for a moment—he would disappear into the shadows again.

"Brave of a certes, sweet one, but the brave light the paths of Eid Kalmut. The dead are no less dead for having been brave."

"Ah, but she is not dead yet."

Sulema shivered, and grunted a little as the bones ground together in her arm. The voices were all coming from the twisted figure in black.

Nightmare Man, she thought. *So you were not just one of my mother's stories.*

The figure drew nearer, though Sulema had not seen him move. She blinked the blood away, blinked again as her vision blurred and she fell to her knees, jarring loose a small, helpless sound that surely did not come from her throat.

"No? Not yet, then. But the venom will have its way with her."

"If the lionsnake had bitten her, she would be dead by now. I think it just kicked her ass."

"I was not speaking of the lionsnake."

"What about this one?" The figure jerked its free arm toward the still form of the fallen vash'ai.

"Kill it if you like." The voice was low and sweet as dark honey.

I know that voice, she thought, and a cold dread coiled deep in her gut. *I have heard it before... but when?*

"You... I know you..." She struggled to clear her head. To stand. Was she standing? She struggled to raise her sword arm. Had she lost her sword? How could she be a sword-sister, if she had lost her sword?

The dark form bent over the vash'ai, and Sulema fought against the darkness like an insect caught in a web. Or like a dreamer caught in a nightmare.

"No," she whispered. "No."

An image tickled up through her memories, like bubbles from the mouth of a drowned girl. This same face looming over her as she huddled deep in a nest of soft blankets, too terrified to cry out.

I wet the bed, she thought, *but nobody ever came.* In her memories, he was a giant.

A blade slashed across her throat—his throat—her throat, and the image shattered.

The vash'ai yowled, a terrible and final cry, cut short, sliced in half. Sulema wailed as her soul bled out into the endless night.

Azra'hael, her heart whispered, broken. *His name was Azra'hael.*

Flashes of blue light crackled across the man's mask like lightning as he stepped back from Azra'hael's limp body and turned to face her. He smiled, or perhaps he screamed without making a sound, and then he threw something at her. Something small and pretty that glittered as it flew, and she snatched it from the air with her good hand without thinking twice.

"A gift from Eth," he said, and then he threw back his head and laughed like thunder, like fire in the tall dry grass.

Sulema fell to her knees—or had she fallen already?—and gasped as the bones in her arm ground together, gasped as she saw what she held in the palm of her hand. A shadow-jewel, a dark crystal the size of a plover's egg, set into a silvery brooch in the shape of a spider. It danced with shadows in the pale moonslight, waving its forelegs at her as if tasting the color of her blood.

She struggled, a fly caught in its web.

"No," she whispered. That was not right. It was latesun, no later, and she had to get Atemi. Had to skin the lionsnake, to take the plumes back to Hannei. She had to save Azra'hael, so that they could become Zeeravashani. "I cannot accept this gift, it is too much."

She struggled...

"No?" He stood over her, smiling, and the sky was dark with regret. "No, then. But your father will be so disappointed."

...caught in its web.

"I know you," she whispered. "Nightmare Man."

The spider crouched and leapt, trailing a silken strand of glistening moonslight. It landed on her injured shoulder and she screamed as its fangs sank into her too-soft flesh.

It *burned*. Venom flooded through her veins like a river of fire, and it burned. The sand rushed up to greet her, soft as her mother's embrace.

Struggled...

Memories crowded forth in a shrill chorus, trapping her in a dark place filled with fire and death. There was no escape. There was no escape. And Mama would not wake in time to save her.

...in its web.

The wagon broke open, and she saw the face of Akari Sun Dragon, white-hot with rage.

She fell.

She burned.

ELEVEN

Daru fell headlong into her tent. "They have found her, Dreamshifter!"

Hafsa Azeina stood, ignoring the pins and needles in her long-folded legs, the angry sound Basta's Lyre made when it fell from her lap, and the manner in which the spirits sewn into her tent strained toward the boy as he lay prostrate on the ground.

"Where was she? Who found her?" She did not ask whether the girl was alive, or unhurt. Three days past she had felt her daughter's screams in the very marrow of her bones, and if the girl had died, she would have known it.

"The First Warrior found her," Daru gasped. "At the Bones of Eth. They have taken her to the Healers' Quarters and Nurati is with her now…"

"Sareta." The woman's name susurrated through the air, whispering along the lines of *here* and *then*, catching her hunter's eye. There was game at the end of that trail… but there would be time for that later.

I am here, Kithren. I was hunting rabbits in the garden. The shadow-dancers are here, stinking of fear and spiders. Paraja is here, as well… best bid the little mouse stay home.

I am on my way. Do not let them touch her.

Best hurry, Kithren, those shadow-dancers are doing something… I will distract them. A silent cat's laugh rippled across their bond.

"Daru, you stay here. I need you to call as many of the shadows away from the healers' rooms as you can."

The boy hesitated. "I will try, Dreamshifter."

She lifted an eyebrow at him. "Try?"

He bowed, and produced his apprentice's flute. "Yes,

Dreamshifter." He sat down, lotus-style, and closed his eyes. She did not miss the tremor that shook his hands, but she had no pity to spare.

She took Basta's Lyre but left the shofar. The golden ram had fed on human flesh, and she did not yet trust his spirit in the presence of blood. Her bare feet carried her up the pass and the path and the steps to the healers' rooms fleet and quick as a girl's, but she could not outrun the smell of her own fear, the images of her daughter bleeding and broken and hurt. It had been four days since Sulema had gone missing, and three since she had felt that scream.

If she dies, Hafsa Azeina thought. *If she dies...*

Somewhere in Shehannam the Huntress lifted her head and smiled.

Warriors and wardens scattered before her as leaves in the wind. One young mother snatched her child up, and the terror on her face only inflamed Hafsa Azeina's wrath.

If she dies...

She will not die today, Kithren. Not of this.

She heard his warning *hnnga-hnnga* even as she reached her destination and threw the doors open with such force that the wooden frames cracked. Before her was such a tableau that, had she not been in such a state, she might have laughed till she cried. Khurra'an had the humans in the room backed into a far corner and was sitting on the shadowmancer. Paraja stood before him, eyes blazing, hair along her spine standing on end, spitting with fury... and the great sire was licking his male-parts as he ignored them all.

Paraja rounded on Hafsa Azeina as she blew into the room, but she ignored her as if the vash'ai queen could not eat her in two bites. Nurati was in a fury as well. If she had had hackles, they would have stood on end, and her black eyes showed whites all the way round.

"Dreamshifter. Dreamshifter, you call off this stinking beast of yours, or I will... *augh!*" Khurra'an shifted in his bathing so that his tail caught her in the face. Paraja snarled.

"Dreamshifter." Again came the soft, low voice of the shadow-mancer, a little out of breath. "If you could just… ugh… if you could just let me up, I might be able to… *mmf.*"

Cat balls in the face to you, sorcerer, she thought. It really was too bad there was no laughter left in her soul. She said nothing, but strode to the pallet where her daughter lay sleeping.

Sulema *was* asleep. Not dead, not even near death, though her wounds were grievous, nor caught in the long-sleep from which few ever roused.

She touched her fingertips to her daughter's face, tracing the bones unbroken, the swollen flesh, the map of pain and sorrows. Victory was here, as well, and fear long buried, and… something else. Something worse.

Nightmare Man, she thought, and the ground in Shehannam trembled. *So you have found her at last.*

"Dreamshifter," Nurati spat, "release us *at once.*"

"Meissati," the shadowmancer implored, "if you would only… *mmmf!*"

That tickles, laughed Khurra'an.

Deep in her sleep, Sulema stirred. Hafsa Azeina reached out to her. *Hush, my darling, sleep now. Mama is here.*

Istaza Ani burst through the wrecked doors, Leviathus at her heels.

"Where is she?"

"Does she live?"

"Shhh. She sleeps." Hafsa Azeina met the eyes of the woman who loved her daughter. "She will live."

My balls are clean. Shall I let this one up? He is not a comfortable seat, after all.

You might as well. There are too many people in here for me to feel the truth of things, anyway. Someone in the room knew what had happened, she could feel it, but too many dreams pressed too close together obscured the scent.

You do not think this was an accident?

There are no accidents. Aloud she said, "This was no accident.

Someone attacked my daughter. See here…" She brushed the braids away from Sulema's flesh. There was a small puncture wound there, almost lost among the chaos of her larger hurts, but to her dreaming eyes it seethed and pulsed with wicked magic.

A strange music floated through Shehannam, catching the attention of the shadows. Some of the lesser ones drifted off to seek its source and even the greater ones swayed, distracted. Daru was playing his flute. Drawing these hungry shadows to himself was a terrible risk, but she shut her heart tight lest concern for her apprentice distract her from the needs of her daughter.

"Move," she said. When Leviathus did not comply, she gave his shoulder a push. *Yeh Atu*, the boy was a young giant. "*Move!*" He did, and she seated herself near the head of the pallet near the still form of her daughter. Folding her sa inward, her ka outward, the dreamshifter rested Basta's Lyre against her cheek.

The First Healer, a woman as wizened and tough as blackthorn bark, hustled over with a scowl. "I need to tend the hurts of the body." Without waiting for an answer, she took a small knife and began to cut Sulema's clothes away.

Hafsa Azeina shut her waking eyes, but the sight of her daughter's wounds pressed against her soul like an unwelcome lover. *When I find the one responsible…*

She stroked the gut strings of the lyre. To her ears—and her ears only—a man's voice wept with pain.

He had been very beautiful.

The greater shadows had been enchanted by Daru's music. They fled hers. Her fingers danced upon the strings, plucking and stroking and teasing live voices from the dead as the gut trembled and wailed and the horned cat's skull let out a long sigh of sorrow and loss. Hers was angry music and sad, a call to battle without hope, a cry for vengeance denied. Hafsa Azeina groped blindly between the sounds of this note and that, seeking her daughter's resonance, for she had long since tasted the song in her daughter's blood. She could find it anywhere.

She found it now.

123

There you are, she thought. As always, her daughter shone like the bright moons against the pale light of Shehannam. Her bright light was tainted by an odd and murky cloud, as if poison had been dropped into a glass pitcher of mead.

Do you see that? Khurra'an asked.

Yes.

What is it? It smells... foul. He drew his black lips back from his tusks in disgust.

Reaver venom.

Can you heal it?

I will try.

I will try, her apprentice had said, when she had set him to a deadly task. She could ask no less of herself. She closed her eyes.

Deep in Shehannam, the Dreaming Lands, Hafsa Azeina dreamshifted. Merged with the form of her own murdered soul to become a thing of twisted hunger and bloodlust, she became a monster, a beast, a thing of nightmares.

When she opened her eyes again, she was Annubasta.

Deep away, far away, the Huntress brought to her lips a golden shofar, twin to the dreamshifter's own, and blew.

Annubasta drew her lips back in a silent snarl, but she remained seated at her daughter's side, claws scraping and gouging at her enemy's guts, playing a lively tune. His heart had been firm and ripe as a plum, and its juices had burst upon her tongue.

The humans gathered in the room were dim shapes to her dreaming eyes, hardly there, mostly asleep even as they thought themselves aware. Their souls shied away from her, though their dull eyes saw nothing but a human dreamshifter playing a gut-strung lyre. The shadows burned with dark flame, hungry and cowardly and cruel. The vash'ai were as glass statues full of dark smoke and vibrant life, their eyes jewel-bright. But the shadowmancer...

If the shadows were a dark flame, he was the heart of darkness, and he burned like the night. His eyes were young suns in an old and angry sky. He stood before her, clad in a cloak of living stars, and he saw her. He saw her, and his smile was the dawn that comes after a night of death.

"Shall we dance?" he asked.

If *danced* is a word that describes what he did next, if *music* is a word that describes the sounds that Annubasta drew forth from her lyre, then *life* is nothing more than a fistful of sand thrown about by the wind.

"Dreamshifter?"

A damp cloth, blessedly cool, dabbed at her face. She reached up to press it to her fevered skin.

Sleeping Beauty wakes at last, Khurra'an laughed. *I wonder—will you eat the world, like the princess in your old stories? Or will you decide to spare us at the last?*

"Coffee," Hafsa Azeina groaned, sitting up and opening her eyes. It hurt every bit as much as she had feared.

Daru pressed a clay mug into her hands and helped bring it to her lips. Across the room, she could see the shadowmancer's apprentice ministering to her master in much the same way.

The things we do for this world, she thought, and washed the bitter thought down with bitter drink.

"Sulema?" she asked.

Daru hesitated. "She is better."

"How much better?"

"The healers say she will live, but…"

"But?"

"There is something wrong with her, Dreamshifter. She woke once, briefly, and her eyes were full of nightmares. There is a darkness…" He touched his shoulder, in much the same place Sulema's wound had been.

"She is bitten." The shadowmancer's voice was a croak. His girl offered a mug of steaming coffee even as Daru had done, but he waved it away with a grimace. "Reaver venom. I have slowed its spread… forgive me, Meissati, *we* have slowed its spread… but this is not a cure. It will seep through her blood." He spread his fingers and stroked along his shoulder, up the side of his neck, and patted his head. "It will grow stronger in her and fill her mind with nightmares, and then they will have her."

"Who will have her?" Daru whispered, his eyes round with horror. Hafsa Azeina took the mug from his shaking hands and took a long swallow of scalding coffee, ignoring the pain.

"Araids," the shadowmancer replied. His apprentice shuddered.

"They will not have her." Hafsa Azeina handed the cup back to her own apprentice and stood, though her legs shook like a newborn filly's. She looked at the battered, troubled face of her sleeping daughter, beautiful as the dawn. More precious than life. "Bring me Leviathus, and Istaza Ani if you can find her."

"Yes, Mistress." Daru bowed low and spun away.

Sulema, she thought, and her dead heart woke just long enough to break.

"You will go to Atualon after all, then?" The shadowmancer's color was terrible, and his eyes bloodshot. He finally took the mug of coffee and choked it down. Hafsa Azeina thought his apprentice was laughing at him, behind those strange eyes of hers.

"We will go. Ka Atu…" She stooped to retrieve Basta's Lyre with her free hand, and shook her head against a wash of dizziness. "Her father will be able to heal her. I have seen him heal people who had one foot already on the Lonely Road." She had seen him heal people who had taken more than a few steps down the Lonely Road, truth be told, but she saw no value in telling the truth.

"As have I." The shadowmancer's star-studded skin glittered, and his smile was as odd as his eyes. "I would travel with you."

She stared at him, and splayed her fingers across the guts of the last man who had lied to her. The shadowmancer's apprentice glared at her, offended, but he just smiled.

"Trust me or not as you will, Dreamshifter. But we of Quarabala have been fighting the Araids for time out of mind. I can help keep the poison back, with my not-so-humble skills. The enemy of my enemy is my friend, would you not agree?"

Shall I trust this man? she asked Khurra'an.

Never. He tried to bribe me with a pig. But you might make use of him, for now. He licked his chops. *The pig was delicious.*

Hafsa Azeina met the shadowmancer's eyes and gave him her brightest smile, the one that sent young children scurrying for their mothers. She raised her coffee mug in salute.

"To enemies," she offered.

"To friends," he agreed.

They drank.

T W E L V E

"It is better to dance with the enemy than
dance to the enemy's tune."

Somewhere out in the vast expanse of sand and savagery, a great cat roared. The sound hung in the air like a promise of blood and death and was answered, first to the east and then to the south.

Leviathus ne Atu, last surviving son of Ka Atu, looked up from the map he had been squinting at and frowned. Something about the way the vash'ai had been calling out to each other felt like the hunt. It stripped away silk and stone and civilization and made a man feel as if he were naked and alone, fleeing an enemy that could end his life with less effort than it would cost him to blow out a candle.

When a fourth cat roared, closer than the others and loud enough to set his ears ringing, Leviathus sighed and moved the lead weights that had been keeping the map from curling at the edges, rolled the parchment, and with gentle care slid it back into its leather tube. He hesitated over the candle in its delicate porcelain lotus. It was not his to take, but the hour was late and he was loath to leave a fire burning amid such precious scrolls and books. At last he shrugged and scooped it up with his free hand. He could always return it later.

He stood and stretched, rolling his neck to ease the stiffness. The woven seat was made for a smaller person with shorter legs, and he had spent the past ten days either sitting in this room or sitting in the sickroom at his sister's side, eating when food was in front of him, fasting when it was not, and entirely shut away from wind and sun. The urge to move was starting to nag at him like one of his father's councilors.

He tucked the leather roll under his arm and crossed the room, careful not to allow wax to drip upon the thick wool rug that muffled his footsteps. The weavings here were as fine as any in Atualon, he thought, and the bright balanced patterns pleased the eye. He made a mental note to have a word with his father about expanding trade with the Zeeranim. For too long they had only relied upon the east for trade goods, and overlooked the barbarian south. If they could figure out a way around the river serpents, perhaps increase the king's protections along the road to Min Yaarif…

The boy who had been sent to guide him to the library was seated at the door, crouched back on his heels and still as a stone carving. He stood as Leviathus appeared, dark eyes flashing in the candle's light, his face as impossible to read as those scrolls written in ancient script. Leviathus smiled and touched the leather roll.

"I would like to take this for the night, and return it later. Would that be allowed?"

The boy studied him for a long moment, and then shrugged. Leviathus motioned for him to lead the way, biting the inside of his cheek as his guide tried to stare him down and, failing that, turned away with a sigh of long suffering. He was used to people all but killing themselves for his favor, and found it both disconcerting and refreshing to be so dismissed by a barefoot slip of a boy.

He followed his irreverent guide through a twisting warren of hallways, and was just beginning to wonder whether the boy was trying to lose him when they stepped through a pair of wide doors and into the mercifully cool evening air. He had spent hours in the library, then… no wonder his back ached and his belly rumbled. The boy disappeared in a flash of white linen and brown feet, and Leviathus shook his head ruefully. He could find his way to his own quarters from here, but not to the kitchens. Another hungry night. Well, perhaps he had some dried meat or something in his rooms somewhere.

The evening sky was beautiful—orange and purple on the horizon arching into a deep, deep blue freckled with the first stars. The larger moon, Delpha, hung low and full in the sky, little sister

Didi peeking shyly over her head. The constellations Eth and Illindra were just winking into existence, taking up weapons in their endless war for dominion over the heavens. Leviathus smiled and breathed deep. The air was sweet and smelled of the river, and small frogs sang a charming chorus. Aside from the river-beasts and land-beasts and young boys who abandoned their guests without first making sure they had been fed, the Zeera was not half as hostile as he had imagined.

The wind shifted, carrying the tantalizing smells of bread and cinnamon, the less appealing stink of some musky animal, and a voice he knew only too well. Mattu Halfmask, son of one of the deposed king's former concubines, a man Leviathus did not trust as far as he could throw the moons.

"The girl is a weakling bastard. No trueborn daughter of Ka Atu would be brought down by such wounds as that. I say she should get on with dying, and let us return home. This has been a madman's quest from the beginning. Do you not agree?"

"They say she was poisoned…"

"They say. They say." Always mocking. "I say no daughter of Ka Atu would be so stupid as to sneak away and get herself killed by one of the kin."

Leviathus stepped around the corner of the building and confronted them. "Lionsnakes are not kin."

Mattu turned his head fractionally, showing the curve of his cheek and sardonic line of his mouth—the only parts of his face Leviathus had ever seen. Tonight he wore the face of a bull, beautifully carved of leather chased with silver. Its sweeping horns almost hid the mischief glittering in that pale blue eye.

"What do you say?"

"Lionsnakes are not kin. They are beasts. Big beasts, to be sure, but nothing more than that." He smiled, a hard smile. "No more than my sister is a weakling bastard. You would do well to keep your tongue in your head, my dear Mattu. And you… Rheodus, is it?"

"Yes, ne Atu." The young Draiksguard had stiffened to attention, and his eyes rolled like a panicked horse's.

"Good, Rheodus, you seem to remember who I am, at least. You should keep in mind that I am my father's voice in this, and I say this girl is my sister." He regarded the two men. "Do you say otherwise?"

"No, ne Atu. M-my apologies." The soldier was stumbling over his own tongue. "I was just... we were only..."

Leviathus waved a dismissal. "Go."

Rheodus left at a half-run, peering over his shoulder at least twice. Well he might. Leviathus would not wish to be in that man's boots when Ka Atu learned that words had been spoken against his daughter. Bastard weakling, indeed... lesser men would hang for such words. But his father had always been blind to Mattu's true nature, and overly permissive with the son of his deposed enemy.

Mattu turned to face him fully. "You are so sure of the girl, are you?"

"What is your game, Halfmask? I know you better than to think you are foolish enough to deny my father's stamp, or impugn Hafsa Azeina's honor. What are you really playing at, here?"

"Perhaps I seek to find discord before it can take root. Does it matter?"

"The words you speak do matter. They matter to me, and they will matter to my father. Do not make the mistake of speaking against my sister again."

"My apologies, *ne Atu*." Mattu folded his arms over his chest and smiled, mouth tight and angry. "I would not have you carry harsh words of me back to my liege."

"Oh, no need to worry about that, Halfmask." Leviathus smiled easily, as if they had been discussing last year's wines. "I will not carry word of this to my father. If you soil my sister's name with your tongue again, I will carve it from your filthy mouth myself."

Mattu Halfmask sketched a mocking bow, turned on his heel, and stalked away into the night.

Does Mattu truly seek to expose the source of this rumor? Or does he seek to further it for his own ends? Not for the first time,

Leviathus wondered whether his father's soft heart would be their ruin. Would he have made the same choice, and spared the lives of his enemies' children? Or would he have allowed the soldiers to slay mere babes, as they had slain the older son?

He watched as the shadows swallowed the half-masked man, and shook his head. Shadowmancer Aasah had warned him against allowing Mattu to accompany them on this quest, but Leviathus had allowed it.

Better to dance with the enemy, he reasoned, *than dance to the enemy's tune.*

The rest of his walk was not as unpleasant. Small stones crunched underfoot and the air was crisp with the scents of lemon blossoms and chocolate mint. Since the day his father had divulged Sulema's whereabouts to him, Leviathus had indulged in fanciful waking dreams of rescuing his sister from a life of privation and danger, but for all of his dreaming, he had never imagined that the barbarians' city might be beautiful. If not for the enormous man-eating and venomous reptiles, the Zeera might be a nice place to live. Yes, it was past time the Dragon King turned his gaze south. Much could be gained through an alliance with the desert barbarians.

Perhaps this land could be tamed and put to good use.

A scrawny form burst from the shrubbery to his right and dashed across the path like a frightened hare. Leviathus snagged the youngster's arm and brought it to a spinning halt. Brown skin, brown eyes wide as moons, long braids and a longer tunic with stick-skinny legs poking out beneath. Girl or boy, he could not say. The child regarded him warily but without any real fear, and without the slightest hint of respect or deference. Leviathus smiled, but the urchin just blinked at him and scowled.

"Do you know where the visitors are being housed?"

A wary nod.

"Would you bring us some food? Please? Whatever is lying about the kitchens unguarded." He reached for the pouch at his waist, and sorted out a few copper slags. "I am happy to pay you."

The child stared at the small coins in his outstretched palm, and gave him a look of pity and disgust before slipping free and dashing off in a completely different direction than the one he had been taking. Or she had been taking. Leviathus sighed. He never would have thought that he would miss the elaborate protocols that surrounded a host's duties in Atualon. Certes, they had never lost a guest to starvation.

Leviathus continued on his way. He ducked through the enameled entry and through a low, wide tunnel, finally emerging into the full light of the moons. The courtyard of the guest's quarters featured a ring of carved stone pillars, each of them graced by a tiny potted tree that had been clipped and trained into a living work of art.

So could we shape and grow this land, he thought, certain the notion would appeal to his father.

Aasah and Yaela were seated in the very middle of the courtyard, in a swirl of tiny night-blooming white flowers. The shadowmancer and his apprentice sat with their legs folded lotus-style, backs straight as saplings, arms folded loosely in front of their chests and eyes closed. They might have been there since the beginning of time, so still were they in the night. Aasah wore a wrap of deepest indigo and his star-studded skin, Yaela a dress of moonsilk and jewels in her hair.

"Statuary fit to grace Illindra's gardens." He joined them without asking, laying the map in its leather sheath to one side, closing his eyes and settling easily into the rhythm of their breath. Let the mind become a pool free of disturbance, he thought, let it reflect the true self.

Still ponds. Starless skies. Leviathus let his mind drift...

His stomach growled.

His nose itched.

Something tickled at the inside of his thigh and he cracked his eye open. In a land of giant cats and snakes big enough to swallow a chariot, it would not do to let the wildlife creep too close to the family jewels.

Aasah had opened his eyes and was watching him with undisguised amusement.

"You made it to five heartbeats. I am impressed, ne Atu."

Leviathus grinned. "I have been practicing."

Aasah was nothing if not a man of the night sky. His eyes, pale as a moon-crocus, were dilated to their fullest, drinking in the thin light and glowing like a cat's. The web of gems that flashed and glowed with their own little fires furthered the impression that the man had stepped down from heavens. As a child, Leviathus had spent long hours staring up into the night, half certain he would find a dark and empty space in the shape of his father's shadowmancer.

If Aasah was a starlit sky, Yaela was his moon. She was Didi, Little Sister, shadowed and round and beautiful, mysterious as a faded dream. Like the moon, she was tantalizingly out of reach, always there, hanging before the eyes like a sweet fruit ripe for the tasting, but as distant and untouchable as the stars.

She opened her beautiful eyes and stared right through him. So had she done since the day she arrived in Atualon, washed up like a bit of flotsam on the tides, to take her place at the shadowmancer's side without a word of explanation to anyone. Not to the gold-masked Baidun Daiel, not to Ka Atu, and certainly not to his magic-deaf son, as if those eyes gave her the right to see and never be seen.

Aasah had explained to him once, after an eternity of questions, that cat-slit eyes were a mark of power where they came from. He would say no more, nor explain whether the magic was a gift of the eyes, or caused them, or what precisely Yaela could see that Leviathus could not.

Sometimes those eyes and their secrets intrigued him. Other times he was sure they mocked him, making him feel small, and ashamed, and angry.

"Have you spoken with my father tonight?" he asked Aasah.

"I have not." Aasah frowned. "I have nothing to convey. I will not tell my liege that his… daughter… is dead while she yet breathes."

The pause was brief, but Leviathus had been listening for it, and for the small catch in Yaela's breathing as well.

So. Even the shadowmancer is not convinced that Sulema is the king's daughter.

"You have not been to the sickroom today?"

Yaela shook her head fractionally, her face as expressionless as ever.

"Not today," Aasah admitted. "The Dance requires a great deal of energy. I have been resting since they brought her back."

Leviathus had been to the sickroom, and had watched the waxen face of his once-vibrant sister as she struggled to breathe, to live. The herbmistress's exact words had been, "*She has not died yet.*" They kept her in a deep sleep, much as his father kept the dragon trapped. *So she can heal,* they said.

"The healer thinks she will live," Leviathus said. "Hafsa Azeina agrees that we may move her, though we will have to travel overland, and that her chances will be better if we can get her to my father. He can heal her, where others have failed. I will travel with her, of course, and I would ask you and your apprentice to accompany us. It may be that you have saved my sister's life, and I will not forget this debt. Nor will my father, when I tell him what you have done for us."

The shadowmancer nodded. "I will be ready, ne Atu."

"Excellent. Thank you, my friend."

At that moment, a stick-thin figure burst into the courtyard, a fat bundle under one arm and a full wineskin under the other. The child stormed over to them, dumped its burdens unceremoniously at Leviathus's feet, and was gone before he could utter a word of thanks. The smell of warm bread and cinnamon rose from the bundle, and Leviathus's stomach growled appreciatively as he reached to unwrap it. Inside he found a small clay pot of honey, half a round of sheep's cheese the color of old bone, and most of a loaf of spiced bread studded with nuts and dried fruit. He broke off a small piece of bread and handed it to the shadowmancer.

"I am glad you will be with us. I am determined to bring my sister home to Atualon alive and well." He emphasized the words *my sister*, and bared his teeth in a hard smile as the shadowmancer and his apprentice shared a surprised glance.

I may be deaf to magic, my... friends... but I am not blind to your ambitions.

Yaela reached for the wineskin. Her pupils had grown so large that only the thinnest ring of iris showed, a flash of green fire in the shadow of the moons.

Leviathus broke off a larger chunk of bread for himself, drizzled some of the honey on it, and filled his mouth with sweetness. The shadowmancer considered him for a long moment before he, too, began to eat.

So, Leviathus thought, *the dance begins.*

THIRTEEN

Ismai dragged his feet all the way from the Youths' Quarter, to which he had been banished until someone figured out exactly what to do with him, through the children's garden and the kitchens, and down the red-stone path to the riverside cliffs, where the herbmistress had her rooms and where Hafsa Azeina had set up her tent. The Mothers had evicted most of the temporary residents, and Aish Kalumm was returning to a quieter level of chaos.

A pair of urchins broke cover and ran full-tilt toward him, brandishing sticks and screaming at the top of their lungs, startling him so that he almost dropped the bag he had been carrying. They came to a skidding and wide-eyed halt as Ruh'ayya poured down from a low wall like spilled shadows, and bounced off in another direction, leaving their shrieks and sticks to tumble through the air behind them.

They run like rabbits.

"Those are not for eating."

I did not say they smell *like rabbits.* She sneezed for emphasis and showed her tusks in a cat's grin. Ismai smiled a little. She had been going out of her way to cheer him up, but it still felt as if he were dragging his heart behind him in a sack.

Finally, and too soon, he came to the arched entrance to the herbmistress's rooms. He swallowed and tapped at the tiles, avoiding eye contact with the bright enameled skulls that grinned at him. When no one yelled at him to go away, he hunched his shoulders up toward his ears and entered.

Ruh'ayya sneezed, and flattened her ears. *I will stay out here. This place smells of a trap. And piss.* She sneezed again. *I never knew humans were so... unclean.*

Hafsa Azeina was seated beside Sulema's bed on a low stool. Her eyes glittered in the dim light, and for a panicked moment Ismai was reminded of the grave-watchers of Eid Kalmut, fabled statues imbued with blood and bone of the living, cursed to guard the remains of their masters for all eternity. She had been there since the day they brought Sulema back from the Bones of Eth, chanting and burning foul-smelling herbs, playing that cat's-head lyre that nobody wanted to talk about, and maybe dreamshifting. He had heard it whispered that the dreamshifter had been seen with fresh blood upon her lips and so he had stayed away all this time.

But nothing was going to keep him from saying goodbye.

He hovered for a moment, staring at her mouth, at the lyre leaning up against the wall, at the dried bundles of herbs and flowers that hung from the rafters, at the bottles and bowls and cups that littered the low table running the length of the far wall, anywhere but the too-still form on the bed.

Ruh'ayya roared outside, her fine voice urging him to courage. He could do this.

The dreamshifter turned her head to regard him, eyes unblinking, and he bit back a yelp of surprise.

"Ismai Zeeravashani," she addressed him.

He bowed low, hoping his knees would not go out from under him. "Hafsa Azeina. Under the sun, I see you."

"Do you?" She smiled. Her teeth did not look bloody. "Do you really? I wonder."

Ismai straightened and shifted his weight from one foot to the other. "I have come to see Sulema. To… to tell her goodbye."

She leaned her head back against the wall and narrowed her eyes to slits. "There is no word for 'goodbye' in Sindan."

"Dreamshifter?"

"In the Forbidden City, you might say *jai-hao*, which means 'until we greet again,' or you might say *jai tu wai*, which means 'until your path returns you to me.' But there is no way to say 'goodbye.'" Her lips pressed together in a wan and altogether humorless smile. "When we left Atualon I had planned on taking

138

her to Khanbul, but we ended up here, in the Zeera, where 'goodbye' means forever."

"I am sorry, Dreamshifter. I do not understand." Nor did he care to. He wished only to stand beside Sulema's bed, to bend down and wake her with a gentle kiss. And perhaps to go back to a time in his life when a wish felt like a possibility.

"Of course you do not understand," she snapped. "You are just a boy. Your path leads from your mother's tent to the kitchens and back, and no further. Just go away, and leave us alone." She closed her eyes the rest of the way, and her tangled river-foam locks fell forward to obscure her face.

Ismai hovered for a moment, torn between fear of the sorceress and the fear of never seeing Sulema again. Then he took a long, slow breath and squared his shoulders. He was Zeeravashani.

We are Zeeravashani, agreed Ruh'ayya.

Thus emboldened, he crossed the room to where Sulema lay, though he kept the bed between himself and her mother. Bravery was all well and good, but to anger a dreamshifter was insanity.

Sulema's left arm was bound in a cast of plaster, but her right arm lay upon the thin coverlet, palm upward, fingers curled gently like a shell that had been dropped and forgotten on the river's edge. He picked up her hand in both of his and turned it over. He risked a glance at her mother and then pressed his lips to the back of her hand. Her freckled skin was dry and pulled too close over her bones, and in the dim light it seemed a ghastly shade of yellow, like a tallow candle once the light has been put out. There was dried blood under her fingernails, and ground into the skin at her knuckles, and at one corner of her mouth.

Ismai had been so angry with her when he thought she had chosen another as her hayatani. Now he just wished she would open her eyes and laugh at him, and if she never chose him for anything at all he would not complain. Let her live, let her be happy, and he would never shadow her footsteps again.

"Sulema," he whispered. "Sulema. I am so sorry. Sulema, do you hear me?" He cradled her hand against his chest and ducked his chin as his face crumpled like a child's. "Sulema? I am leaving today. My Ruh'ayya chose me, above all others. I am Zeeravashani now, do you believe it? Do you hear me?"

He wanted to say so much more to her. To brush her hair out and wash it and braid it again, and tell her that she would be the finest Ja'Akari ever. To thank her for not laughing at him and his stupid dreams of adventure. But the words congealed in his throat and it was all he could do to keep from crying.

He held her hand for a long moment as Hafsa Azeina sat in the shadows, hair tumbled over her face and so still she was hardly there at all. He willed Sulema's sunken eyes to open and see him, wished her fingers to tighten upon his, wished her cracked lips to smile, to speak, to frown and tell him to go away already. Anything. He willed her awake and well with all his heart, but the shallow rasp of her breathing was the only sound in the room.

She has gone, he thought, *gone and left me all alone.*

Tears spilled from his eyes and pooled in the palm of her hand, but the screaming of his heart was not enough to wake her.

Ismai brought her hand to his cheek, and then kissed her tear-washed skin one more time before tucking her arm next to her body. He smoothed a few strands of dull orange hair back from her forehead, wishing he had the courage to kiss her slack mouth one time. Perhaps she would wake if he did, and beat him silly. But her mother was close, and the teeth showed slightly in her half-open mouth, and Sulema looked so lifeless and hopeless and gone that he could do nothing more than pat her shoulder and wipe his face on the sleeve of his tunic.

"I am going," he told her, and then, "*Jai tu wai.* I will see you again."

Did the sorceress smile at that, did she peer at him through her tangle of bone-white locks? Ismai could not have said. The words that had gotten stuck in his throat spilled from his eyes, and he stumbled half-blind from the room.

There was a soft noise behind him. Ismai clapped his hands over his ears and walked faster. Nothing in the world had ever terrified him as much as the sound of the dreamshifter crying.

Ruh'ayya brushed against him, almost knocking him over. He clung to her neck and pressed his face into her hot, prickly fur, letting the rumble of her breath and the great booming drum of her heart calm him.

She was your mate? Ruh'ayya asked hesitantly. She was not very familiar with the silly ways of humans and hated to seem ignorant, but his distress was hers now.

"She was my friend." Ismai pulled back and sniffled, glad there was no one to witness, and scrubbed his face again on his poor sodden tunic.

But not like Cub-in-Shadows.

He smiled a little, and his stomach growled. How could he be hungry when Sulema lay so close to death? "Not like Daru, no."

We could bring her meat, she offered helpfully.

Ismai sighed, and then bowed formally because it seemed like the right thing to do and because she liked it when he showed respect in the human way. "Thank you, Kithren, that will not be necessary. My… friend… cannot wake to eat. But the thought is kind."

Ruh'ayya dipped her head. The black tip of her tail swayed back and forth in a lazy pattern, and her eyes shone with pleasure. She tipped her head to one side, round ears flattening for a moment and then flicking forward again.

Dairuz says I must tell you that Tammas tells him we will be going soon. She blinked, and the tip of her tail twitched. *I am not a bird, to carry messages.*

Despite his heavy heart, Ismai grinned. "Tammas? Tell him I have one more person I would like to see before we go."

Her tail jerked again, harder this time, and she stared.

"Please? Beauteous one?"

She flattened her ears.

Ismai bowed low. "If you would be so kind as to grant me this favor, O jewel in the night, we will stop at the kitchens on our way back and I will beg meat for you."

Her ears flicked forward at that. *Pig meat?*

"A nice fat leg of pig for you," he agreed. "Please."

Very well, she agreed loftily. *I like pig. I do wish you humans were just a little smarter, so you could tell him yourself.* Her eyes took on the dreaming look that told Ismai she was conversing with another vash'ai. When she was finished, she gave him a sly look from the corner of her eye and began to clean one of her paws, flexing so that the cruel blue-black claws slid free of their sheaths. He knew better than to ask whether there had been a reply.

As he stepped through the low arch and into the first light of morning, Ismai nearly crashed into Hannei. He caught himself on his toes at the last possible moment, arms pinwheeling, once again nearly dropping his bag as he tried to stop his forward momentum from tumbling them both down the steep path. Hannei laughed and reached out to steady him, splaying one hand against his chest.

"*Yeh Atu*, Ismai, always in such a hurry."

"You are looking well, Ja'Akari." She was—her face was still a bit pale, the shadows under her eyes and cheekbones told of weight lost too quickly, but after Sulema's still form she seemed full to bursting with life.

"Under the sun I see you, Zeeravashani. That is a lovely friend you have there." She nodded to Ruh'ayya.

I like this one. She smells of smoke and meat.

Ismai shuffled his feet, wishing he could leave without seeming rude. Hannei glanced toward the herbmistress's rooms.

"You have been to see Sulema?"

"Yes. She is… sleeping."

"Is the dreamshifter still…"

"Yes."

"Ah. Well, I should go and… I need to say goodbye."

"*Jai tu wai.*"

"What to who?"

"*Jai tu wai.* It means… until your path brings you back again. Not goodbye."

"I like that. *Jai tu wai.* I suppose you will be leaving with Tammas?"

"Yes." Such a difference a tenday could make. "I wanted to find Daru first, and say…"

142

"*Jai tu wai.* Be well until our paths cross again, cousin." She surprised him by leaning forward and planting a kiss on either cheek.

"She will get better," he blurted.

"Of course she will." Hannei clenched her jaw and blinked. "She is Ja'Akari, and we are no easy meat." She bowed to him, and again to Ruh'ayya, and then ducked past.

Ismai rubbed his cheek reflectively and started down the path to the river's edge. He had become Zeeravashani, and he might some day be Ja'Sajani, but he would never, ever understand girls.

The dreamshifter's tent was not far down the path, off to the side of a little clearing that was used in the summertime for drying and smoking the giant *am'kal.* Thousands of the little bones crunched underfoot, and the path was slippery with silver scales. Ismai had fished for am'kal with his father, when he was a small boy, and smiled at the memory. Perhaps some day he would be a father, and would brave deep waters and hungry serpents for an afternoon spent fishing with his own son.

First, though, he would need to figure out how to get a girl to look at him twice.

He looked up at Ruh'ayya's growl. The sound was high and whining, and set his teeth on edge. She crouched on the path, staring at the dreamshifter's tent, hairs bristling in a fine line from the back of her skull to the tip of her tail, which lashed wildly from one side of the path to the other and sent the glittering scales aflight.

"Ruh'ayya?" He stepped closer. Her face wrinkled almost comically as she pulled her lips back, exposing her white tusks, red tongue lolling.

He comes.

The creatures embroidered all upon the tent of Hafsa Azeina writhed and billowed, and the tent flap was blown aside as if by a great wind. The massive form of Khurra'an flowed from the darkness, glowing as his dappled golden fur seemed to catch fire.

Ismai raised his brows, puzzled, as the king of cats raised his head and regarded them, the black tuft of his tail swaying gently back and forth. His tusks, long as a woman's forearm and banded with gold, gleamed dully in the morning light. "Is he not your sire?"

Yes. Her thought was a whisper, trembling in his mind. *My sire.*

"I do not understand."

No. You do not.

Khurra'an wrinkled his lips back and began a series of grunts that led up to a bone-rattling roar. He stared at Ruh'ayya, who had closed her eyes and flattened herself along the path, before giving a final, satisfied grunt. His tail curled upward and he turned away, strolling with an air of absolute unconcern toward the river.

Ismai realized he had been holding his breath and let it out with a whoosh, as wide-eyed and awake as if he had drunk an entire pot of coffee. "What was that all about?"

Ruh'ayya opened her eyes the tiniest slit. Her hackles were standing straight up in the air.

I was not supposed to choose you yet. I am in trouble.

"In trouble?" He thought of the times he had earned extra chores, or had privileges taken away. No dessert, no weapons practice, no sneaking off to the bachelor's band to try imprinting a young stallion.

It is rather more serious than that. Her tone was dry. *He may decide to kill me.*

"Kill you?" He gaped.

It is our law. But he will probably allow me to live. The end of her tail twitched. *He has not killed me yet.*

"I will not let him kill you." He had meant to sound more gallant and less panicked. The thought of his life without Ruh'ayya...

You will not let him kill me. The thought was warm and rich, suffused with laughter and no small amount of love. Cat-love, fierce and possessive, all sharp and pointy. *Go on, little manling, say your not-goodbyes to the little dreamshifter and let us leave this place.* She settled herself and began to groom.

"Are you not coming in, then?"

She stopped mid-lick to stare at him, tongue hanging out in a comical manner. *You would have me cover my sire's musk with my scent? I have no desire to look upon my own intestines, but thank you for asking.* Her eyes gleamed. *Every time I decide you are not completely hopeless…*

"Yes, O beauteous one." He bowed to her, grinning. She ignored him as only a cat can, sticking one leg high in the air the better to groom some delicate part. Chuckling, he ducked into the dreamshifter's tent.

Daru was in the middle of the tent, wrapping bright glass bottles in scraps of cloth and packing them into a wooden crate with trembling hands. His face was white and his breathing seemed fast and shallow.

Ismai frowned. "Are you all right?"

"Is Khurra'an gone?"

"Yes."

"Then I am all right." He placed both hands on the lip of the crate and sagged in the middle, every line of him shouting relief.

"What is it with you and Ruh'ayya?" Ismai stepped closer, still frowning. The younger boy's breathing was all wrong, and he had already come close to losing two friends. "Khurra'an will not hurt you."

Daru looked at him with those strange, sad eyes. "Will he not? Ask Ruh'ayya."

He had never attempted to speak with his kithren when he could not see her, but it could not be all that complicated. He closed his eyes and concentrated.

WHY IS EVERYONE SO AFRAID OF KHURRA'AN? HE WOULD NOT REALLY HURT DARU, WOULD HE?

STOP SHOUTING! she snarled in his mind. *And stop asking stupid questions. Cub-in-Shadows is wise to be wary of the vash'ai. They see him as weak. Most would kill him, given the chance.*

MOST… BUT NOT YOU?

They see him as weak. She sounded smug. *I see him. Now, go away until you have learned not to shout.* Just like that, she was gone from his mind. He told Daru what the vash'ai had said.

145

"I told you so." The younger boy sounded weary.

"Well… Ruh'ayya likes you."

"Too bad I am to travel with Khurra'an, and not with you." Daru sighed an old-man sigh. "Do not worry about me. I am used to it. Are you looking for the dreamshifter?"

"No, I came to say goodbye. But I think I will say *jai tu wai* instead." The words came easily to him now.

"Ah." A smile lit Daru's small face. "*Jai-hao, insuke Ismai. Kuokenti shi.*" He clasped his hands beneath his chin and curled his back in an odd little bow.

"You speak Sindanese?"

"I speak Sindanese. When you are sick as often as I am, you have a lot of time to study."

"Ah, little sage, but have you ever studied weapons?"

Daru stared at him as if he had grown fur and feathers. "Weapons? Me? No. I am too… I am too small." He took a deep breath, and repeated softly, as if to himself. "I am too small."

"Too small for a sword, maybe. At least for now." Ismai made a face that was meant to be funny, but the boy just stared at him. "My mother says that if I eat fish, I will grow as big as Tammas. Perhaps you will, as well."

"You will grow as big as Tammas. Bigger." Daru stated this as a fact. "I will always be small. And… weak."

"Oh, but you are not too small for these." Ismai felt a grin split his face as he dug into the bag and brought forth the leather-wrapped bundle. He handed it to the boy, hardly able to contain his excitement. "Go on, open it."

"What is this?" Daru turned the bundle over in his hands, staring. It made a dull clinking sound when he shook it.

"Open it and see."

Ismai watched Daru as he slowly unrolled the leather. He had cleaned churra pits for a week in exchange for this gift, and was repaid a thousandfold at the look that crossed the boy's face.

The leather rolled open to reveal six knives, each with a handle of bone carved in the shape of a different animal and a blade as long as a man's hand. Daru reached out to touch the nearest, the one shaped like a hawk.

"They are beautiful," he breathed, but in the next breath said, "They are too fine. I cannot accept this gift." His hands belied his words, twitching as if they itched to caress the smooth carvings, to test the edge of the gleaming blue steel. The knives were sharp enough. A slice along Ismai's own thumb attested to that.

"They are yours." Ismai held up his hands to stave off further protest. "I say they are yours. Daru… they belonged to your mother."

The boy stopped breathing, and his eyes went wide as the night sky.

"They have been sitting in one of my mother's rooms for a long time, so I asked. They belonged to your mother. Now they are yours."

The small boy launched himself in a tumble of arms and legs, hitting Ismai in the midsection and hugging him so hard his ribs creaked. "Ow!" He laughed. "Daru! *Ow!* Let me breathe. You like them, then?"

Daru spoke against his chest, voice small and muffled. "I have never held anything of hers before." He stepped back, embarrassed. Ismai looked away so that the boy could wipe the tears from his face. "Never. Thank you, Ismai. Thank you so much."

Ismai cleared his throat. At this rate, it would take a year and a day to dry all the tears from his tunic.

"You are welcome, little cousin. I hope they make you think of us, when you are far away in Atualon learning all there is to know." He ruffled the boy's hair. "You will come home safe, and tell me all the adventures you have had and all the things you have learned."

"Home." Daru was smiling now. He glanced around the tent, and made a face. "I had better finish packing, or we will never be able to leave. If we never leave, we will never be able to come home again."

"True enough." Ismai laughed. His spirits had lifted as if a new sun had risen in his heart, and it seemed to him in that moment that all would be well with the world. He would be Zeeravashani, and Sulema would heal and be her bright self again, and their paths would lead them all back home sooner rather than later. It would be as if they had never left… only better.

Daru rolled the knives up and clutched the bundle to his breast, smiling beatifically. "Until your path brings you back again, cousin. Be well."

"Be well," agreed Ismai. "*Jai tu wai.*"

He turned and strode out into the bright morning, whistling as he went.

FOURTEEN

Tsun-ju Jian, the pearl diver's son, became Daechen Jian in the four hundred and ninety-ninth year of Illumination, during the reign of Daeshen Tiachu. The emperor's historians maintain that under his golden fist the rivers flowed with milk and honey. Jian would later recollect that the rivers—and the streets, and the walls—ran not with milk and honey, but with blood.

The emperor bade his people rejoice and so they had, flocking to the city in twos and tens and by the hundreds, a shrieking mad-eyed mass of humanity pooling about Khanbul, staking out territories, posturing, breeding and eating and making a mess of the place until the tenth day of the Feast of Flowering Moons. On the eleventh day, the hung-over, penniless, and exhausted population abandoned Khanbul. They threw salt and worried looks over their shoulders as they hurried away, and with good reason. On the twelfth day, the emperor would hunt. Any citizen-slave too sick, or old, or drunk to flee—and there were always a few—would disappear on that day, never to return.

Or so the stories claimed. The son of a Bizhanese pearl diver had never really believed. Daechen Jian soon would.

"It was a fine, fat harvest this year." Xienpei informed them over bowls of golden rice and salted fish. "The Yellow Palace will be filled to bursting." One of the lashai ladled tea into a tiny porcelain cup and offered it to her, bowing low. She accepted the cup without acknowledging the servant's existence, the last two fingers of each hand tipped delicately away from her face as she breathed in the heady fumes.

"When will we be moving to the Yellow Palace?" Perri accepted his tea and glanced up at the servant with a smile, and then flushed and looked away. "Now that our... now that the commoners have all left, there is nothing for us to do here but rattle around in the walls and fight." The boy was slight for his age, and his round yellow eyes were even stranger than Jian's. Jian had stepped in when he found Perri cornered by a pair of pig-farm boys from Hou, and the smaller boy had dogged his heels ever since.

Naruteo scowled. He was taller than any boy there save Jian, and muscled like an ox. Naruteo had grown up in Huan, close to Khanbul, and considered the rest of them to be far beneath him.

"We will leave when the emperor wishes us to leave, and not a sandspan earlier." *Peasant*, his eyes added.

Xienpei laughed, displaying every gem-studded tooth in her head. "The emperor does not know you exist, little Daechen. Nor does he care. You are less than ants in the shadow of a dragon."

"When will we leave, then?" Jian asked. "If it please you, Yendaeshi."

Xienpei favored him with a nod. "When we have separated the dirt from the wheat, and then the wheat from the chaff, those who remain will be allowed to move on to the Yellow Palace."

"Not all here are Daechen." Naruteo did smile, then, and his flat eyes reminded Jian of a snake's. "And not all Daechen are worthy. Most of you will not make it."

Some of the other boys shifted and muttered, exchanging worried glances. Jian caught Naruteo's gaze and held it, but addressed his words to their yendaeshi.

"What happens to those who are not chosen? Will they be allowed to return home?" The room stilled at that, and most eyes turned toward Xienpei, some worried, others hopeful.

Xienpei reached out one long, lacquered fingernail and touched the pearls at Jian's neck. "Your mother is tsun-ju, is she not? A pearl diver?"

Jian nodded, wary.

"Does every oyster she finds contain a pearl?"

"It would be nice if every oyster had a pearl in it, but most do not. Some have sand, or pebbles."

"Or nothing."

He nodded.

"What of the pearls? Are they all as fine as these?" She tapped his necklace again.

"No, Yendaeshi."

"Ah, so those lesser pearls, what happens to them? Does your mother return them to the sea?"

Jian shifted, uncomfortable as the other boys began to stare at him. Perri was white as a gull, and Naruteo smirked into his tea.

"No," he answered at last. "She sells them at market."

Xienpei nodded and sat back. "So. Some will be used to make jewelry, and some will be sewn into clothing, or used to decorate masks. Or given to a small boy to play with."

Jian stared at her, the tea he had drunk curdling in his belly like sour milk.

"Others will be ground into powder and used in medicines, will they not, Daechen Jian?"

"Yes, Yendaeshi." He wanted to vomit.

"Every pearl your mother finds belongs to the emperor. Every pearl serves a purpose, even if that purpose is to become something less than what it thinks it is. So." She set her cup down with a clack for emphasis, and the lashai hurried over to fill it.

Xienpei turned her head and looked deliberately at the gray servant, and then back to Jian. Her smile was kind, but her eyes cruel as a hawk's.

"Even if that purpose is to be ground into dust."

That night Jian dreamed that giant hands strung him on a fine thread with hundreds of other pearls, as his mother began to pluck them loose and, one by one, drop them into a mortar. She was humming under her breath as she worked, and as her hands worked their way closer and closer Jian found himself unable to move, or call out, or do anything at all to save himself.

Then came the day of winnowing.

It began well before dawn. Jian was roused by one of the ubiquitous pale servants and ushered from his room still yawning and rubbing his eyes and wishing for some hot tea and a toothbrush. The hallway was packed with other boys, shuffling and jostling one another, some of them demanding to know what was happening to them. He was reminded, uncomfortably, of goats in a meat pen.

They were herded through the halls, down the stairs, and outdoors, trotting along barefoot and packed shoulder-to-shoulder, chest-to-back, a sea of yellow silk, bobbing dark heads and frightened eyes. The yendaeshi emerged from the lower rooms, carrying long poles with hooked blades at either end, some with merry faces and some looking grim. Jian saw Xienpei poke a boy back into place with the end of her staff, laughing, and was not reassured.

Finally they were marched and prodded and jogged into a large square and allowed to stand in place, steaming in the cool morning air. Jian juggled from foot to foot, grimacing at the cold hard ground and rubbing his arms as he looked around. He recognized this place. During the Feast of Flowering Moons, it had served as a marketplace for meat animals and child slaves.

Someone tugged at his sleeve. He looked down to see Perri, dancing from foot to foot and shivering. "I do not like this."

"*Hsst.*" Jian warned. "Neither do I."

The yendaeshi had been all friendly smiles and kind words before this day, though Jian had suspected them of a darker motive. On this morning each was resplendent in a silken robe of deepest gold, with a stooping black hawk upon the breast and the snowy white bull of the emperor embroidered across the back. The hooked staves they carried were put to good use, striking out here at a face, there at a leg, until the boys were huddled together like livestock in truth, and no few of them bled or wept in fear.

"Stay close," Jian whispered.

Naruteo stood a bit in front of them and off to one side, dressed in silks that made Jian feel shabby in comparison. He turned to stare at Jian and Perri, and drew one finger slowly across his throat. Then he dismissed them utterly, squaring his shoulders and turning to face what was to come.

Never before that day had Jian felt so vulnerable, as if he were but one of a thousand fish in a bait ball waiting to be picked off by the sharks. He glanced at Perri, shivering in wide-eyed fear beside him, and for the first time in his life caught the peculiar burned-sweat scent of fear.

That decided him. His heart might be racing, but he did not have to meet his fate cowering like a rabbit in a snare. He would bring honor to his mother's name, though he felt like a rabbit wearing the wooden mask of a sea-bear.

"*Hsst*," he whispered to Perri, and gave him a sharp nudge with his elbow. "Courage."

Perri stared right through him, mouth trembling. *Courage*, he mouthed back. He dropped his skinny arms to his side and clenched his fists.

Then the seven gates of Yosh opened, and there was no more time for courage.

Doors slid open all around them, silent as mouths, and disgorged an army of lashai. Each gray-clad, white-faced servant bore a tray of steaming cups, and the sharp tang of bitter tea washed toward them. Jian felt his stomach clench, and his gorge rise. Whatever was in those cups, he did not want to drink it.

Xienpei looked over her shoulder at him as if she had heard the thought. Her eyes were lit with amusement and her red lips curled in a cruel smile. She covered her mouth with a dainty hand and winked at him before turning back to witness the spectacle.

The lashai drifted closer, so smoothly they seemed to float on a current of air, bearing the enormous trays as if they weighed nothing. They reached the edge of the crowd of wide-eyed boys, and held up their trays, and waited.

The bald man who had been laughing with Xienpei spoke. His voice was surprisingly deep, and powerful enough that it bounced off the walls surrounding them. "Each of you take one cup," he said, "only one. And drink."

No one moved.

"Now."

The lashai pressed closer, and one boy reached out toward the trays. His hand hovered for a moment before snatching a cup. Then he brought it to his mouth, hand shaking so hard Jian could see it from such a distance, and drank.

Nothing happened.

The boy made a face, shook his head a little, and returned the cup with a grimace. The boys to his left and right began reaching out for their cups and downing the contents as well. Some of them made a face or gagged at the taste, but that seemed to be the worst of it.

"Maybe it is some sort of ceremony?" Perri whispered under his breath. Jian remembered Xienpei's smile, and shook his head fractionally.

"I think not."

The first rank of boys was peeled aside by the yendaeshi with their hooked poles, so that the second rank could drink, and the third, and the fourth. By the time the lashai reached the middle ranks, where Jian stood ready, the first boys had begun to look pale. Jian took the cup with his fingertips, trying to tell himself that it was dragonmint tea, nothing more. As he brought the cup to his lips and the scent hit him full in the face his whole body disagreed and he hesitated. He tried to make eye contact with the lashai, but those brown eyes were half-lidded and empty—there was nothing there at all. Those eyes frightened him more than whatever was in the tea.

Xienpei stood behind him, her lips at his ear. He had not seen her move.

"Drink," she said. Her breath was hot and smelled of mint, and Jian could see the flash of metal as she brought the wicked curved blade of her staff to rest against his cheek. "Drink. If you spit out so much as a drop, I will gut you like a fish."

Jian drank. From the corner of his eyes, he saw Perri do the same. Naruteo reached for the tray almost eagerly and shot them a look of spite as he tossed his drink back and dropped the delicate cup, and then he crushed it with his bare foot.

Xienpei chuckled and removed her blade. "Courage," she mocked. Then she was gone.

I am Tsun-ju Jian, he told himself, *son of Tsun-ju Tiungpei, the pearl diver of Bizhan. I have braved deep waters and sharp teeth. I have seen the face of shongwei. In my veins flows the blood of the Issuq...*

One of the first boys to drink the tea dropped to his knees with a shout, a cry that became a gargling shriek as he bent over double and began to vomit bright splashes of red upon the gray cobblestones. Another succumbed, and another. The air grew thick with the smell of sickness and blood and panic. There was a commotion off to one side as a boy near the walls tried to break away and flee. Jian watched in horror as two of the lashai took his arms and a third grabbed him by the jaw and forced him to drink. Though the boy struggled and screamed, the three pale servants were no more moved than adults holding onto a small child, and their faces remained as blank and still as smooth waters.

This scene was repeated over and again as someone tried to escape or to fight back, and always with the same result—a boy defeated, sometimes bloodied, with his belly full of tea and his eyes full of fear. One boy, a larger youth that Jian recognized with a shock as one of the pig-farm boys from Hou, thrashed his head from side to side and howled, fighting the servants who held him down. The noise was cut abruptly short as one of the yendaeshi stepped forward. The bladed staff licked forward and down like a lizard's tongue and opened the pig-boy's belly like a sack of grain, then up again and sidewise across his throat. Red bloomed against yellow silk, like a dream poppy in a field of buttersweet, and the boy fell forward to thrash in a spreading pool of his own blood and entrails.

Two more boys met similar fates as the lashai and yendaeshi swept through the ranks subduing, dosing, and occasionally butchering boys as they went. As they were finishing up, Jian felt the first pangs in his gut, pains like those he had experienced once after eating the wrong kind of eel.

It is not so bad, he thought as the pain bloomed and receded first in his gut, then in his chest, and finally in his kidneys before starting up in his gut again. *Not so bad. I can handle this.*

Then the pain had its way with him.

One time, when he was very small, Jian had pattered down the moons-lit path from his mother's house to the sea. The gulls were calling to him, and the waves, and the low and mournful voice of some great beast far out to sea, lifting its head above the waters to sing for him. It sang of loneliness, and need, and of home far away. Little Jian had waded into the sea in search of the song's owner, and the sea had claimed him.

The tide had been cold, unflinching, an unnatural greedy mouth that sucked at his feet, his legs, and finally opened to swallow him whole. Jian would remember for the rest of his life how it felt to be sucked in and rolled about by the water, end-over-end with his arms and legs flailing like an abandoned rag doll, utterly without control.

Now, as Jian fell to his knees and then toppled to his side, boiling from the inside out as if he had swallowed a cup full of sea nettles and slag, he was gripped by the same feeling of helplessness. He would die, or he would not die, and there was nothing he could do about it either way.

The cool rock felt good against his cheek. He smelled blood and shit and death, and he smelled the bilious stink of the thick black stuff he retched up. People were screaming, people were dying, but the stone was cool and quiet, so Jian pressed closer and closed his eyes with a sigh.

He heard the creaking of heavy wooden wheels, very near, and footsteps hurrying back and forth, so close he was kicked and tripped over any number of times. The pain came in like the tides, advancing and receding, advancing and receding, taking small bits of him away with every wave. During one of the moments of relative calm he had enough left of himself to wonder whether Perri had died, and whether he would die as well, alone on the stones with vomit in his hair. But he could not rouse himself to care.

Soon enough the pain claimed the last of him, and he was gone.

Eventually the pain came to an end. It was not a sudden end, a shock of bliss and blessed numbness, and neither was it a fading end like sunlight gone to the moons. It was a violent end, full of death and anger as the pain tried to keep its claws in him, to take one more bite, to wrest one more scream from his bloody throat.

As soon as Jian understood that he was screaming, he stopped. His had been the last voice. No one else screamed, or wept, or moaned. It seemed as if his harsh and labored breathing, the pounding of his heart, and the scrape of his fingernails against stone were the last sounds in the world.

Then something grunted, and snuffled, and grunted again. Jian could hear the sound of claws dragging along the ground. Hot breath seared his face and wet flesh touched his skin. Jian tried to recoil, to cry out, to escape, but the best he could manage was a shadow-thin wail as his eyes cracked open.

His vision wavered and danced as if he stood behind a waterfall in the dim light, and what he saw made no sense. Golden slippers and gray, a forest of slippers, soaked in blood and worse. Standing between the slippers and his face was a smallish creature in a golden harness, some breed of tusked dog, or maybe a kind of pig. It had thick, wiry-looking gray hair, and a long naked tail like a rat's, and a long flat snout with curling flat tusks that clacked and gnashed together as it peered at him with round, bright eyes. It nuzzled his face again with a flat, wet pink nose, and squealed, and wagged its tail, as pleased with itself as a lady's lap-dog that had just learned a new trick.

"*Dahwal*, Jinjin, good girl." Jinjin, if that was indeed the creature's name, whipped its tail back and forth so hard the hindquarters danced along with it. "This one is Daechen. And," the voice sounded surprised, "it is awake."

Gray slippers glided close. Hands grasped Jian under the arms and hauled him upright until he stood, supported by a pair of the lashai. He swayed and would have collapsed had they not been holding him upright, yet the servants—both considerably shorter and slighter of build than he—seemed to bear his weight without effort.

"Ah, young master Jian." Xienpei's face swam into view. Jian felt a shudder run through him, and the servants gave him a shake that set his head lolling to the side. "I am so pleased to see you alive. And awake. I am claiming this one," she added to someone behind her. "I have the sea things this turn and this boy is pure Issuq. Look at those eyes."

She turned back to him. Something glittered in her hands. "Hold him still," she snapped to the servants who bore his weight. "I will not have him damaged." She stepped close, so close he could smell the sandalwood and cinnamon of the oils she used in her hair, and something cold touched the side of his face. He would have pulled away if he could, but it was all Jian could do to breathe in and out, in and out. There was a *kachunk*, and fresh pain blossomed in his ear, but it was a small and warm kind of pain, almost comforting after all he had been through.

His mouth tasted of bile, and bitter herbs, and of blood. Jian tried to spit, wishing he could get away from the taste and the horrors of the day, wishing he had the strength to spit into the round and smiling face of the yendaeshi. But his tongue felt thick, and his mouth would not work properly. The best he could do for now was drool disgustingly down the front of his ruined yellow silks.

"Charming." Xienpei laughed, a sweet and girlish sound that made the hairs prickle at the back of Jian's neck. "Strip him, wash him, make him presentable," she told the lashai. "Daechen Jian will be riding back to the palace with me." Her smile was honey and poison. "I have plans for this one."

The servants half-led, half-dragged him across the market square. He stumbled over the stones, and his own feet, and once he stepped on an outstretched hand. It was cold underfoot and did not move, and as Jian slipped and staggered through the bloody ruin he realized that he was crying.

This is what it means to be a Prince of Khanbul, he thought, weeping. *A Prince of the Forbidden City.* How his mother would tear her hair to see him now. How the bullies of Bizhan would laugh to see Daechen Jian, blessed by the emperor himself. He did not stop weeping as they stripped the silks from his body and threw them in a growing pile of gold and yellow rags that had been the finest clothing of a thousand young men.

Jian tried to pull free from their hands as they led him to the wash racks that had served to bathe meat animals before they were sold, but they were too strong. He stood as little chance against his handlers as a yearling steer.

In the end he stood stripped of clothing and pride as they dumped buckets of cold salted water over his head, over and over again, and the tears continued to wash down his cheeks as they scrubbed him with handfuls of salt and sand, dried him with less care than the butcher might show a slab of meat, and rubbed scented oils into his skin. One of them pried his mouth open and scrubbed his mouth out with something that tasted of mint but stung his cheeks and tongue where he had bitten them earlier. Strangely, this new pain, and the throbbing in his earlobe, helped him to gain control of the sobs that wracked his body. The tears still spilled over, now and then, but he was no longer heaving and gasping like a child.

Other boys were dragged and carried over for much the same treatment. They were stripped, scrubbed, dried and oiled like so many redjaw during a spawn. Jian saw Naruteo being carried by three of the lashai, and to his relief he recognized Perri as they dragged him past, limp and bloodied but apparently alive. None but Jian were awake, however, and as he looked around he realized that the boys being washed and laid aside represented only a small fraction of those who had drunk the tea.

"Where are the others?" he asked. His voice was a broken whisper. "The other boys... where are they? Where have they gone?"

He hardly expected the lashai to answer. They never had, before.

One of them turned his head—or her head, it was hard to say—and some strange emotion flickered behind those dull eyes. Jian thought that behind its impassive mask, the lashai was laughing at him. It lifted one hand, slowly, and pointed.

It was then that Jian saw the covered wagons. There were a score of them, or more, enormous things crudely fashioned from dark wood and bound in iron, each pulled by a team of surly-eyed, stub-horned ghella. All in a line and facing the gates, they were piled high and covered with ugly brown sacking. Jian's gut clenched and he would have been sick again, had there been anything left to sick up.

Beneath the covers, something was moving. Some *things* were moving, and Jian knew what those cloths concealed, just as clearly as if he had seen them beaten and cut and tossed like offal upon the carts. As if he had put them there himself.

The carts began to roll, drivers swearing and shouting and cracking their whips over the heads of the sullen ghella with no more concern that they would have shown had they been hauling barrels of salted meat. They rolled through the gate one by one as an oily black smoke began to rise somewhere in the distance, and Jian could no more stop the wagons and save those boys than he could stop the trembling in his legs, or save himself.

The lashai stared. Jian dove deep, deep into the cold depths of his terror, and there he found a perfect black pearl, big as the last joint of a man's thumb. A prince's courage. He closed his fingers about the pearl. It was warm to the touch, and smelled of the sea. In the back of his mind he heard the gulls cry, and his mother singing as she mended the nets. He surfaced, looked into the servant's dead eyes...

And smiled.

It was a small gesture of defiance, a candle against the dark night, but later Jian would remember that moment and think, *That is when it really began.*

The lashai turned and led him away from the wagons. His defiance spent, Jian sagged with relief at that and nearly stumbled over his own feet. They walked across the stones and through a small doorway tucked away in one corner. He found himself in a plain room of gray-and-white stone. A long, low counter ran along one wall and a bench along the opposite. Jian swayed dangerously on his feet and the lashai pushed him to sit on the bench before picking up a small brass bell from the counter and ringing it, startling him with the pretty little sound.

A small door opened and a young woman stepped into the room. She stopped and blinked at the sight of Jian.

"Ah," she said. "You have brought me a live one. How... unusual."

Jian was painfully aware of his nudity. The bench was cold, and he fought not to weep. He was finished with weeping, with feeling like a mewling babe exposed to the elements and left to die. Unfortunately, it seemed, the world was not finished with him.

The lashai only waited. The girl began pulling wrapped bundles off the shelves, never once looking at Jian. Each package was shown to the lashai, and then the girl would make a mark on the rice paper wrapping and set it aside in a growing pile. Jian watched it all from a great distance, and wished he dared lie down on the bench and sleep. He was so weary, and so tired of being frightened, and the thought occurred to him as he watched the girl and the lashai that if by killing them both he might make an escape, he would do so.

At long last the girl turned to him and snapped her fingers. "You," she said, "stand."

He tried to obey, tried and failed. How had he thought to kill them and make an escape? His strength, as his defiance, had come to an end.

"I cannot." His voice was raw, his eyes were raw, and tears began spilling down his cheeks again.

The girl stared and for a moment her face went slack with pity. Then she glanced at the lashai, set her mouth, and shrugged before reaching for one of the larger bundles. She unwrapped it as she crossed the room, set it on the bench next to him, and pulled him to his feet. The room lurched dangerously.

"Stand," she told him again, and he found that he could. Barely.

She dressed him as if he were a child, or a corpse to be laid out for burial. Yellow silk again—Jian found that he had come to loathe the sight of it—a long robe, fine in quality and make but plain and unadorned, falling well past the knees. Black silk trousers, loose through the leg and gathered at the ankle, and tall boots of pressed felt with upturned toes and leather soles. A shorter robe of sheer black spidersilk went over all, and a wide belt that tied at the back.

When she had finished the girl stood before him, fussing with the belt and the lay of the cloth. Jian glanced at the lashai. The gray servant seemed indifferent. Still, he kept his voice low.

"What is this? What is happening?"

She would not meet his eyes.

"Do you know?" He caught her arm. "Please tell me. Please."

She shrugged away from his grip and shot him a look that mixed anger and fear and guilt in equal measure. "I cannot say."

"Please."

"I cannot say." She put her hand against his chest and gave him a little shove, so that he staggered backward and half-sat, half-fell upon the low bench.

The girl turned to the lashai and bowed low. "He is finished. I will have the rest sent up to the Yellow Palace." She barely waited for the servant's nod before turning to flee through the door by which she had entered.

The lashai looked down at Jian with mocking eyes. When it turned to leave he staggered to his feet and followed, defeated.

Xienpei was waiting for them.

"Leave us," she said. The servant bowed and walked away without a backward glance. Xienpei turned to Jian and smiled. "Let me look at you. Up and walking about as if nothing had happened. Oh, these are yours." She reached into the pocket of her robe and drew out Jian's necklaces of jade, and amber, and pearl, and looped them over his head. None of it felt real. "Come, walk with me. It will help move the *tsai-si* through your blood."

A tremor passed through Jian, and he thought his legs would collapse from beneath him. Xienpei put her hand on his shoulder to steady him, and then took his arm and led him away. The market square was dotted with kneeling servants, each with a bucket and brush and paddle, washing away every trace of the day's events. He realized with fresh horror that this place was the scene of such slaughter every year, this place he had visited with his mother time and again to buy honeyed ice from the mountains and laugh at the fools' plays. He should have known. Somehow, he should have known. Next year, in the very place he had fallen, people would laugh, and flirt, and bid on livestock, and watch the jugglers...

"Is it not a beautiful day?" Xienpei's eyes were bright, and her jeweled smile blinding. "Come, come, I want you to see something." Together they crossed the square and walked through the gates, which had been flung wide and left unguarded, and into the Princes' District of Khanbul. The black smoke still rose in the west, but she took his arm and pointed eastward, toward the palaces of the Daechen rising yellow and white and black. Beyond that he could just make out the shining walls of the Forbidden City and the golden dome of Taizhen Dao, the Palace of the Last Dawn.

"Do you see this path?"

It was more of a road than a path, cobbled and well kept, wide enough for five carts to drive abreast. He nodded.

"This path is five thousand years old," she told him. "Five thousand years ago, our first emperor had these very stones set down, that those few who were worthy might one day find their way to the palace. To learn the ways of Daechen, to walk the paths of day and night, of roses and moonlight, to pass through the courts of the soul and kindle the fires," she touched one hand to her heart in an odd gesture, "and add to His Illumination. You cannot understand what I am saying yet, but you will. I am telling you, Daechen Jian, that five thousand years ago the emperor laid this path for you." Her smile turned inward.

"This is not a foretelling. Perhaps I am mistaken, and you will die before the sun goes down. I will still be here, either way. Oh, do not give me that look. You should be thanking me—you are still alive, after all. Come, come, we must not be late."

As she led, so Jian followed, head spinning and occasionally seized by a spasm of pain that would leave him gasping and weak. Xienpei urged him to walk, and walk faster. The shadows that filled his mind were receding, only to be replaced by a blinding headache. When they came to a place where two paths met and turned toward the center of the city Xienpei bade him sit, and settled herself down beside him.

They did not wait long. Dust rose in the distance, and before long Jian could see shapes moving toward them. A low rumble grew into the rattling cacophony of wooden wheels against stone. Jian thought the carts had come for him and tried to stand, to flee. Xienpei clamped a hand down on his arm.

"Stupid boy," she hissed at him. "Sit."

So he sat, and waited, and before too long he could see that these were not the corpse-wagons. These were smaller and more finely made, white and gold in the sunlight and pulled by teams of graceful white horses. They moved at a brisk trot, high-stepping and smooth. Each cart carried a score or more of young women, girls the same age as Jian, dressed in yellow and white silk. Most lay asleep, or senseless, and those few who sat upright clung together, or wept, or stared numbly into the distance. Jian looked up into their faces as the wagons slowed and passed, and knew they mirrored his own pain.

"Who…" he began.

"Hush! Look. Look!" Xienpei pinched his arm. He looked.

Then he saw her.

She was seated at the back of a wagon, slumped against one side, boot-clad feet dangling behind as if she would jump from the wagon and run off if only she could gather her strength. Her face was a perfect oval, high cheekbones marking her as mountain-born. Her hair was black and glossy, and her eyes… her eyes. Jian knew those eyes, had seen them staring at him from his mother's mirror, from every still, deep pool he had ever looked into. She saw him as well, and sat bolt upright, staring with her mouth open in a perfect little O as they drove past and dwindled into the distance. Jian gaped after the girl long after she was gone from his sight.

"She is Daezhu," Xienpei said, satisfaction coloring her voice. "You did not think only boys were ever born during Nian-da, did you?"

"I…"

Xienpei stood and hauled him to his feet. "This is your road, the only one open to you now. The paths lead on, and none leads back to the life you had before. That way lies only death." For the first time since Jian had met his yendaeshi, she was not smiling. "The choice is before you. Remain where you are, and die. Look behind you, and die. Or move forward… and live."

Jian looked to the east, down the path to the girl and the palaces and a life he had never wanted.

"That is not much of a choice."

Xienpei laughed without a trace of humor. "It never is."

FIFTEEN

He called for her in the moonslight hours, when the world was cool and still.

She was deep in Shehannam, tracking the hare that was Umm Nurati's soul-twin, and keeping a wary ear attuned to the world around her. The Wild Hunt had not been through this region in an age, but that meant nothing. So when Khurra'an interrupted her dreamshifting and dragged her back into the world, she was angry enough to take a bite out of his ear.

You could try, he suggested, laughing at her.

Daru was curled at Sulema's feet like a scrawny kitten, only half asleep. His dreams were a gossamer shroud, and she was well pleased. His presence would serve to keep the girl safe from the shadows, and Khurra'an would eat any threat posed by the physical world.

The dreamshifter stepped from her warm tent and onto the cold sands, scowling up through her hair at Leviathus. He was dressed for travel, in an Atualonian kilt and the gold-and-white cloak of the ne Atu.

"There had better be coffee," she said.

He smiled a little and handed her a full mug.

"Walk with me," he said. "Please."

"Do you not know it is death to wake a dreamshifter?"

Leviathus grinned. "That is a story you made up so that no one would bother you in your tent. You never really sleep anyway, do you?"

"I do not need much sleep." She had not slept in years, not in the way he was thinking, but that was nobody's business but her own. "I do need privacy, and rest. What brings you here, and all alone?"

"I wished to speak with you."

She gestured toward her tent, but he shook his head.

"Let us walk. The camp has a thousand ears."

They walked. Didi paled and her darker sister faded into the sky as it paled from black to indigo, and then the first angry streaks of dawn broke free. Akari Sun Dragon, it seemed, was no happier at being woken from his slumber than she had been.

"Are we still family, Zeina?" he asked.

"Family is not like a dream from which you can wake."

"No matter how hard you try?" His voice was bitter. "Zeina, I have missed you. I missed you… so much. You have no idea."

She stopped and turned back toward her tent. Leviathus took her by the arm, careful not to move quickly, careful to let go when she shrugged away.

"I cannot be away from Sulema for long. She is not out of danger, yet."

"No, stop, please. I did not come tonight to argue with you. It is just… this is wretched, Zeina. Here we are walking together before the rest of the world wakes, just like we did when I was little and unable to sleep." He had been an anxious child, prone to bouts of insomnia. "Before Tadeah's death, and the politics, and the… politics. We should go, just go."

"Where would we go?"

"We would go fishing. Or hunting! Show me where you slew the golden ram. Take me to this Valley of Death I have heard so much about. Even that cannot be as bad as politics. Just let us go."

"Eid Kalmut is a peaceful place, *ehuani*, so long as you do not disturb the Guardian. I have seen more of the world than you have, this world and the next. Perhaps that has cured my wanderlust. Besides, we both have lives that cannot so easily be cast aside to run away and sleep beneath the stars."

"Still the stern mother." Leviathus smiled ruefully. "And yet there was that time we slept in the atrium, so you could teach me the names of the stars, do you remember? And the concubines came down to dance with Father? You did not want me to get in trouble, so you threw your robes over me…"

"That was long ago."

Leviathus laughed. "That was the first time I had ever seen a woman naked, and I was a little bit in love with Jamandae from that day on."

"I was a terrible influence," Hafsa Azeina said, and frowned as she remembered the deposed king's youngest concubine. "I was young and foolish."

"You were wonderful," countered Leviathus. "Zeina…"

A shadow passed over them, and a mournful cry sounded in the dark skies above. The song was answered to the north and, faintly, to the west. Leviathus looked up and squinted into the dark.

"Bintshi?"

"Lesser wyverns, and they are mating, not hunting. If it was a bintshi, you would be dead already." She shook her head. "Leviathus, why have you come here? The Zeera is no place for you."

"I have come because my father desired to know his daughter. I have come here, tonight, because he is troubled by events in the world. The Daemon Emperor…"

"Wyvernus would not be so troubled by events in the world if he would leave the world well enough alone," she snapped, irritated. "The Sindanese have kept to their Forbidden City since the Sundering. Why does Ka Atu think they will venture forth now, after all this time? Unless he has given them cause."

"Do you remember Archmaetreus Mundaya?"

"I remember." Hafsa Azeina spat. Mundaya had been found guilty of selling babies on the black market.

"Her sentence of death was commuted," he said. "In return, she agreed to spy for us. She works as a midwife in Sindan and tends to their… more unusual births."

"And…?"

"The Sindanese emperor is breeding a Daechen army. Women are encouraged to lie with daemons, and bear half-human spawn."

"An army of children? Unless they mean to use soiled wrappings as siege weapons, I hardly see cause for concern."

"Children grow up."

"What does Ka Atu propose we do about this? Ask the Sindanese women to stop bearing young? Sindan is a slave empire, and the women all belong to the emperor. It is death for any to refuse him. Besides, the stories tell us that the Dae are magical lovers. That one night of passion may be the only joy those women experience in their miserable lives."

Leviathus frowned. "You are not taking this seriously."

"I am not taking your father's concerns seriously. There is a difference. Tell me, what does your father propose we do about this army of infants?"

Leviathus looked uncomfortable. "Some among the Senate have proposed we should poison the villages' wells, perhaps, or we could train special midwives—"

"Do they think the Sindanese emperor would not notice a horde of women descending on his land with their midwives' gear?" She made a silencing motion with her hand. Her eyes felt hot, she was so angry. "Murdering innocent children… the idea is monstrous. Those children are less a threat to the land than your father's meddling."

"I do not agree that my father should go along with these plans, Zeina. I tell you so that you may dissuade him, or come up with a solution that does not involve spilling the blood of children."

She shook her head. "My days of persuading your father to do anything are over. This is a task for the queen consort. Take your concerns to her, whoever she may be."

Leviathus stared at her. "You truly do not know?"

"There are many things I do not know. Which thing is this?"

"There is no queen consort. When you left, Ka Atu retired his concubines, and he has refused to take a new wife. His fortress Atukos was dark for a year and a day, and he refused to light the fires. He would not listen to reason. It is a good thing he did not know back then where you had fled to, because he swore to lay waste to any who sheltered you."

Hafsa Azeina knew there had been a price on her head, but it had never occurred to her that Wyvernus might spend the rest of his days alone. The thought was surprisingly painful.

He pressed on. "Jamandae tried to reason with him, but then she was killed, and for a while we all feared for our lives. The mountain began smoking again, and the soldier beetles on the northern slopes swarmed. Those were bad times."

"I am sorry."

"Will you explain nothing? I cannot believe it was all a lie. You loved us. You loved me."

She could give him that much, at least. "Of course I loved you." She hesitated. "I still love you. But it changes nothing."

"It changes everything," he protested. "Zeina, why did you leave us?"

"I did not leave you. I left Atualon."

"You left me behind."

"You were not mine to take." She raised her hands and pushed the hair back from her face. "Leviathus, why do you come to me tonight? Have you come to walk down these old paths? Because I will not. I cannot."

"Will you not tell me why you left?"

"No." She bit the word in half.

"You do not plan to stay, do you? You will just leave us again." She said nothing.

"Zeina, we need you. I need you. My father needs you… These are troubled times, and he needs your advice."

"Your father has a kingdom full of people who are more than happy to advise him. He hardly needs my voice added to the din."

"That is just the thing." Leviathus ran his hands through his hair, clearly frustrated. "The matreons and patreons have their own interests at heart, and the Imperators always want war. The il Mer have grown too powerful, and one out of three of our soldiers are paid by the salt folk. Their loyalty is questionable. There is no one the king can trust to give him pure advice, from the heart."

"From the heart." Her laugh was bitter as blood. "If you only knew. What of the Quarabalese shadowmancer? Is he not a wise man?"

Leviathus hesitated and lowered his voice. "He is a foreigner, and his ways are strange. My father trusts him, but…"

"You do not."

"I do not."

She sighed. "I would like to help you, Leviathus, I really would, but I am no longer queen consort. I am not the woman you once knew, the young mother who took you fishing and taught you the names of the stars. My daughter and I are no longer of Atualon. Perhaps once he sees me, your father will realize that it is time for him to move on. Past time for him to choose a new consort and produce a new heir, an echovete child that he can raise up to rule in his place. And sooner is better than later. The child will have to learn to control sa and ka. I know your father thinks he is invulnerable, but even Ka Atu is mortal."

"It is not that simple, Zeina. I am not to tell you this but—"

"What?" she snapped. "Leviathus, it is time your father lives his own life, and it is time I return to my daughter. She needs me. He does not."

"It is too late for my father to take a new consort, too late for him to sire an heir." His voice broke. "Zeina, he is dying."

For a moment Hafsa Azeina could not breathe. She remembered holding in her hands the portrait of a foreign king, a red-haired man with a ready smile and mischief in his eyes. She remembered telling her father that she would take this man for her own, and she had. She had sailed across the perilous sea, and they had fallen in love at first sight, just like in the stories.

Yet stories, even love stories, do not always have happy endings. She had learned that long ago, and much to her sorrow.

Somewhere high above them, the wyvern screamed.

SIXTEEN

Leviathus ne Atu was a learned young man, and he loved maps. In his dreams he had traveled the Dibris, had tasted the exotic food and drink of the desert prides, had found his sister and brought her home again a thousand times and one.

He knew of the plumed lionsnakes and the vash'ai, *mymyc* and wyverns and spiders big enough to entangle sheep in their webs—Atualon did a brisk business in spidersilk—and he knew the desert was as wide and deep as Nar Bedayyan. But tracing the Zeera on a map was one thing. Dragging one's sunburnt and parched ass across it was an entirely different matter.

The Zeeranim were as a slow-moving shadow rolling across the land. Half a thousand set out at the same time, most of them barely grown youths and fierce-eyed huntresses. There were no Mothers in this group, no pregnant women or children clinging to skirts. These precious and vulnerable members of the prides remained behind in the river fortress Aish Kalumm. A wise choice, perhaps, but Leviathus's books told him that once all of the desert people had been free to wander at whim beneath the desert moons, and he felt that something beautiful had been lost.

They moved north, staying far enough to the east of the Dibris that they might avoid most of the larger serpents, but not so far that their path would take them into the territories of the wild vash'ai. These people depended on the cats' aid and sufferance for their very survival. To trespass was blasphemy.

Though it often seemed to Leviathus that the worst blasphemy these people could imagine was moving with a purpose. They wandered more than traveled, a haphazard tangle of stubborn and hot-headed people who had more or less decided to move in the same general direction, until some of them decided to go home, or stop and take a nap, or go tarbok hunting instead.

If the lack of discipline was maddening, the Zeera herself was every dream of adventure he had ever had as a boy. This far from the Dibris, water was nothing more than a fond memory. The world was wind and sand under the sun, wind and sand under the moons, and stretched ever on and on as far as the dreaming mind could reach. And it sang. It was one thing to hear tales of the singing dunes, and another altogether to stand in the light of the pregnant moons, feeling the sand beneath his feet shift and swell to their pull, and listen to the slow and mournful dirge of the desert. At night the song was a mother's lullaby, sometimes. Other times it was a man with a voice like thunder singing to his lost love.

When the sun came up the voices took on a sharp, snapping quality. They crackled like fire, they called the heart to war.

By day the ground burned and shimmered like gold in the jeweler's forge. With each step, Leviathus's body reminded him that this was no place for life, certainly no place for such a small and insignificant life as his. Well could he imagine Akari Sun Dragon from the old tales stretching his wings across the thin blue sky, while Sajani Earth Dragon burned beneath their feet as she dreamed of her lover's touch. The Sleeping Dragon would wake and split the earth asunder when she emerged to rejoin him in their dance across the heavens, unaware of the small lives that burned in the glory of her rebirth.

Unless, as it was said, Sajani Earth Dragon really was the mother of the desert prides. In that case, she was as likely to sleep until the end of times, or wake and decide she did not care so much for Akari Sun Dragon, or choose to go goat hunting instead.

Somehow, despite all the chaos, the lot of them managed to wake and break their fast each morning before sunrise, early enough that the sands were still cool and friendly, late enough that most of the night hunters had given up drooling around the ring of fire and swords and slunk off to find softer prey. Leviathus never saw aught of these beasts save spoor, but those claw-marks and drag-marks and piles of dung as big as tents were enough to make him glad for the presence of the vash'ai. Without the big cats, humans in the Zeera would have been hunted to extinction long ago.

By the time they passed the territories of the Nisfim, the northernmost pride, their party had dwindled to perhaps a hundred people and a score of vash'ai. Leviathus traveled with his own small horde as befitted a man of his station. These included six of the Draiksguard and four of the Baidun Daiel, as well as Aasah and his apprentice. The men of the Draiksguard insisted on wearing their scale tunics and snarling helms despite the heat. Rheodus was not among them—Leviathus had left the young man to guard the ships when it became apparent that Mattu would be traveling overland with them.

Leviathus was not about to let Mattu Halfmask sink his claws into the Draiksguard.

He wondered whether the Zeera had ever seen such a strange troupe, and upon what stage their stories would play out. His father's ward, Matteira, would no doubt have written them all into a puppeteer's play for the amusement of their great-grandchildren. He smiled to think of it.

How, he wondered, *would she portray her twin?* His smile faded as he looked at the man himself.

Mattu Halfmask wore the face of a fennec today. The oversized ears and pointed face lent an air of sly mischief that suited him well. Leviathus saw more than one of the Ja'Akari eyeing the man with speculation, and wondered whether those girls hoped more for a peek under Mattu's mask, or his kilt. He hid a smile and wished them much luck. Mattu's secrets were notoriously well guarded.

As were those of Hafsa Azeina.

The woman who had been closer to him than his own mother stalked the edges of the camp like a wraith, silent and brooding, her face a masterpiece of maskery beyond even Mattu's skill. He saw her at mealtimes, she and that big cat of hers that had the other cats cringing in his presence. He saw her riding during the day off to this side or that, farther from the party than Leviathus thought safe, and she brought back meat more often than any other hunter.

He saw her every night in the healer's tent, when he paid his visit to Sulema. During those times she sat on her haunches silent as death, eyes staring out as if she looked upon some dark and distant landscape. It was so difficult for him to reconcile soft memories of warmth and moonsilk with the reality of this harsh woman with skin spotted like a cat's, and the scent of blood clinging to her robes.

Her little apprentice, Daru, was another story begging for an audience. Such an unlikely pair could scarce be imagined outside of a Dae-tale—the cat-woman and the mouse-child who feared and loved her. For wherever the sorceress went, his eyes followed, and he seemed to tremble in Zeina's shadow as if he expected her to eat him at any moment. Leviathus could never remember having felt such fear, not even when he was small and his father had taken him to the coast to watch the sea-bears hunt, and he felt sorry for the boy. The dreamshifter's apprentice had a hard path ahead of him, and likely a short one. Neither the Zeera nor the Zeeranim seemed tolerant of weaklings.

On the seventeenth day of their journey, when they had reached the point along their route closest to Nar Bedayyan and just before turning east toward the Great Salt Road, Leviathus found a circle of short standing stones and built his fire in the very midst of them. The shadows danced to the song of the dunes, looking for all the world like young girls dancing in a ring around the Seeding fire, and he settled his back against a sun-warmed rock with a skin of wine to one hand and a bag of scrolls to the other.

He was distracted. Sulema's color had been good, and she had begun to mutter and cry out in her long sleep. The healer thought she would wake soon and had ordered them all out so that she might rest, which made no sense to him at all. He wanted to be close when she opened her eyes, wanted to hold her hand and talk to her and see that she was still in there. One of his father's grooms had taken a kick to the head, years ago, and had woken from the long sleep with a mind as empty as a sucked egg. Leviathus could not bear the thought of his bright sister snuffed out so, not when he had finally found her.

He sighed and pulled out a scroll at random. It was a treatise on the emperors of Sindan.

"*The Palace of the Last Dawn,*" it began, "*is the oldest man-built structure in the Known World, and said to be among the most beautiful. Slave-built over the span of two hundred years or more, said to be haunted by the spirits of those who died during its construction, the Palace of the Last Dawn lies at the heart of the Forbidden City and has never been seen by human eyes. The first Daemon Emperor, Daeshen Baichen Pao, also known as the Golden Fist...*"

Leviathus raised his free hand to rub between his eyes. He needed knowledge, true knowledge, not a storyteller's conjecture. He did not need to know the color of the Daemon Emperor's windows— or the fit of his underthings—half as much as he needed to know how many soldiers the emperor had at his disposal.

Look, here the idiot referred to the fourth emperor as Daeshen Tiachu. Unless the current emperor was more than three thousand years old, which hardly seemed likely, his father's venerable mistress of records either needed to retire or find herself a new scribe.

He put the scroll back and chose another, this time selecting a work that was meant to be a playful ballad. For in fiction, as in the best of lies, lay many important truths. This particular scroll was a master's piece by the mysterious scribe known as the White Crow, and had come to his father's libraries all the way from Khanbul.

Leviathus had been fascinated with Khanbul as a child, likely because the thought of a Forbidden City had caught his imagination. He had been a boy drawn to the forbidden: sweetcakes before dinner, the Queen's Atrium, the women's baths. Come to think of it, those things were still fascinating.

He grinned to himself.

Daeshen Tiachu had sent a trade delegation to Atualon some years back. Leviathus had expected to find them exotic, even frightening. He had not expected to find them beautiful—but they were, every one of them, even the ones who peered through veils with eyes too large or too round or too vibrantly colored to belong in a human face. They moved with an eerie grace and spoke with voices harsh as a crow's laugh, or sweet as the ocean sighing at sunset, and managed to convey damnable arrogance with exquisite courtesy so that not even the volatile Ka Atu could be anything but charmed. They had come into his presence bearing arms, and had walked away bearing gifts.

These days Atualon imported a great amount of Sindanese pearls and jade, amber and bamboo, and enough wormsilk to clothe every man, woman, and child in Atualon. In turn, the wagons bound for the Far East were laden with the wealth of the mountains—red salt and white, gemstones and black iron, spidersilk, and, most precious of all, saltware.

The kilns of Atualon were famous for the urns and jars fashioned of red salt clay. This clay, when fired, would keep food unspoiled for weeks, and water sweet for years. In a world seared by a dragon's song, the red salt clay was life itself.

Leviathus yawned over the scroll, beautiful as it was, and reached for the next. Better to dance with the enemy than dance to the enemy's tune. Better still to learn the steps of the dance before the music begins.

"What are you reading?"

Leviathus looked up, startled. The boy was a mouse indeed, to move so silently. He unrolled the scroll further, that Daru might better see the delicate letters and vibrant illustrations.

"*The Dreams of Dragons*. My tutors would be furious."

The boy tipped his head to one side, eyes bright with reflected flames.

"Why?" He spoke Atualonian, and his words were only lightly accented. Leviathus smiled. Of course, any student of Zeina's would be well tutored.

"I should be reading histories. This is a ballad." He recited:

> "Listen, O my people, to the Dreams of Devranae daughter
> of Zula Din, that
> brought boundless grief upon the Zeeravashani. Many a
> brave warden did
> it send hurrying down the road to Yosh, and many a Warrior
> did it yield a
> prey to wyrm and serpent, for so were the counsels of the
> Grandmothers
> fulfilled from the day on which Davvus, king of Men,
> and great Devranae, daughter of the Huntress, first set eyes
> upon one another."

The boy smiled and tucked his hands behind his back in a stance familiar to any schoolboy. He answered, in a voice as pure as a mountain stream:

> "And which of the Four was it that set Beauty before the
> Beast? It was Thoth, son of Eth
> and Illindra. He was angry with the sons of Men and set
> a geas of love to doom the people, because Jesserus father of
> Davvus
> had mocked Iftallan his priest. Now Zula Din had
> come to the houses of Men to free her daughter, and had
> brought with her a thousand of her Hounds: moreover she
> bore in her hand the
> Bow of Akari, and wore upon her brow a crown of
> blackthorn, and she
> sounded her horn for the blood of the Baidun Daiel, but
> most of all the man Davvus,
> who was their chief."

Leviathus shoved the scroll back into the bag and laughed. "Well played, boy. That will teach me to measure my own shadow against the sun. Sit down, sit down. It is always a pleasure to speak with another scholar. You are young to have read the *Dreams*."

The boy sat across the fire from him, flushed with the praise.

"I was often sick as a child. The dreamshifter would tell me tales to shut me up."

"To shut you up, or to put you to sleep? Aeomerus was a tedious old fart. Though this White Crow tells it well."

Daru burst out in shocked laughter, quickly smothered. He did not seem a child who laughed often, or easily, and Leviathus was glad to hear it.

"I like the *Dreams*. And I like *Siege of Dreams*."

Leviathus thought he could guess why. "Davvus was a great warrior."

Daru nodded eagerly. "I wish he had found the dragon. Do you think we ever will? Find her, I mean."

Leviathus raised his eyebrows. "What do you think?"

"Ah, you answer a question with another question, like Dreamshifter." The boy rolled his eyes. "Next you will say my mouth is too small to speak of such big things."

"And not to cast your fishing net at a dragon. And not to shoot an arrow at the stars." Leviathus laughed. "Zeina used to tell me those same things when I was your age."

The boy's jaw dropped and his eyes goggled so they seemed in danger of falling out of his head. "You were her apprentice?"

"Not at all. I am surdus. Do you know what that means?"

Daru looked down at his feet. "It means you cannot see magic."

"It means I cannot *hear* magic," he corrected him, "although it is much the same thing. Hafsa Azeina is… was… she is married to my father."

"She *whaaaaat*?" The boy's voice was an incredulous squeak. "You lie."

"Sometimes," Leviathus admitted, "but not about this. Zeina is my father's most beloved wife. When my mother died—"

"She is a *wife*?" the boy squeaked again. His face had gone three shades of pale. "What kind of man would marry *her*?"

Leviathus could not help it. He burst out laughing. "You make it sound as if my father had taken a lionsnake to bed. She was not a dreamshifter then. She was just a girl from the Seven Isles of Eiros, and wed to him to seal an alliance. They fell in love and he set his other concubines aside for her. It was quite the scandal."

"You do not simply wake up one day and decide to become a dreamshifter. You either are, or you are not." The boy bit his lip and scowled at a thought. "If Hafsa Azeina was married to your father, that makes you and Sulema…"

"Brother and sister. I am surprised nobody has told you this before."

"Nobody tells me anything." The boy sighed, and then his thin face lit up. "I cannot wait to tell Ismai. He will be so relieved. He thought Sulema had chosen you as her…" and he choked, blushing. "I mean, he did not know you were her brother."

"Ismai, is it? Is that not the young man who got in so much trouble for taming a vash'ai as we were leaving?"

"Tame the vash'ai?" The boy's eyes threatened to pop right out of his head. "You had better not let them hear you say that."

"Not tame? How do you live safely among them if they are not tame?"

The boy gave him a look that was pure Hafsa Azeina—mingled patience and exasperation.

"Who told you they are safe? You do not know much about the Zeeravashani, do you? Oh!" He blushed again, red as a pomegranate. "Oh, I am sorry, that was rude. My mouth rides faster than my brain can walk, sometimes."

"No need to apologize—you are right. I have much to learn, and my tutors hardly know more about the Zeeravashani than I do. Tell you what," he nodded to the bag of scrolls. "Ride with me during the day and teach me. At night, I will let you read these… if you like."

The boy's eyes lit with delight as he stared at the bag of scrolls, but he hesitated.

"You will not forget?"

Leviathus kissed his fingertips and held them up to the sky. "Under the stars, I will not."

Daru opened his mouth, but the words choked off as his body arched and shook. His eyes grew wide and sightless, lips drew back in a rictus grin. Leviathus lurched to his feet, scattering scrolls across the sand and perilously close to the flames, but the fit passed before he could take a step. The boy looked at him, trembling and panting as if he had run for miles, and tears spilled from his eyes to roll unheeded down the thin face, leaving little trails in the dust.

"*Sulema!*" the boy gasped, scrambling to his feet.

Leviathus dropped the scroll and ran.

SEVENTEEN

Sulema had hung suspended, away from song and sun and sand, for as far as she could remember. Wrapped head to toe in some soft, silken stuff she swayed back and forth, back and forth in a wind she could neither hear nor feel upon her face.

Free yourself, a voice barked in the darkness. But struggling against her bonds had never done any good, so she slept instead.

She dreamed of the night she and Hannei had walked soft-foot and laughing among the drowsy stallions of Uthrak. The moons lit their way through the endless night like firebugs caught in a spider's web. She and her friend had braided shining beads into the manes of swift Zeitan and sweet, brave Ruhho. Tradition held that if these beads went undetected until Hajra-Khai, they would be granted breeding rights to the best stallions in the Zeera. They braided their dreams into those wind-knotted manes, and the whispered promise of a golden future. A promise that Akari Sun Dragon would wake and spread his wings over the world once more, that tomorrow would come, and fillies and colts and children, honor and glory and songs at the day's end, a thousand and one tomorrows alike as grains in a handful of sand.

And if Akari does not rise? the voice persisted. *What then, O warrior under the sun? Will you free yourself and bring light to the world? Or will you hang here in the darkness and become meat?*

Sulema felt it then, a third presence in the void, felt it as a shiver along the web that held her fast. A dreadful cold emptiness, always angry, always hungry, and it was aware of her now. There were no stallions, no cousins or warriors to help set her free. She had only herself to rely on, and she knew herself to be unreliable.

"I cannot free myself," she cried out, and the words froze in her throat. "I have tried."

Have you? I think not. A laugh barked nearby. Sulema found that she could open her eyes, and turn her head. She found herself face-to-face with a fennec, a tiny white fox with ears as big as its head. A creature of the moon, pale and beautiful, with eyes like starlight on the water.

All around them, woven into and out of the darkness further than her mind could stretch, shimmered a vast and intricate web. It was from this that Sulema hung, head-down, one foot tucked behind her knee and hands behind her back.

"Help me," she asked the fox. "Please."

Help yourself. Better hurry, he is coming. That one has been looking for you for a long time. The fox tipped her head to one side and swiveled her enormous black-tipped ears.

Sulema realized that she was hanging upside down from an impossible spider's web, talking to a fox in the middle of nothing. The web went ever on and on, beyond all imagining. Threads of starlight and moonlight and blood and gold shimmered and shivered and pulsed to the beat of a great and powerful song. Silvery globes were threaded all along the strands of web, like beads of magesilver braided into a stallion's mane, bright little lights that did not detract from the soft dark.

There were black strands tangled into this great web, too, strands that pulsed with silent malice, a darkness so bright it burned her eyes. These strands trembled and swayed under the weight of the terrible presence. Something, some vast and evil Thing, had noticed her struggles… and it was hungry.

"Are you real?" Sulema asked the fox. "Or am I dreaming?"

I am neither. I am Jinchua. Are you real? the fox mocked. Or am I having a nightmare? Really, you two-legs have the most ridiculous imaginations. Is this the best you can do? Or the worst?

"If you are a dream, you are the most annoying dream I have ever had." Sulema closed her eyes. "I am going to wake now."

What is your hurry? You have been asleep most of your life. Safe in your mother's tent, in a cradle of bones, dreaming to the sound of a bloody lullaby.

Sulema fought the strands that bound her arms, and began to spin slowly around. "You leave my mother out of this!" Even as she said the words, an image flickered across some of the closer globes—a monster with the head of a horned cat, glaring at her with her mother's eyes. In its hand it held a blade of dark flame, though whether it meant to free her or slay her Sulema could not have said.

Would you turn her out? The fennec lolled her tongue in a sardonic smile. *That might not be wise. You deny her even as the heart's blood of your enemies burns sour in her mouth. Would anyone else find such value in your life? I think not. That one would have made a good fox.*

"I do not have to listen to you," she told the fox. "You are nothing but a dream, and when I wake I will tell Hannei all about it and we will laugh."

Will you laugh when next you meet Hannei Two-blades? I think not. You will not wake at all, if you do not free yourself quickly. He is coming, and the song in your blood is driving him mad with hunger. Nobody can wake from the dream after they have been torn to pieces and gobbled up.

The wind howled now, and though she still could not feel it on her face it caused her to sway back and forth like a toy held up to tease an infant. The wind mocked her struggles.

Your father will be so disappointed, it said.

You almost had it! You were almost there! The fox stood on her hind legs, and pressed her cold nose against Sulema's forehead. This close, Sulema could see the slit pupils of her eyes and her white, white teeth. Her breath smelled, oddly enough, of cardamom. *You need to free yourself now. There is no more time.*

Sulema twisted her hands behind her back, straining at the silken bonds till it felt as if her shoulders would pop loose. "I cannot!"

Not like that, the fox snapped. *Stupid two-legs. To break your bonds, you must first accept them.*

Sulema could feel the Thing drawing nearer, could feel the web shudder under its weight and smell the carrion stink of its intent. She bucked and struggled wildly as panic rose in her throat. "I cannot!"

No? The fox sat and curled the soft brush of her tail daintily about her paws. *If you cannot accept those things that bind you in life, then you surely must accept your death.*

Sulema stopped struggling and hung still for a moment, suspended at the heart of all things. "I do not understand."

A cub could understand. Life, or death? Life, or death? Why is this so difficult for you? It is time for you to choose.

The air rippled and parted like a tent flap, and a shadowy figure stepped through. The cat-faced being that was—and was not—her mother crouched close and she gagged at the carrion stink of its breath. In its hand the monster held a wicked-looking black knife. Sulema could not help but think it wished to taste her flesh. The blade flashed once, twice, three times. Sulema jerked against the web, trying to escape the knife, but the cuts had not been meant for her. Some of the strands that had bound her floated away into the night.

"Help me," Sulema begged. "Please."

The cat-thing sat back on its haunches, it looked at her through her mother's eyes, spoke to her with her mother's voice.

"I can do no more," it growled. "You will have to free yourself." And it faded away.

The web shimmered, its strands crackling and shrieking in protest as more of her bonds fell away and the Thing began its final descent. She could hear it now, the thin, high voice gibbering in anticipation of her blood, the rasp of its legs against the silken strands that bound her.

"I do not know how!" she wailed.

The fox lunged forward and nipped Sulema sharply on the nose.

There is no time, she barked, and Sulema could hear the Thing shrieking with glee, could feel the web sag under its weight. The little silvery globes shimmered in the dark, and they rang with the sound of a thousand thousand voices.

Then she understood, in a moment so clear and sharp it cut

her heart. The globes were worlds, they were *all* the worlds... the world of Man, Shehannam, even the Twilight Lands, worlds without number, lives without end. Every creature was bound to the web of life, every sound in every world was a perfect note in one great song.

Sulema stopped struggling and stared into the fox's bright eyes. The Thing did not matter, the web did not matter. There was only this one choice, and Sulema had made her decision long ago. She smiled. The fox smiled back.

"Life," she whispered. She closed her eyes and relaxed against the silken strands that held her fast. "I choose life." As easy as that, she was free.

The sun warmed her face. Sulema opened her eyes to find herself once more in the Zeera.

I know this place, she thought. *I could make it home by dark.* But a storm was rising in the west, and another was blowing in from the north. Sandstorms, killing-storms.

Follow me if you wish to live, the fox cried, as it ran on ahead.

Sulema dug her heels into Atemi's sides and took after the fox in a hard gallop, flying over the desert as lightly as a stone skipping across the river. The little creature kicked up puffs of sand as she ran, the brush of her tail daring them to catch her, but no matter how Sulema urged her mare on they could not quite seem to close the distance between them.

"Jinchua!" she called. "Jinchua!"

Catch me if you can, laughed the fox.

As she rode, the world on either side of them fell away, the world behind them fell away, the world beneath them fell away. Sulema leaned into Atemi's neck, her mare's sweat-slick hide hot against her cheek and lather flying into her face as they tried to outrun the howling wind. When she glanced down, Sulema could see the land laid out beneath them like a painting, like one of Leviathus's maps—rivers of blue ink and gold foil sand, the tourmaline splotch of an oasis, the tiny sketched figures of her people struggling to maintain their foothold in a hostile world.

She saw the wild vash'ai ranged about Aish Kalumm in a wide crescent as if they were herding the people into the river to drown. She saw her sword-sister Hannei, the shadows of two swords laid across her back like a curse, drinking from a golden cup. She saw the thick black snake of a funeral procession winding its slow, sad way toward the river, and watched as Tammas laid flowers upon a pyre. Paraja and Dairuz stood by his side. The vash'ai turned their heads to watch as Sulema and her mare raced past.

She flew over the camp of the Ja'Sajani, busy keeping the people's lives in order. She saw Ismai and his pretty vash'ai queen racing and tumbling after one another along a line of tall dunes, like cubs at play, and she smiled to see him happy.

Sulema flew past Istaza Ani astride her big red stallion, riding north away from the people. The youthmistress wore a look of grief and granite, and her eyes were red from weeping. A wild vash'ai stalked the pair, ranging now behind and now to the side, and though Sulema could feel his regard he spared not a glance as she and Atemi thundered past.

She swept east over the slow blue waters of the Dibris. A lonely ship sailed against the wind, a dragon-faced ship with gold-striped sails. All the crew lay bloated and blackened in death. At the helm stood a shrouded ghost with a metal face and eyes that burned.

I know him, Sulema realized, and his face began to turn toward her as if he sniffed out the thought. *I know that ship.*

Come away from there, barked the fox. *Come away now, you are not ready for that yet.*

Sulema passed the vessel with its dead crew, soared across the Dibris, and skimmed along the burned red ground of the Seared Lands before turning north, as the fox flew, north toward the sea, and Atualon... and her father.

A beautiful woman slept beside the sea, a blue-skinned woman in silk and jewels wearing a white-gold crown. The waves danced and sang about her skirts, begging playfully for her attention, and all along the shore flowers bloomed for the love of her. Her face was peaceful, and soft dark curls were held back from her face with a web of starlight. Lashes black as soot brushed her pale cheeks, and her breast rose and fell as she slept.

The winds fell away behind them. Sulema brought Atemi to a halt, and dismounted.

She stood upon a beach in the light of the moons, and watched the lady sleep.

"What is this?" she wondered aloud. "What is this?"

This is Sajani, the Sleeping Dragon, the fox explained. *She is the reason you are here.*

"I do not understand."

Do you not see the danger? Open your eyes. Let go of those things that bind you, and open your eyes.

Sulema closed her eyes, and opened her eyes, and *saw.*

An intricate tangle of twisted black wires stretched from horizon to horizon, the first strands of a web that would capture the world. A thousand shining spiders danced about, spinning and weaving, spinning and weaving, weaving a cocoon of death around the shining lady who dreamed on, oblivious to the danger.

Sulema started forward. "We must wake her!"

Wake her? the fox barked. *Wake the Dragon, and you die.* She stood and shook herself. *We all die.*

"What do I do?"

Why are you asking me? I am only a fox. Why do you need to do anything at all? Stay here, if you like. There is game, there is food and water. You have your horse, and your bow, and the company of a lovely fennec. What more could you ask? Do nothing, become a warrior, return to the Zeera and ride with the Ja'Akari. Is this not what you want?

Sulema realized that, indeed, she held her bow. It seemed to her that she had but to turn around, and she would be back in the Zeera. She could hear her sword-sisters laughing, so close, could smell cooking meat and sweet mead. There was nothing to keep her from joining them…

She gestured helplessly to the sleeping lady and the spiders, busy with their webs. "If I do nothing, she will die!"

Is this not a good day to die?

Sulema threw her bow to the ground. "It is a good day to live!" she yelled at the fox. "Stop trying to trick me."

The only trickster here is you, silly girl. Is your choice made, then? Do you choose life, pain and all?

"Yes."

Then pick up your bow.

Sulema bent to retrieve her bow, but as soon as her fingers curled around the wood she knew something was not right. In her hands she held now not a bow, but a staff of blackthorn nearly as long as she was tall, and big around as her wrist. It was not unlike her mother's dreamshifting staff, though this one was topped with the carven head of a fennec, and tiny foxes chased one another up and down its length.

Heavy, she thought, raising the staff up before her eyes. *I never knew it was so heavy.*

She was alone. The sleeping lady was gone, and the fox, even the sound and smell of the warriors' camp had disappeared. She stood bereft and abandoned in a clearing of grass ringed by rocks and trees.

"Jinchua!" she called. "Jinchua!"

Wake up, you silly girl. You chose to live, now you must live with your choice.

"You cannot leave me here like this! Jinchua!"

Wake up...

"But I *am* awake," she protested, and the sound of her own voice startled her so that her eyes flew open.

"She is awake! Sulema is awake!"

"Hush, you, stand back and give her some air."

"Is she all right?"

"Let me through!" This last voice, more of a roar really, was her mother's. As Sulema's eyes adjusted to the interior of her mother's tent she was shocked to find it full of people. The crowd parted as her mother pushed through them all, using her staff as a club to move those who did not get out of her way quickly enough. Sulema saw tears in her mother's golden eyes as she dropped to her knees.

"Sulema. Oh, my daughter." Sulema was shocked again as her mother drew her close and nearly squeezed the life back out of her in a warm, if bony, embrace.

She patted her mother's back feebly, not sure how she should respond.

"Water," she said, and was dismayed to hear her voice so weak. "Please."

Hafsa Azeina turned to snap at a young Ja'Akari. "Girl... Saskia! Bring water. The rest of you, out! Sulema, what is this?"

"Oh." Sulema sighed, and shifted the blackthorn staff that had begun to dig into her side. "Oh, this." She sighed and ran one finger along the line of laughing, running foxes. "It was not a dream, after all."

Hafsa Azeina looked away with a grimace.

"Mother?" Sulema hated how her voice cracked. After all these years, one would think she would be used to rejection.

When her mother looked at her again, she seemed older. "I had hoped for an easier path for you. An easier life than I have led." Hafsa Azeina laid a hand on Sulema's forehead, touched her as she had not in years beyond counting. She looked at the staff, really looked at it, and her mouth quirked in a reluctant smile. "A fennec?"

"A fennec," Sulema agreed. She relaxed into the cushions, wincing as her body's pains began to make themselves known. "Her name is Jinchua."

EIGHTEEN

Hafsa Azeina and Sulema had been gone for a moons' turn when First Mother Nurati came waddling out to Ani in the bachelors' pasture, carrying Ani's sword and bow and trailing a sullen-faced Hannei. It was not right that a woman so close to her in years, and so close to giving birth for the sixth time—the sixth!—should look so beautiful. But there it was.

"We have a problem," Umm Nurati said without preamble. "That lionsnake Sulema killed was female."

Paraja padded over to sit near Nurati. She curled her thick tail about her feet and went still as only a large predator can. Ani glanced uneasily at the vash'ai, and then at the lovely and eternally expectant Umm Nurati, and knew she was not going to enjoy the rest of this conversation.

"Oh, for the love of rain. And nobody noticed before now?"

"Apparently not. The outlanders skinned the beast and salted the hide, and it was not before I unrolled it that anyone thought to look. Her underbelly was yellow as buttersweet."

"*Za fik*," Ani swore. "She had a nest, then."

"And eggs set to hatch, if they have not already. I need you and Hannei to find that nest and destroy it, either way."

Ani stared. "The two of us, kill a clutch of lionsnake whelps? You do know the little fuckers can kill, right? Is this girl even healed enough yet to ride? Spare me a warrior or three, at least."

"Would that I could. Many of my Ja'Akari are out hunting to replenish our stores—those outlanders eat like greedy children—and the Ja'Sajani are out debating and marking the prides' territories. With the slavers as active as they have been, I need every warrior I can get my hands on to defend Aish Kalumm. Hannei is the best of those who remain, and all I have to spare.

She swears by Akari that she is well enough to ride, and this one will not swear the sky is blue unless she has painted it herself."

"*Za fik,*" Ani swore again, but without conviction. Then she sighed. "Might as well die today as tomorrow, I suppose."

"As well die tomorrow as today." Nurati smiled grimly. "I have seen you do more with less. Did Theotara herself not train you? Were you not champion in your day? Youthmistress, I would not ask this of you were there another choice."

"I know." She sighed again and turned to her horse. "Talieso, it seems we will be riding today after all. We will take the southmost way."

Nurati frowned. "That way is much longer. The eggs…"

Ani cut her off. "The eggs are likely hatched already. I will not follow such a large party as was bound for Atualon so soon— their leavings will have attracted a swarm of predators by now. We will take the southmost way. It should take us—" she pursed her lips and stared up into the sky, thinking "—three full days of riding each way, one day to kill the little beasties, one more for luck. Give us a halfmoon or so before you send someone out to look for our bones."

"Have it your way, Youthmistress." Nurati bowed.

"Hah. If I had *my* way, I would be lounging by the river with Askander Ja'Sajani fetching me coffee and sweets, not chasing off to the Bones of Eth after a clutch of lionsnake whelps." She shot a mild glance at Hannei. "Why are you still here? Do I need to write your name in the sand, girl? Go get your horse." She snorted as the young Ja'Akari bowed and trudged away, shoulders hunched. "I see that one is still sulking about being left behind."

"She blames herself for her sword-sister's misfortune. In her mind, two girls doing a stupid thing together is better than one girl being stupid on her own."

"Sulema will be fine. That one is as tough as her mother." She reached out to take her bow and sword. "And far too stubborn to die."

Nurati handed the weapons over without meeting her eyes. "I know you are fond of the girl."

"I am fond of all my girls."

"Of course," Nurati agreed, face smooth as river stones, and she bowed.

"I have been meaning to speak with you about this year's crop of younglings…"

"Perhaps we will speak on this when you return, Ani. Right now, you need to go clean out a lionsnake hatching and I need to get to the kitchens and deal with the latest emergency."

"What emergency would that be?" Ani checked her bowstring. It was a bit worn… she would take two spares.

"I have no idea. There is always an emergency in the kitchen. Two days ago, one of the cubs hid a russet ridgeback in one of the big pots—"

"Gah!" Ani shuddered. "Spiders! Forget I asked."

"Do you remember Istaza Theotara and the time we put ridgeback eggs in her bedroll?"

"Remember? *Ehuani*, my backside still hurts from the thrashing she gave us." Ani laughed. "If I ever find out who told on us…"

"You never knew?" Nurati gave her a strange look. "Your face gave us away."

"My face?"

The First Mother shook her head and stretched, rubbing her lower back with a grimace. "Your face always gave us away. You are a terrible liar, Istaza Ani." With that, she bowed again and waddled off.

Ani sighed and leaned her forehead against her stallion's copper-red shoulder. Talieso shifted his weight from one side to the other and curved his neck around to nose her. He stood with one hind leg cocked, content to doze in the sunlight while the younger stallions sparred and pranced. She realized with a pang that her stallion's face had started to gray, just a touch about the eyes and above his soft nose.

"Do not go getting old on me, sweet boy." She kissed his cheek and he nudged her again, hoping to shake a treat loose. "We are too young to be going gray." She put her hand on his crest and gave it a little shake. "Look at that neck, you lazy thing, going all to fat. Just as I am going all to bone and gristle. When did this happen? Did we blink?" She reached deep in her pockets for the treat he knew would be there. "Look at us, old and lazy in the sunlight, and another batch of cubs sent off like seeds on the wind, to take root where they may. The girl, Talieso, our girl is gone, did you know? Her mother has taken her away from us after all." She buried her face in his neck and breathed in the deep scent of her horse as he nodded his head, sucking on the sweet and making funny faces.

"You are more her mother than Hafsa Azeina ever was."

Ani startled upright and whipped around.

"*Khutlani*, girl." She scowled. "You are not so tall that I cannot kick you in the head, you know. It is rude to sneak up on an old woman… rude, and dangerous."

"Yes, Youthmistress." Hannei bowed, fist to heart and unrepentant. "But it is truth, all the same."

"Where is your horse?"

"Tied near the churrim, and with your tack and all of our supplies ready to go." She cleared her throat. "Mekkia is in heat, so I will be riding Lalia. She is new to me but seems well behaved."

"Lalia? I know that filly. I am surprised that Rama Ja'Sajani let her go." The Uthrakim were notoriously tightfisted when it came to their mares.

Hannei shifted uncomfortably beneath her gaze. Ani knew her girls to the marrow of their bones, and this one was hiding something. Well, there would be time to ferret it out as they rode. She sized up her companion and made a mental bet with herself that if she did not have the full story before the day was out, she would ride to Askander Ja'Sajani and pronounce herself ready to bear his children.

Again.

They tacked up their horses and started out at an easy trot along the southeastern route toward the Bones of Eth. If they took this way past the Bones they would eventually come to Eid Kalmut, the Valley of Death. The southwestern route would take them instead across the Dibris to Min Yaarif, a den of outcasts and slavers. Beyond that city of ill repute lay the jagged peaks of Jehannim and, eventually, the Seared Lands.

Hannei was quiet, even for her. The girl's silence might be excused away as the need to concentrate on riding a new horse, but Lalia was a sweet little thing, uncomplicated for such a young mare. Nevertheless, Ani decided against pressing her with questions. Though never as openly rebellious as Sulema, the dark-haired beauty could be as stubborn as any rock in the Zeera.

They ate as they rode, and their pace was easy enough. Over the miles a comfortable silence grew between them. Ani had trained four crops of cubs during her years as Youthmistress, and one would think that by now she was used to the shock of transformation as her girls grew into capable young women overnight. But each time was like a new year's pressing of jiinberry wine, bitter and sweet, with a hard kick to the gut and well worth the headache.

The sun was getting old and coppery in the second day of their journey before Hannei pulled close on her gray filly. Ani slowed Talieso to a lazy trot, which was much easier to do than it had been in his youth. Their youth.

"Youthmistress?"

"Hannei Ja'Akari." She smiled. "What bothers you?"

"I wish you would not read my mind like that." The girl scowled, half in jest. "I want… I need to ask you something."

Ani nodded and kept her eyes to the ground in front of them. There had hardly been any spoor all day. It was unusual, and change made her nervous.

"What do you think of…"

"What do I think of what?" she prodded.

"What do you think of… Sulema?" The name came out in a rush, and Hannei looked away. "Do you think she will live?"

"If anyone has the will and the power to heal her, it will be Ka

Atu. Hafsa Azeina tells me that his magic is very powerful. And he is her father, after all."

Hannei nodded, still not meeting her eyes.

"I also think that is not the question you truly wish to ask. I hope you know that when you are ready, I am here." She gave Talieso his head, but had to press his sides before he picked up his pace. "I spoke true when I told Nurati that I care for all my girls, Hannei."

Hannei had never been a talkative child. She had let her sword-sister chatter on for the both of them. Bold, bright, audacious Sulema, first to jump into a pit, last to look for snakes. Sometimes Hannei had followed in Sulema's wake, sometimes she stood apart, but always she kept her silence, even when being a tell-tale might have spared her backside. She rode easier as the day wore on, but she kept whatever was troubling her locked behind those big brown eyes.

She has her father's eyes, thought Istaza Ani. He had been a churra-headed pain in the ass, as well.

Akari Sun Dragon grew red and lazy in the west. They were not far from the Bones of Eth, but Ani had no desire to be near that accursed place after darkfall. She began to cast about for water. Her ka was not particularly strong, but she knew there was a small oasis nearby. It should be easy to find, even with her limited abilities. She spared a glance at Hannei and nodded approval at the girl's half-lidded, unfocused look before closing her own eyes.

Talieso jogged on, unconcerned, his warm sides pressing gently against her calves. So strong, her boy, so sure of himself. Though the Zeera was ever-changing they had ridden this way before, and his senses were much better than hers. She touched his presence as she allowed her own to roll out like a thin mist upon the desert, clinging, stretching, seeking... She felt his aura as a cool green-blue, her own a fairly dull red, the color of clay, shot through with streaks of brown and green.

This was Dzirani magic, sung into her bones with her first taste of mother's milk. Her secret—and her death, if it were known.

Each land had its own magic, but bonesingers were welcome in none of them.

Talieso turned his head to the north just as she caught a ripple of pale blue at the far edge of her sensing.

"There." She opened her eyes to find Hannei pointing. "Water, not sweet but not too stale. Do we camp tonight?"

Ani nodded, once. "You have been to this oasis before?"

"No, Youthmistress. I have been to the Bones of Eth, but we have always taken the northernmost way."

"Then that was well done, young Ja'Akari."

Hannei flushed with pleasure, but the praise was not enough to loosen her tongue.

They camped that night in a strip of green, in the shadow of the Bones of Eth. Once a jewel of the Zeera with trees and tarbok and small flocks of birds, the oasis had lost battle after battle against the long heat until now it was little more than a rattle of dry grass in the dead wind, a puddle of water with a stale, boiled taste to it. Talieso snorted, unhappy, but drank his fill several times over. Hannei's filly was not as easily convinced. She roared through her soft little muzzle and stared at the two-legs, plainly indignant. When no sweeter water was forthcoming she finally drank, but with such an expression of disgust that Ani had to smile. Mares could be such silly creatures...

...and so could young girls. Hannei scouted dutifully, fed the horses their measure of grain, built a small fire shielded for stealth, dug out the food and waterskins, but kept her eyes averted and her mouth shut the whole time. Istaza Ani sat on a bit of dried deadfall and watched the performance with pride, admiration, and irritation.

"Listen, girl..." she began.

"Hannei Ja'Akari, not *girl*." She handed Ani her ration of waybread and pemmican, and met her eyes square for the first time that day. "I will take first watch tonight, *Istaza* Ani. Shall I wake you at sixmark?"

Ani accepted the food with a smile, and a rueful shake of the head. "Wake me at three. We will leave the horses here and walk the rest of the way while the sands are still cool and the hatchlings still slow." She cracked a flat of waybread in half. "Are you going to tell me what is bothering you, or do I have to beat it out of you with a stick?"

Hannei's lips quirked. "You would have to catch me, first."

"You are an insufferable brat." She washed down a mouthful of bread, and made a face. "And this water is stale."

"It is. The hearthmothers say the salt jars are not keeping it sweet."

"*Za fik.* We will have to send a delegation of Ja'Sajani to Salar Merraj, I suppose." One more thing to worry about.

"I overheard Umm Nurati speaking with Hafsa Azeina about trading for more jars, before they left. She said they would be passing through the Saltlands." The girl found sudden interest in her handful of pemmican and began poking through it, looking for berries. "Youthmistress?"

"Hm?" She turned her head and looked toward the grazing horses, the better to let the girl speak.

"They say Sulema was hurt in her head, not just her body. Before the healers put her into a sleep, she was screaming about... strange things." She hesitated. "Talking to someone who was not there."

Ani thought she understood the girl's worry now. A warrior had to rely on and trust her sword-sister. Those who had been broken in the head through illness, or injury, or a cruel twist of fate were not suited to a warrior's life.

"Hafsa Azeina is a skilled dreamshifter. Sulema is in good hands."

"But dreamshifting is not a healing magic, is it? It is a killing magic... and Hafsa Azeina was born an outlander."

The last word was spoken with distaste. *Outlander.* As if foreign ways were wicked ways, to be feared and reviled. Ani tried not to let the alarm show on her face. Such old hatreds rang in her ears with the lingering screams of massacre.

"I have never heard you speak of outlanders in such a way. Where is this coming from?"

Hannei shrugged, clearly unhappy.

"Hannei, listen to me. You are a good girl, and you are a smart girl. If someone is spreading such thoughts among the Ja'Akari..." She struggled to rein in her lecturing tone as the girl's eyes went opaque and her mouth set in a stubborn line. "Hannei, you must tell me. Who has been saying such things to you?"

"No one, Istaza Ani. It was just a thought. Forgive me." Hannei tossed the handful of pemmican into her mouth and washed it down with stale water. Her face was blank. Ani had lost her.

"Hannei..."

"Hannei Ja'*Akari*." Hannei touched her oiled temple with one finger. Ani sucked in a sharp breath at the insult. "You should sleep, Youthmistress. It is late, and I have first watch."

It is not as late in the day as you think, girl. I was Ja'Akari before your mother decided to chase your father round the campfire. But Ani did not say the words. She got up to check on her horse—not because Talieso needed checking on, but because if she did not take a great many deep, slow breaths she was going to kick the brat's ass from here to Aish Kalumm—and then chose a low, smooth place for her bed.

There she lay, wrapped in her saddle blanket and her aggravation, listening to the crackle of fire and the laughter of stars, cold and very far away. She closed her eyes and drank deep of the cooling night air, but it was long before she slept, and her dreams were troubled.

In her dreams she was busy lecturing her girls—naked but for a pair of blue trousers, though it made sense at the time—and then someone grabbed her by the scruff of her neck and shook till her teeth rattled. She gagged at the hot, wet stink of carrion.

Wake. Wake. I like my prey to see me before I eat it.

Ani opened her eyes and looked death straight in the gullet.

NINETEEN

"If I die today, I will die facing my enemy."

Istaza Ani was gone.

Hannei woke from a deep slumber to find that the Youthmistress had left her behind as if she was the smallest of children. Judging by the spoor, Ani had been accompanied by a warrior and her vash'ai.

The Ja'Akari burned with shame. It was inconceivable that she might lie asleep as strangers entered their camp, spoke with the youthmistress, and left again. Worst of all, her sword and bow lay untouched—a blatant insult.

She tugged the laces on her vest tight—though it made her healing ribs ache—grabbed her weapons and the brass box Umm Nurati had given her, and gave Lalia and Talieso the briefest once-over before taking off toward the Bones at a dead run. She stepped in the other warriors' footprints, an old Ja'Akari trick meant to confound an enemy.

These tracks led straight and true toward the tormented shadows of the Bones of Eth. The morning air was still cool, so she slung her bow across her back, tucked the box in tight against her body, and ran.

The way was short, and her legs long, so she was not much winded by the time she reached her destination. She slowed her steps, lightly, lightly on the sands, a whisper only, pulling in her ka so as not to alert her quarry. She opened her mouth as wide as she could and breathed out long, slow, gentle breaths.

Nobody here but the wind, she sang silently, *nobody here but the sand...* and the towering and twisted Bones of Eth clawing forth from the Zeera like the flesh-stripped hand of some monstrous felldae.

Sweat poured down her back, under her arms, between her breasts. She grimaced—lionsnakes could taste a body's heat upon the air—but there was nothing to be done for it now save put one foot in front of the other, down the twisted path and shadows that chilled the heart but never the body.

Halfway down the path, she heard the most dreadful sound, a strange ululation that rose and fell before trailing off into a whooping scream. The scream broke off, and then… nothing. Her heart tripped over its own shadow, but Hannei pressed on.

If I die today, she thought, *I will die facing my enemy.*

As she stepped between the ugly striped rocks, she could feel the air cooling and clotting about her like dead blood. It stank, and it hummed with the voices of a handful of lesser scavengers—buzzards, sandgulls, the yipping bark of a fennec. The wind kicked up sand-dae and they swirled mockingly about her ankles, promising to scour the flesh from her bones once she was dead.

A small and bug-eyed shape streaked by, screeching and shaking bright plumage in a show of defiant terror, before she could react. So, the whelps had hatched… but where was the youthmistress? Where was the warrior who had come upon them in the night, and left her sleeping?

She heard the songs of three bright souls then, one after the other, a song woven warp and weft by the deft golden fingers of the Zeera. The first song was the desert herself, a low and throaty croon, like the song of a mother to her favorite child. Long had Hannei been dancing to this song, the dance of her life, and always it had soothed her soul.

The second song was a wyvern's cry, a sweet and mournful note, and triumphant. It is known that the wyvern will only sing to its prey when it is sure of the kill. This second song brought her up short, to the delight of the sand-dae, who skipped in small circles and danced the Dance of the Fainthearted Warrior.

The third song stopped her heart and made it wait three beats before allowing it to start up again. It was the roar of a vash'ai, a deep, rumbling bellow that shook the sands and caused the very ground beneath her feet to recoil. For a moment after there was silence, the deep silence of a well gone dry, of death in the night, the silence at the end of all hope.

It seemed to her, for the first time, that life was rather too short. But she would face death like a warrior, under the sun she would. With trembling fingers she found the laces holding her vest closed, and tugged them apart, baring her breasts in a show of contempt for whatever enemy lay in wait.

It was a good day to die.

"Show me yours, bitch!" she shouted, glad that her voice did not betray her fear. The Bones swallowed her bold words and gave her nothing in return. Not an echo, not an answer, not a hint of what might lie ahead. Hannei dropped the brass box, drew her yet-unblooded shamsi with the faintest whisper of death, and ran to meet her doom.

The air cleared as she passed through the pillars, and Hannei leapt onto the hot yellow sands with a defiant yell.

The scene that met her eyes was so utterly wrong that she stumbled to a halt, gasping as the parched air sucked her lungs dry.

There, in the far dark corner of the most cursed place she knew, stood Istaza Ani, covered in blood and entrails. The youthmistress was crouched on the balls of her feet, wielding a long leg-bone club. Her mouth stretched wide in a rictus snarl, and she stood facing the biggest and most disreputable-looking wild vash'ai Hannei had ever seen, a massive sire with a broken tusk.

The cat opened his mouth and roared, and Hannei flinched at the power in his voice. He shook his head and swiped sideways at Istaza Ani with the speed of a striking serpent. Ani bent backward so fast it seemed she would topple into the sand, and her braids whipped about like a dancer's as she spun sideways with a high kick, light as a silk flower, fingertips of her free hand brushing the ground.

Hannei had never seen Cub Paints the Sky so flawlessly

executed. She stood in open-mouthed amazement, sword dangling forgotten in front of her.

Istaza Ani threw her head back and let loose with the same strange singing, screaming ululation Hannei had heard earlier, then whirled as quickly as the vash'ai had struck, lashing out with her club. The weapon hit something with a wet thunking *crunch*, and sent a small grayish form shrieking through the air. When the hapless lionsnake whelp hit the ground, dazed, the vash'ai pounced like a kitten and bit it in two with one snap of his great jaws. Istaza Ani straightened, trilled again, and then she threw her arms wide open to the sky, tossed the blood-slick braids from her face, and laughed.

"Blood and bloody entrails!" she whooped. "That was a fine bit of goatfuckery!" She turned toward Hannei. "A good morning to you, Ja'Akari. Did you have a nice sleep, while we were killing the whelps for you?" She gave her club an efficient flick, and flung a viscous string of red-black gore upon the pale sand.

"I… I…"

"Yes, yes, I know. Close your mouth, there's a good girl, and take your box and go get that last whelp. I stunned the little fucker, so it should not get far."

"Youthmistress?"

"You are still here? You are still talking? Run, girl! Oh, but keep your eyes peeled. There's a young wyvern flapping around somewhere. He's got a belly full of whelps and he's afraid of Inna'hael, here, but he's big enough to be nasty." She smiled fatuously at the vash'ai, who was rubbing his face in a puddle of blood.

Hannei shut her gaping mouth, bowed to Istaza Ani, bowed again to the massive sire, and spun on her heels. She had no idea what had just happened, and a simple task was exactly what she needed.

Get the box, track the hatchling, catch the hatchling. That much she could manage.

It was as Istaza Ani had said. The little creature, long as her arm and weighing about as much as a bag of grain, lay panting on its side not far past the Bones. Hannei pinned its head to the ground with the flat of her sword, grabbed it firmly behind the jaw—even more firmly once she got a good look at its needle-sharp fangs—and proceeded to learn that lionsnake hatchlings are stronger than they look, that the hooked claws on their forearms are just as nasty as one might imagine, and that little lionsnakes do not appreciate being stuffed into boxes.

By the time she returned, Hannei's arms—and her dignity—were shredded beyond recognition.

Her mission accomplished, she dropped the hissing, spitting box in the shade, though by then she did not much care whether the daespawned little fucker lived or died. She squared her shoulders, took a deep breath, and walked across the hot sands to the dark corner where the youthmistress stood with the broken-tusked vash'ai. Shame was a weight she dragged behind her, but she would not allow that to slow her steps. She was a full warrior, now, not a child to avoid the consequences of her dereliction. She halted and bowed, but neither woman nor cat took any notice of her. They stood in the darker shadows, staring at a pile of fresh cracked bones.

"Youthmistress," she began.

"*Hsst.*"

"But I…"

"*Hsst!*" Istaza Ani held up a hand. "Not now, girl. Tell me, what do you see?"

Hannei rocked back on her heels and caressed the hilt of her sword as she studied the pile of bones. Any Zeerani would recognize *those* bones.

"Vash'ai," she said. "Young. Very young. And… oh." She stepped closer and felt her gorge rise as she studied the skull. *Oh, no.* She dropped to a crouch and leaned as close as she could get to the remains without disturbing them. "No, no, no. This is not right. He was—"

"He was *butchered.* Skinned." Istaza Ani's voice was low, and hoarse. She reached out and touched the vash'ai on the shoulder. The massive sire was so caked and matted in blood that his pale mane stood out in red-tipped spikes. He might have looked ridiculous but for the waves of fury that boiled the air about him.

The hair stood up along Hannei's arms, and at the back of her neck. The young vash'ai *had* been butchered. Nothing else would leave such neat hack-marks at the ends of the bones, nor explain how they were arranged so neatly with the big ones all in one pile, topped by the skull. And worse had been done.

"His tusks," she whispered. "Who would… who would…?"

The vash'ai growled, a low rumble she felt through the ground. His yellow eyes flickered with a furious grief that pierced her shallow human heart. Istaza Ani looked at him, and then closed her eyes.

"This was his son," Ani whispered. "His name was Azra'hael. He came here seeking his kithren."

"Oh." Then, "Oh, *Sulema*." Pain lanced through her heart. To lose your vash'ai at bonding… what would that do to a warrior?

The big cat stood, shook himself, and stalked off. The older woman watched him go, eyes unfathomable.

"Istaza Ani, forgive me, but are you and he…? Are you…?"

The youthmistress raised both eyebrows at her. "His name is Inna'hael."

"Are you… are you and he… are you Zeeravashani?" She had never heard of one so old bonding with the vash'ai. Then again, before today she could not have imagined anyone butchering a vash'ai, any more than she could have imagined taking a blade to the flesh of a child.

Istaza Ani almost smiled. "We have… an understanding. Beyond that, who can say? His son has been murdered, and I have agreed to help him find whoever is responsible."

Hannei felt as if the world had tipped to one side, and everything she knew was out of place. "Murder a vash'ai? Who would do such a thing? Who *could* do such a thing?"

A roar shook the sky. It was a heart-sound, a soul-sound, thick with rage and grief.

"You are asking the wrong questions." Istaza Ani's eyes had gone flat. Hannei had seen that expression on the other woman's face once before, when a young girl's rapist had been caught and the man handed over to her for justice. He had died... eventually.

"Youthmistress?"

Istaza Ani stepped toward the bones, and kicked one away from the pile before Hannei could object. Then another, and another.

"You ask *who*. You should be asking *why*." She picked up the vash'ai's skull. It was unbroken, save where the tusks had been broken out. "Why would someone kill a vash'ai and desecrate his body? Why leave it where he was sure to be found, sooner or later, by his kin? Think, girl. How will the vash'ai answer this abomination? What will the Zeeranim answer be, when we find those responsible?"

Drums sounded deep in her heart. "War."

"War is always the answer. War with the vash'ai. War among the prides. Or war with Atualon... How do you think that war would end for the people?"

Hannei thought of the great ships, the gold-masked mages, the soldiers' armor bright in the sun. "Not well," she admitted.

"Not well. That is one way to describe total annihilation." Youthmistress Ani snorted. "You begin to understand what is at stake now. Someone killed this cub and left him here in order to wound us, to anger us, perhaps even to cause bloodshed between the two-leggeds and our sweet kithren. They killed him, they desecrated his body. They took his tusks." She stared into the vash'ai's empty eye sockets, and the hand that touched her sword trembled. "See the hatchmarks here, and here. They took his skin as a prize."

Hannei wanted to throw up. She wanted to cry.

"They took his skin." She stepped toward the pile of bones, and something rolled beneath her sandal. She moved her foot and bent to pluck the object from the sand.

Her head spun, and she was seized with a strange feeling, one of those odd dark moments like the echo of a dream, of a life already lived, of following one's own footprints. She balanced a strange knife in the palm of her hand. It was an evil-looking thing with a half-moon blade, hooked on one end and pointed at the other. This blade was set crosswise into a haft of heavy red wood carved into the shape of a pile of human skulls, the topmost of which was jealously clutched by a golden spider with a cluster of glittering rubies for eyes.

Air hissed between the youthmistress's clenched teeth.

"Flayer."

Indeed the blade was made for it. Hannei could see that the thin crescent would be used for cutting through flesh and scraping it clean, and its sharp hook for the more delicate acts of flaying—the initial incising of the carcass, the pulling out of veins and tendons, and cutting around the orifices of the skin. Her own skin crawled at its touch. This was a wicked thing, made for more than the skinning of game. It was heavy in her hand and smelled of murder.

"Do you remember the stories you used to tell us," she asked the youthmistress, "late at night when we were far from camp and you wished to scare us witless? Terrible stories of Arachnists, cult-priests with knives such as this." She forced these words out between stiff lips. The priests worshipped Araids, giant man-killing spiders of the Seared Lands, and were served in turn by their foul not-dead Reavers. Creatures of legend and nightmares. "The Arachnists come from Quarabala, do they not? Same as that outlander shadowmancer. This must be his." She was so angry her hands shook.

Istaza Ani held out her hand, and Hannei surrendered the blade gladly.

"The shadowmancer? Perhaps. Perhaps not. Such a blade might as easily belong to that apprentice of his, or to another of the Atualonians. It may have been dropped here in order to draw suspicion toward the outlanders. But it does seem certain that Sulema's encounter with the lionsnake was no accident. She was lured here to die."

"By the outlanders."

"That seems the most likely explanation, but let us not be too hasty to jump into the pit…"

"…until we know what kind of snakes are there." Hannei favored her teacher with a humorless smile.

"Ah, so you *were* listening. You were always so quiet, sometimes I wondered."

"I was listening." Hannei stared at the pile of bones, the cat's skull with its missing tusks and telltale hatchmarks, and then at the knife that Istaza Ani held in her hand as if it might bite. And again at the bones. She could not meet her teacher's eyes.

"Hannei." The youthmistress's voice was gentle. "What are you thinking? Do you know something of this?"

She looked to the side just as the wild vash'ai padded back into sight. He was magnificent, and broken. Yellow eyes met hers and she could feel his pain singing deep in her own heart.

"No. I do not know." She took a deep breath. "Maybe."

Istaza Ani rocked back on her heels and waited.

"I heard the First Warrior speaking with First Mother. Before we left." The words felt as if they were being dragged from her chest. "They were speaking of… I am not certain, but I think they were speaking of Sulema, and of her father, the Dragon King. Umm Nurati said that if Ka Atu rises, war will come again to the people. The First Warrior said, ah, she said, 'that heart of Atualon will be the death of Atualon.' She said that the outlanders would wake the Dragon, and then the world would die." She looked down, away from the pile of bones, away from the knife, and especially away from the youthmistress.

"I see." Istaza Ani was as still as death, but her eyes were bright. "And did they know you were there?"

"No, Youthmistress."

Istaza Ani touched her shoulder. "Hannei. Hannei Ja'Akari."

Hannei straightened her back and raised her eyes. "Istaza Ani."

The older woman nodded once. "Ja'Akari, do you know what must be done?"

"I must warn Sulema. She may be riding into a trap."

"This is bigger than Sulema, girl. What do you know of our history of Atualon? Of the Sundering?"

"The Sundering?" She blinked, confused by the change in subject. "Only what you told us when we were young. There was a war between Sindan, and Atualon, and Quarabala, and the outland sorcerers went mad and killed everyone they could. They poisoned the air and the water, and they burned the land, and they made the kin so angry they started attacking humans. A lot of people died, and everyone thought it was the end of the world. But that was a long time ago."

"A long time ago." Istaza Ani stared at her. "A long time ago? Have I failed you so badly, then?"

"Youthmistress?" She was confused. What had she done wrong?

"The Sundering is as real for us today as it was a thousand years ago. Why do you think there are so few of us left? Why are there more ghosts in our cities than there are children? Why do so few vash'ai choose to bond with humans?" She nodded to the great cat. "Inna'hael was a sire grown when last Atualon warred with Sindan, and the daeborn took his people to sell as slaves. Ask *him* whether the wars were 'long ago.' Ask my people, as well. The Dzirani caravans once stretched across the desert like jewels on a woman's necklace... Now we are memory and song, our daughters sold into the Zeera to keep them from ending up as slaves, or worse."

Hannei lowered her eyes and bowed low. "*Ina aasati*, Istaza." She had not meant to cause pain.

Istaza Ani snorted. "Oh, stand up. Not your fault I taught you too much about the tenets of honor and not enough about your own history. But it looks as if that history is opening its mouth to take another bite of us, and we need to think before we act. I will carry this warning—and this knife—to Hafsa Azeina. Like as not, the dreamshifter is knee-deep in this horse shit. You will return to Aish Kalumm and report our success here to Umm Nurati, and say nothing of any of this. Keep your wits sharp, your eyes open, and your mouth closed."

"What will I say when you do not return with me? Do I tell them you have gone to Atualon?"

"No. Tell them…" She glanced at the copper box and smiled. "Tell them I have gone to the outlanders' markets in Bayyid Eidtein, to sell the whelp. Such a thing would be worth many salt jars, and our need is great."

Hannei could feel the Bones of Eth pressing in upon her, as if the giant's fingers would curl closed and crush her. Akari Sun Dragon felt far away, his light thin and weak. Perhaps he had turned his face from her for her treachery.

"As you say, Youthmistress."

Istaza Ani studied her face. A strange little smile upon her lips. "You are Ja'Akari now in truth, and as honorable a warrior as I have ever met." She bent her head, just a little. "Under the sun I see you, Hannei."

"Under the sun I see you… Ani." Hannei bit her lip hard. "I will do as you say. And anyhow, as you are always telling us, it is a good day to die."

Ani laughed. "Indeed it is a good day to die, Hannei Ja'Akari. But always remember this: it is a better day to live."

Hannei had much to think on. "Istaza… Ani. You do not think the First Warrior and Umm Nurati had anything to do with all this, do you?" She gestured to the pile of bones. "It would be… abomination. Unthinkable. For one of the people to harm vash'ai…"

Inna'hael, the wild vash'ai, curled his lips back from his tusks in a silent snarl.

"Unthinkable, yes," agreed the youthmistress, shaking her head.

She did not answer the question.

TWENTY

I *have found her kima'a.* Khurra'an's physical body lay stretched out beside Sulema's still form. His voice rang with the echoes of Shehannam.

Hafsa Azeina looked up from the new-strung lyre. *Is she injured, or is she held?*

Both.

Shifter magic, or atulfah?

Neither, he answered. *But this magic tastes of spiders. It is draining her sa. Best come quickly.*

Spiders. She set Basta's Lyre upright, one ridged horn resting against her cheek. *So Sulema's dream was a true one—we are dealing with an Arachnist. The cult of Eth has risen once more.*

So it would seem.

Hafsa Azeina let her fingers rest against the gut strings for a moment. The harp was eager, but she was worn from the journey, from the worry, from a life of bloodshed.

Damn the Araids, what have they to do with this? I have no quarrel with the spider folk. Or had none, until now. *Can you find Ani for me?*

Will you give me the boy?

Never.

It was worth a try. Khurra'an twitched in his sleep as his laughter faded from her mind.

Hafsa Azeina snugged the lyre closer, let her eyes go soft, and began to play. The notes were sweet, low and mellow as his voice had been.

The minstrel had wandered into Shahad a half year past. His mouth was filled with stories for children, his bags full of exotic trade goods, and his eyes full of flattery whenever they lit upon her. She could almost see his face, the high cheekbones and bright smile, and his breath smelled of honey and spices and sweet lies.

I can help you, he had whispered, reaching up as if he would brush the hair back from her face. *I can help you both, keep you safe, just tell me where the girl-child is and I will keep you safe.*

His words had not been so sweet once he started screaming, and his heart had tasted neither of honey nor of spices, but the lyre cradled against her cheek had a lovely voice nevertheless. Strings made of human gut had a resonance none other could match. Hafsa Azeina closed her eyes and played a song of triumph and redemption sharp enough to make the Zeera weep.

So smoothly she slipped into an open state these days, easy as a drink of water. How little there was tethering her soul to this plane. She envisioned her *intikallah* as flowers on a vine that twined up and about her spinal column and bloomed one after the other, each blossom brighter and more complex than the last until the final blossom—the heart's-eyes *kallah*—unfurled into a ball of such radiance she could feel it spilling from her flesh-eyes. This light caught on Khurra'an's jeweled tusks, wreathing his beloved face in a halo of redgold sparks. She closed her waking eyes, and opened her dreaming eyes, and beheld the path to Shehannam. Down it led, and into the dark. Hafsa Azeina broke free of her body and let herself be sucked into the otherworld.

How many times had she done this, how many hundreds of times? And yet she still felt a faint urge to glance over her shoulder at her body, slumped now in the middle of her tent, breathless and cold as a corpse. The music hung in the air about her, one last note to hold time still, and this note was all that would sustain her body until her soul returned. She could have opened a door between worlds and made this journey in the flesh, but she had broken the laws of Shehannam time and again, and the Huntress was hot on her trail. Safer to leave her body behind.

Safer, Khurra'an agreed. *Not safe.*

The light failed as the way to Shehannam closed behind her and for a moment she was suspended weightless in the dark. The sky began to clear, and the light from a younger sun filtered in through the darkness all around her and she was floating, flying, lighter than a child's last breath. She knew that if she looked down she would see no feet, no body, but these things no longer interested her. She focused her will and swooped lower, feeling the wind rush past her face and her outstretched arms even though in this time and place she had neither.

There. Khurra'an had marked the path for her with his own essence.

True friend. She gathered her will, and plunged down.

The air had a strange, shimmery quality to it, and the sky was sticky and wet. She found herself wanting to swim through it with arms her mind kept insisting were there. She was buffeted by winds that should have passed right through the mist of her thoughts and her descent was slowed to a painful crawl. Determined, she gathered in the tendrils of her aura and plunged down, down.

A quick shift, a moment of red pain, and she stood on the lush green grass wearing a golden collar, her golden shofar, and the face of Annubasta. She could not hide her true nature in Shehannam. She tightened her claws on the skull-topped staff and flicked her tufted ears this way and that, seeking her prey, wary of the Hunt. A slight breeze rippled through her fur and teased at the hem of her skirts. She lifted her face, wrinkled her lips back, and tasted the wind.

Sulema.

She tucked her staff close to her body and loped down the path, claws digging deep furrows in the rich soil. She could feel atulfah ripple through the twilight sky as Ka Atu searched for his daughter, and closed her mind up tight, though not without regret. If not for her need to protect Sulema from the dangers in Atualon, she and the Dragon King might have faced this enemy together.

The thick grass gave way to a stand of trees, a bit of the Old Forest. Hafsa Azeina pushed and clawed her way through the thick growth and into a small clearing ringed with jagged crystalline rocks and enormous shaggy mushrooms. A young fennec lay asleep in the middle of the clearing, blood staining her white fur. The dreamshifter pushed through the circle with her staff and opened her waking eyes. The fennec blurred, and for a moment she could see her daughter lying naked and wounded upon the forest floor.

Sulema wore a headdress as elaborate as that of the First Warrior but all in white, and she was bound from chin to ankle in a spider's web, thick as the strings on her harp and pulsing with malice. There were other things binding the girl, as well—the blue and gold weavings of her father's magic, the starlight web of a shadowmancer, the wicked spiny tendrils of a blackthorn vine.

More bonds than any girl should have to suffer, she thought.

Fewer than yours by far, Kithren.

Hafsa Azeina brought her free hand up to her mouth, and bit down hard. Pain and blood welled forth, and with blood upon her lips she called, *Belzaleel.* And, *Belzaleel.* And thrice: *Belzaleel.* She had no breath in this place, but her words made the air tremble, like dark stones dropped into a clear pool. With her third summoning a heavy dagger of dragonglass appeared in her hand and immediately suggested that she might like to stab herself in the leg.

Stop that, she told him. *I have work for you. I must free my daughter from these things that bind her and prevent her from healing.*

What do you have to offer in return?

Hafsa Azeina brought the blade to her mouth and gave it a bloody kiss. The blade hissed and seemed to shudder in her grasp. Nothing pleased Belzaleel more than the taste of her blood.

Very well, it agreed. *I will give you what you seek... if not what you need.*

Hafsa Azeina wiped her fouled mouth on the back of her hand and waited.

You cannot cut all these bonds, the blade went on. *That would kill her. Some of these need to be left in order to anchor her to your world, and others she needs to cut for herself.*

Which to cut, then? Answer me true, wicked thing, or I will shatter you and leave you to be hunted for the grief you have caused.

The dagger was silent for a moment, and then it responded.

The father smooths a path to destruction, but those bonds are not yours to cut.

The Web of Illindra stretches in both directions farther than the eye can see, farther than even I can see. You may save her if you cut through those, but you may kill her. I would suggest leaving those be, for now.

The blackthorn bindings must never be severed, not by you, not by her. They bind her to another and those bonds may save you all.

The Shroud of Eth... cut that. Do it now. Let no part of it touch your skin—to do so is to alert the Huntress to your presence, and you are not ready to face her yet.

Hafsa Azeina knelt by her daughter's side, wary of Belzaleel's sharp edge and fickle nature. As she cut through the Arachnist's bindings, careful to peel the vile stuff aside with the dagger's blade, she could not help but think that Sulema looked so alone here, so young and vulnerable. She longed to kiss her daughter, just once, like she had when the girl was very small. When was the last time she had touched her daughter in kindness? The thought was sharper and more dangerous than Belzaleel himself.

Just once, she thought, *what would it hurt?* The girl would never know. The temptation became unbearable. She leaned in close and kissed her daughter. As she did so, the girl started to fade. When she was gone, the little white fennec jumped to her feet, barked at her angrily, and ran off into the forest.

Will it be enough? she asked the blade.

Perhaps it will be enough. Or perhaps you have failed, and she will die. The blade dissolved with a laugh, and the last bit of black web fell to brush against her hand. A horn sounded, far away: once, twice, three times. She knew the voice of *that* horn. Its twin rested upon her hip.

The Hunt was on.

Khurra'an padded into the clearing. *I see you have released the girl. But at what cost, Dreamshifter?*

The price is mine to pay. I will pay it gladly, if it saves my daughter. Tell me, my friend, did you find Ani?

I did.

She touched his shoulder. *Take me to her.*

They flew.

They found Ani's *kima'a*, a prickle-bear, sleeping too near the Bones of Eth. Hafsa Azeina spat a mouthful of dream-dust over the sleeping spirit, made a circle of her thumb and index finger, and looked through it into the woman's dream.

A small child sat on the back of a Dzirani wagon, dangling her feet out the back. A woman was singing nearby. The girl looked up at Hafsa Azeina, frowned, and spoke with Ani's voice.

"Balls on a stick, Zeina, you know I hate when you invade my dreams." The little girl scowled and blinked at her in the green light of Shehannam. "And why do you always show up looking like that?"

"What are you doing here?" She spoke aloud for her friend's benefit.

"That is private. *This* is private."

"Not *here* in the Dreaming Lands. I mean so close to the Bones of Eth."

The dream shifted, and they were standing near the Bones. Ani was a woman again, but Hafsa Azeina was still a monster.

Ani made a wry face. "Thank you for that. I was enjoying that dream far too much."

"What are you doing here?" she asked again.

"Hannei Ja'Akari and I were sent to chase down a hatching of lionsnake whelps. Turns out that old lionsnake bitch of Sulema's had a clutch. We got them all, though. How is the girl?"

"She is alive." Hafsa Azeina felt Khurra'an's alarm even as she felt a foreign mind brush hers. "Who else is here with you?"

"Oh, that must be Inna'hael. He is about here somewhere…"

Inna'hael! Here? Khurra'an vanished, and the presence of the strange vash'ai winked out as well.

That was interesting.

Ani stared at her. "What was *that* all about?"

"I do not know, and I have no time to find out. Tell me, Youthmistress, did you find anything at the Bones of Eth besides a lionsnake hatching?"

"Yes, I did. A knife, a wicked thing with a curved blade of red steel and a golden spider…" As Ani spoke, Hafsa Azeina could feel the wicked thing stirring, as if their words had caught its attention.

"*Ssst!* Do not talk about it here! You must bring it to me in Atualon."

"That was the plan. Dreamshifter…" She hesitated.

"Yes?"

"I do not know whether I should tell you this, but… Hannei lied to me."

"Lied? Hannei lied? The girl is *ehuani* made flesh."

"She lied by omission only, and I understand why she did it, but still it struck me as strange."

Ani told her of the conversation Hannei had overheard, and of the vash'ai bones, and her own suspicions.

Hafsa Azeina narrowed her eyes, and the pale sky boiled with clouds.

"A murdered vash'ai. The knife of an Arachnist. Someone is hunting in *my* territory, now. Tell me, Youthmistress," she growled, "who told you to go to the Bones of Eth? Was it the First Warrior?"

"Sareta? No, she is off taking census with the Ja'Sajani. It was Umm Nurati who sent us." Then her mouth dropped into an O of dismay as she realized the import of what she had said… and what the dreamshifter would do about it. "Zeina, no. Zeina, *no*, you cannot do this."

Hafsa Azeina raised a furred hand and held up three claws, one by one.

"Nurati sends a secret envoy to Ka Atu, and tells him where to find us. Umm Nurati tells the First Warrior of a small lionsnake that needs hunting… only it turns out to be a big old grandmother of a beast, and my daughter is attacked with Araid magics. Now she sends you to the Bones of Eth, and you find an Arachnist's flensing knife. Three lies speak truth—Umm Nurati has made herself my enemy. She chose this path, not I."

Ani's face was terrible with grief. "Dreamshifter, I beg you… we do not know for sure that any of this was deliberate. Hafsa Azeina, she is pregnant! What of the babe? No. Please, for the love you bear us… she is with child."

Hafsa Azeina unhooked the golden shofar from her belt. The shadows at her feet stirred in anticipation. It had been moons since last she had killed, and they were hungry.

She was hungry.

"I am sorry, Ani." It was not wholly a lie. She would rather keep the truth of her dark nature hidden from the one woman who still called her *friend*. "She should have thought of that before she tried to kill my daughter."

It was time to hunt.

Hafsa Azeina brought the golden ram's horn to her lips…

…and blew.

TWENTY-ONE

Nurati shifted in her low-backed chair as the babe kicked insistently at her backbone. Once in a while it would hook its wicked fingers into her rib cage and *stretch* against the confines of its fleshly prison, and pain would dance up and down her spine like a naughty child. She supposed the coffee was not helping, but there was nothing to be done for that.

You have to sleep sometime.

She glanced at Paraja, who lay stretched out at her ease upon Nurati's own silken pillows and churra-down bed. *You sleep enough for the both of us.* The child kicked again, a direct hit to the bladder this time, and she made a soft noise of irritation. *For the three of us.*

Sleep is good for the cub.

"A living mother is good for the cub." She spoke aloud, as if releasing words into the air would make it so.

You fear the dreamshifter.

You do not?

Paraja bared her fangs, in mockery or warning. Nurati remembered the day, the glorious day, when she had slipped the golden bands onto the lovely queen's tusks, and felt for the first time the weight of gold bands on her arms. So long ago.

Long ago, her queen agreed. *We were cubs, chasing butterflies in the sunshine.* She rolled over onto her side and stretched so that her long black claws extended to their fullest. *You are still a silly cub, and the prey you stalk now is beyond you.*

Nurati took up the quill again, one of the pretty red-and-blue ones made from the feathers of a lionsnake. They had been a gift from the First Warden some years back, and held their shape well. She dipped it into a jar of lovely purple ink and began adding flower-petals along the margins of a page.

For each of her children she had written and illustrated a story-book, and this child seemed to urge her toward flowers and fancy script. She felt certain that she carried another daughter beneath her heart. Another little girl to dress and to teach and to love. Fat cheeks to kiss. First steps to guide.

A she-cub, agreed Paraja. *Your last?*

Nurati wiped the nib on a soft cloth, and sprinkled sand across the dainty violets.

I know you are planning something, her queen complained, *yet you keep your secrets from me. Are we not one?*

We are one, she agreed. *We are Zeeravashani.* She blew the sand onto the table, and set the little book down. Nearly done.

The tip of Paraja's tail curled up, and then slapped back down.

"If a neighboring pride threatened your cubs, what would you do?" Nurati asked aloud.

Paraja flexed her paws again. *By tooth and by claw, I would kill them.*

"Just so. This outlander king, this Ka Atu, is a threat to my children. All my children." She rested a hand on her belly, and leaned back with a sigh. "If he dies without an heir, atulfah runs rampant and we are lost. If he dies with an heir, and this new Atualonian daemon decides to invade the Zeera, we are lost. Our Ja'Akari and Ja'Sajani together can hardly keep the greater predators at bay, much less fend off an attack from the north. I am no warrior. I have neither tooth nor claw. So what is a Mother to do?"

She opened her sa to Paraja's touch, and let the cat rummage through her mind. Her thoughts were reflected back to her by the queen. She saw herself as a strong young vash'ai, flagging her tail at a powerful sire.

"Just so," she agreed, laughing. "I will take their king as a consort, and he will give me a child. Surely an heir to two thrones is a threat to neither." Such a child they would make—beautiful and powerful. Powerful enough to shake the world to its very roots.

There is no throne in the Zeera.

Nurati smiled. *Ages pass. The world changes. There was once a throne in the Zeera, the throne of Zula Din.*

You think to become another Zula Din?

No. She stroked her taut belly. *Not I.*

What of the dreamshifter? What of the dreamshifter's cub?

She did not answer. She did not need to.

You should have stuck to hunting butterflies, Little Sister. There was such sorrow in the thought.

The child in her belly rolled over again, and then fell into a fit of hiccups that had Nurati gritting her teeth. This was going to be a long night. She picked up the little silver bell that would summon her errand-girl with more coffee.

Long into the night she worked, as the moons rolled across the sky and past her window, as Paraja snored on and the errand-girl slept in the corner. The oil lamp flickered, and her eyes blurred, even as she finished the last line of the last rhyme in her little girl's first book. Tomorrow she would ask the smiths for gold foil, to brighten the edges of the pages. Tomorrow she would... tomorrow...

In the end, Paraja was right. She had to sleep sometime.

The quill slipped from Nurati's fingers and landed on the rug, staining the pale wool.

Her head lolled back, and her hand slipped from her belly.

The lamp spluttered, burned low, spluttered again, burned out.

Golden eyes burned in the dark, waiting for her.

A queen hunting butterflies.

TWENTY-TWO

Hafsa Azeina had left before dawn, her little apprentice informed Sulema when she went looking for her mother.

"She cannot rest with so many people nearby. Can I help you, Dreamshifter?"

"I have a headache. Can you give me more of that tea?" She had ten headaches, and they were having a grand party together inside her skull. "And do not call me that. I am no dreamshifter. I am Ja'Akari."

Daru shrugged his bony little shoulders. "As you will. Dreamshifter said no more dragonmint tea yet. It has been only half a day and you are supposed to take no more than one cup every two days. Dreamshifter said—"

Sulema held up a hand and tried not to scowl, because it was not this child's fault her mother was the way she was, and because scowling made her headaches worse. "Did she say anything that would be of use to me, Daru? If you cannot give me anything for this headache, I am going to go lie back down and hope to die."

The boy pursed his lips and looked at her a little too closely. "Dream—ah... Ja'Akari, are you unable to sleep?"

"Yes. It has been so noisy since the Atualonians joined us." In truth, she had not slept at all for quite some time, and it was no fault of her traveling companions. The whispers and grunts and farts of a soldiers' camp were as much a lullaby to her as the singing dunes. Worse, much worse, was the noise inside her mind. It was as annoying as the ringing ears she had once gotten from a kick to the head, and as inescapable. She was not, however, going to admit this to her mother's apprentice. She was Ja'Akari, and she would rather die Ja'Akari than live one day as a dreamshifter. "If you cannot help me..."

"Wait." Daru bit his lip and looked away. "When there are too many people nearby, Dreamshifter cannot sleep, and she gets headaches. A long walk away from camp will help. That is why she goes hunting so much."

Here I thought she just liked to kill things, Sulema thought, crossing her arms over her chest and scowling despite the headache. "For the last time, I am no Dreamshifter, boy. I just have a headache. I was almost killed by a lionsnake, or had you forgotten?"

Daru looked her straight in the eye and raised one eyebrow, just as her mother might have. "Even so, Ja'*Akari*. You did spend time in Shehannam, and that will affect you just as much as a wound to the flesh. Would you have left your arm to heal on its own?"

Sulema had just been chastised by a child. Worse, she realized he was right, and she had been rude.

"I am sorry, Daru. I know you are just trying to help."

He shrugged again. "I am used to your mother. *You* do not scare me."

"So what do you suggest, O Daru Stout-Heart?" she asked with a smile.

"Go for a bit of a walk, or better yet, a ride. Being around animals sometimes helps. They are quiet in a way that humans have forgotten. It helps to touch your bare feet against the sand. It helps to be near water, but I have not felt water in days, have you?"

"No. And that is strange. Ani taught us that there were water-holes all along this road."

"That is what I had read too, though I thought maybe I remembered that wrong. No matter. The desert is as calming as flowing water, in her own way. If you ride a way out and sit for a while, just still and quiet, with your eyes closed, that should help. Oh, and wear this." He reached into his thin tunic and drew forth a large chunk of pinkish rock on a thong, then slipped it over his head and held it out to her. "When it starts to feel heavy, bring it back and I will cleanse it."

Sulema hesitated. "What is it? It looks like salt."

"It *is* salt, red and white. It will clean the... oh, just take it, it will help."

Sulema put the thong around her own neck and tucked the lump into her vest, though she felt foolish. "Thank you, Daru. I will return it."

"No need, Ja'Akari. I have several. Besides, I am doing this as much for myself as I am for you."

"Hm?"

"I am not afraid of you, Ja'Akari... but I *am* afraid of your mother."

"That makes all of us." Sulema tried to smile again, but it probably looked more like a grimace. "Thank you, Daru."

"You should probably not ride far. Your arm—"

"I know, Daru."

"And Dreamshifter says there are greater predators near—"

"I *know*, Daru." She rolled her eyes.

"I know you know, Ja'Akari," he told her, and his voice was very soft. "But a warrior who has lost her vash'ai will often take foolish risks."

Sulema stared at him. She had told nobody about Azra'hael. *How does he know?*

"The shadows told me," he whispered as if she had spoken aloud. "I have not had a chance to talk to you before this, but I wanted to say..." His eyes were dark pools of sorrow. "I am very sorry for your loss, Zeeravashani."

Zeeravashani.

Sulema turned on her heel and fled before a single tear could fall.

Sulema had to admit, it was better once she was out and away from the camp. The only voices left in her head all belonged to her, and had been with her for as long as she could remember. Voices that nagged and picked at her every fault and reminded her, like a children's song that goes round and round without end, of every thing she had ever done wrong in her life. The worst of these she imagined as a twisted shadow perched behind her on the saddle, sharp of tooth and wit as it mocked her in a shrill whisper.

Azra'hael, it whispered. *You failed him. You killed him. You never deserved him and now he's gone, gone, gone.*

Gone, gone, the other voices laughed. *Gone.*

Not even Zeeravashani for a day, it hissed. If it were not for you and your stupidity, Azra'hael would still be alive.

Azra'hael, the others agreed. *Azra'hael…*

…Azra'hael…

Consumed as she was by despair, Sulema did not notice when Atemi perked her ears forward and went stiff all through the neck as if she, too, could hear the whispering voices. She did not notice the little dance her mare did with her feet or the tension that shuddered through her hindquarters, loud as a shout to any warrior who knew her horse. Sulema was listening to the false voices in her mind, not the true voice of her good mare, and so she did not heed her friend's warnings.

Thus it was that the moment she realized that the whispers were not all inside her head, that there was a strange smell on the wind and a strange feel to the air, was precisely one moment too late. Atemi launched herself straight up as if she would jump the moons, and Sulema found herself tossed through the air like a basket full of wheat.

Her first reaction was shocked indignation. The first rule of the Zeera is that a warrior never comes off her horse. Her second was trepidation, as she had just enough time to realize that it was really going to hurt when she hit the ground. Her third reaction, as her not-yet-mended flesh struck the earth and she rolled ass-over-end-over-ass down the dune, was to scream.

Fortunately she passed out before she could do much more than suck in a mouthful of sand, and the dark veil lifted from her eyes as quickly as it had come. It occurred to her later that had she screamed, or had she lain senseless and vulnerable for more than a heart's beat, surely her story would have ended there. Her next stroke of good fortune came when Atemi, more curious now than spooked, followed her rider down the dune as if to ask why she had decided to fly away.

Sulema pulled herself to her feet with a stirrup, and into the saddle with sheer stubbornness. Though she wanted nothing more than to ride back to camp and have her hurts tended to— her arm inside its cast felt distinctly *wrong*—she could not ignore the sounds that came to her ears now that her mind had quieted. The whispers had grown into shouts, and the unmistakable ring of steel on steel, and cries of pain and panic. Slavers, most assuredly, and their party was riding right for them. Her duty as Ja'Akari came before duty to self. Of course, such duties would be more easily carried out had she not ridden out alone and unarmed.

Stupid, the twisted shadows whispered. *Stupid, stupid girl.*

Enough, she whispered back. *I do not have time for your lies.* Sulema banished the fell voices from her mind, and rode cautiously toward the sounds of battle. *One look,* she thought, *one look and I will ride back to camp and alert the others. One look, and I will go.* Keeping the nervous Atemi at a tight walk, she crested the top of the dune.

One look, and she knew that her luck had run out.

There were slavers, sure enough, a largish band of raggedy-looking men, heavily armed and poorly mounted, but they were not setting up an ambush for the Zeeranim. Rather, they were under attack by a knot of *things*. Nightmare creatures that were shaped like men, that stood upright and dressed like men, but the sight of them sent a wash of cold horror up Sulema's back and froze her mind in a moment of gibbering panic.

The things' skin shone pale and hard as a scorpion's chitin in the rich moonlight. They spoke in a harsh chittering buzz, and when they moved—she watched one of the things scuttle sideways and then leap onto a slaver with a thin shriek—when they moved, she wanted to puke up every meal she had ever eaten. They looked wrong, they sounded wrong, and worse—they *felt* wrong. Like poison in sweet wine, like living flesh gone rotten.

An oily smell like burnt cinnamon and blood rose to meet Sulema, and Atemi flew into a panic. Sulema let her have her head, hissing between her teeth as the mare bolted back the way they had come. Pain knifed up her spine and through her ribs and ground its teeth in her broken arm, but she knew she had to return and warn the others.

As they labored up the next dune, Atemi balked and came up in front, nearly unseating her rider for the second time in one day. Sulema grabbed the mane with her off hand, letting loose a string of curses that would have done Istaza Ani proud, but broke off mid-*guts-and-goatfuckery*, heart in her open mouth, stunned to the marrow of her soul. A hundred warriors, more perhaps, crested the dune and poured down the side toward her and Atemi like a flood of water from the old stories. They were the desert made flesh in their golden robes and bright breastplates of wyverns' scale, bleached and stiffened hair swept back from their faces like the manes of the wild vash'ai that flowed among them, eyes ringed about with kohl so that they burned like cinders in a funeral pyre. They were more deeply dappled and powerfully muscled than any warriors Sulema had ever seen. Beside them, First Warrior would have seemed a frail old lady with feathers in her hair. These were the Ja'Akari of legend, the golden warriors, the First Women, fierce and proud and free. They were everything Sulema wanted to be, and her heart leapt even as they rode her down.

The riders in front glanced her way as they passed by, but looked away again without so much as a nod. As if she were a child, mud-streaked from a game of aklashi, and they the true warriors riding out on Ja'Akari business. It stung. It stung, because the dismissal she read in their eyes rang true. Had she not ridden out this day unarmed and heedless as a milk-breathed brat? Wounded, unhorsed, and now fleeing an enemy? Oh, it stung. As the last of them rode past, Sulema swung Atemi round and followed.

Not safe, her mind suggested. *Not a good idea.* But she could no more have resisted following these women than she could have resisted touching her mother's dreamshifting staff, when she was small and lonely and afraid of the dark.

The golden Ja'Akari coursed silent and sure across the desert. They broke upon the manlike creatures steady and sure as Akari spreading his wings across the sky, and as the Sun Dragon throws back the night so too did they throw back the enemy. If there were screams, they did not come from the warriors, grim-faced and true.

Nor did the creatures seek to flee. Outnumbered as they were, they turned almost in unison, and their pale hard faces shone with fell glee as they leapt bright-eyed and open-mouthed to meet their doom. No quarter was given, nor was any sought, as the sight of each force drove the other into a frenzy of bloodlust. The few remaining slavers, cowering, were trampled beneath the hooves of the Zeeravashani as the warriors swept like bloody rain across the sands, shamsi flashing with delight, then wheeled to charge again.

Sulema rode with them, lifted up light as a feather by the song in her heart. *This,* she thought, and *this,* and *this.* One of the warriors grinned at the look on her face, and tossed her a sunblade hilt-first. She caught it in her off hand and shouted as she drove Atemi into the melee.

Time slowed and her head spun as if she were once again caught in the spider's web, watching the events unfold from afar. Her blade rose and fell, rose and fell like the moons, like the desert tides, singing a song of blood, sweet and harsh and true. A monster looked up at her from the belly of a gutted horse and hissed, and leapt. She swept the head from its shoulders as if they were playing a game, and laughed at the look on its face as it bounced away. The sky dimmed, the world clenched around her until it was nothing but a fistful of sand and blood and white, white bone. She ducked a thrown blade, and kicked away a hand that would have dragged her from the saddle, and for a while she fought muzzle-to-tail beside a thin warrior whose mouth was a bloody snarl.

When the fist opened and released them all, a handful of bright warriors and three vash'ai lay upon the sand unmoving among the bits and pieces and torn bodies of the chitinous things, blood and ichor soaking into the soft sand. Somewhere, a man was screaming, a nerve-scraping sound that grew weaker, and weaker, and gurgled, and finally stopped.

Several of the warriors had dismounted and were poking at the bodies, dispatching those monsters and slavers that still had a bit of life left to them, and dragging the dead into a pile for burning. Sulema slid from her saddle to join them and then wished she had not, as her knees buckled and she sat down, hard. She would stand, and join these strange and wonderful warriors, she would find out who they were, where they had come from, why she had never heard of them... just as soon as the pain let up.

As she sat splay-legged on the sand, Atemi pawing impatiently near her leg, a pair of beaded wyvern-hide boots stepped into view. Sulema looked up and saw a swirl of golden robes, a shining bone-and-scale breastplate in the olden style, and dark eyes in a dark face, bright with good humor above a stern mouth.

"So, little softlander." Her voice was low, her words oddly clipped, as if she did not wish to waste a bit of breath on them. "Lost and alone, a stranger under a strange sun. What to do with you, little lost kitten?"

Sulema made as if to stand, but the stranger rolled her wrist easily, and the point of a shamsi brushed against her throat.

"*Ehla, yeh* Adalia, *neyya*, this one is our guest. A wounded warrior, yet she fought well today... for a softlander." Another woman— taller and older than the first, with a heavily scarred face—stepped into view and patted Atemi on the rump. Sulema recognized her as the warrior who had tossed her a shamsi. "Well mounted, too... though perhaps next time she will bring her own sword."

Sulema reclined near the fire, washing down honeyed locusts with the harshest usca ever to set fire to a warrior's belly, and pondered the great knot of confusion her life had become. Mere moons ago she had been a simple girl with a simple life, looking forward to riding alongside her sword-sisters and betting on which of them might first lose her virginity, and to whom.

Now the world was a tangled mess of spiders' web and blackthorn, and she was caught in the middle with no way out.

"More usca?" Ishtaset smiled, and the scars on her face and the glint of firelight in her eye made it seem conspiratorial. "I find it cuts through the most complicated of riddles. Sometimes before I pass out."

Sulema found it hard to imagine this woman ever losing control of her faculties, and shook her head, setting aside the clay mug.

"Thank you, no. I have suffered a recent blow to the head…"

"To your arm, and your face, and your ribs as well, I can see. Fall off your horse often, do you?"

"A lionsnake fell on me, actually."

"Did you win, at least?" This from the woman Adalia.

Sulema shrugged. "I am here. She is not."

"False modesty in a false warrior." Adalia snorted. "Look at her, with her outlander hair and her outlander eyes… a boughten child, no doubt." She spat, a shocking waste of water.

"Adalia, you may leave." Ishtaset put her horn of usca aside. Her eyes were no longer smiling.

"*Rajjha…*"

"Leave. Now." When the other woman huffed off, the warrior made a strange little gesture with her hand. "I will not apologize for her, *ehuani*. Her mother was killed by outlanders, and she will never forgive your kind."

"My kind? I am no outlander. I am Zeerani. I am Ja'Akari, like you."

"Ja'Akari, those children who claim to live under the sun, but live between walls of stone and roofs of clay?" Her laugh was harsh as a crow's. "Ja'Akari, I? I think not. I am Mah'zula, girl. We are Mah'zula."

"Mah'zula?" Sulema gaped. "The First Women? They have been gone for a hundred years. More. The Mah'zula are lost in the wind."

"Are we? Who says this thing?" The warrior's scarred face twitched with open amusement.

"First Warrior—"

"Ah yes, Sareta."

If Sulema's mouth hung open any wider, she could have swallowed a lionsnake. "You know Sareta?"

"I know of Sareta Ja'Akari. I also know of the moons-haired dreamshifter from the northern lands, and of her flame-haired daughter. A warrior always knows her enemies."

These women, these warriors were the sa and ka of every dream Sulema had ever had as a young girl. "I do not wish to be your enemy," she said. *I wish to be you,* she thought.

"Do you not?" The woman saluted her with the mug of usca, and a sardonic smile. "We shall see."

They spoke of many things, long into the night. Ishtaset described a pure, nomadic life lived by the tides of wind and sand and moons. Never staying in one place for long, never building settlements.

"Roots are for trees, not for women," she laughed. "Does Akari sit in one place in the sky, and grow fat and soft? No, and neither shall we, his true warriors." She spoke of running with the wild vash'ai, bound to all and to none, hunting as a member of the pride. She guessed at Sulema's lack of sleep, the waking nightmares that had plagued her since the Bones of Eth, and suggested that the vash'ai healers might cure her better than any human king.

"They have their own magics, bound to thorn and moonslight, and more powerful than we can know," she said.

Ishtaset went on to suggest that Sulema might live among the Mah'zula, one of them, free to roam with the wandering stars. Free from the Mothers, and her mother, free from the shadow of the Dragon King her father.

Free.

Long after Didi had rolled away to her little bed, Ishtaset roused the single surviving slaver, a youth not yet old enough to have grown a beard. She bound his wrists before him and tied him behind her horse, a rangy red mare with a deep chest and snarky look. He rolled his eyes in terror of the beast, but when he would have spoken Ishtaset backhanded him casually across the mouth, and laughed at the look on Sulema's face.

"I know you softlanders allow your males a loose rein," she teased, "but you really should train them young. It is easier on them if they learn their place in life early on. And this one is less than a man, he is a slaver." She stared at the boy, and a slow smile warmed her face. "*Was* a slaver."

When they came to the edge of her mother's camp, Sulema was surprised to see how exposed it seemed, how noisy and chaotic and out of place with the outlander soldiers and even the Ja'Akari running about like children, calling her name. She should have felt guilt at having been gone for so long and causing such worry, and she knew it, but what she felt most was embarrassment.

Ishtaset laughed again, doubtless reading the thoughts on her face, and leaned from her saddle to give Sulema a hug, just as if they were sword-sisters.

"Softlander or no," she said, "you are welcome among us, Sulema Firehair. Return to us some day and we will make you strong and teach you the way of the true warrior, not this pale imitation of life you have been living." She handed over the boy's leash, and slipped away into the night.

A part of Sulema's heart rode away with her. She wondered if the word *ehuani* would ever taste so pure again, or clean, as it had when she was among the Mah'zula.

TWENTY-THREE

A *camp never sleeps,* the king's son thought to himself. *Someone is always sharpening a blade, or braiding a pair of sandals, or eating, or farting, even during times of war when stealth is needed.* And this was no tactical camp, but an odd assemblage of people—many of them young soldiers, armed and dangerous, some of them old politicians, sleek and deceitful. Statesmen, family men, and at least three different kinds of sorcerer. The air seethed with suspicion and magic and lust. A potent mixture, not conducive to a restful night.

Leviathus gave up trying to sleep and rose from his bedroll with a grimace. He had to pee, anyway.

He made his way to the hastily dug latrines, face heating as he passed through the Zeerani camp. Eyes gleamed out at him from the dim circles of their small and shielded fires—cats' eyes, women's eyes, lingering upon him with open hunger so that he wished he had dressed in more than a long tunic and sword belt.

There was a single guard at the stinking sand pit, and he was relieved to see Zeina's little apprentice. The Ja'Akari did not know to turn away and give a man the courtesy of a private piss, and holding it in was painful.

The boy sat with his back against a stack of baskets and boxes, eyes wide against the night. He flushed and looked away as Leviathus emptied his bladder, hugging bony knees to his thin chest. When Leviathus was finished, he turned to the child and grinned.

"Pulled guard duty tonight, did you? Shitty luck, that." He chuckled at his own pun.

Daru shrugged, still not meeting his eyes. Leviathus wondered whether perhaps the boy considered him a threat. He thought about the sort of threat a grown man might pose under cover

233

of dark, especially to a vulnerable child. What had Zeina been thinking, to give the boy such a task?

"I find myself unable to sleep tonight," he said. "What do you say I take over your watch, and you go catch some sleep? Your mistress will not mind, I am sure." *And I will have a word with her about this in the morning.*

The boy shrugged again and seemed to draw in upon himself. Was this the same child who had laughed with him over old poetry? "Daru? Are you all—"

One of the big baskets tipped over, spilling its contents onto the sand. Leviathus gaped to see the captive slaver cowering between them in the thin torchlight. He was young, very young, ragged and terrified.

Ah.

Leviathus sighed. "Daru…"

"*Sssst!*" Daru jumped to his feet, holding his finger over his lips in a shushing motion. His eyes darted, pleading, between Leviathus and the young slaver.

"Daru, you cannot let him go," he whispered. "There are wyverns and worse out there, you know. Even if he survived the night, he would be hunted down at first light. Better he should live as a slave."

"No." Daru's voice trembled, but his chin took on a stubborn set that Leviathus knew well. "Zeeranim do not own other people. It is not right."

"Daru…"

"It is not *right*," Daru insisted. Tears welled in his eyes, and he scowled as fiercely as his mistress might have. "If Sulema keeps a slave, it will not just hurt him." He waved a thin hand at the trembling slaver. "It will hurt her sa. It will hurt all of us. We are all connected." He pointed from the captive, to Leviathus, to himself, and then to the camp. "Do you not see?"

"I see a boy who is going to get in trouble over something that is none of his business. He is a slaver, Daru. What do you think slavers do? Why do you think he was here, in the first place? His kind steals children and sells them at market. He deserves his fate."

"He did not choose to be a slaver."

Leviathus stepped closer to the trembling captive. *This one is even younger than I thought,* he realized with some chagrin. *Not much older than Daru.* He hardened his heart.

"There is always a choice. This boy would have taken my sister captive, had he the chance. He would have taken you. Would he have shown you the same mercy, I wonder?"

"There is always a choice," Daru agreed. He stood, and his shadow stretched tall in the pale torchlight. "*My* choice is mercy, no matter what his might have been."

"You are determined to do this?"

"I am. Are you going to stop me?"

"No. I am going to help you." He sighed. "Of all the nights to need a piss."

The sky was beginning to burn a little about the edges as Leviathus cut the slaver's tethers and handed him the bag of provisions Daru had stashed away.

"It is not enough," he warned the lad, in the tongue of traders and slavers. "You would do better to stay with us."

The captive shook his head, clutching the bag to his chest, his eyes deep pools of fear. When he spoke, it was in a boy's voice, high and breaking, and his speech had a rough western edge to it.

"I have to get back. If I do not…" His voice choked off.

"There is nowhere for you to run. Come back with me, and I will see that you are well cared for."

"I cannot." The boy sobbed. "They have my sisters." He took a long, shuddering breath, and squeezed his eyes shut tight. "I cannot." Then he opened his eyes, and bowed low. "I owe you my life. As they say, *ehuani.*" He turned and fled, narrow bare feet kicking up puffs of dust until he was lost to sight.

Leviathus sighed. "I fear you owe me nothing but your death, but so be it."

"What do you owe *me*, outlander? That slave was not yours to free."

Leviathus spun round, drawing his sword, but it was knocked from his hand as a powerful blow sent him flying. He landed some distance away, gasping, groaning at the pain that blossomed in his chest even as the first rays of sun kissed the eastern sky.

Stupid, he thought, *stupid. Unarmored and alone. Stupid.*

"I see you are considering the error of your ways." She spoke Atualonian with the barest hint of sand and honey.

He looked up, up past the stomping, snorting mass of horse that had just kicked half the life out of him, past the golden robes and gleaming breastplate, and into the grinning face of a warrior ridden straight out of the old stories.

"*Huh...*" He coughed, and dragged a breath in, hoping his ribs were merely bruised.

She looked across the desert, after the fleeing slaver. A great cat roared, and was answered by another, and she smiled.

"Your little mouse runs, but I do not think he will get far. As for you..." She drew a blade, long and wicked, from its sheath across her shoulders.

A horn sounded, long and low, calling the hunt, calling to battle, calling the lost ships home.

Her smile widened, full of dark promises. "Save me a dance," she said. "We will meet again, you and I." She blew him a kiss, and raised her sword over her head, and rode off laughing into the dawn.

TWENTY-FOUR

"There, see? The blue Fairuz." Askander First Warden pointed toward the bright water on the horizon. "We need but cross the river, and *za hanu*, we have reached Bayyid Eidtein."

Ani looked up from the path and smiled. She was stuck, as always, with a pang of attraction that never seemed to lose its edge no matter the distance or the number of gray hairs between them. "I am obligated to you once more for accompanying me, First Warden. Talieso and I would not have made such good time without your help."

"I did not accompany you to incur obligation... Youthmistress." He grinned at her, the same wicked flash of teeth in a sun-loved face that had caused her heart to skip all those years ago, when he had been a handsome youth and she a round-eyed cub looking for her hayatani. He had been no easy meat, but she had been a most persistent huntress. "Ah, I see you still blush like a girl."

"I still kick like a girl, too, *ehuani*." She stuck her tongue out at him and they shared a laugh, comfortable and warm as the autumn sun.

She had not exaggerated when she said they had made good time, despite a rough start. It had been long and a day since she had ridden so far north. The paths had shifted and many of the oases she remembered had been swallowed up by the hungry sands. At first Ani had been forced to push Talieso harder and farther on less water than she had wanted. By the time they had stumbled across the Ja'Sajani taking census she and her stallion had both been footsore, butt-hurt, and seriously out of sorts with each other. First Warden had replenished her stores, guided her to better paths, and had offered assistance more graciously than she accepted it.

She was glad now for his company. Askander had proven himself willing and able to lend a hand. Both hands, in fact, and on more than one occasion. Her mood had mellowed, and although she was saddle-sore and loath to rise in the mornings, it had been, all in all, the most enjoyable ride she had had in years.

She would be glad of his presence, as well, when she delivered the knife to Hafsa Azeina. Ani had not spoken to the dreamshifter since that fateful night, and guilt chewed at her heart.

If only I had not spoken to the dreamshifter about my suspicions, she thought, *perhaps I might have gotten an explanation from Nurati. If only Zeina would have at least waited for the child to be born. If only Nurati had not meddled in the dreamshifter's affairs...*

Inna'hael growled.

If only you would learn to quiet your mind, he grumbled. *You make more noise than a cub hunting spiders.* He shimmered into being to her right, nearly invisible against the russet sands. Talieso snorted and danced to the left. Although he had never objected to the presence of other vash'ai, her stallion had not warmed to this wild sire and always kept one eye rolled in his direction. His ears flattened and he crowhopped, announcing his willingness to stomp the cat into mush at the first sign of a threat.

The wild vash'ai ignored the horse completely. He ignored Askander as well, and treated Askander's Duq'aan with such contempt that the smaller sire had scarcely been seen since they had left Riharr. Ani had attempted to chide the sire for his rudeness, but he had laughed at her with his eyes.

Get rid of that thing, he urged, as he had done many times since she had taken up the flensing knife. *Throw it aside. Bury it. Let it lie forgotten until stars dim and moons fade. It stinks of soul magic. Get rid of that snake, too. Better to kill a thing than keep it in a box.*

The lionsnake whelp screeched and thumped as if it knew they were discussing its fate, and Talieso flattened his ears, letting her know again what he thought of being forced to carry such a thing across the desert.

"A live lionsnake whelp is worth ten salt jars in the Zeera, and twice as much to the outlanders," she retorted. "We will be rid of it once we reach the market, and I am taking the knife to Hafsa Azeina."

Ah yes, the dreamshifter. Inna'hael growled again, a low rumble she felt more than heard. *Kith to Khurra'an... I do so look forward to seeing him again.*

"How do you know Khurra'an?"

Khurra'an and I are old... friends. Even as he mindspoke the word, red flashed across her vision and the taste of hot blood filled her mouth.

"Wait, no... wait, you. I will not get involved in some kind of war between vash'ai."

War? War is a stupid human concept. You stalk an enemy until you have him by the throat, and then agree that he may keep his queens. Stupid humans. He lifted his tail and let his lower jaw drop, displaying massive tusks. *Why would you be involved in a war, sweet one? You are no queen, you are a huntress. You bring meat for the pride and watch over the cubs. You hunt, you guard, and you do as you are told. Why else would I have chosen you?*

A sudden wind kicked up a faceful of sand, and both horses spooked. Inna'hael became one with the squall, faded away until he was no more than a pair of yellow eyes and a saber-tusked grin, and then he was gone altogether. The wind died. Talieso whipped her leg with his tail and stamped, furious with her for not doing something about that cat.

Askander whistled softly through his teeth.

"I do not envy you your companion," he said. "It is hard enough with a bonded vash'ai. I cannot imagine what it must be like to face down a wild sire, much less a *kahanna*. I thought your dreamshifter was a bold one, but this! You have some tits, woman."

"Wait... kahanna? What is this?" Ani had the sudden, sinking feeling that she was about to hear something she did not really wish to know.

"Kahanna. You know... a vash'ai sorcerer."

"*Za fik*," Ani swore, with feeling. "Of all the goatfucking, sword-sucking, maggot-infested, gut-wounded, nut-licking animals in the world, why did this one have to choose me to pick on?"

Askander threw his head back and roared, startling a golden hare from a pile of rocks. "Oh, Ani, you precious thing, he doubtless chose you for your sweet words and gentle manner."

Ani scowled at him. "Males of any species are a pain in my ass."

Talieso stretched his neck back and bit her foot, hard.

The sound of their laughter, the sun in Askander's hair, the way his eyes curved into half-moons as he laughed at her. These things would become a memory to be treasured, bottled up and hoarded. A memory to light her way in dark times.

The faint path they had been following for so long now had become a wide avenue of footprints, hoofprints, claw-marks and wagon-ruts. As they drew closer to the river and to the wide arch spanning its steep banks these tracks gave way to a groomed, hard-packed avenue and finally to a cobbled stone road. They kept their horses to the side and gave them their head. Encouraged by the smell of fresh water and sweet grasses, their stallions fell into a strong trot. Askander's eyes took on a faraway look for a few heartbeats, and then he looked at her and smiled.

"Duq'aan has found a pride of young and unattached queens to flirt with until we are ready to leave. Will Inna'hael accompany us into Bayyid Eidtein, or will he remain outside the city walls?"

"He will do as he will do." Ani shrugged, reluctant to admit that although Inna'hael spoke to her as he wished, he rarely chose to do so. "We are here, and that is what matters now." She could feel the fell knife, wrapped and bound in leather and hanging from her belt. She had not wanted to leave it in her saddlebags, but touching or even looking at its naked blade made her flesh crawl. "Now we must find Hafsa Azeina and give her this blade, and that will be an end to it as far as I am concerned." She pushed the thought of Nurati back down to the dark deeps of her mind.

"Ah, yes, the dreamshifter." Askander set his mouth in a thin hard line and picked up the pace.

Ani stood in her stirrups and held a hand up to shade her eyes as the bridge to Bayyid Eidtein came into view. "Look, oh look, it is just there. It is so big! I had not known it was so… big!"

Askander snickered. "Not the first time I have heard those words from you."

"I was not speaking of your ego, First Warden. I was speaking of the bridge. Half a troop could ride abreast with room to spare. But there are no guards… just look at the low walls of the city! And they have planted trees from the river banks to the wall." She clucked her tongue. "A single pride could take this place in a single day and have time left over for a game of aklashi."

"Yes, but who would want to take Bayyid Eidtein? It is known as a den of rogues and miscreants. Travelers and traders from Quarabala to Rah Kuwei come here to drink and whore, to gamble and fight…"

"Why have you not brought me here before?" She grinned. "It sounds like my kind of place."

"Which is precisely why I have not brought you here before. Bad enough we should let you influence our younglings, without turning you loose on the poor tender outlanders."

Ani was spared the need to reply as they drew close to an ancient olive tree which squatted next to the road like a wide and ancient grandmother napping in the sunlight. A voice hailed them from its gray-green boughs and both Talieso and Akkim spooked to the side like silly young colts.

"*Yassa!*" A smiling and heavily tattooed brown face peeked out from the foliage. "O good travelers, how my heart delights to see you! How I could kiss your cheeks and weep with joy!"

Ani raised her brows at Askander. "He seems happy to see us. Why do you suppose that is? Do you think perhaps he is a brigand and means to rob us? I suppose we should shoot him."

Askander reached for his bow. "He did threaten to kiss us. I suppose it is only prudent."

"No… no!" The boy squeaked, and practically tripped over his own tongue, so quickly did he speak. "O honored pridesmen of the Zeera, please have pity on a poor traveler…"

"Pity. Yes, that is the word I was looking for." Askander agreed. "Pray tell, why are you perched up in that tree like a songbird?"

"The better to beg for a kiss?" Ani guessed. "Fly down here, little bird, and ask me to my face. Perhaps I will kiss you with my knife."

"Ah, beautiful lady. I, ah, I find myself in a deplorable state of undress at the moment... and I would never dare to beg a kiss of such a lovely—"

"I would stop right there," Askander warned, "before she decides to cut you after all."

"*Ehuani*, Askander, I believe he was speaking to you." She clucked to Talieso. "Let us leave this little bird to his singing."

"A moment! Please!" The boy sounded near tears. Ani pulled her horse around with a heavy sigh.

"Make it quick, outlander. We have business in the city."

"The... city." The boy blinked. "Of course. As I say, I find myself, ah, sadly without..."

Askander urged Akkim under the tree and looked up. "Clothes. Naked as a fish. Caught with another man's lover, hey?"

"His daughter," came the woeful reply. "She was willing enough—"

"Dumped you off out here for the bandits and barbarians without a stitch to cover your hide, did he?" Ani laughed.

"Yes, and he stole my horse, as well." The boy indeed looked woebegone.

"Ah, the folly of youth." Ani reached back to rummage in her saddlebag. "I suppose I can... Here. It will be a bit short on you, I suppose, but at least your balls will not be hanging out in the wind." She tossed him an old tunic.

A brown and surprisingly muscular arm shot out from the tree, and he caught the garment neatly.

"O great lady, the birds will sing your praises!" He favored her with an impish grin. "Especially this bird." He pulled the linen over his head and dropped from the branches. A lanky youth, at the most twenty years of age. "If I could beg one further favor..."

Askander glanced at Ani and sighed. "I suppose you are going to insist on holding his hand all the way to the city. Give you a brat with big brown eyes, and you go soft in the head."

Ani looked the youth over and hid a smile. Her girls would be fighting one another for a shot at this one, for sure, curly black hair and mischief to the bone. "Perhaps he will be of use to us. Tell me, boy, do you know Bayyid Eidtein?"

"I do, O beauteous one." He started to bow, seemed to think better of it as the hem of her tunic rode up his thigh, and settled for a flourish of his hands instead. "Let me be your guide. I know the city well."

"If you do not stop trying to flatter me, I will take my shirt back from you and let you walk naked."

His face fell a little at that. "Walk? I had hoped…" He eyed their horses.

"Do not push your luck, brat. This woman's bark is bad enough, but her bite is much worse." Askander turned so Ani could just see the mark her teeth had left on his shoulder, just this morning. If only she had something to throw at him…

"No outlander may touch our *asil*," she informed the brat. "You will walk beside us. Tell me, have others of our people arrived recently? Warriors, and an injured girl, and a woman with golden eyes?"

The boy stopped and stared at them. "You are with the barbarian sorceress? I cannot go with you," he said. "I am sorry, I am most abjectly sorry, but I cannot. A dreamshifter, and ne Atu, and that… that girl…" He backed away, eyes huge.

Ani showed her teeth. "Did I ask whether you wanted to come with us? You will walk, or we will tether you like a goat and you will drag behind. But you are coming with us." She turned to Askander. "Did you bring rope?"

"Did I bring rope?" He clucked his tongue. "Did I bring rope. Did I bring water? Food? A bedroll, perhaps?"

"Smartass."

"I will come."

"Excellent choice. Talieso does not like dragging people, and often shits on their heads in protest. What is your name?"

"Soutan Mer." His voice was sullen.

Mer, she thought. *Why is that name familiar to me?*

"Mer?" Askander's brows rose at that. "Of the salt merchants?"

"Yes."

"Interesting. Tell us, Son of the Salt, you know of the people we seek. When did they arrive in Bayyid Eidtein? Are they still there?"

"Four days ago. And no, they have gone on to Atualon." He looked up at them speculatively. "Is it true that the queen consort has been living among the desert barbarians as a dreamshifter? Why has she come? Why is she with the children of Ka Atu? Are they her prisoners? Does she hope to take his throne? They say he is ill. Is that girl really his daughter?"

Askander pursed his mouth and looked at her from the corner of his eyes. "This was your idea."

"*Za fik,*" she swore softly. "I told you males are a pain in my ass. *Het het!*"

Ani laid her leg along her stallion's side and urged him to a walk fast enough to keep the boy from asking more questions. She schooled her face to stillness, schooled her heart not to fly, to sing, forced herself not to urge Talieso into a headlong and heedless gallop.

She had heard the fear in the boy's voice, had seen the look in his eye at the mention of Hafsa Azeina, and these things were not to be ignored. The winds of fear might fan the embers of war to flame. But right now, in this moment, Ani could not bring herself to care about such things. For the youth had carried the words she was most desperate to hear.

Sulema was alive.

TWENTY-FIVE

The tintinnabulation which at first seemed to echo so musically from the blacksmiths' tents had become a cacophony of pain that lodged itself between his ears and throbbed in time to the constant ringing of hammer against metal.

Worse, the air was thick with the smell of meat from the smoke-tents, and him with a belly full of pemmican, journey-bread, and flat water. His first journey into adulthood was three times cursed—word had come through the vash'ai that slavers' ships had been seen in the waters near Aish Kalumm, so the First Warrior had taken her warriors and left the Ja'Sajani, the craftmasters, and the disgracefully young new-bonded Zeeravashani bereft of female companionship.

A shamsi hung from a belt at Ismai's waist, a sword of the Sun Dragon forged of red steel from the Seared Lands. His mother had handed him this sword with her own two hands, had kissed him upon both cheeks and called him the child of her heart in front of Tammas and half the pride. The blue veils of a Ja'Sajani's touar slapped at his face and got in his mouth when he tried to talk, but in that moment Ismai had been glad of them, for they had hidden his tears.

That was then. Now, the blue robes and headdress of the Ja'Sajani seemed to gather all the heat and stink of the day and hold it close to his body, and the veils wrapped so closely around his head likewise held in every unhappy and sleep-deprived thought. His shamsi, the sun-forged and salt-quenched Quarabalese blade that marked him out as his mother's favorite son, was heaviest of all. It was not an especially heavy blade, but as Istaz Aadl ran them through the first three forms over and over and over and over again, Ismai's shoulders burned hotter than the forges at midsun, and his arms trembled like grass in the wind.

"Enough!" the youthmaster bellowed. He never spoke to the boys in his normal voice—if he had a normal voice—and he never spoke to Ismai at all except to threaten or demean him.

Jasin groaned and dropped his sword in the sand. "Why do the rest of us have to suffer just because this *majdoube* does not know his forms?"

The youthmaster closed the distance between himself and the boys and backhanded Jasin across the mouth. "Pick up your sword, you limp *gewad*. Go on. Now you will hold your sword in Catching the Cat stance until I tell you otherwise."

Jasin looked as if he had bitten into horse shit, but bowed to his Istaz and did as he had been told.

Catching the Cat was a more advanced stance than Ismai had yet managed. One foot was meant to be tucked behind the other, a body's weight carried on the ball of the forward foot, with a twist at the waist and hands upraised as if to catch a cat that had been springing at one's back. Add the weight of a sword and Ismai winced in sympathy. Not that it would win him any friends. His ineptitude among the youths, most of whom would become wardens this summer, stuck out nearly as much as the blue robes that marked him out as a full Ja'Sajani.

The elders had not known what to do with such a young Zeeravashani. He had not trained with the younglings who hoped to become wardens, but they could not turn out a bonded man in the white robes of a child. This was their compromise— that he should have the outward trappings and some of the responsibilities of a warden, while attempting to catch up in his training like a newly tapped youngster. This explanation did nothing to appease his new pridemates, who had trained together for years and resented both his unearned status and the extra work his clumsiness earned them.

"And you!" Istaz Aadl thrust a beefy index finger toward Ismai. "You park your ass right here until you can perform Sun Burns the Flower without fucking it up, or I am going to burn your ass with the flat of my sword." His gaze raked across the other boys. "The rest of you goat-fathered idiots go find something productive to do. Now!"

The students scattered with scarcely a backward glance. Ismai had made no friends among the other boys, nor was likely to as long as his robes and his bond with Ruh'ayya set him apart. Neither had he made friends among the Ja'Sajani proper, men twice his age or more with whom he had little in common, and whose scars suggested they were not likely to be impressed by his new status. Tammas and Dairuz had gone back to Aish Kalumm with the Ja'Akari almost as soon as they had arrived. His brother was likely in the City of Mothers even now, dining on flaky whitefish wrapped in sweetgrass, and washing it down with a horn full of mead.

Ismai sighed and flowed as best he could into Flower Stance, wobbling a little as he brought his feet close together. He was hot, and tired, and hungry, and he felt more foolish than flowery. He ignored Jasin's derisive snort, and brought his rear leg forward into an exaggerated step while raising his arms up to his sides, wrists toward the sun, right fingers curled lightly about the hilt of his sword. On the first day, he had nearly chopped off his own toes so many times that Istaz Aadl had forbidden him to practice with his own blade until just this morning.

Ismai put his weight on the front foot and attempted a pivot, a move that ended with him ass-up in the sand.

This is impossible, he thought.

Not impossible. Ruh'ayya rumbled merrily in the back of his head. *Merely improbable. You look like a newborn tarbok trying to stand for the first time. That reminds me... I am hungry.*

Ismai picked himself up and brushed off most of the sand, wishing he dared remove the heavy touar. But the last time he had attempted to tie the headdress without assistance, he had nearly hanged himself.

"You are such a child," Jasin spat. "The Ja'Sajani probably have to wipe your ass... now that your mother is not here to do it for you."

247

Ismai spun, mouth hanging open. The other boy had not moved. He held Catching the Cat as if the human body had been intended to twist just so, and his blade shone against the midsun sky. It was a plain blade, new-forged, identical to any number of blades meant for Ja'Sajani who had mastered the Twenty. Ismai felt his lip curl, and his stomach growled.

Shall I eat him for you? I really am hungry.

No, thank you. I do not need you *to wipe my ass, either.* He picked up his sword. "Your mouth is too small to speak of my mother." He stared at the other boy deliberately, and smiled. "And far too pretty."

Jasin hissed between his teeth and snapped upright. "Would you draw steel against me, then?"

Ismai held out his shamsi, still staring at the other boy, and dropped it contemptuously upon the sand. "You are not worth my steel... you limp gewad."

Jasin howled at that and tossed his own blade aside. The boys flew at each other headfirst.

Like hill goats in rut, Ruh'ayya noted with approval. *Bang your brains out, then. I hear human brains are delicious.*

Jasin had trained among the Ja'Sajani for years, but Ismai was a younger sibling in a family of warriors. He might not yet be able to hold Fish Stance without falling over, but his opponent had never had to wrestle an older brother and sisters, and had never learned to fight dirty.

Ismai ducked aside from a punch as if his little sister Rudya had thrown it, and came up swinging with a hook that took Jasin full in the face. He was horrified—and gratified—to feel the larger boy's nose crunch beneath his knuckles.

Now you have done it, Ruh'ayya observed. She padded into view just as Jasin sank to his knees, yelling and clutching at his face. Blood spurted and dripped from between his fingers. *You broke one of them. I do not think the sires will be pleased with you.*

Once again, Ruh'ayya showed herself to have an excellent grasp of human nature. An enormous hand grabbed Ismai by the back of the neck. He was lifted high into the air and then shaken like a girl's rag dolly.

"Enough!" The voice was loud enough to set his ears ringing. "If your hands are idle enough to be at one another's throats, I will give you something to fill them with. You." He pointed at Jasin. "The privy pits want work."

"He broge by dode!" wailed Jasin, hands still cupping his face.

"With a face as ugly as yours, it can only be an improvement. Stop by the healer's tent on your way to the privies. I said go!"

Jasin retrieved his sword and hurried off, shooting Ismai a look of pure loathing as he passed.

"And you!" The smith glowered. "I expected better than this from you. You should expect better than this of yourself. Fighting in the dirt like some outlander urchin. Spilling your cousin's blood! Were you half again as big, I would beat some sense into you. Were you half again as smart, I should not have to."

Ismai felt a sulk welling from his chest, try though he might to hold it back. "He started it."

"He started it? Did you just tell me 'he started it'? You, the favored son of Umm Nurati, the brother of one of our finest wardens?" Mastersmith Hadid hawked and spat. "Little cousin, it is high time you let go of your mother's teats and grew a pair of your own."

Grow your own teats? I did not know human males could do this.

Ismai bit the inside of his cheek to keep from laughing. *Are you trying to get me killed?*

Mastersmith Hadid turned his face and stared straight at Ruh'ayya until the vash'ai turned her head away and began licking dust from between her toes. "And *you*! Whatever you were thinking to bond this one so young, he is yours now. You are not to encourage this type of behavior, do you understand?"

Ruh'ayya stuck her leg up into the air and began cleaning her nether parts. The big man snorted.

"Hopeless, the pair of you. Do you at least understand what you have done here, son of Nurati?"

"I defended myself from an attacker." Ismai scowled at the way his words rang in the air, hollow and without conviction. "It is my right."

"Perhaps when you had milk teeth and women washing your bottom when you soiled your clothes, but no longer." He stepped close, and Ismai only flinched a bit as the big man took a big fistful of his blue robes. "What do you see when you look at this? What do you see when you look into the water?"

Ismai stared at him uncertainly. "I see... touar?"

"Yes. You see touar, the robes of a Ja'Sajani." Mastersmith Hadid released him, and sighed deeply. "What do you think young Jasin sees?"

Ismai shrugged.

"He sees a boy who has been given everything in life, everything he might hope to ever win through sweat and blood, and a great deal more besides. You are the son of Umm Nurati, the most powerful woman in the prides, a mother of six living children. Six! Brother to Tammas Ja'Sajani besides."

"Oh, yes, Tammas." Ismai hated the sound of his own voice, even as he said the words. How could he explain to this man how it was, growing up in the shadows of the handsomest and most talented man in the pride? What mother would not wish her youngest to be more like the oldest? Even as he thought this, Ismai caught sight of his red sword lying in the sand and felt a moment of shame.

"Yes, Tammas, whom you favor more than you know. Such a family you boast... while most women cannot bear one child to term, your mother births six. Two of your sisters fertile, as well—and young Tammas, himself a father thrice over, *ehuani*. It can be expected that you will sire at least one child in your lifetime, if not many. You have this pretty beast—" he jerked his chin toward Ruh'ayya, who lifted her head from her important business and showed a bit of fang "—though you are too young to have earned the bond.

"You have a fancy sword which you have never learned to use, you have the blue robes that Jasin has worked to earn since he was five years old, and already the women's eyes follow you about the camp. You have everything, and you leave the rest of them nothing."

Ismai hung his head, willing the tears to go back where they had come from. "I did not think…"

Ruh'ayya heaved herself up from the sand and came to stand by him, nudging his shoulder with the top of her head.

I still love you.

"You did not think. I know this, having been young and bone-headed myself." Mastersmith Hadid reached up to rub his smooth scalp, and tug at his Master's lock. "But you are a man grown now, whether any of us likes it or not, with a man's responsibilities. It is time to set the idiocy of youth aside. We are too few, little cousin, to allow you the comforts of childhood any longer. Do you understand how few we are? Nine smiths for all the prides. Nine, when there used to be hundreds. Less than ten thousand Ja'Sajani, perhaps half again as many Ja'Akari and that only because so few of our women are fertile. Do you remember the words? 'I fight against my brother…'"

"…but I fight with my brother against my cousin…" Ismai continued.

"…and I fight with my brother and my cousin against outlanders," Mastersmith Hadid finished. "Precisely. Here is the thing, young Ismai. We Zeeranim are so few in number now that every drop of blood is precious to us. Every man among us is a brother. Do you know why we are so few?"

"The Sundering."

"The Sundering, yes. Wars and earthquakes and worse, and do you know how the Sundering started?"

Ismai had not really paid much attention to his history lessons. "A wicked sorcerer?" he half-remembered, half-guessed. "He brought down the fury of Akari Sun Dragon upon the world, or… or something like that. There are many stories of the Sundering." He could only remember half of the stories he had been told, and understood fewer than half of those.

Mastersmith Hadid rubbed his face. He did not look angry now so much as he looked tired. Tired and sad. "Many stories, yes, but they are all the same at the heart. There was a sorcerer in Atualon, and he called himself Ka Atu, the Dragon King. During a war with Sindan, this king used the magic they call atulfah, he used too much of it, sucked the world dry like you would suck an egg... and the magic fought him. The battle between this Dragon King and his unnatural magic raged across the land, searing Quarabala and freezing the northern wastes, causing the seas to rise so that they covered the land in some places, where in others the water disappeared altogether."

"But that was so long ago," Ismai protested. "The people survived, and we are stronger now."

"The people survived, but are we any stronger now than we were a hundred years ago? Two hundred?" The older man shook his head. "In my grandmother's mother's time, one in every three women gave birth. Now, perhaps one in every four or five women bears a living child. This is what we ward against, Ja'Sajani, my youngest brother. As you take census, year after year, you will come to see that we are failing as a people. We are dying."

This is true. Ruh'ayya's voice in his mind was slow and sad. *Among the vash'ai as well. Among the kith, and the kin, and even the lesser beasts... the world is dying.*

Ismai stared at Ruh'ayya. "But... what can we do?"

"Do? We can do as we have always done. Serve and protect. Take census, make note of the fertile men and the fertile women, and suggest pairings so that we may build another generation. It has been enough, or almost enough, until now." Mastersmith Hadid laid a heavy hand upon Ismai's shoulder, and stared into his eyes with such profound pity that Ismai took a step back, alarmed.

"Why now? What has happened?"

"It is not what has happened, it is what will happen... if it is not happening already. Ismai Ja'Sajani, everyone knows of your... fondness... for Sulema Ja'Akari, the daughter of Hafsa Azeina."

"Yes..." *Everyone knows?* he thought, dismayed.

"Sulema has been wounded. Perhaps she will die." He held up a hand to forestall Ismai's protest. "Yes, I know you will her to live, but she may die on the road to Atualon, or she may die once they reach the city. If she does not die, if she survives… what then? What then, Ismai, warden of the people?"

"If she survives…" *When she survives,* he thought stubbornly, "I suppose she will meet her father and then return home. She is Ja'Akari."

"She *was* Ja'Akari, Ismai. She is the daughter of Ka Atu, and the Dragon King has no heir. He has only the one son left to him, and that son is surdus… deaf to the song of sorcery. He cannot wield atulfah, and so he can never be king. Do you really believe Ka Atu will simply allow this daughter of his to leave, to ride off again into the desert firing arrows into the sunset? After he has spent so many years and so many men searching for her?

"Istaza Ani told me once, and this was years ago, that Hafsa Azeina had killed more than a hundred men to keep her daughter hidden away. A hundred men, and all of them sent by Ka Atu to seek this girl out and force her return. Does it sound to you as if Sulema will be free to leave? Once she reaches Atualon, boy, she is lost to us. Best you think of her as lost to us already."

"But the dreamshifter is so powerful," Ismai said, stunned. The world tilted beneath his feet. "Her mother will keep her safe."

"Keep her safe? Boy, have you been listening? Ka Atu is like the Sleeping Dragon in the old stories, powerful enough to crack the world open and destroy us all. His daughter will be Sa Atu, the Heart of Atualon, a sorcerer-queen. It is no longer a question of how to keep Sulema safe from her father. Now it is a question of how we will keep the world safe from Sulema." He squeezed Ismai's shoulder and then let his hand drop away. "I am sorry to tell you this, *ehuani.* I rather liked the girl, myself."

Ismai stared for a moment, then turned and walked slowly to where his sword lay, half-buried in the sand as if it meant nothing to him. He picked up the blade and looked at it for a long time, watching sunlight ripple and dance upon the bright steel, the swirls of color that drew the eye in. It was a beautiful sword, sweet to behold and balanced in the hand, and he felt shame for the way he had behaved earlier.

"You should spend some time with your vash'ai," Hadid said.

Ismai looked up, startled. "What?"

"New Zeeravashani are expected to spend some time alone getting to know one another. Perhaps you and Ruh'ayya should walk out for a day or three. Your brother would tell you as much, but as he is not here…" The big man nodded. "No camp, no chores, no jealous looks, hey? And no hammering for a while? Just a short walk, mind you. Practice your forms while you are gone, that will make Istaz Aadl happy." He unfastened a large leather bag from his belt and tossed it to Ismai. From the feel of it, the bag was mostly full of food and waterskins. "You have had many changes in your life, in a short amount of time, and I daresay you have much to think about. I, myself, find it much easier to think when I am not surrounded by other people."

I would like that. Ruh'ayya had ceased insulting Mastersmith Hadid with her bath and was sitting straight, ears perked forward with interest. *I would like that very much. We could hunt and would not have to share the meat.*

Ismai nodded, unable to speak for the lump in his throat.

The smith began to turn away but stopped, a slow grin spreading across his coarse face. "We are not far from Eid Kalmut, you know. The Valley of Death. When I was a boy, I was hot to ride out and see the ruins, but of course we were forbidden. I suppose no one has thought to tell you that it is *khutlani*?"

"No," Ismai sheathed his sword. "But if it is forbidden, I promise I will not—"

"Ah-*aat*!" The smith held one hand up in warning. "If no one has thought to tell you a thing is forbidden, you can hardly be faulted for doing it. I do not want to know your plans, boy. So, go, spend some time with your vash'ai. When you come back to us, you will have to leave all this boyish nonsense behind. You will dedicate yourself to your training, and we will find you a horse of your own, and you will be Ja'Sajani in truth. You understand this."

Ismai nodded.

"Good. Then go, be a foolish boy one last time. When you return, perhaps you can tell me tales of the Valley of Death." The mastersmith of the pride winked, and then he turned and strode away.

Valley of Death? Ruh'ayya yawned and stretched, digging her long black claws into the sand, and then she shook herself and showed her tusks in a pleased smile. *That sounds promising.*

"You are a very strange cat," he told her. He loosened the cords that tied the bag shut and looked inside. It held maybe three days' worth of fish-and-jiinberry pemmican, which was his least favorite food in all the world, two fire bundles, and several wax-stopped waterskins. He would be sleeping under the stars with little food in his belly and no tent, no bedding, no companionship besides an enormous saber-tusked cat who had never promised not to eat him.

Perfect.

Perfect, Ruh'ayya agreed.

He shrugged the bag onto his shoulder, reached up to ruffle the soft fur behind Ruh'ayya's jaw, and they set out to the north and east, toward one last great adventure.

The sky was wide and blue, blue as the robes that billowed and flapped about him like a bird's wings in the thin wind, drawing cooler air up and against his skin. His new boots, still bone-white, shuffed softly against the sand. His muscles were sore, but it was a good sore, the kind of ache that comes from being young and hale and pushing the limits.

Without warning Ruh'ayya swatted him, claws-in, and sent him rolling down a steep dune. He tumbled ass-over-touar, limbs flailing. He lost his headdress, he lost his bag, and any semblance of dignity that had been left to him as well. When he finally came to rest at the bottom of the dune, face planted firmly in the sand, butt-high and with his legs splayed, Ruh'ayya laughed at him in his head and took off running, tail held high in an invitation to play.

What could he do but spit sand, collect his belongings, replace the touar as best he could, and give chase? His legs pumped and burned as he tore up the next dune after her, the air burned in his lungs, and he roared with vengeful laughter.

They were Zeeravashani. The world was theirs.

Ours, agreed Ruh'ayya. She paused, poised at the top of the next dune, tail still dancing. *But only if I agree to share it with you*. Then she was gone again.

They played like this for some time, Ismai never quite able to catch the taunting young queen. They ran laughing from the noise and stink and demands of humanity, from the weight of other people's minds as they looked on and thought, *Too young, too foolish, too lucky, too loud*. There was only the sky, and the Zeera, and Ruh'ayya who loved him.

A shadow passed overhead, and for no reason he thought of Sulema. It was as if she ran with them, and felt so real that it seemed she would be waiting for him with a skin of pilfered mead in one hand, two drinking-horns in the other, and a smile wide as the sky. Ismai was suddenly overwhelmed by the certainty that she was waiting for him, just ahead. But when he reached the top of the next rise and stopped, chest heaving, there was only Ruh'ayya.

Of course he had imagined it. Just as Mastersmith Hadid had imagined that she might ever pose a risk to her own people. "*Now it is a question of how we will keep the world safe from Sulema.*"

Ismai snorted, and removed his touar and shook it free of sand before rewrapping it as best he could. It was still lopsided, but at least it sat firmly where it should. Keep the world safe from Sulema? She was a terror to the kitchens, and a headache to Istaza Ani, but she was a danger to no one.

Ruh'ayya jogged up the hill and shook herself so vigorously that sand stung his eyes. *You are thinking of your mate?*

Sulema is not my mate.

If you say so. She showed a bit of tusk. He stuck his tongue out at her. *We should hunt. I am tired of dead fish and stinking fat. I want meat, red-blood meat squealing and hot.*

"*Za fik*," he swore aloud, disgusted with himself. "I forgot my bow!"

Oh, however will we hunt without your puny bow? she mocked. *Surely we are doomed to die. We should lay down right here and let the buzzards eat our guts.* Ruh'ayya stretched, extending her proud black claws and showing every inch of gleaming white tusk. *Or you could find a watering hole so that we can hunt.*

Ismai shook his head at her, grinning. *I could... if I wanted to.*

She blinked her great shining eyes at him and waited.

He let his eyes unfocus and allowed his ka to blossom in the desert heat, unfurling like the petals of a blackthorn rose. He could feel Akari Sun Dragon looking down upon them, could feel the thrum of the desert song, he could feel Ruh'ayya blazing like a fire, and he could feel water, water and life, not too far to the east. An oasis, though not much of one by the feel.

Ismai came back to himself slowly, and set out at a slow jog toward the oasis. Ruh'ayya trotted along with him, sometimes to one side or the other, sometimes bounding ahead a short distance, and now and then dropping behind. This last trick made the hairs at the nape of his neck prickle.

Would you stop that?

She laughed in his mind again, but quit her teasing and came up to run at his side.

Ismai was winded by the time they came within sight of the oasis—not much more than a puddle in the sand flanked by a few blackthorn bushes, really—and dropped the bag from his shoulder onto the sand. He dug out a waterskin and took a long pull at it. Perhaps the water at this place would be sweet and he could refill the skin, perhaps not. He would not be away long enough for it to matter, in any case.

Ruh'ayya's ears swiveled forward and she tensed, her body fairly humming with excitement.

Meat! She dropped to her belly, haunches wiggling as she prepared to launch herself downhill. Ismai followed the line of her stare, and his heart leapt like a stag.

Wait! Wait! That is not meat. That is a horse! Not just any horse, either. She was a dream, a vision, shimmering in the air before him as pale and perfect as a shell at the river's edge. She raised her head from the water, ears flattening along her neck and then pricking forward again, poised for flight. Ismai looked at her and understood, after all these years, what it meant to love a horse.

But it is not your *horse,* Ruh'ayya protested. *She is young, she is tender, she is sweet!* Then the vash'ai glanced up at him and blinked, and her tail sank to the ground. *Oh, scat and offal. Very well, if you must have her, you must. It will be interesting to watch you try to catch her, at any rate.* She relaxed, sinking fully onto the sand, and folded her paws beneath her chest, eyes shining with amusement.

Ismai shouldered his bag again, not wanting to lose it, and took a deep breath, trying to loose the tension in his gut. His hands were shaking and his mouth was as dry as if he had caught an accidental glimpse of Sulema bathing again. He slowly unwound the upper belt from his waist and knotted one end into a simple halter, and then, heart in his mouth, he began the long, slow walk down to the water.

The little mare lifted her head immediately and followed his approach with her enormous dark eyes. She was gray, the color of smoke against the sky, or river-foam among the willows. Her body was limber and sleek, her legs like a dancer's, her mane and tail a rippling waterfall of silk.

Enough, Ruh'ayya complained. *There is no excuse for bad poetry.*

"*Ehuani,*" he breathed. Beauty in truth. So would he name her. "Ehuani."

The mare absorbed him with her eyes, flared her nostrils and drank in his scent. She was not afraid of him, that much was apparent.

"Ehuani," he named her three times. He closed the distance between them slowly, letting his eyes remain soft, his intentions clear. *I would never harm you, beautiful one.* She was a pale moon in a pale sky, glowing with the promise of spring. She was...

She was very clear about her intent not to be caught by a stripling boy, flatterer or no. Ehuani—for that was her name now—flagged her tail disdainfully before wheeling and trotting away with a toss of her head that reminded him exactly of Sulema's reaction, that one and only time he had approached her with a stammering admission of love.

Ruh'ayya brushed past him, shoving him with her shoulder as she passed and nearly knocking him down. *Well, what are you waiting for?* She laughed. *Let us go catch your horse.*

The mare led them on a merry chase. Had he not already spent one half of his energy at his morning's training, and the other half playing with Ruh'ayya, it would have been exciting. As it was, the excitement soon gave way to miserable, teeth-gritting, scowling exhaustion and even a little irritation as Ehuani played her game with obvious enjoyment.

She was no wild horse—she was too well groomed, well fed, and too obviously not afraid of either of them for that—but neither was she compliant. She would stand for a bit, allow them to approach, flick her ears forward at Ismai's outstretched fingers, and then she would be off again, bucking and kicking and squealing as if his offer of friendship was deeply insulting.

Still, every time the mare stood still it was for a little while longer, every time she let him near it felt like *this* time when he reached to touch her, his fingers would not brush empty air still swirling and warm with her scent.

In this, too, she was like Sulema.

Finally, just as Akari Sun Dragon turned his thoughts and his gaze toward the western horizon, Ehuani allowed him to touch her. It was a whisper, the slightest brush of her velvet lips and the tickle of her whisker against his outstretched palm, but the sight and smell of her so close, the heat of her breath against his palm, the promise of touching such beauty gave Ismai the heart and energy to continue.

He turned to Ruh'ayya with a grin. His touar was falling off one side of his head, the bag of food and waterskins weighed him down as if he was carrying Mastersmith Hadid across the Zeera, and the shamsi had bruised his hip and thigh so that it felt as if he had lost a sword fight with his shadow. But he was so close.

Then he saw the way.

Ruh'ayya, O my beauty, he cajoled, *if you would angle off to the side and drive her toward that tangle, I could come at her from this side, slowly, and I think this time she would not run away...*

Tangle? What tangle? She narrowed her eyes as he pointed.

Due north, beyond the tangle of brush and bones, he could just see the dark line that was Eid Kalmut. *Za fik,* no wonder he was so...

BONELORD!

Ruh'ayya pinned her ears and screamed, bringing herself up into her shoulders so quickly she almost stood on her hind legs.

Bonelord? His brain stopped still. It was as if he had been turned into a solid lump of stupid. *Bonelords are children's stories. There is no such...*

The air was rent with a hiss, a whisper of wind in the reeds at first, then the cries of birds, the whistling of all the tea-kettles in Aish Kalumm come to a boil at once. The tangle of bones began to shake and grow as something shook itself free of the desert sand, something so big and so utterly wrong that Ismai's mind shied from it as Ehuani had shied from the touch of a rope.

The mass thrashed and grew, an oasis of carrion, a forest of bones, and then a cavern opened in its side, tall enough for a man to walk through without ducking, wide enough that four might walk abreast. The cavern stretched wide, and wider still, and then emitted a bloodcurdling shriek thick with hatred and despair. The cry brought Ismai's heart to his mouth, and tore the veil from his mind.

The thing emerging from the Zeera was big enough to swallow a herd of tarbok. It was long and flattish in shape, like a leech, and covered all along its length with bones and branches and entire rotting carcasses. Ismai saw the hips and legs of a man, the tusked skull of a vash'ai, the long, delicate ribs of a huge lionsnake.

Run! Ruh'ayya screamed.

Run, agreed his mind. But his body refused to answer. His blood ran cold and slow as the river after a killing rain.

Then Ehuani screamed, a silvery cry ringing out against the horror, and thundered past the thing's gaping maw. The bulk of the thing twitched and twisted, bones flailing and waving about like willow trees in the wind, and it turned to follow her. Its flat sides rippled across the desert in an oddly graceful dance as it moved with a speed that belied its size.

Ismai dropped the bag, drew his sword—though it was shorter than any but the smallest teeth in that stinking, gaping maw—and ran downhill screaming at the top of his lungs, ready to die in defense of a horse that wanted nothing to do with him.

Stupid boy! Ruh'ayya snarled in his mind. *This way.* He saw at once what she was about and angled his path to meet hers. This way would take them to the west a bit and then north again, hugging the midsection of this line of dunes, and bring them to the very mouth of Eid Kalmut just in time to die. *Stupid, stupid,* she repeated. But she ran beside him nonetheless, tusks gleaming red with the dying of the sun.

His boots pounded sand as they curved upward, around, and down. The dunes flattened out as they reached Eid Kalmut as if they wanted nothing to do with the Valley. He tucked his elbows and ducked his head, lungs screaming, heart pounding, legs burning like iron on the smiths' anvils as they raced to cut the bonelord off and then—

Ruh'ayya disappeared in front of him with a flick of her black-and-bronze tail. She stretched out above the Zeera, swift as thought, brave as thunder. Ismai's heart flew with her and he slowed—how could he ask her to do such a thing?—but Ehuani screamed in fear, rising up on her back legs and thrashing the air in terror and defiance as the bonelord raised its bulk high in the air above her, emitting a thin wail of bloodlust and victory.

Ruh'ayya came to a skidding stop between the mare and their doom, hackles raised all along her spine, mouth gaping to reveal her beautiful, deadly tusks, and she yowled a cat's death-song, terrible and wild and proud. Ismai sprinted to her side, one last mad dash, and then lifted his sword and shook it full in the face of death.

This close, he could see bits and chunks of rotting prey clinging to the rows of hooked and inward-curving teeth, could see a cluster of eyes bright as a beetle's just above the apex of its gaping maw, and most of all, he could smell it. Worse than offal, worse than latrine pits, worse than a week-old corpse. It smelled of disease and rot, of unclean death and the musk of endless terror.

Ismai sucked in a final breath and used it up again in a defiant scream.

"Come at me, then, you miserable vomitous mass! You venomous sack of entrails! *Show me yours!*"

The thing paused in its swaying, and turned its head—if such a thing could be said to have a head—toward him. Its flesh pulled back from the tooth-studded hole of its mouth, and it gurgled and hissed, a long, low, drawn-out sound so like a laugh that all the hair on Ismai's arms, his scalp, and down his spine stood on end. It reared higher, horrid bulk blocking out the last rays of sunset, dropped its jaw open with a sloppy, sucking noise…

…and stopped. It stopped swaying, and hissing, it stopped twitching, even its little beetle eyes held still.

Ehuani dropped to all fours and stood, sides heaving, roaring through her nostrils. Ruh'ayya breathed in soft little grunting snarls, and Ismai's heart pounded in his ears like a war drum, *tha-rump tha-rump tha-rumble*, but the bonelord did not move.

Tha-rump, tha-rump, tha-rumble…

Then it sank down, down, down, sinking and shrinking and seeming to draw in upon itself. The mouth closed and the eyes pulled inward defensively. The thing's sticky-looking gray hide crawled and shrank as it sank down into the sand, down down down till it was the faintest tumble of bone, and then it turned and swam away through the rippling desert sands just as the last red ray of light winked out and left them shrouded in darkness. Ismai shook so much that he had to hold his sword with both hands, lest he drop it and shame himself.

"What," he said aloud, "just happened?"

"Venomous sack of entrails?"

He spun about so fast that he *did* drop the sword, and scrambled to pick it up again. "What! Who!"

A slight figure stood before him, a little wisp of a thing, one slender hand stroking his horse's nose. She was dressed in robes of many colors, a patchwork of spidersilk and wormsilk, linen and cotton and cloth-of-gold, fine materials but tattered and mismatched and worn. She was swathed in veils so that only her eyes showed, enormous and dark in the fading light, and enough skin so that he could see the dreadful scarring, the bright pale patches of pink and bone-white against darker skin.

She ducked her head and looked away.

Do not look at her. Ruh'ayya warned. Her voice was very soft, as if her very thoughts might be overheard. *Do not frighten her.*

Do not frighten her? Ismai had to remind himself to close his mouth. He used both hands to sheathe his sword, slowly and gently as if he stood before not one, but two wild fillies. He stepped forward, careful not to step too close, and laid a hand upon Ehuani's shoulder.

The horse snorted but did not try to pull away. She was soft, soft as silk, and he was still alive to touch her. His skin tingled—he was alive—his heart beat, breath still filled his lungs. He had not yet soiled himself. All in all, the day had turned out better than he had any right to expect.

"I am Ismai," he told the horse. She swiveled an ear and rolled her eye. "Ismai," he said again. He named himself to her three times, binding his fate to hers. "I am Ismai."

"Ismai." The girl whispered, eyes still averted as she stepped back from the horse. "His name is Ismai." She turned half away from him, thin hands disappearing into the folds of her robe.

Ismai stroked his horse's neck, her shoulder, under her jaw. He scratched the spot on her chest that horses so love, and smiled as she fought against making a funny face, still not entirely willing to trust him.

"Lovely girl. My lovely girl. Look at you, just look, you are a breath of morning, you are wind made flesh, just look at you, my lovely girl." He loosed the halter that had become so tightly wound around his hand that it had turned his fingers white, and held it up so that she could see. The mare rolled her eyes at that, and tossed her head in a most haughty manner, obviously recognizing the halter for what it was and just as obviously wanting nothing to do with it.

"Shhhh, pretty girl," he soothed. "I will not hurt you. I will never hurt you. My tent is yours, my water is yours—" He had to smile at his own words then. "—if I can find it." He rubbed the soft rope against her softer hide.

"You called Arushdemma a 'venomous sack of entrails.'" The soft voice was a bit closer now, though the girl still stood some distance away and poised on her toes as if prepared to flee his presence. He reminded himself that this delicate child had just faced down— and frightened away—a beast so monstrous his bowels still ached to think of it. Still, she seemed younger than and far more timid than his next sister, Dennet, who had just seen her thirteenth winter. "You called him a 'miserable vomitous mass.'" Then she did an astounding thing. She laughed. Her laughter was the lightest, prettiest, and altogether most delightful sound Ismai had ever heard.

"Arushdemma? That thing has a name?" He brought the halter closer to Ehuani's face, and she stretched her neck high to avoid him.

"Of course he has a name. All things have a name. Even you." She shrank away from him again, gliding backward over the sand as if a breath would carry her away. "Even I have a name."

He moved the rope back down to Ehuani's withers and rubbed her with it, on the itchiest of itchy spots, and finally the mare twisted her lip upward, baring her teeth in a comical grin.

"You know my name."

"Ismai," she agreed, and relaxed a little when he did not ask for hers in return.

"I dropped my food and water out there on the sand," he told the horse, and not the girl. "I might find it, if I had a torch."

Or you might ask the vash'ai, who has excellent night vision, Ruh'ayya reminded him, amused.

The girl hesitated. "You will not follow me?"

"Never," he assured her.

She was gone with the next breath, dissolved into the deepening twilight like a drop of ink into a river of dark water. Ismai stayed where he was, letting his horse get to know him, enjoying the sound of his own heart beating and the feel of air in his lungs and wind in his hair. It had been an excellent day to die, but it was far, far better to have survived.

Just as he slipped his arm about Ehuani's neck, and the halter over her head, just as she shook her head and blew softly through her nostrils and allowed him to tie it, the girl reappeared in front of him, carrying a torch that spluttered and spit and cast an odd reddish glow. Ruh'ayya spat and slunk away into the darkness, but Ismai was glad for the light. He kept his eyes averted as the girl drifted close, closer, close enough almost for him to touch, and when he reached to take it he was careful not to brush her fingers with his own. Ehuani did not care for the flame, but neither did she pull away.

Ismai held the torch in one hand, and Ehuani's lead rope in the other, and he bowed as if he was facing every Mother in Aish Kalumm, and all the wardens besides. The girl laughed again, and again the sound pierced and lifted his heart.

"Will you come with me?" She was small, and all alone. He had to ask.

The girl drifted close again, and laid her hand upon Ehuani's soft muzzle.

"Go with him," she whispered. "Be good to him. He has a kind heart." Ehuani snorted and nodded her head, and the girl's eyes crinkled with what might have been a smile. Ismai wished she would laugh again. Those eyes met his, briefly.

He was falling, falling through the dark. He opened his mouth to cry out...

...and she looked away. "Arushdemma will not come near, as long as you carry my torch. But he has your scent now, and you have insulted him. That was not a wise thing to do." Her eyes crinkled again. "But it was funny."

"Can I come back and see you again?" Ismai bit his lip as soon as the words were out, but he could not take them back. Nor, he realized, did he wish to.

Her eyes met his again, the briefest glance. This time he stayed put. "If you do, bring the torch."

Ismai bowed again, and turned to follow his own footprints back the way he had come. He could feel Ruh'ayya's brooding presence, and the dark closing in all round, and the moons as they prepared to rise full and brilliant, and the stars so far away, so cold and indifferent to the yearnings of a young boy's heart.

"Char."

"Hm?" He half turned back to face her. Dark eyes flashed in the light of his torch.

"Char," she told him, and then a third time, binding their fates together. "My name is Char."

TWENTY-SIX

Hafsa Azeina rode through the massive bronze-and-gold Sunset Gate of Atualon with one hand on the golden shofar and a snarl on her face that should have sent the cheering crowds before her running for the protection of the cold stone walls.

It had been half a lifetime since she had endured the presence of so many people at once, and their wants and dreams pressed upon her like a dead weight. Keila, her dapple-gray mare, snapped at any who drew near, be they horse or man or even vash'ai. The Imperators who had been thrust upon her as an honor guard had learned to keep their distance from the ill-tempered beast.

They kept a wary eye on her horse, as well.

She remembered coming here as a young girl, how pretty and bright the little houses seemed with their neat white walls and colored-glass windows, brass roofs gleaming in the morning light, and how the people cheered for her as she was led up the wide avenue. The houses were as charming in the dying of the day, little oil lamps hung in the windows so that Atualon looked like a well-lit jeweler's shop.

The flowering trees were as fragrant as she remembered, the black mountains wreathed in smoke and magic were as breathtaking, but she knew Atualon now for what it was—a trap. She clenched her jaw and followed the winding road ever upward toward Atukos, the great black fortress of Ka Atu and the mountain for which it was named. At either side the people of Atualon pressed close, too close, too noisy and needy, spooking the horses and causing Khurra'an to lash his tail in aggravation. They gaped at the vash'ai, at her, at the people, like children watching a troupe of fools.

"Look at those teeth!" cried a man in a merchant's smock, pointing at Khurra'an.

The better to eat you with, thought the cat. *You owe me a fat pig for this, Dreamshifter.*

"*Ai yeh,*" one of the Ja'Akari whispered close behind her, "these outlanders have no manners at all."

As they had ridden past the outlying farms and villages, now they rode through the city proper without stopping, winding round and round through the foothills of Atukos. Eventually the Merchant's Circle and the slaves' quarters and the lesser houses fell behind and beneath them, and the sky-sweeping Dragonglass Gate of the Greater Quarters opened to enfold them into a lover's embrace.

A false lover, she thought, and at her dark look the guards closest to her shied away. She was still astride her mare, and still scowling, when Imperator General Davidian, flanked by a double fist of Baidun Daiel and as many Draiksguards, materialized out of the gloom and informed her that Ka Atu commanded her presence and that of his daughter.

Ka Atu *commanded* her. Hafsa Azeina could feel her jaw set.

"My daughter has been injured," she replied. "She needs food, and rest, and a bath. Tomorrow is soon enough for Wyvernus to go poking at her." *If he cannot be bothered to meet us himself, he can just sit on his blasted chair and wait.*

"Meissati..."

"Meissati? You forget yourself, Imperator. I am Queen Consort. *Have* you forgotten?" She shifted the staff in her lap. "Or do you deny me?"

Aasah swayed in his saddle, and his little apprentice stepped up beside him. They had been dancing their shadow-magic every night, every single night since Sulema had been injured, trying to hold back the Araid venom that still threatened to consume her. Hafsa Azeina heard the Ja'Akari muttering among themselves, heard the *clop-clop* of hooves on cobblestones as the Ja'Akari drew up behind her, as the Baidun Daiel began to chant under their breaths and sway.

"I have forgotten nothing, Issa. I was there to greet you the day you first arrived in Atualon, as I am here to greet you now. And I am very much your servant." He swept a low bow. "No one here will deny you a thing, but your presence is most urgently... requested... by Ka Atu."

Let me eat him, Khurra'an laughed. *He is caught between a dreamshifter and the Dragon King... it would be a mercy killing.*

Let me have him, suggested Belzaleel. *Just a taste.*

Hafsa Azeina was startled enough at that to jerk upright in her saddle. If Belzaleel could speak to her here and now, she was more tired than she had thought. And if the daemon blade wanted this man dead, she would be well advised to guard his life.

Hafsa Azeina dismounted and handed her reins over to Daru. "Watch over Sulema," she told Leviathus. "Keep her safe."

Leviathus bowed. "Of course, Issa. I will take her to your rooms in the Queen's Tower."

Davidian did not hide his distress. "Queen Consort, my orders—"

"Insist all you will, Imperator, I am her mother, I am dreamshifter of the Shahadrim, and I say she will rest now. Or do you claim a higher authority than mine?"

Imperator General Davidian bowed again, a defeated look on his lined face. She should have felt some sympathy for the man, would have, in years gone by—Davidian had always been kind to her, and she respected the old soldier—but if he had wanted kindness from her, he should have led her to the baths and given her a cup of coffee before ordering her around like a kitchen slave. Perhaps Atualon had forgotten what it meant to have a queen consort in residence.

When Davidian turned as if he would lead her, Hafsa Azeina dismissed him and the Draiksguard with an impatient wave. She pushed past them and past the Baidun Daiel as well, not bothering to brush the hair back from her face or the dust from her robes. Wyvernus wanted to see her? Fine, then, let him see her.

Let him smell me, too. He should have let me take a bath first.

"Do not bother," she told them all. "I know my way to the bedchambers of Ka Atu."

Indeed she did. The black glass walls streaked with gold, smooth floors warm underfoot, even the smell of fresh bread lingering in the halls that led to the kitchens still haunted her dreams. Did she close her eyes, her feet would know the way. Did she lose her feet, her heart would know the way. She ignored the guards who flanked her and the serving folk who fled from her, scowled her way past any who looked to hail her, and startled one midnight-haired young beauty so badly that the girl dumped wine down the front of her sheer rose gown.

I know her, she thought, startled. Matteira has grown into the promise of her beauty. *But what is the sister of Mattu Halfmask doing in these halls, in the dying of the day?*

A fist of young guardsmen hurried to offer assistance to the girl, and Hafsa Azeina fought the urge to smile. There was no reason she should feel amused, or safe, no reason to feel she had come home after too long away.

No reason at all? The thought seemed to come from the very walls of Atukos. *You* are *home.*

That stopped her in her tracks. *You stay out of my head!* She shoved Wyvernus out of her mind and slammed the doors shut. She could hear him fluttering just beyond her ward like a bird outside the shutters, laughing at her. *Damn that man.* She drew herself up, eyes blazing so that the pretty girl and her admirers all remembered that they had important business elsewhere...

...and stopped so abruptly that Khurra'an bumped into her leg. She had not checked for traps since riding into Atualon, and that was arrogance enough to get her killed. She had enemies in this city, many of whom were probably close enough at this very moment to hear her if she screamed. One of these enemies was the shade of her former self, whispering of laughter and love and long, slow caresses in the dark.

The Wyvernus she had loved would never have wished her harm, but the handsome young man with fire in his heart was as dead and gone to dust as his golden-eyed princess with moonlight hair. So Hafsa Azeina opened her intikallah, and studied the palace with her dreaming eyes.

There it was, the web of magic that held this city together and bound the world to its will. At every meeting between two strands hung a gleaming droplet of atulfah, shimmering and trembling like a little globe of magesilver, endlessly reflecting this world and every other, bridging the strands of might-be and will-be and are. Her trained gaze skimmed over those tempting jewels. They were a byproduct of the dream, a naturally occurring trap, and posed little threat to one such as her.

What she searched for, and what she found—here, and here, and here—were places where a dreamshifter or mage or shadowmancer had altered the path of the web by adding new strands, or burning away the old.

What is this? She drew closer to the web, to a place where the strands had been torn asunder. Hidden in the shadows, someone had—

"Are you going to stand here all night with your eyes closed? Or will you go to him at last?"

Her eyes snapped open, and she glared at Khurra'an. *Why did you not tell me he was there?*

Khurra'an showed a bit of fang. *Why did you not sense him yourself?*

"I do hope you have not lost your way… Queen Consort." Mattu Halfmask was wearing the face of a crocodile. "If you like, I would be your guide."

Hafsa Azeina reached up as if she would touch his mask. He tensed, but did not flinch away as he once might have. "Thank you, Halfmask, I believe I can find my own way. Your sister, however, may be grateful for some assistance."

He went still all over. "My sister?"

"She spilled a bit of wine on herself, back there." She pointed. "Fortunately, her distress was witnessed by a handful of young men. Unfortunately, it was witnessed by a handful of young men.

By now, I am sure she would appreciate it if you would rescue her from all the help."

"The day my sister needs rescuing, I will eat my mask. You did not answer my question."

The lights in the walls flared suddenly, flickered and went out.

The sire of this rock grows impatient, Khurra'an noted.

The sire of this rock can stuff a sandal in it, Hafsa Azeina retorted. *I will get there when I get there.*

In the dark, she could hear the rustle of fabric as Mattu Halfmask stepped close, smell the oil in his hair and, oddly, the sharp musk of a man's fear. "Hafsa Azeina," he whispered, so low she had to strain to catch his words, "whatever else I may be, I am not the enemy. Not *your* enemy, at any rate." He dared touch her arm. "Tread softly, and with great care, Queen Consort. More blood has been spilled in this foolery than even you know." He turned on his heel and strode away, white cloak fluttering behind him like wings.

Hafsa Azeina started again toward Wyvernus's rooms and was not surprised when the lights in the walls flared back to life. Nor was she surprised to find the halls now cleared of traffic.

"Oh, hold on to your kilt, you old grouch," she muttered. "I am coming." One of the guards snickered, and she spun to face them. "*You!* Find someone else to shadow, or I will find something interesting for you to do. That means you, too, Davidian. Or do you fear for the safety of your liege, in the presence of one woman?" The ringing of boots on stone described their hasty departure.

Perhaps they had not forgotten her, after all.

The lights flickered again, and she knew Wyvernus laughed.

She strode down the hallway and into his chambers like a queen, though perhaps not the queen he remembered. *This* queen had a vash'ai at her side, a song of death in her heart, and blood on her hands. The Queen Consort had come prepared for battle.

❖

As it turned out, she had prepared for the wrong battle.

The smell of his chambers curled about her in that first moment, stopping her in her tracks, stripping away too many of her defenses. Olive oil and lemon, smoke and fennel and mint. Strongest of all, weaving itself into the very fabric of her, the scent of the man himself.

This man is my enemy, she reminded herself. The trap had been baited well, but she was no longer a princess bride, wide-eyed and trusting.

He sat as he always had, in a low-slung chair carved of blackthorn and inlaid with ivory, a goblet of wine in one hand, watching the door and waiting for her. She looked at him, and her jaw dropped open.

"Your hair," she gasped. "What happened to your *hair*?"

The Dragon King of Atualon threw his head back and laughed. He slapped his thigh, and sloshed wine upon the white fur rug, and laughed as if he had not spent half her life sending assassins to die at her hand.

The Wyvernus she remembered had a shock of curly red-orange hair, as hopelessly wild and tangled as her daughter's bright mess. This man's scalp was smooth and bare as an egg. He set his goblet down on a low table, and stood to greet her, wiping tears of merriment from his cheeks. His cheeks…

"You said you would never grow a beard." It was a fine beard, too, bright as the hair on his head had once been, and with streaks of white at the sides.

"This?" He stroked his face, still grinning. "This is not a beard, at all. The hair on my head moved south."

And so she found herself, weary and wary and smelling of horse and a long moons' travel, face to face with the lover she had left behind so long ago. He set his wine down and stood, holding his hands out to her. She hesitated.

So much blood.

"Zeina," he said softly. "Welcome home." He took her hands in his, and pulled her close, and kissed her on either cheek. She closed her eyes and tugged her fingers free.

So much stood between them. Murder and worse, betrayal and worse. What carnage they had wrought, the two of them, through the song and dance and the games they played. Here she was, and there he was, and a river of blood flowed between them.

"You look tired," he said. "Tired, and beautiful." He said nothing of her wizard-locks, nor of her scars, nor of the look in her eyes. "Come, sit with me, have a drink of wine. Let us talk."

She let herself be led to the low chairs.

"You look well," she lied awkwardly as she took one of the chairs. Her chair, the one he had made for her, and laughably decorated with a bit of her failed embroidery. It had been a joke between them.

Khurra'an padded over to stretch out by the fire. Wyvernus glanced at him, his face betraying neither surprise nor alarm.

"I look old," Wyvernus corrected her. "Old, and at least as tired as you are. Whatever else we do to each other, let us not begin to lie." He picked up a small brass bell, and rang for a servant. "I had your chair put away the day you left. And I had it brought out this afternoon."

Hafsa Azeina drew in a deep breath, and leaned forward. "Sulema needs healing. She has been bitten—"

"Araid venom. I know." Wyvernus smiled, and picked up his wine, and leaned back into his chair. "I will heal her, of course. She is my daughter, and my only heir. But what of you?"

"What of me?" she asked. "I was promised amnesty. Or was that a lie?"

"I never lie. I promised you amnesty..." A slow grin spread across his features. "But I never promised you freedom."

The trap snapped shut.

TWENTY-SEVEN

Leviathus took the stairs two and three at a time, forcing the door guards to scramble before him and his Draiksguard to jog along, clattering with every step.

He had chosen his own costume that morning with no little care, knowing that this would be the day of their arrival. He wore a tunic of fine white wool embroidered in gold beneath his draikscale armor, battered from use but polished and sharp. The white-and-gold cape of ne Atu flared behind him, and he kept a spring in his step and a wide grin on his face no matter how his legs and his cheeks ached from the effort.

He was tired, bone-tired, sore and worried sick about Sulema, but he was home, and that meant he had to be at his most alert. He wanted nothing more than to deliver his sister into their father's care and collapse at her side with his belly full of food, but the heart's yearnings laid easy paths for an ambush.

He caught the arm of one of his most trusted soldiers, and pulled him close without breaking stride.

"Thaddeus," he said, "send mantids to the members of the Third Circle. I will have them attend me in the Sunset Chamber."

"Yes, ne Atu." Draik Thaddeus touched the pommel of his sword. "Will Mattu Halfmask be attending as well?"

Leviathus raised his eyebrows. The boy was sharp.

"Yes, I believe he should. Good call."

"Shall I send food?" An insolent grin flashed beneath the snarling dragon's helm. "Pemmican perhaps, and stale water?"

"Food of a certes, soldier, but if I so much as smell pemmican I will personally feed your ass to the soldier beetles. Is that clear?"

"Sir!" Thaddeus slapped his leather breastplate and dashed away.

Someone bumped into Leviathus's hip, nearly bowling him over.

The attack has come sooner rather than later, he thought. He drew his short sword and pivoted…

…and stopped short, sword point a scant hand's width from the face of Hafsa Azeina's small apprentice. The boy's chest was heaving, but he did not so much as glance at the weapon.

"The shadowmancer told his apprentice to tell me to tell you," he said, quickly and quite out of breath, "that there is a problem with the horses."

"The horses? What problem is that?"

"Your people are trying to touch them."

"My people are *supposed* to touch them," he explained. "That is what they do. We have grooms to care for our horses, here in the city."

"Your horses. Not our horses. It is death for outlanders to touch the asil."

Leviathus rubbed at his face. He did not have time for hard heads or small minds, not this night. He turned to his third-in-charge.

"Hekates," he sighed, "I need you to go tell my father's grooms to stop trying to touch the Zeerani horses, before someone gets killed and eaten."

Hekates hesitated. "Stablemaster Ippos…"

"Probably looks like a suckling pig to a barbarian who has eaten nothing but pemmican and moldy bread for so long. Take this." He wrenched the signet ring from his finger, and handed it to the Draik. "This ought to shut the old windbag up. The Zeeranim are to be shown around the stables and pastures, and will be taking care of their own animals. Go! *Go!*" Hekates saluted and ducked away, and the boy turned to leave. "No, not you," Leviathus said, and put a hand on Daru's shoulder. "You come with me. Keep your eyes open…"

"And my mouth shut." The boy nodded.

"Good lad. Can you keep up?"

"I… yes."

Leviathus led the boy and the remaining guards through the hallways at a pace that was just short of a jog, and so they arrived at the Sunset Chamber well before the others. The chamber was richly furnished, and designed with an eye toward catching the last rays of sunlight. The western wall to his left was a series of narrow arches left open to the night breeze. On the eastern wall a masterwork of painted tiles depicted a shining Sun Dragon stretching his wings over a wide blue sea. From the ceiling hung a riot of red and gold magelight globes brought all the way from the Forbidden City, and a heavy stone table of white-and-gold marble dominated the center of the room. The far wall was dominated by a white marble fireplace in the shape of a dragon's snarling face, but on this evening no fire was necessary.

Leviathus took his usual seat at the head of the table, his guards in a tight semicircle behind him and Daru seated on a low bench at his side. The servants appeared with food just as members of the Third Circle began to arrive. Mattu Halfmask was first, mismatched eyes snapping and angry in his crocodile's face. Leviathus nodded to the patreons as they entered the chamber. He helped himself to food and wine, and made no move to stand.

Loremaster Rothfaust, as was his custom, was last to arrive. The loremaster had leaves in his wild hair, and in his wild beard, and ink stained his fingertips. He took his place at the end of the bench, gestured to one of the comelier serving girls, who dimpled at him—Loremaster Rothfaust was ever popular with the ladies— and then nearly knocked the ewer of wine from her hands as he spread his arms wide.

"Leviathus, my boy! Word in the kitchens is that you have succeeded in your quest. Our lost lamb, home at last! I have my apprentices setting aside the very best of this year's hatchlings, and I will see to the selection and training of her mantid myself." He took the proffered wine and smiled again at the girl over the lip of his cup. She blushed prettily and looked away. "Every one of us here is delighted to hear you have returned our queen consort to us. The girl—how is she? When might we meet her?"

Leviathus arched a brow at the man. The loremaster had been close to Hafsa Azeina all those years ago, and doubtless had helped effect her escape.

"My sister is at least as delighted to be here as we are to have her,

Loremaster. But she has been ill, and needs to rest." He nodded to Master Healer Santorus, who inclined his head gravely in return.

"The girl needs rest, and quiet." His voice rumbled like far thunder, and he beetled his brow at the other patreons. "And of course, Ka Atu will wish to spend some time alone with his daughter before you lot begin parading her about the city."

"Eh? What is this?" Ezio, his father's Master of Coin, peered suspiciously about the table. "The girl is ill? Is she sickly, then?"

Aasah spoke up from his seat nearest the head of the table. "Sulema *ne Atu*," he spoke the title pointedly, "has grown up these many years among the barbarian Zeeranim. She is as hale as one of our prince's soldiers, here. The girl was injured as she attempted a foolish quest."

Leviathus watched the shadowmancer's face closely, and noted that Mattu did the same. Oddly enough, Yaela shook her head fractionally and a shadow crossed her smooth features.

"The girl was very brave," she said. It was the closest Leviathus had ever heard her come to disagreement with her master. "She battled a lionsnake alone. And killed it."

"Indeed?" Loremaster Rothfaust set down his empty glass. "Well, she will hardly be battling such beasts here in Atualon, where it is perfectly safe."

There was a moment of complete silence at that.

Leviathus cleared his throat. "In the interests of preserving the peace and maintaining the safety of our city," he said, ignoring Rothfaust's snort, "we need to deal with the Zeeranim who have traveled so far to deliver my sister into our care. Many of them are seasoned warriors, while the rest are either highly respected persons or new-made warriors."

"Likely to cause trouble," Mattu added.

"Likely to cause trouble," Leviathus agreed. "We need to host them, feast them, thank them, and send them on their way with full bellies and a suitable reward—and no blood spilled on either side if we can help it."

"No blood, and no seed." Santorus scowled. "We have enough

problems maintaining our population without an explosion of halfbred brats overrunning the city this time next year."

"Master Santorus." Leviathus leaned forward. "The Zeeranim are my sister's people. If you sharpen your tongue against them again, I will have it out."

The master healer spluttered. "I was simply—"

"*Out,* Master. Either hold your tongue, or I shall have Draik Brygus hold it for you."

Santorus bowed his head and remained silent.

"Very good. Now, as to their reward…"

"Salt." Yaela's jade eyes flickered up to meet his, then found her hands again. "Forgive me, ne Atu. I speak out of turn."

"No, no." He waved the apology away. "I would hear your words."

"The magic of the salt jars in Aish Kalumm has begun to fail. The water goes flat in three days and stale in ten."

"If we paid them in salt jars…" Rothfaust mused. "Sweet water is life in the Zeera. Life for life."

"Life for life," agreed the Master of Coin, beaming. "Fifty salt jars should…"

"One thousand."

All heads turned to Mattu.

Ezio spluttered. "One thousand salt jars? One thousand! Do you know how much…"

Mattu held up one hand. "The Zeeranim have raised a daughter of Ka Atu as one of their own. Fed her, clothed her, and by all accounts loved her. At the very least, they seem to have been able to keep the girl alive. Think on this—if the girl is echovete, Ka Atu will have his heir. If the Zeeranim have saved Sa Atu, the Heart of Atualon, they have saved us all. I say anything less than one thousand salt jars is an insult and unworthy of Atualon."

Well, that *was unexpected.* Leviathus pursed his lips and listened to the labored breathing of the boy beside him. "Have some food," he whispered under his breath. "Have some wine. Do not fear—it is well watered." His own pitcher was, in any case. That which he had served to the patreons was less so. The boy reached obediently, if timidly, toward a platter of rainfruit.

"The salt jars are failing everywhere." Rothfaust spoke to the ceiling above them.

Aasah turned to him. "What is this? I have heard no such thing."

"I am fond of the kitchens." The loremaster patted his belly. "So they are fond of me. I hear things. The jars in the kitchens and the market no longer keep water sweet, and the new firings are… flawed. They come from Salar Merraj blackened, or cracked, or malformed, and sometimes they give the water a bitter taste."

"It is true," Ezio mused, "that the price of the jars has risen steeply of late, and there are not as many to be found. The Salarians tell us that production is slowed, or that there has been some damage to the kilns…" He shrugged as the others stared at him. "I thought they merely sought to drive up the price. Those salt folk are notorious thieves and hagglers."

"How much more this gesture will mean to the barbarians, then." Aasah purred. A strange smile played about his mouth, and the stars in his skin glimmered. "One thousand salt jars. I agree." He held up two fingers of his left hand, calling for a vote. The patreons raised their hands one by one, save Ezio.

"It is agreed that Atualon will pay one thousand salt jars to the Zeerani prides, in accordance with law and custom," Leviathus said. He held the Master of Coin with his eyes.

Ezio sighed and bowed his head. "As you say, ne Atu. I do wonder, though, how delivery of such a large shipment of pottery into the Zeera will be managed. The king does not maintain roads farther south than Bayyid Eidtein."

"I have full faith in you and in your magic, Master Ezio."

The old man sighed again. "I was afraid you were going to say that."

Master Santorus tapped his wineglass hesitantly against the table. "If I may…" He fiddled nervously with the fruit on the platter before him. "It occurs to me that the failure of these salt jars may be a symptom of a weakness in atulfah. My blood mages have been complaining to me for some moons now that some of their treatments are less efficacious. Particularly those cures needing a little song and dance." He spread his hands wide. "I have not noticed any difficulties in my own work, and had dismissed the complaints. But now..." He shrugged.

Leviathus turned toward the shadowmancer. "Have you noticed anything amiss?"

Aasah's face was inscrutable. "I have not. But then... my magic comes from a different source than yours. Perhaps it is a regional failing."

"Perhaps it is a passing thing, like the seasons..." Ezio suggested.

Yaela smiled at that, just a flicker of emotion, the flash of teeth beneath still waters.

Rothfaust banged his glass down so hard that Leviathus winced.

"Salt magic is failing. Blood magic is failing. My mantids become wilder and more unmanageable every year, and they darken earlier. I have heard this song so many times that I cannot get it out of my head... can you not hear it? Are you all surdus?"

The loremaster stopped short and sucked his breath in, flushed from his fantastic beard to the roots of his unruly hair. "Ah, Leviathus, I am sorry..."

"*Are* we all deaf?" Leviathus held his hand up for silence. "No, wait. I shall have to think on this some more. My father tells me that more and more children are born without ability to hear the song every year. Loremaster, what do your books and scrolls have to say on this matter? What songs do your little mantids sing to you? Surely these things have happened before."

A triangular head no bigger than a man's thumb peeked out from behind the loremaster's ear at the word "mantid," and cheeped hopefully. Rothfaust handed a tidbit to his little pet. If Leviathus did not know the loremaster better, he would have said the man was stalling.

"Well, speak up," urged Mattu, cracking a pomegranate open so that the juices ran down his forearms like blood. "You have so many words, surely you can spare a few for us."

Leviathus leaned forward, forearms on the table. "Loremaster Rothfaust," he asked, "in all your readings, have you found mention of such a thing as the failure of magic? Has such a thing happened before in the history of Atualon?"

"I have found mention of such occurrences in one book. Only one book," he held his hand up as if he would apologize, "but it describes our situation exactly. Blood magic, water magic, salt and song, all seemed to lose their strength. Like the weakness in the limbs of a sickly child."

Leviathus heard Daru's sharply indrawn breath, but a quick glance at the boy's face showed nothing. Loremaster Rothfaust was not an unkind man. Why would he say such a thing?

"No, no," the loremaster mused, stroking his beard with one hand, and gesturing with his wine cup with the other. "Not a weakness, precisely, not an illness... a flicker. Like a torch in an airless chamber. The flicker of light before it goes out completely, and leaves you in darkness."

There was a second moment of silence. Two in one council meeting—that itself was probably a historical moment.

"What book?" Aasah asked. He leaned forward, eyes like blue fire in their intensity. "What book, what scroll, describes these things?"

Rothfaust was silent.

Leviathus put his hands on the table before him and leaned forward. "What book, Loremaster?"

"*The Dragon Cycle*."

"Heresy!" spluttered Ezio. "Rubbish! Nonsense! That book does not even exist!"

"Bad science!" Santorus roared. He looked as if he might fall victim to an apoplexy. "Bad science!"

"*The Dragon Cycle*," Mattu repeated. "You are telling us that you believe these things are happening because the dragon is preparing to wake after a thousand years trapped in slumber? Is this your claim?" He leaned back and took a careful sip of wine. "If this is the case, I suppose we should take emergency measures to prevent that from happening. Pray tell us, Master Rothfaust, how exactly *does* one convince a dragon not to wake?"

Yells of "Bad science!" and "Preposterous!" shook the chamber walls.

"I am telling you that the only book I have found which refers to such a pattern of events is *The Dragon Cycle*," Rothfaust replied, unperturbed. "That does not mean you need to make an ass of yourself, Mattu Halfmask."

Ezio choked on his wine, and the master healer pounded him on the back. Daru was as still as a mouse in a room full of cats.

"Patreons, please," Leviathus held up both hands. "Let us hear the loremaster out."

Rothfaust shrugged. "I am telling you what a book says. What the words say, and the stories, and the songs. Something is happening in this world, do you not feel it? Do you not hear it? The magics are failing. Women and infants die in childbirth, our crops fail, and our fishing fleets return with empty nets—when they return at all. The daeborn gather in numbers greater than at any time since Davvus, and someone has been calling up bonelords in the desert. I have heard on three separate occasions that the Great Hunt has been seen in the east—"

"The Great Hunt! Bonelords and dragons!" Santorus threw his hands up in the air. "Rumors and stories and myths! We are trying to govern a kingdom, and you bring us children's stories, Loremaster."

"All truth is found in stories," Rothfaust insisted. "Where else?"

Leviathus was too tired to watch old men hurl wine-cups and insults. He brought his own cup down upon the table, harder than he had intended. A small chip flew off the stem and flicked against his cheek, narrowly missing an eye.

"Masters," he said, "Patreons. Esteemed shadowmancer. I have been riding a long while, and I am weary. We have a great deal to discuss, but perhaps some other time?" He softened the tone with his best and most disarming smile. "I would dearly love a bath and a bed. Let us take a while to ponder these things, and perhaps our loremaster may pursue this line of research further." Rothfaust nodded.

"Excellent," Leviathus concluded. "I can assure you, I will take these concerns directly to my father... once I have seen the baths."

Mattu coughed discreetly. "Perhaps not tonight, ne Atu? I believe your father is entertaining company at the moment."

Leviathus frowned. Mattu made it sound as if his father was...

Oh.

Oh.

The last rays of sun filtered in through the dragonglass columns, lighting the room with sparks of gold and bronze. The silk lanterns from Khanbul glowed softly as Akari Sun Dragon plunged into the sea in search of his long-lost love, and behind him, the fireplace roared to life. Leviathus stood, smothering a yawn, and the patreons rose with him.

"Very good, then, let us adjourn, and continue these discussions another time." The servants filed in and began removing the foodstuffs. Leviathus kept a genial smile on his face as the rest of the Third Circle—having been rather abruptly dismissed—rose, bowed to their prince, and left the chamber.

All of them, that is, except Mattu Halfmask. He remained behind, even as the servants brought in rags and buckets and began scrubbing the stone table.

"Might I beg a moment of your time?" he asked. "A new troupe of fools has just rolled in to one of my establishments, and I think you would find their tale most... illuminating."

Leviathus was too tired to play his cousin's games. "Later, perhaps."

Mattu stepped close, so close that Leviathus's sword hand twitched. "Ne Atu. You really need to see this. Come with me." He glanced down at Daru, and gave a mocking little bow. "Do bring your guest. I am sure this will be of interest to his mistress, as well."

"Halfmask..."

Mattu reached for the hilt of his sword, and drew...

Leviathus drew as well—and found himself guarding against a bright spray of silk flowers. Mattu laughed and tossed the bouquet to Daru, who plucked it neatly from the air.

"Oh, come along now. I mean you no harm, O favored son. My sister *adores* you, for whatever reason, and I would show my true face before I ever caused her a moment's sorrow. Besides," he winked at Daru, who stared solemnly over the flowers, "I would never harm a child. Shall we?" He turned and walked from the room, whistling. After a moment's hesitation, Leviathus sheathed his sword and followed, with Daru at his heels and the Draiksguard close behind.

They left the palace through a low door most commonly used by merchants and kitchen-lads. Mattu drew his hood up so that only his mask peered out, but Leviathus left his face bare.

They walked quickly down an alley between two rows of well-appointed merchants' houses. The bright light spilling from colored-glass windows onto pale cobblestones gave their path a merry look. It was time for a late supper, and the smells of roasting pig and fish stew—and of some lemony dish from one house—reminded Leviathus that one light meal after months' worth of travel was not a sufficient homecoming.

He knew this alley well, had spent many an evening with friends in these elite establishments. Mattu led the way up some stairs and into a well-lit bathhouse. The guards who had followed them remained in the street.

"I did not need to come this far for a bath," he grumbled. "I do have a tub in my rooms."

"And a girl waiting to help you," Mattu agreed as he held the door open with a mocking flourish. "I know, I sent her there myself. I must warn you, though, Ginna is a spy in my sister's employ. Why do you think I am so close with my own... business?" He let the heavy doors bang shut behind them. "I have given my staff each a copper and the night off, save old Douwa. At her age she has no more need of coppers than she has of gossip." He laughed.

They shed their clothing. Leviathus threw Daru a towel, which he wrapped about himself with a grateful look, and they walked down the steps, through the proud enameled columns, and into a blinding cloud of steam.

Leviathus tensed, half expecting an attack as Mattu led them around the pit of steaming rocks and toward the figures seated on the wooden benches at the far side of the room. As they stepped closer, and the figures resolved themselves through the fragrant steam, he stopped dead in his tracks. He did not recognize the youth with the salt-clan tattoos, though the boy seemed familiar, and neither did he know the older Zeerani man, but he knew the woman who sat between them. Knew her, and could not imagine the reason for her presence.

"Istaza Ani." He bowed, nonplussed. "I had not expected to find you here." Nor had he expected to see her naked. For all her years, the woman had a startlingly fine figure, lean and muscled and curved like a girl's. He tried not to stare.

"Impressive." The youthmistress smirked at him. "Your scar, I mean. A man is so much more attractive once he has a few marks on his hide, do you not agree, Askander?" The middle-aged man beside her, lean and scarred as an old stallion, snorted a laugh without ever opening his eyes.

"A reminder never to get too close to a sea-bear." Leviathus resisted the urge to touch the ugly marks that nearly bisected his torso, and took the bench farthest from the Zeeranim. "I had thought you were to remain behind."

"That was the plan," she agreed. "Plans change."

"Istaza Ani." Daru chose to sit with the desert folk. "Sulema has woken. She is weak and tired… but the Dragon King has agreed to heal her."

Istaza Ani smiled at the boy. "I had heard, thank you, Daru."

"Will you tell us *now* why you have come?" Mattu Halfmask asked. The sweat beaded in his hair and dripped down his mask, causing it to look as if the crocodile shed tears. "I am pleased that you sought me out in the market, but I am afraid I cannot bear the suspense a moment longer."

The older Zeerani man—Askander—opened his eyes then, and

gave Mattu a look like a hawk sizing up its prey. Istaza Ani placed a hand on the man's thigh. She glanced at the salt youth, and at the half-masked man, and then shrugged and reached for a bundle of leather at her side.

"I found this in the Bones of Eth, at the very site where Sulema was... wounded. I had thought to bring it to Hafsa Azeina, but the idiots at the gate would not let me see her and I thought it might be rude to kill them."

"One does not simply walk into Atukos and demand to speak with the queen consort." Mattu laughed.

"Ha. She squats in the sand just like any woman. I would know." Ani unwrapped the bundle. "She would not thank me if I turned back without first giving her *this*."

The cloth fell away to reveal a blade, a wicked thing made for a wicked purpose. Red as blood, carved all over with tiny human skulls, it had a golden spider at one end and a blade meant for stripping hide from flesh at the other.

Mattu grimaced to look upon it. The salt-clan lad reacted even more strongly, scuttling away from it as from a scorpion exposed to the sunlight, mouth open and eyes wide and white as boiled eggs.

"Interesting." Leviathus leaned in, though wary of touching the fell thing. "A nasty-looking weapon. You say you found this in the bones of something? Where that lionsnake attacked Sulema? I am afraid I do not see a connection."

"The Bones of Eth," murmured Mattu Halfmask. He stared at the knife. "A place of ill reputation, to be sure. May I?"

Ani hesitated, and then placed the thing upon his outstretched hands, wrappings and all.

"I would not touch it, if I were you. It feels... wrong."

"I have no intention of touching it." Mattu handled the knife as if it were a venomous snake, and very much alive. "Exquisite craftsmanship. It turns the stomach, to be sure, but it is beautifully made. Look here, you can see tiny hairs on the spider's legs, as if it had been crawling about one day and then *poof*! Turned to gold. And the eyes." He turned the blade, careful not to let it brush his skin. "The eyes seem to follow you. I do not think I would sleep well with this in my bedchamber." He returned it with a shudder. "Horrible thing."

"It is horrible," the youthmistress agreed, "but do you know what it is? What it is meant to do? This is not a weapon meant for combat, but it hardly seems a bauble."

"I know what it is," Daru whispered. His eyes were enormous in his thin face, and he shrank a little as they all turned to look at him. "That is a blade of Eth. I saw a drawing of one once. In a book." He swallowed.

"Let me guess." Mattu's voice was dry. "It was a book you were not supposed to be reading."

Daru shook his head.

"I have heard of such a thing, as well." The tattooed youth looked as if he wished himself far away. "Very bad. Very bad." He shook his head. "Chop it up. Throw it away. Throw it into the sea. It is evil."

"A thing cannot be evil, though it may be used for an evil purpose." Leviathus frowned. "In any case, I would like to take this to my father. If someone is playing at Eth-worship, Ka Atu needs to know about it."

Istaza Ani shook her head. "You will give this to Hafsa Azeina. She is waiting for it."

Leviathus raised his brows. "My father—"

"She is right." Mattu raised his hands as Leviathus turned toward him. "Wait, cousin, hear me out. If you take this to Ka Atu, he is going to give it to his shadowmancer for study. And Aasah…"

"…is a priest of Illindra," Leviathus finished. "Consort of Eth."

"He was born and raised in Quarabala." Mattu raised a hand and adjusted his mask. "You know what the priests of Eth did to his people. If he suspects that the cult of Eth has arisen from the ashes…"

"He would tear Atualon apart to find them."

"He would tear the world apart," corrected Mattu Halfmask. "Shadowmancy is powerful magic, and Aasah would not be the king's shadowmancer if he were not a dangerous man."

"I will take the blade to Hafsa Azeina," Leviathus decided, and accepted it carefully from the Zeerani woman. "If she believes these people are threatening my sister, she will find them."

"And eat their hearts," Ani agreed. "And use their guts to string her lyre." The woman leaned back, breathed the steam in with a smile, and twined fingers with the man sitting next to her. "Your stonemasons should build such baths as this in Aish Kalumm. For the Mothers, of course. A fine gift for the people from Atualon." She smiled, eyes half-closed.

"Ah," Leviathus said, as he wrapped the knife again and sat it down on the bench. "As it happens, Atualon will be making a gift to your people. To express our gratitude for keeping my sister safe, all these years."

Askander glanced toward Ani from the corner of his eyes. The youthmistress had lost her smile.

"There is no need for gifts," she said, rather stiffly. "Sulema is a daughter of the pride."

"Of course," Leviathus agreed. "But she is my sister as well, and we are… I am… delighted to find her well and happy. You have no idea what this means to us. What it means to me."

The woman scowled and said nothing.

The man at her side brought her hand to his lips. "Their ways are not our ways," he reminded her gently. "He means no insult. Let the boy make his gesture."

"Oh, very well." Her scowl darkened, but she relented. "What value would you place on one Ja'Akari, then?"

"Ani…" Askander warned.

"One thousand salt jars." Leviathus smiled. The salt-clan youth squawked and nearly fell from the bench.

The three Zeeranim stared at one another in open-mouthed shock. It was Askander who finally spoke.

"One. Thousand."

"One thousand salt jars," Leviathus agreed.

"You cannot know…" Ani swallowed. "You cannot know what this means to us."

"Life." He smiled. "Life for life. You cannot know how precious my sister is to me, so I suppose that makes us even."

Ani looked at him for a long moment, and then slowly inclined her head. "I must apologize, Leviathus ap Wyvernus ne Atu. I have misjudged you."

Not the first time that has happened, he thought, but said only, "It may take some time for us to complete such an order. I understand that there have been difficulties in production lately. As for delivery..."

"I believe I can help with that." The tattooed youth grinned, bright teeth in a dark face full of mischief. "I apologize, ne Atu, for we have not been properly introduced. I am Soutan Mer ne Ninianne il Mer. I believe we have met, only," and he winked, "never under such circumstances as these."

"Son of the Lady of the Lake." Leviathus laughed. "Of course! I did not recognize you without an angry husband shaking his fist in your face. I hardly dare ask how you ended up involved in all of this. What was it this time? Or should I ask, *who* was it this time?"

"You should probably not ask. There I was, naked in an olive tree..."

"Again?"

"Again—"

"As fascinating as this is," Mattu Halfmask interrupted, "the hour grows long, and we should not risk discovery any longer. My staff will be returning to their duties soon, and it would be best if we were not here."

"You are right, of course." Leviathus collected the fell knife, and the wickedness of the thing dampened his mood. "You will have to tell me your story another time, Soutan Mer. If you would escort our friends to quarters here in the Merchant's Circle...? Thank you. Atukos is in your debt."

Istaza Ani yawned and stood, and laughed when the Atualonian men made themselves busy looking anywhere but at her breasts. "I should not linger, in any case. Inna'hael is outside the city walls, hunting, but I cannot guarantee that he will only take four-legged prey. Best we return to the prides as soon as we may. I had hoped to see Sulema…"

"I can bring you to the palace tomorrow, if that would be acceptable." Soutan Mer glanced at Leviathus, and received a nod. "I can arrange the sale and delivery of your salt jars as well, and maybe even convince my mother to give you a fair price. Fairer than is her wont, at any rate." He shrugged. "As many times as she has threatened to toss me into the Salt Lake, still she is rather fond of me, and I dare say she will appreciate my return. You desert folk seem to have a gift for returning lost things. Shall we?" He nodded to Leviathus, and left with the Zeeranim.

"Was that so wise?" Mattu Halfmask asked, rising from the bench.

"We had agreed that the gift was appropriate."

"I am not speaking of pottery, ne Atu. I am asking whether it was wise to advise our enemies that they should go home and prepare for war. That is what they will do, you know, once they have thought about the cult of Eth and what that might mean."

"Enemies? They are not our enemies." Leviathus frowned. "I had thought to seek an alliance with them."

"Oh, by all means, seek an alliance. Treat with them, trade with them, breed with them, if you feel so inclined. Atu knows, we need the children. But never forget this, Leviathus ap Wyvernus, ne Atu. We are the People of the Dragon." He smiled, and tears ran down the crocodile's face. "The world is our enemy. What is that word they use in the desert? *Ehuani?*"

"There is beauty in truth," Leviathus agreed softly. The knife felt heavy in his hands. "*Ehuani.*"

The boy Daru gave a sudden shudder. He was so quiet, Leviathus had half-forgotten he was there. "Are you all right, child? Forgive me for keeping you up, I am sure you are…"

The boy looked at him, eyes wide and wild and dilated. "It is Sulema," he said. "They are taking her to the Dragon King."

"Now?"

Daru nodded. "Dreamshifter says you should come, right away."

Mattu Halfmask had an odd smile on his face. "You had best hurry."

"Hurry?" Leviathus frowned. "Are you expecting trouble?"

"Trouble?" Halfmask laughed, odd eyes glinting. "Your father, Hafsa Azeina, and that hot-headed sister of yours, all together for the first time in years... what could possibly go wrong?"

Leviathus grabbed a towel and ran.

TWENTY-EIGHT

The baths of Atualon, like everything else in this strange place, were so big, so magnificent, that neither the eye nor the mind could take it all in at once. It was, she thought, like the tale of Zula Din eating the lionsnake. Too big, too much. She ducked her head under the water—*so much water*—and resolved to conquer this strange new world as the hero of old had conquered her deadly meal—one bite at a time.

A chamber just for bathing, a pool of running water like a slice of river picked up and set in stone just so one person could wash away the dirt. It was wasteful, it was wonderful, and a little ridiculous. The blue and gold and red tiles, cut and placed just so, made a pretty picture of water beasts playing beneath the waves, and every other surface seemed to be of dragonglass or silver or some other precious thing. A statue of a woman sat at the end of the pool, one foot dipped into the water, a pile of linen towels and little bowls of soft soap cradled in her lap.

A lifetime of this, she thought, *would make me as soft and useless as that soap. But I would smell very nice.* How her sword-sisters would laugh to see it—and how much more pleasant it would be to share this with them, these bowls of fruit and bread and soft ripe cheese, a skin of *avra*, a horn of *usca*, a pretty man or three to liven things up. It was a pleasant thing to soak away the stink of long travel, but she missed the company of her sword-sisters.

Sulema was fumbling at her braids with her left hand, cursing roundly under her breath, when Saskia walked in. She, too, was freshly bathed, her braids still damp, and her eyes were big as a digger-owl's as she looked about the chamber.

"*Ai yeh*," she breathed, "all this for you? You could hold a *sharib* in here." Her voice echoed oddly in the long, tiled hall, and she stepped forward to test the waters with a toe. "The water is *warm*. Ooo, the Mothers would love such a thing, can you imagine?"

"The Mothers are welcome to it," Sulema answered. "My fingers look like dried dates."

"They sent me to fetch you. As if I were an errand-boy." Saskia tossed her head. "But it is good that these outlanders do not see you looking so weak and pale. These wounds should have healed by now, and have you been eating? Here, let me help you with your hair." She knelt by the edge of the pool and began undoing the tight braids.

"Thank you," Sulema said, and she meant it. "This business of having one good arm is horse shit. Dreamshifter tells me that this Ka Atu will be able to draw the shadows from my wounds, and then I will heal faster." She wriggled her fingers at the end of her cast, wishing she could take the blasted thing off and scratch. The itch was worse than the pain, sometimes. "It has been so long since I danced the forms, I will likely fall on my face."

Saskia finger-combed Sulema's hair loose, and began to scrub at her hair with the soft soap. "He may heal the bones, *ehuani*, but will he be able to fix all that is wrong with you?"

Sulema went very still. Her mouth wanted to ask, *What do you mean?* but her warrior's heart knew that the question would be a lie.

"You cannot hide such things from your sword-sisters, Sulema Ja'Akari." Saskia's voice was soft, the words heavy with regret. "You do not sleep. When you do, you cry out with nightmares. I, myself, have watched three times as you nearly fell from your saddle. Waking, you are lost in dreams, and your eyes move back and forth, watching things that are not there. I have seen this."

"Everyone knows?"

"Only your sword-sisters, *ehuani*. Never would we betray you." Saskia dunked Sulema's head under the water once, twice, three times, rinsing the soap from her hair, and then began the task of braiding. "But, Sulema, you cannot be broken and remain Ja'Akari. You know this."

"I know this. You worry about nothing."

Saskia said nothing, but helped her from the pool. Sulema snatched up a towel and dried herself awkwardly with one hand, waving away the other girl's offer of assistance. *The Dragon King will heal me,* she thought, stubbornly. *He owes me that much. He will heal me, and I will ride with the Ja'Akari once more.*

But she did not speak the words, for fear they would taste like a lie.

Dressed in clean warrior's garb—not the clothing that had been laid out for her, silly stuff fit for Mothers or invalids—Sulema followed Saskia through a warren of wide hallways, with high, arching ceilings and rounded doorways set with heavy wooden doors.

Sulema delighted in the doors, the narrow windows of colored glass, the bright tiled murals, but most of all the dragonglass fortress itself. Though the black stone seemed opaque, it glittered in the early sunlight and seemed to glow as she passed, lit from within as she padded silently behind Saskia.

Welcome home, the walls seemed to say.

I am just visiting, she assured them.

She ignored as best she could the crowd of people who followed in her wake like serpents behind a fishing-boat. Dragon-faced guards like those who followed Leviathus around, women in bright robes that dragged on the stone floors behind them, men in short kilts that showed a shocking amount of leg, and a girl in a funny hat who clutched a large wooden box and panted in her efforts to keep up with the adults. Sulema had to pee, but she had no idea where the latrine pits might be dug, or how to get outside, and she had no desire to relieve herself in front of an audience.

"Where is Atemi?" she asked instead.

"There are some nice pastures here, on a low hill. Most of our warriors are with them," Saskia replied. "These outlanders keep trying to touch our asil… and no person in her right mind would want to sleep under so much stone. It feels as if the entire mountain might come down on us at any moment." She glanced up at the high ceiling with a shudder.

"I am sorry to be such trouble." Truly, it shamed her that so many would leave their homes and their lives just so that she might meet her father and be healed. One warrior did not merit disruption of an entire pride.

Saskia shot a sympathetic look over her shoulder. "You would do the same for any of us."

Ehuani.

They came at last to a pair of wooden doors tall enough for a wyvern to enter without ducking its head, and a pair of gold-clad soldiers in short kilts and helms more ornate than any she had yet seen bowed them into what seemed a very great hall. A long carpet of red and thread-of-gold, flanked by the Draiksguard, led to a high dais where Sulema's mother was seated beside a bald man in simple robes of white and gold, a thin circlet of gold upon his brow.

"Good luck," Saskia whispered.

"He is just a man," Sulema whispered back. She did not want to face this alone.

"I fear no king of men," her sword-sister answered, "but your mother scares the lionsnakes out of me. I think I hear Istaza calling my name." She slipped away.

"Ah, I am not too late."

Sulema turned toward the newly familiar voice, unable to fully conceal her relief. "Leviathus!" Her brother stood beside her, damp-haired and looking as if he had dressed in haste, flanked by a panting and disheveled Daru. *Thank you,* she mouthed to her mother's apprentice. He shrugged and blushed.

"You do not think I would leave you to face this walk alone, do you?" Leviathus offered his arm.

The way was not as long as it had seemed, with an ally by her side. As Sulema approached the dais, her mother and the man seated next to her both rose. Hafsa Azeina stepped down to meet them, her face, as usual, unreadable. She took Sulema by the hand—her uninjured hand, and when was the last time she had done that?— then turned to face the man who stood above them all.

Sulema held her breath. Judging by the room's silence, she was not the only one.

The man descended slowly, never taking his eyes from her face.

Those eyes, Sulema thought, and her heart was pierced through. *I know those eyes.*

"Ka Atu," her mother said in a voice that betrayed nothing, "This is Sulema an Wyvernus ne Atu. Your daughter."

The man stood before Sulema. He reached a hand to her face. He touched her.

"Of course she is," he said. He pulled her away from her mother, and her brother, and he enfolded her in a warm embrace. "My daughter." Then he held her at arm's distance, hands strong on her shoulders, face wreathed in a warm smile and a beard as red as her own hair. "My daughter!"

The room erupted in cheers, and for the second time in as many moons Sulema saw fear in her mother's eyes.

Sulema had been walking forever, ever since she had broken free from the web. How long ago was that? Moons, years, lifetimes? The path she walked stretched out farther than she could see or imagine with her tiny human mind.

Khutlani, child, your mouth is too small to speak of such things.

The sharp rocks cut her feet. They were bleeding, and the path behind was slick with her blood. But the path before her was stained red too, and Sulema was sure she had never been this way before. Had she? She knelt to touch the ground, and as she did so realized that the path was carpeted with the red robes of battle-mages.

Baidun Daiel. Sleepless. Soulless.

The thought was not her own, and she looked about for its source.

Azra'hael?

That one is long gone, the voice chided. *Gone down the Lonely Road. Do you not see his tracks?*

Sulema pushed aside one of the red cloaks that obscured the path, and jerked her hand away, startled, to see the gold mask beneath. Masks… thousands of them, laid side by side, end to end, like cobblestones of gold. Though no eyes stared at her from behind the masks, though they had only a mere suggestion of a mouth, she was certain that behind each was a person, screaming forever. She tugged the cape back, stood, and walked on, trying not to think of the faces beneath her feet. The road wound ever on and on, and she had to see it to the end, no matter how it was paved.

Then he was there, just a few steps before her, golden cloak rippling in a breeze she could not feel, hands clasped behind his back. He spoke without turning.

"Are you my daughter?"

"Are you my father?" she countered. "Truly my father?" She closed the distance between them, every step an agony.

"Tell me, child. What do you see?"

Sulema took her place at his side, and the breath caught in her throat. She stood at the very summit of Atukos, at the mouth of the living mountain. Below her, before her, stretched a great lake of magesilver, still and pretty as a mirror made of dreams, so wide that the far shore was a jagged shadow. The hot breath of a living dragon poured up toward them, bubbles breaking the surface and lingering like misty little ghosts dancing upon the bright surface.

"Tell me, child," he said again. "What do you see?"

She looked down. Clouds were reflected upon the surface of the lake, and trees, and the exposed flesh of Atukos. The sun swam overhead, but though its warmth lay upon her shoulder like a hand, she saw nothing of herself, not so much as a shadow.

"Where am I?" she asked, puzzled. "Father, where am I?"

Akari Sun Dragon stared back at her. His eyes were molten bronze and copper, and his teeth swords.

"You are home, Ja'Akari," he answered, and Sulema screamed as his breath melted the flesh from her bones.

The dragon seized her in his great talons, and Sulema could feel the bonds that held her to the world, to the people, to life, snapping and withering at his touch. She screamed again as he raised her high above his head and tossed her back down the mountain. The red cloaks were burned away, and the screaming gold faces rose to meet her.

She fell.

She died.

"Is it done?" Her mother's voice, cool as the river on a hot day.

"It is done." Akari answered with the voice of a man. "I have loosened the Araids' hold on her and frozen the venom within her blood. She should recover much of her strength now, with rest and care and a great deal of food."

"Will she ever truly heal?"

"I cannot be certain. I was able to put the Arachnist's magic into a deep sleep, but it lies dormant within her blood."

"When can I take her home?"

"Oh, my dear." The man's voice was wearied beyond the reach of sleep, but he laughed. "Did you not hear the dragon speak? Sulema is home. You are both home."

Sleep now, came the voice of Akari. *Little Ja'Akari. I am well pleased with you. Sleep.*

The moons chased each other round and round the Web of Illindra, and she slept.

The first thing Sulema felt was her head—it felt as if the dragon was trying to hatch from inside her skull. The second thing she noticed was that her skin itched as if she had fallen asleep on a nest of ants. The third was that Akari Sun Dragon was prying at her eyes. She opened them.

"How do you feel?" The voice swam up through her mind like the bubbles of dragon's breath.

"*Ung,*" she answered, and made a face. Her mouth tasted as if something had crawled in there and died.

"Here." A cup was pressed into her hands, and she drank. Coffee.

"I love you," she croaked, blinking a crust of hard sleep from her eyes. Then she saw him. *The Dragon King.* "Oh…"

"I love you too, Daughter." His smile was fond, and mischievous, and made him look years younger. "How do you feel?"

"Like the sheep's head in a game of aklashi. After it has been given to the vash'ai to eat. And shat on by a horse." Then she realized to whom she was speaking, and her face flushed hot with chagrin.

"Ah, you are your mother's daughter." The Dragon King laughed, a great full laugh from the belly, and slapped his knees. "Delightful girl." He held out a hand, but stopped short of touching her. "Do you mind?"

She shrugged. Was she allowed to say no to a king?

He touched her arm, now free of its cast, and then the pulse at her throat, and finally his fingers pressed down upon her forehead. It made her feel dizzy for a moment, and stars danced before her eyes, but when he drew back, the king—her father—looked well pleased.

"Very good," he told her. "Better than I had hoped. You will need food, and you must drink as much water as your belly will hold, and sleep as much as you can."

"I have not been able to… oh." She *had* slept. And she had dreamed.

"As I thought. Your sleep had been stolen from you, and your dreams, and replaced with… well. There will be time for that later, when you have had a chance to rest, and to eat. And perhaps another cup of coffee?"

"Yes, *please*," she said, and he laughed.

"Oh, you *are* your mother's daughter. And mine, too. My daughter." He picked up her hand and cradled it against his chest. "Tell me about yourself. Tell me everything." His blue eyes were warm as an oasis at midsun, and as welcoming. "I want to know my beautiful daughter."

The dragonglass walls glowed with warmth and welcome.

The trap snapped shut.

TWENTY-NINE

The dreamshifter had been fighting with the outland patreons again. Daru could see it in the way she let her hair fall in a tangled mass over her eyes, and in the quick, angry movements of her hands as she stripped flesh and tendon from a large bone.

He had seen her do this before, return from Shehannam with bone or hair or hide, loops of purple-gray intestines, skulls with flesh and fur still attached. The skulls were the worst—some of them came from *people*. Hafsa Azeina would strip the bones clean, and then close them up in a box filled with sand and flesh-beetles, and later she would boil them and do… other things.

Whenever she returned with these things, he knew, somebody had died in their sleep.

She turned the bone over in her hands, and he saw the ball-end of a leg bone. Daru touched the little bird-skull flute tucked away in his sleeve, and ducked his head in shame. He was her apprentice, and he should be learning how to do the things she did, but he did not want to kill anything.

A movement caught at the corner of his vision and he looked up. Khurra'an was watching him, watching and twitching the end of his tail. The big cat let his mouth drop open and the light from the fireplace glinted off the gold bands of his tusks as his pink tongue lolled out and he slowly, deliberately, licked his chops. Daru imagined that he heard giggling among the shadows in the corner.

"Khurra'an," Hafsa Azeina said aloud and without looking up, "stop." The big cat grunted and closed his mouth, but the shadows still peered out from behind his eyes.

Daru scooted to sit closer to the fire, where the shadows were fewest. The rooms that had been given to Hafsa Azeina were huge, big enough to house a number of people, but there were only the two of them and Khurra'an. There was a sleeping room for the dreamshifter, and a washing room with tubs and basins, even a tiny room for doing... *that*. Daru wondered where the poop and the dirty water went, but had not yet worked up the nerve to ask the outland servants.

Daru had his own little room, all to himself, a soft mattress piled high with woolen blankets and a heavy dark brown fur with claws and tail still attached, and a wooden table and chair, and a little colored-glass oil lantern. He would have preferred to curl up in there and look at the map of the city Sulema's brother had given him, but the vash'ai stretched out in front of the doorway and mocked him with his wicked eyes.

"Dreamshifter." She looked up at him, gold eyes snapping, and he swallowed. "Are you hungry? I could bring you some food."

"*Maashukri*. Do you know the way to the kitchens?"

He nodded.

"Mmmf. Meat, bread, water or wine. Nothing spiced, nothing sweet. Have them send up a leg of something for Khurra'an." She caressed the bone in her hands. Daru tried so hard not to see it that his eyes hurt. "You need to eat, as well. You are getting too skinny again. The Mothers will not thank me if I let you fade away." Her mouth curled up, and he knew that she meant for him to laugh, so he chuckled obediently.

She really did try to be kind, sometimes.

"Yes, Dreamshifter." He stood, and tried not to flinch when Khurra'an stretched, extending sharp black claws as long as Daru's hands. "Stop it," he told the vash'ai, and burned with shame as his voice quavered.

"On second thoughts," Hafsa Azeina said absently, tearing a tendon from the bone with her fingernails, "have the kitchens send up a whole pig instead of a leg. Send a servant up with my food instead of bringing it yourself. You should not return until Khurra'an has gorged."

302

"Yes, Dreamshifter." He bowed, and skirted around the edge of the room. When the cold wall at his back gave way to an arched doorway, Daru turned and fled.

There were fewer shadows in the hallways. The walls glowed gently, lit from within, a glow that brightened at his presence and faded as he passed. Hafsa Azeina had told him that this was one of the properties of the dragonglass palace, and that if Ka Atu were absent, or died without an heir, the palace would go dark and they would need to use torches. She also said that the lights had been much brighter in years past.

For his part, Daru was just happy for anything that might keep the shadows at bay. He flitted down the halls, counting the turns on his fingers—left at the unicorn tapestry, left and down at the big pot full of flowers, left again at the little square door with sheaves of wheat painted in gold all round the lintel, then right, then down a steep flight of stairs. That last bit was always full of shadows, and they pulled at his feet as he passed, so he held tight to the balustrade and fairly flew down them, and then—*pop!*— into the big, bright room crowded with tables and benches, and with the kitchens at its far end.

This room was Daru's favorite so far. It was round, and boasted a high, arched ceiling set with beams of pale wood smudged from all the smoke and grease, hot and bright from the fires and the ovens and the cooks' colorful patchwork aprons. A whole pig was roasting on one spit, and another spit was strung with ducks like beads on a necklace, and round loaves of rich dark bread were stacked higher than his head in an alcove next to the ovens.

Daru watched the greasy smoke rise up and disappear through a hole in the ceiling. He wondered where the smoke went, and if someone had rooms over the kitchens, and whether the smells made them hungry all the time or if they got tired of it after a while. He thought it might be nice to be a cook, though he felt sorry for the little pigs in their wheels, trotting and trotting and turning the meats round. He hoped they had not known the pig that was roasting.

Even at this late hour, there were people at the tables. A knot of Draiksguard in their red-and-white robes sat at one, their grand dragon-faced helms propped on the table or benches beside them. A bunch of pretty women sat at another table pretending not to notice the soldiers. Other outlanders were scattered all about, but there were none of the red-robed Baidun Daiel staring at him through their blank gold masks.

He heaved a sigh of relief and trotted toward a group of Zeeranim in a far corner. They stood out like hunting cats in a herd of goats.

The people looked grim-faced and sober, and Daru could see shadows clinging to the edge of the group even in this bright light. Someone had died, someone they knew.

I hope somebody died in an accident, and not in their sleep, he thought.

Someone knocked into him from behind and sent him sprawling across the wooden floor. He hit his chin and bit his tongue, and a flower of red pain blossomed in his mouth.

"Oh! Oh, I am so sorry!" Struggling to his feet, Daru turned his head to see a plump and pretty girl. She was not much older than himself, he guessed, though considerably taller and already round as a woman. Her aprons were a riot of color her face was screwed up in embarrassment. Daru tasted blood in his mouth, but he did not want to spit in front of her, so he swallowed it instead. "Are you all right?" she asked.

He shrugged and brushed at his tunic, checked to make sure his whistle had not been crushed. His face felt as hot as the spit-fires. "I am fine," he muttered, "thank you."

"You are one of the visitors, are you not?" She smiled wide, standing too close and fluttering her hands over his clothes and hair like one of the child-minders. He shrugged away from her, but she followed him with her big eyes and her dimples. "Are you sure you are all right? I am sorry if I hurt you. I did not see you there, you are so skinny! Did you really travel with the Heart of Atualon? They say your people are all warriors—is the Heart a warrior? You look hungry—are you hungry? Can I get you anything?"

"I am… I ah… ah…" Daru froze like a tarbok caught in a cat's stare. "Hafsa Azeina sent me for some food. And a pig."

"Some food *and* a pig?" Her grin widened, and Daru took a step back. "Is a pig not food, then? Do you want a live pig, or a dead one? Perhaps that one?" She jabbed her finger toward the pig roasting over the fire. "Surely you do not mean to eat the whole thing. You are so skinny! You speak Atualonian well. Are you a warrior, too?"

A heavy hand clamped over Daru's shoulder. He squeaked and jumped half out of his skin. The girl's eyes went huge and she grabbed her aprons and bent almost double. Daru looked up and into the half-masked face of an owl. The man's eyes crinkled at him, though his mouth did not smile. Hafsa Azeina had warned him to stay away from this one.

"Is Marisa bothering you, young sir?"

The girl squeaked and bent lower.

Daru went tense all over, and sighed a small sigh when the man took his hand away. "No, ah… no." He was not sure how he should address this man. Surely "Halfmask" was not his real name. "She was asking if I needed anything."

"Do you? Need anything." The eyes crinkled again.

Daru glanced at the girl. She was trembling, and he could not see her eyes. "Yes, please. Meat and bread and, um, food for Hafsa Azeina. Nothing spiced or sweet. And, ah, a pig for Khurra'an. Dead, and um, fresh. Not roasted."

The man patted him on the shoulder again. "Your dreamshifter, yes?" He glanced at the girl. "Marisa, you are dismissed. Unless you wish to feed a pig to one of their giant cats? No?" His eyes were bright as he watched the girl dart away. "I will see to your mistress's food myself, young sir, and send some men up with a pig. Marisa is right, though. You are too skinny. I assume you are to eat, as well?"

Daru ducked his head.

"Very good. Go on, then, fatten up on milk and honey." The owl's face turned aside. "I am sorry for your loss, by the way. She

305

was a very beautiful woman." And he walked away.

Daru stood frozen in place. *Sorry for your loss.* Surely Sulema had not died? Not now, when it seemed so certain she would recover? He imagined himself telling the dreamshifter that her only daughter was dead, and all he could think of was Khurra'an licking his chops.

No... that was ridiculous. He shook himself free and walked slowly toward the people. The dreamshifter would have known already. She was always the first to know of a death. And she had said nothing.

Whoever it was, then, had likely died in their sleep.

He held his mind's eye firmly shut against the image of Hafsa Azeina turning the bone over and over in her hands. People died all the time. It meant nothing. The bone may have come from a tarbok, or from a slaver who threatened the people.

You know better, the shadows whispered. *You know.*

Saskia scooted her butt over to make room for him at the end of the bench, and Daru slid into place with a grateful nod. She nodded back as he reached dutifully for a trencher of flat bread piled high with duck and roasted onions. The smell made his mouth water, even though his stomach still felt like it was full of sand.

There was no talk at this table, no laughter. Saskia's eyes were red and raw, and her face was splotchy. Daru tucked his chin and stared at the food in front of him. He needed to eat. He had been told to eat. He sighed and picked up a sliver of duck with his fingers.

He really did not want to know.

"Who?" he whispered.

"You do not know?" Saskia whispered back. Her voice was hoarse and broken. "You really do not know?"

"No."

"Umm Nurati is dead. First Mother is dead." She began to weep. Kabila put her arm about the younger Ja'Akari's shoulder, and hugged her close.

Daru could feel the shadows watching him, waiting to see what he would do. He put the duck in his mouth, chewed, swallowed, and reached for another piece. It tasted like nothing.

"Why should he care? He is not of the people." Duadl Ja'Sajani spat like one of his churrim. "He is hers. Has your dreamshifter killed recently, boy?"

"*Khutlani*, Duadl. Hold your tongue. Your mouth is too small to speak of such big things." Kabila reached in front of Saskia to give his arm a squeeze. "It is not for us small ones to order the movements of the stars, eh, Daru?"

Daru managed a smile and tried to shrink in upon himself. The food was sand in his mouth, sand and dust and old leather. He ate every bite, even the bread trencher. It settled in his stomach like a fist to the gut, and he washed it down with water that tasted of copper and iron and sulfur. When he had finished, he sat at the table and stared at his hands. The people talked among themselves in low voices. Saskia wept quietly, and she was not alone. The only one who sat alone was Daru, the dreamshifter's apprentice.

Umm Nurati was dead.

He would never see her again, never hear her soft voice or words of encouragement. She would never smile again, or laugh, or do anything at all.

His stomach clenched. He remembered a night not so long ago, when Paraja, eyes glowing, had stalked him down an alley between the Ja'Akari barracks and the armory. He could smell the wet feathers and fowls' blood from the fletcher's rooms, and hear the *ting, ting, tap* of a small hammer against metal, and once again saw her jewel-bright unblinking eyes emerge from the gloom. She moved in a half-crouch, shoulders working back and forth beneath her gold-and-black dappled fur, and she flashed her tusks at him, daring him to run.

He had pressed his back against the building, and she crouched low on her front claws, hips wriggling… and then the barracks door had opened, and the light spilled out, and a knot of half-drunk warriors had staggered laughing toward them. Paraja had lashed her tail and faded back into the night. Now that Nurati was gone, would Paraja linger about the city, perhaps take another as Zeeravashani? Or would she return to the wild vash'ai? Daru closed his eyes and wished to never see her again.

But Nurati…

Umm Nurati, First Mother, the mother of all the prides. She was beauty, she was grace, she was a soft song in the night when a little boy was wracked with bloodboil fever, the hand that lit a candle and chased the shadows away. Hers was the voice that laid down the law against exposing infants at birth, no matter the omens, no matter their deformities, no matter their weakness. She held every babe born to the pride, she kissed every wrinkled little face and counted every finger, every toe. Sulema had told him that Umm Nurati had cradled him in one arm and banged her staff down in anger when the old ones had insisted he be buried with his mother—a sickly child, so weak and ill-omened that even her own vash'ai had wished him dead.

A tear splashed down onto the table between his hands. Daru could feel the bands tightening about his ribs. His next breath came labored, and the shadows pressed in. Pain lanced through his chest, and again, and he sat upright and threw his shoulders back to give his lungs some room. Almost, he could see her face among the shadows, cheeks hollow, eyes hungry. Had Tammas been there to sing her bones to sleep? He was her eldest child… and then another blow hit him, harder than the first.

Her child.

He tugged at Saskia's sleeve, gasping weakly. She turned to him, and her eyes widened. She elbowed Kabila, who took one look at him and stood very quickly, frowning and wiping her hands on her tunic.

"Daru? Child, are you all right?"

"Weak…" muttered someone at the end of the table. Duadl grunted and turned away with a disgusted look.

Daru clung to Saskia's arm. The pressure built in his ears, and he knew what would come next—a rush of noise like black wings in his ears, and dark fog closing in until he could scarce see his hand before his eyes. He pushed at the weakness like an infant wrapped in the coils of a serpent.

"The baby," he whispered to her. "Baby..."

Saskia reached and supported him with her arms as he toppled from the bench. The shadows swept in, delighted at this chance, and he fought to remain upright.

"Hold him... here..." Strong arms lifted him, lifted him as if he were a swaddling infant. Tears curdled in his throat as his arms went limp and he began to shake. He heard Saskia's voice, muffled and far away.

"He was asking about a baby."

Kabila's breath was warm against his cheek and she held him close. Her heartbeat was strong and beautiful as it sang to him. *Live. Live. Live.*

"Baby? Do you mean Umm Nurati's baby?" She clutched him tighter still. "She lives, a fine strong girl. She will grow to be beautiful like her sisters, and you will grow to be wise, and powerful, and keep her from harm. You will be our dreamshifter, and watch over us as we sleep."

"Yes," he heard himself whisper. *While you sleep.* Then the wings rushed by, and he was flying.

First, he fell. He fell through the arms that held him, through the stone floor and the room beneath and the floor beneath that, faster and faster through chamber and stone and water and then stone again, as the earth grew warmer and thicker and then opened up beneath him, and then he remembered that he could fly.

He snapped his wings open and felt the muscles in his back and chest wrench as he caught the air and pulled himself from a dive into a sharp upward swoop and then hovered, heart racing, and peered into the gloom. He was far, far beneath the surface of the earth. He could feel it pressing down upon him. Down here, the rocks shifted and stirred in their sleep, muttering in the long dreaming, and he could feel the molten veins of the dragon bursting with dormant life. He was in an ancient cavern full of dust and stagnant air, studded with stalactites no taller than a short child, stunted and twisted and coated in a pale slime that glowed and throbbed and stretched out tiny blind tentacles, searching endlessly and vainly for life, for sustenance, for light.

Men had been here before, men in the ancient long ago. Their hands had hewn the rock, had sliced into the living earth and carved out row upon row upon endless row of niches and shelves and shallow graves in the floor. And graves they were, each of them stuffed with a corpse shrouded in cloth gone to dust and mold and foul air. He felt the back of his neck prickle, and his heart squeezed shut as he looked upon the bodies.

Hundreds of them, thousands even, more than his mind could guess at, every one of them swaddled and draped in red, and with a golden mask upon the face. The silk on most of them had gone to rot and red dirt, but the bodies were whole, hands folded primly over their chests, gazing forever into the gloom, brooding over their dark thoughts. Whatever they were, whoever they had been, they were bad enough that not even the shadows came here. The place was as empty and still as a dead man's mouth.

Daru made a sound in the back of his throat, a scared little whimpering breath, and one of the corpses turned its head and stared at him, blank dead eyes dry and flat behind the dusty mask. Daru opened his mouth to scream and fangs sank into the top of his skull, just above his eyes, a great mouth clamped shut on his head, squeezing, squeezing, and he was dragged from the chamber of horrors up, up, up into the light of day.

Thank you, my friend. Where was he?

Down. Deep in the slumbering earth. There is something there that should not be. Like an infection in the bone, a dark stain in the blood. Something foul.

Araids?

No. Old, older than trees' roots. And vast... the ground is riddled with it like a bone full of bloodworms.

The boy is lucky you were there.

There was no answer to that.

If I am lucky, Daru thought, *I am the unluckiest lucky person the world has ever known.*

Hush, he wakes. And you owe me a pig.

Daru was curled on his side, soft bedding and slick fur pressed against his cheek. He felt the air burning in his lungs, and his heart's labored efforts to keep beating, like a bird in a too-small cage. He tried to open his eyes, but they were caked with dust, the same foul stuff that coated the inside of his mouth.

"What?" he croaked.

Hafsa Azeina's strong, bony arm supported him, helped him to a sit up. She wiped his face with a warm, damp cloth, and held a cup of cool water to his lips. He sipped, then drank greedily. The cool water seemed to spread through his limbs and into his fingers and toes, making them tingle and come back to life.

"What?" he asked again. "What happened? Where was I?"

"*What* is fairly simple to answer: you had one of your fits." Hafsa Azeina took the cup from his fingers and turned away, toward Khurra'an. Her locked hair glowed in the firelight. "*Where* is a bit more problematic to answer. What do you remember?"

"I was in a place… down. Under the ground. Very, very far underground." Remembering, he shivered. "A big cave—and there were more caves, I think. Like a rabbit's warren, or spiders' tunnels. There were dead men. Or… not dead. One of them turned to look at me. But I may have dreamed that part."

He had not dreamed it. Even now, those dead eyes bored into his, wanting something from him. Hungry, and angry, and very, very old.

She turned her face toward him, and he flinched from the intensity of her gaze. "What else?"

"They were… they seemed to be… wrapped all in red. And." He

swallowed. "Gold masks. Like those battle-mages."

"*Ahhhhhhhh.*" The breath hissed from her, and she turned to look at Khurra'an. "So. Now we know."

The cat just stared at them, flipping the back of his tail back and forth and not blinking.

Hafsa Azeina moved away and folded her legs to sit staring into the fire. Her face went smooth, as smooth and clean as a golden mask, but he was not afraid. Daru had been staring at that face for as long as he could remember, watching the golden eyes flick back and forth as if they followed things that nobody else could see. Many times he had fallen asleep as she sat staring into the fire, and sometimes when he woke her face would be bloodied, or grim, and soon after she would begin making a new instrument out of a bit of bone, or gut, or skin. Daru never asked what she had done, because she watched over them all as they slept.

Her gaze turned to him. "Daru."

He sat up straight, letting the blankets fall away from his shoulders. "Dreamshifter?"

"You have seen the Baidun Daiel. You are to stay away from them, as far as you can, at all times. Never speak to them. Do not look at them, or speak of them, or think of them if you can help it. Especially when you are tired, or falling asleep. Never, never let them touch you. Do you understand?"

Daru nodded.

It was not enough. Her eyes went sharp as a hawk's. "Do you understand?"

"Yes, Dreamshifter."

"Also, I have been neglecting your body. You are thin and weak."

He burned with shame, that the dreamshifter would think of him so. Khurra'an grunted. To Daru's surprise Hafsa Azeina stood, and walked across the room, and tucked her knees underneath to sit beside him on her pallet. She touched his cheek with the back of her hand, looked into his eyes, touched him gently between the eyes with one finger. Her eyes were softer than usual as she sat back upon her heels and regarded him.

"You really are an exceptional child," she told him. "Remember this—I chose you as my apprentice for a reason."

He realized that he was gaping at her, and snapped his mouth shut. She smiled, and a little bit of it leaked into her eyes.

"You are an exceptional child," she repeated, "and this city is a dangerous place for exceptional children. I want you to keep close to the people at all times. Ware all outlanders, not just the red mages."

"Yes, Dreamshifter." He had an uncomfortable thought. "Even Leviathus?" He liked the tall, red-haired man.

The smile left her eyes. "Even Leviathus. Even Sulema." She glanced at Khurra'an. "We need to make your body strong, stronger than it is now. If you are fainting away in front of people, you are vulnerable. This mountain air will be good for your lungs. I will have you walking every day, climbing stairs. Carrying things. Kabila will help you with this, and keep an eye on you when I have none to spare. You will take long baths in the mineral pools, to heat and strengthen your blood. You will eat meat, as raw as you can stand it." She stood. "You are nine years old now. It is past time you learn a weapon. Not the sword, maybe." She looked at him and frowned. "Not the staff. A short bow, and perhaps… knives?"

Daru was so excited he could hardly sit still. *Weapons!* The dreamshifter finally, *finally* thought he was strong enough to learn weapons. He felt his eyes glowing from the inside out, and scrambled to his feet despite the trembling in his legs. "I have knives, Dreamshifter!" He caught her amused glance and blushed furiously. "I mean, yes, Dreamshifter. Ismai gifted me with a set of knives before we left." He swallowed. "They were my mother's."

She smoothed the hair back from her eyes with both hands. "Let us see, then."

Daru fairly skipped into his little room and fumbled for the rolled leather pack that held his knives. He skipped back as well, and then stood for a moment clutching them to his chest. What if she did not approve? What if she changed her mind?

What if… what if she took them from him?

She stared at him, holding her hands out patiently as if she read his every thought. He handed the package over reluctantly, and fairly held his breath as she let the leather fall open, revealing his only treasure.

The knives were even more beautiful than he remembered, bone handles gleaming. Hawk, snake, fennec. Horse, owl, sandcat. The edges of the blades swirled blue-green and orange if you turned them just so in the sunlight.

"Ahhhhh." Hafsa Azeina breathed softly. Her hands hovered over the knives, but she did not touch them. "I had forgotten that she had these. Interesting, that they should find their way to you now." She handed them back to Daru. They were heavy and warm in his hands as if he held a living thing. "Knives it is, then."

Daru clutched the knives to his chest and returned to his little room, wondering whether perhaps he was still dreaming.

The next morning when he awoke the knives were still on the little table by his bed, but now they were sheathed in a fine black leather harness meant to be worn diagonally from shoulder to hip. Daru dressed, and over his tunic he buckled the harness. It fit perfectly.

As he left the dreamshifter's rooms, he saw Hafsa Azeina seated before the dragon-face fireplace using a leather strap to polish the long bone. She glanced up, nodded approvingly at Daru and his knives, and went back to her work.

He broke his fast in the kitchens, thanked Saskia for her care and concern, and smiled when Kabila ruffled his hair and teased that she would be making a man out of him after all. Nobody took any notice of his knives or called him a weakling. Nobody mentioned Umm Nurati or the dreamshifter.

When he returned, the dreamshifter and Khurra'an were gone. In their place was a short woman, an outlander with curly dark hair tied back from her pale face with a leather thong, and enormous gray eyes darkened with kohl. She wore soft leather boots laced to the knee, and loose linen trousers, and a leather harness much like his own buckled over a short blue tunic. She looked at him, put her hands on her hips, and scowled.

"This is what they give me to work with?" She clucked her tongue and advanced. She moved like a vash'ai on the hunt, low and smooth and silent. Daru froze where he was. He was not supposed to talk to outlanders.

"Your mistress has sent me to you," the woman explained. "After this day, you will come to me. I will show you, yes?" Her Atualonian was heavily accented. She poked his shoulder, clucking her tongue again as she felt the muscles in his arm, poked him in the belly, stared hard at his face. Daru wondered if she was going to open his mouth and look at his teeth. "A challenge, yes. They give me straw and expect me to spin it into sunlight. *Pah!* What do we have here?" She reached for his knives.

"These are mine." Daru clutched the knives to his chest and took a step back.

The woman arched both brows at him and her gray eyes danced merrily. "Oh, it has spirit, does it? Good. I was wondering whether they had sent me a boy or a mouse. I do not teach mice, not even for what they have offered to pay me. Hah! Not even for that! Well, boy, let us see what they have given me to work with. Show me how you would hold your knife."

Daru reached hesitantly toward the top knife, the one shaped like a horse, and drew it from the sheath.

"No, no, *no!* Put it back." She scowled ferociously. "Not like you are some cook, chopping vegetables. The first thing you have to do is stand. Like this." She grabbed his shoulders and pushed them down so that he stood with his knees bent a little, and kicked his feet apart. "Shoulders back, back straight… no, *no.* Loose like a snake, not stiff like a piece of wood. Loose, yes, so you can move your hips. So you can slide your feet. Yes!

"Now hold your belly in… no, no, do not *suck* it in, you are not a fat man trying to impress a pretty girl. Hold it in. Use your muscles. Press your belly toward your spine. No, no, not like a piece of wood. Yes, like that! Now, breathe. First you must learn to breathe, and then we will teach you how to fight so that you can keep on breathing, yes?" She chuckled at her own joke.

They kept at it until Daru could hardly stand straight for the fire in his belly and back, till his legs cramped and his neck cramped and the knives in their harness felt so heavy he could barely get down to the kitchens, and groaned to think of the climb back up.

When he was back in his room, he dragged the belt off, laid it across the little table, and fell asleep so quickly he did not have time to grieve, or worry, or even wonder where Hafsa Azeina and Khurra'an had gone.

The next morning Daru learned that the woman's name was Ashta, that she was not a weapons-master at all but a journeyman *mantist*—whatever that meant—and that her father had taught her to dance with knives. He learned that she had been easy on him the first day.

After the midday meal, Kabila found him and announced with a big grin that it was time to get to work.

THIRTY

"Kaapua," Xienpei said, gesturing toward and across the wide blue waters. "The River of Flowers."

The land at their feet sloped gently toward the river. Here the trees had given way to scrub and shrubbery and colorful grasses, and the land all along Kaapua was aflame with red and yellow and orange dream-poppies, waist-high rhododendrons in violent scarlet and deepest purple, cobra grass with hoods of pale green and yellow-spotted throats, flowers that burst like fireworks, flowers that looked like small wisps of colored smoke.

Even so late in the spring Jian could see the occasional raft or basket of blooms making its journey to the sea, stragglers from the mountain villagers' fertility rites. One particularly elaborate creation spun and bobbed its way past them, trailing streamers of cloth and laden with offerings of guava and pomegranate blossoms. Some woman had wished for a child, a girl-child.

Jian felt his heart squeeze painfully and he wished that the stranger's prayer might be answered, that she would be blessed with a strong and healthy daughter, and that the little girl would be born well past the days of the Two Moon Dawn.

None of this showed on his face—not the beauty of the land, his joy at being so close to water, not even the thought that if he drove his knife through the throat of Xienpei, he might throw himself into the water and escape. Or better yet, drown. He let the flowered raft slip by beneath his gaze, lest the touch of his regard bring misfortune to its maker.

"Why have you brought me here?" he asked instead. Not that he expected Xienpei to answer, or would trust her words if she did.

Her laugh was as light and sweet as the wind through the flowers. "As a reward, why else? Do you think I tempt you to make an escape? I am unarmed." She spread her arms out to either side and laughed again. The sunlight caught in her teeth. "I like to come out here and breathe air that does not stink of sweat and fear. I like to be near the water. I am hoping you might run so that I can hunt you down and eat you. Take your pick." She lowered her arms, sank gracefully to the ground, and closed her eyes.

Jian studied his yendaeshi as she meditated, hands resting lightly on her knees, face as smooth and guileless as a sleeping child's. He wondered whether she really wanted him to run, and what might happen if he did.

The raft shed its flowers into the river as it spun gently out of sight.

A hummingbird danced about him for a while, thinking perhaps that he was an enormous yellow flower, before taking its place amongst the honeybees.

A hawk circled lazily overhead, hoping to startle a hare into flight.

Jian closed his eyes, listened to the wind, and waited.

"You are getting better at this," Xienpei said after a while, without opening her eyes. "You are learning well. You may swim, if you like. I know how the water calls to you."

"Yendaeshi?"

She did not answer. Jian stared at her for long moments more, then shrugged and walked down the gentle slope toward the water, stripping his clothes off as he went and letting them fall to the ground. He could feel the muscles shift and curl beneath his skin, and the ache at the side of his neck where Naruteo had struck him two days earlier. He shook his hand: still a little numb. He shed his left sandal in the grass and his right sandal in the mud by the river, and then the water slapped at his feet, inviting him to play.

Jian froze mid-breath, his entire body shocked by a pleasure so sharp it was closer to pain. The water was sweet and shallow and fickle, it sang of mountaintops drenched in rain and locked in ice, of flowers and frogs spawning in the reeds, and the long deaths of rocks. It did not sing to him with the voice of the sea, but it sang, and for now it was enough.

Shedding his human existence as carelessly as he had shed his clothes, Jian slipped into the river and let the water carry him away. All his life he had been called Issuq, a sea-thing's child, but not until this moment had Jian felt the truth in those words.

Not a day of it had come easy. The Daechen had been moved into the Yellow Palace the very same day as the winnowing, and by the third day Jian thought he was going to die as well. During the first few days, he had been given purges and potions and foul-tasting teas that made his eyes water, his tongue swell, and his hair fall out in clumps. One day he would break out in an angry red-and-white rash, and the next his body would try to rid itself of every meal he had ever eaten, from both ends at once.

He was confined to his room at first, and when the boys were finally dragged to the main dining hall, he saw that their numbers had been cut by nearly half again. Jian was happy to see that Perri had survived, though the smaller boy was a mass of bruises and cuts and walked bent over in an old man's shuffle. He was even happy to see Naruteo's swollen, sullen face. The laughing boy from Shenzou, the weaver's boy from Tienzhen, the pig-farm boys from Hou… in the end they had been nothing more than a handful of lesser pearls, ground into dust.

The following weeks had brought no relief. The purges and medicines stopped, and were followed by a blessed few days of rest and bland food and even the occasional walk outside, but every moment and every movement took place under the watchful stare of the yendaeshi, and the slightest wrong glance brought swift and painful punishment. Jian learned quickly to keep his head down and his mouth shut. Naruteo, whose neck was stiff as a bull's, was slower to yield his will and often absent at mealtimes.

Days bled into weeks, each turn of the moons bringing a new torment as he was poked and prodded and tested and beaten for infractions he could not have guessed at or avoided. Asking after his mother had earned Jian a leather strap across the face. Looking up toward the sun had earned him a five-stroke caning and the loss of his clothes for three days. The morning he watched both Naruteo and Perri stripped, bound, beaten, and dragged bloody and unconscious from the exercise yard, he knew he would not survive the Yellow Palace. He wondered whether they would send his bones to his mother, or whether she would take her tea at the beach during Remembrance, and smile, thinking him alive and well.

That night, Jian dreamt of the sea. In his dream there were no yendaeshi, no yellow silk or blood-soaked sheets, no Yellow Palace, no emperor. There was only Jian, and the sea, and life. He dove down, down, into the mother's embrace, feeling the warm salt water tickle and rub against his thick fur, peering wide-eyed through the tourmaline gloom. He was not alone, for once in his life he was truly not alone.

He could hear the cetaceans calling each other by their beautiful names, hear the vast weave of their lifesongs circling round and round, never-ending and ever-changing as the sea herself. Lives that were so infinitely small or so incredibly vast his mind could not map them, and that was just fine. None was more important, or less important, than his own.

They were.

He was.

A bullfish flitted by, and he thought about eating it. A shongwei passed beneath, and thought about eating him. He was strong, he was fierce, he was home. He ate the bullfish, and it was good. He was eaten, in turn, by the shongwei... and that was also good. There was no pain, no regret, there was only the sea.

The next day Jian woke early, feeling better than he had since he had come to Khanbul. He felt... clean. As if he had been swallowed and spat forth again, whole and healed. Even Xienpei noticed the change. She had had him beaten in case he had been planning an escape, and then with her own hands she brought him a plate of fish and seaweed and rice with saffron, and praised his stamina.

"Your successes are mine," she had explained to him as they dined together that evening, "as are your failures. I never fail,

Daechen Jian." Jian had nodded as the lashai poured another cup of salty tea. He could almost feel the muscles flex beneath his fur as he reached for it. He was almost surprised that he held the delicate porcelain with a man's hand instead of powerful black claws. He did not need Xienpei to tell him that this tea had been made with seawater. It was good.

From that time forward, Jian had grown in strength and skill as quickly as a toddler learning to walk. His muscles grew heavy and lean under the harsh hands of the combat and weapons tutors and the watchful eyes of the kitchen staff. On Xienpei's instructions he was fed generously on meat, fish, or fowl at every meal. Before a turning of the small moon he could run from the front doors and up the spiraling stairs of the tower without stopping once. By the turning of the big moon he could run back down, as well. His hair grew sleek, his skin glowed with health, and Jian began to hope he might survive the Yellow Palace.

Xienpei had ordered that he be taught the gentle arts as well—script and poetry, music and dance. This last he performed gracefully enough if he was allowed to move slowly, like a bear, and his singing voice was a bear's as well, low and growly and coarse. He was no more apt with any of the wind or stringed instruments they tried him on, so finally they settled on the skin drums, which suited him well. It was a pleasant change to sit cross-legged in a quiet corner with the heavy drum in his lap, and feel the wood shiver and rumble at his touch.

As he became more and more proficient at the tasks his yendaeshi set him, and more pliant to her commands, Jian was allowed some small freedoms. No longer was he to be observed as he bathed or slept, nor required to keep his hair cut short to the shoulders, and he was allowed the freedom of going barefoot as had been his preference for as long as he could remember.

Best of all, if there was time left in the day after his chores and lessons and punishments were complete, he might be allowed to go for a walk outside the palace. When he went to the river he was always accompanied by Xienpei, and a pair of lashai with short bows. He was also made to understand that if ever he tried to escape, Perri would share in his punishment. Even so, Jian looked forward to these outings with an eagerness that shamed him. The smallest flawed pearl may be precious to a man who has no other treasure.

The moons tossed and turned across the sky, lean and full and lean once more, and as one moon bled into the next Jian found that he was sleeping through his nights and performing through his days like a bear trained to the chain and the whip and the beastmaster's sharp voice. As his body adapted to this new life, so did his mind, to the point that he shied away from all thought of home or escape, and hardly flinched when one of his yearmates was beaten for some minor infraction or shortcoming.

Sometimes a boy's place at the table would sit empty for a day or two, and sometimes his chair would be removed altogether. Jian kept his eyes to his own plate and said nothing. The sun shone just as brightly either way.

He reached the bottom of the river and twined his arm about a thick strand of serpent grass, anchoring himself against the current. The mud was cool against his skin, the river stones smooth and soothing as small hands massaging away the day's hurts.

He let the water have its way with him, tossing him this way and that, playful as a child with a new toy. He looked down, away from the surface and the sunlight and the land creatures, and for a moment allowed himself to imagine that he was at the bottom of the sea. A curious pike emerged from its home underneath an old hollow log and hung suspended in the water, face-to-face with him, its sleek body undulating, red-and-green fins twisting this way and that as it held itself in place and studied him.

Eventually it lost interest and swam away in search of a meal. He closed his eyes and turned his face into the current.

"Jian," he whispered, and felt his name turn to bubbles and be washed out to sea. "Jian."

He stayed as long as he dared. When he surfaced, Xienpei was not alone. Naruteo was there, hands bound behind him with a leather thong. He was collared as well, and a sturdy lashai at each side held a leash. The look he shot Jian was pure venom. Another of the yendaeshi stood beside Xienpei—Jian recognized the bald man who had laughed at them as they were culled, and his breath caught. As if she scented his fear, Xienpei turned to him and smiled.

"Now you see, Tsa-len? My boy can be trusted. He is a good boy. Is that not right, Daechen Jian?"

A chill wind rippled over his skin, and Jian repressed a shiver. He bowed his head low.

"Yes, Yendaeshi." His legs and feet were covered with mud from the river, and Jian was painfully aware that he stood naked before the others.

"I prefer to raise mine up with a bit more spirit." The bald man chuckled. His voice was smooth as a cat stalking its prey. "Toughens them up, eh, boy?" Jian heard the slap of flesh on flesh, and Naruteo's grunt of pain.

"Yes, Yendaeshi."

"I will wager that my Jian is as tough as your… boy… any day."

Jian held his breath as a cold sweat broke out all over his body. He had heard rumors of the yendaeshi pitting their charges against one another, in fights to the death.

"Oh? What will you wager?"

"I will wager this jade pendant against that ruby of yours."

"Ah, Xienpei, I am disappointed in you, wagering baubles when we have fine young flesh to hand. Perhaps what they say is true… you are losing your edge."

Jian heard Xienpei hiss at the insult. He felt the fear coiling in his belly, rising up his throat like a snake…

…and he let it go. Just like that, he let it go, breathed it away into the mud and the wind and the river. What would be, would be, and if this day ended with his body dumped into the river and borne out to sea, so be it.

323

"So you say. What would you have, then?"

"My boy against yours, for training rights. My boy wins, I take yours. Your boy wins, you get this one."

"I have no use for your land-locked bullock. I want the girl."

"Ah." The man laughed. "So it's a matched pair you want, is it? I am delighted to find the rumors of your demise are... premature. So be it. My boy against yours, for the girl. You!" he barked at Naruteo. "Strip!"

"Jian!" Xienpei snapped. "To me, now."

Jian trotted quickly to stand before Xienpei, dismayed at the sight of his muddy bare feet near her immaculate gold slippers. She lifted his chin with two fingers and stared straight into his eyes. Hers were as bright as a child's at a festival. He had never seen her so animated, not even at the winnowing.

"Jian," she whispered. "Daechen Jian. This is your moment, do you understand me? Your day. Do you wish to live?"

"Yendaeshi?" His thoughts moved slowly, as if his head was clogged with mud from the river.

She slapped him hard enough that he tasted blood. "What are you? Are you a piece of shit washed up by the sea, or are you Daechen?" She slapped him again, snapping his head to the side. "Are you a corpse rotting on the beach? Or are you Issuq? Live?" She slapped him a third time. "Or die?" She raised her hand again. "Live?"

Jian reached up and trapped her wrist in his hand. He was strong, he realized, strong enough to snap her little bird-bones with a simple twist. He stared into her face, daring her to strike him again.

"I will live," he growled at her.

Xienpei smiled at him and wrenched her hand free. "Then fight, you little bastard. Fight, and win, and I might just let you live." Swift as a serpent's strike she grabbed him by the shoulders, and whipped him about, and gave him a strong push just as Naruteo, unbound and naked, staggered toward him.

Then he understood.

Their eyes met. Naruteo's face twisted into a mask of rage, eyes small and red as a bull's, and Jian felt his own bloodlust rise in answer. As the other boy bellowed and charged, head down, Jian roared a challenge and ran to meet him. They collided with a bone-jarring crunch. Jian was lifted off his feet, but twisted away and landed upright in the mud at the river's edge. He roared again and held both arms out as if to embrace his enemy as Naruteo shook his head, turned, and charged again.

The river sang in his blood and the wind sang in his lungs, and Jian twisted, snarling, as Naruteo closed the distance in three short strides. Power exploded in his chest, his back, his legs and he struck toward the enemy with his hand open, fingers splayed like claws, fully intending to knock the other boy's head from his shoulders. The blow connected with a satisfying crunch and Naruteo spun with the force of it, slipped end over end, and flew backward into the river with a splash. He bellowed and thrashed, trying to right himself.

Jian did not wait, but threw himself on his opponent and pinned him on his back in the shallow water, kneeling on the other boy's shoulders and grabbing him by the throat. He ground his teeth, peering through a red curtain of fury and blood as Naruteo choked and gasped, flailing like a fish dying on the end of a harpoon.

"Enough!"

The river rushed in his ears as he pressed Naruteo's head back, back into the water. The other thrashed and fought, bloody foam at his mouth washing away and eyes bulging in fury—but his struggles grew weaker, and Jian knew he had him. Power surged in him again, blood and victory, and he bared his teeth as he pushed his advantage, pushed Naruteo's face beneath the water.

Someone pulled at him, struck at his shoulders and his face and the back of his head, seeking to deprive him of his prey. Jian snarled at them and tightened his grip. His enemy's struggles grew feeble. Just a moment longer...

"ENOUGH!" Xienpei's voice lashed at him, and Jian fell back, shuddering and breathing hard. Hands reached past him to drag Naruteo from the water, and he snapped at them.

"Enough, Daechen Jian. Back, now." Her hand was at his shoulder, pulling him away. Jian allowed himself to be led, though he growled at them through his teeth. She cuffed him on the side of his head, almost fondly, and he subsided.

The river called to him, its voice soft and sorrowful. He sat back on his haunches and let the cool water wash the mud and blood from his fur.

Fur?

As the lashai and the bald man dragged Naruteo's limp form from the river, Jian brought his hands up before his eyes. His hands, not a sea-bear's claws as he had imagined, a man's hands covered in mud and blood. Naruteo rolled over on the beach, retching up water and groaning. Jian almost sobbed in relief.

I am a man, he thought. *A man, not a beast.*

Xienpei stroked his hair and murmured to him in a low voice. "There, there, my good boy. Shhh, let it go." He did not look up, but he could hear the smile in her voice. "You did well today, Daechen Jian—I am pleased. Very pleased." She patted his shoulder and then walked along the river's edge to the other yendaeshi, who stood over Naruteo with a murderous scowl.

She did not bother to look back.

THIRTY-ONE

"Are you ready?"

"I have some questions."

"Good." Wyvernus smiled across the low table at her, his teeth very white in the moonslight. "Ask me anything you like. This is a test, nothing more, and a very simple one at that."

"That is all?" Sulema frowned at the silk-covered mounds between them.

"That is all."

"This is magic?"

"Very small magic, yes. I already know you are echovete—you used to scream your head off when you were a baby and I was working—but I need to determine how strong you are, and how your power balances out between sa and ka."

"Will it be anything like dreamshifting?" She had experienced a taste of her mother's magic, and wanted none of it. The fox-head staff she had banished from sight, if not from her mind.

"*No.*" The chamber rang with his denial.

She wanted to squirm like she had as a child and Istaza Ani was teaching maths—but he *had* said she should ask him any question that came to mind.

"I thought you wore the big mask to work magic?"

He smiled at that. "This is just a small magic, as I said. Very small. I do not need the Mask of the Sun Dragon—or the Baidun Daiel—for something like this."

She took a deep breath. "All right, I am ready. What do I do?"

"I will sing a note, and when I tap the table, you tell me which bowl feels most alive to you."

Sulema blinked, and Wyvernus laughed at her surprise. Then he closed his eyes and began to sing.

The Zeeranim are very fond of music. The desert sings as the dunes swell and recede to the pull of the moons, the warriors sing as they ride out to the hunt, young Mothers sing to the children they hope to bear. They sing of life, and death, and all the little moments in between… but Sulema had never heard anyone sing like her father. His voice rose into the air, lifting her spirits up to the moons, a single note clear and sharp and bright as the sword at her waist.

This one, she thought, and reached out without hesitation to touch one of the covered bowls. She could not have said how she knew, any more than she could have explained the difference between red and blue, or hot and cold. She just knew.

Wyvernus let the note fall away, and smiled.

"Very good," he said, "and very fast." He reached to draw away the silk, and laughed when Sulema recoiled. The silk had concealed a very old bowl, reddish-brown with age, made from a human skull inlaid with silver and precious stones. "Come now, you will hurt poor Yoric's feelings."

"Yoric? The poet? You *knew* him?"

"Alas, not well. Ah, you should see your face!" He laughed, and his laughter was as beautiful as his song. "Ah! I am teasing you, child. These bowls are ancient beyond knowing. Their owners are long gone to dust. A king simply does not have time to go about lopping off people's heads, just to make bowls."

She found herself laughing along with him, and as they were revealed one by one the row of jeweled skulls grinned too, enjoying their game. Rob's head was full of rocks, Natan full of air—not *empty,* her father had chided—Jonnus held cinders, Tracia a live mouse that scampered away as she was revealed, and Olivia was full of… dead spiders. Sulema shuddered when her father stuck his finger in the bowl and stirred them around, and found herself thankful for the morning's fast.

"Ugh, spiders."

"Oh, these are not just any spiders. Look." He picked one up between thumb and forefinger and held it entirely too close to her face. "See how it glitters in the moonlight?"

"Almost like metal."

"*Almost* like metal, very good. The Araids use blood magic to

328

fuse flesh to metal, and so turn an ordinary spider into a weapon." He dropped it back into the bowl with a clink, and wiped his hand on the front of his robes with a grimace. "Fell things."

"*Ew*. I had never imagined there could be anything worse than spiders." At her father's laugh, Sulema pointed to the last bowl, larger and more misshapen than the last. "And that one?"

"Ah yes, I saved the best for last. Last test, and tell me true if you sense anything. Most people cannot, so do not feel bad if you feel nothing."

"I am Ja'Akari," she assured him, stung. "My words speak only truth."

"You are Atualonian," he replied, "so that will likely change. Now, listen."

He closed his eyes, and drew a deep breath, filling his chest, his belly, tilting his head back and letting his shoulders fall loose. Sulema expected his powerful voice to bellow forth like her mother's shofar, but the sound that rolled over his tongue and into the deep night was the slightest call, the softest cry, the last sad notes of a shepherd girl, playing her lonely flute.

No man could ever make a sound like that, she thought, stunned. *A dragon, maybe, but not a man.*

The bowl on the table sang back.

"I hear it," she whispered, and might have wept for loss when Wyvernus let his song die away. For it had been a song, a whole song in a single note. "I heard it."

"You heard it." His voice was as rough as a warrior's after battle. "Of course you heard it." He drew back the white silk to reveal a skull white and smooth as polished alabaster, crowned with a pair of small and delicate antlers. "Amrit il Mer," he named her, for surely no man's skull could be so beautiful. He reached into the bowl with both hands and drew forth a delicate orb, a globe fashioned of rose-colored rock and set with jewels. "This, my dear, life. No echovete can hear it unless they are powerful—very powerful—in sa. Yet you were able to hear the masculine ka as well. Truly, you are exceptional."

The globe held Sulema's attention. She was seized with the desire to snatch it up, to claim it as her own. "What is it?"

"It is life. The resonance of life, to be more precise. See, it was fashioned from red salt and white, and turned to stone by some art we no longer possess. This is our world as Akari Sun Dragon might see it. Look here." He turned the globe over in his hands and traced a line where the pink salt was nearly white, and tapped a tiny chip of onyx. "This is us, this is Atualon. This is Nar Bedayyan, and this little vein of lapis is the Dibris, and right here? That is your City of Mothers."

"*Ai yeh*," she breathed, and reached for the globe.

"*Aat-aat*, not yet, you are not ready for this yet, my girl. This stone has power all her own, power even I do not fully understand. But this, right here, this is what I wanted to show you." He pointed to, but did not touch, a scorched and broken area not as wide as the palm of his hand. "Do you know what this is?"

"Quarabala?" she guessed.

"Clever girl. What caused this damage, do you think?"

Sulema frowned and looked from the globe to his face, though it was not easy to look away from the stone. "Surely whoever made this fashioned it so?"

"Not at all. This stone mirrors our world exactly. If the Dibris were to bleed dry, the little vein of lapis would disappear. If Atukos were to crumble into the sea, this bit of onyx would disappear as well."

"*Ai yeh*," she said again.

"Exactly. So I ask you again, what caused this damage? To the stone… to our world?"

"The Sundering?"

"Well, yes. And no. This damage, the cracks here, and the burns, and the brittle nature of the surface, all happened at the same time. The Sundering was not caused by a human war, Sulema—the war was a part of the Sundering. Humans are not big enough, not powerful enough, to effect such change." He placed the stone carefully back into the bowl. "Only a dragon could do such a thing. That seared and broken place is where Akari Sun Dragon breathed fire upon our world in an attempt to wake his mate, to make her hatch. He very nearly succeeded. Kal ne Mur nearly died trying to sing the dragon Sajani back to sleep. As it was, the draik's efforts tore the world in half, creating two worlds that are part of and yet separated from one another. These two worlds have been drifting farther and farther apart since that day."

Sulema blinked. "Two worlds? The Twilight Lands are *real*?"

"As real as ours, and in as much danger. They have no sun, save that light that filters through the veil to them, and we have no magic save a pale shadow of past glories. If the dragon wakes, the veil will be shredded, and..." He held his two fists together, then drew them apart with a jerk and held them open, palms-up. "Neither will survive. Nor would we survive the physical act of the dragon hatching, any more than an egg survives the chick.

"Do not doubt, Sulema, the dragon *is* waking. All the signs are right here for us to see." He tapped the globe with one finger.

"If the dragon wakes, we die. Can we kill the dragon?"

"Spoken like a barbarian warrior." He laughed. "Just how big do you think a dragon is, Sulema?"

"Well, bigger than a lionsnake, I imagine—"

"Yes, bigger than a lionsnake. Bigger than Atukos. Bigger than the *world*, Sulema. Our minds are too small to hold such wonder. We have no more hope of killing a dragon than an ant has of killing us for stepping on its anthill. Even if we could kill her, what then? If the chick dies within the egg..."

"It rots."

"It rots," he agreed. "Our only hope is to keep the dragon alive and asleep for as long as we can. She has been asleep for as long as our world has existed, and she can sleep until the end of time, as far as we know. The only way to keep the dragon from waking is to sing to her through atulfah. The only one who can do this..."

"Is you," she whispered.

"Is you," he corrected gently. "My time is nearing its end, sooner than I might wish. Truly, daughter, you are our only hope."

"*Za fik*," she swore. "There is no choice for me, is there?"

"There is always a choice," he told her. "I cannot compel you to learn atulfah, or to use it to sing the Dragon to sleep. You could choose to deny your birthright and return to the desert, free as a sparrow in the wind.

"I cannot, however, allow you to leave untrained or able to wield atulfah, a sword for whomever chooses to claim it. Your mother kept you shielded from atulfah for all the years you were gone. You could be shielded again—sealed for all time. But you would be cut off from the song as if you had been born surdus, unable to sense sa or ka. Cut off even from the smallest magics—you would be unable to seek water in the desert, unable to bond to one of your great cats."

"The Dragon would wake."

"And destroy the world, yes. Most definitely."

"This is no choice, this is horse shit." Sulema scowled, not caring whether or not one was allowed to say "horse shit" to a king.

"I never promised you a *good* choice," he replied. "Sometimes your only choice is, as you say, horse shit. Sometimes it is a choice between death and death. Sometimes it is a choice between two different deaths. But there is always a choice."

"So. Remain in the trap and die, or chew off my leg and bleed to death." Sulema thought that the skulls were mocking her, safely dead and exempt from the struggles of the living.

"I said much the same thing, when I was your age." Wyvernus clasped her hands between his, and his eyes were full of moonslight and sorrow. "None who bear such burdens as ours do so lightly, or without pain. Are you the woman I think you are—the warrior your mother claims? Will you bear this burden, knowing that you alone must pay the price?"

She stared at the Dragon King, his face deeply lined with strain and worry, aged before his time like dates left too long in the sun. His hands, cradling hers, trembled like an old woman's. His eyes, it seemed to her, had seen far too much. Those eyes said that when death came, it would not be too soon. Because she had her mother's stubborn chin, and her father's stubborn red hair, because she belonged to both of them but belonged, at last, to herself, she drew her hands away and stood.

"It may not be much of a choice," she told him, "but you say it is my choice. I will not make it until I have had time to think."

He stood as well, and bowed to her as if she were king and he a stubborn child.

"As you wish."

THIRTY-TWO

The wind was born of a dreamshifter, playing a leg-bone flute. Fingers as nimble as a young girl's danced across the smooth bone, its owner now gone to song and dust and tears and the memories of her children. But the sunlight that warmed her back was still the same. Akari Sun Dragon spread his wings over Atualon just as he did over the Zeera, blessing the mother, the child, and the murderess alike.

Born of pain and betrayal and the ferocity of a mother's love, the wind danced in defiance and grace along the walls and ramparts of Atukos, sparking it to dark flame and a life of its own—a small life, snuffed and smothered as quickly as it kindled. The little fires deep within knew that theirs was a false life and short, and burned ever the brighter for it, for such a life has no time for regret.

The wind whistled and hissed through the wide, arched windows and doorways of the dreamshifter's rooms. Red spidersilk curtains billowed in the wind, they writhed like wraiths from Tai Damat come for the blood of men. Cruel shadows, still warm with the day's lifeblood, caressed the dragonstone floors and walls to a semblance of life, ran sharpened claws gently over the thick white fur upon which she sat, even dared to ruffle the long black feathers dangling from her cat's-skull staff. Yet for all their muttered curses and promises of death, they never quite dared touch the dreamshifter. They wailed in defeat down the wide corridors, off in search of softer prey.

The wind was sickly sweet with sweat and laughter, and the day's long dying, and the dreams of young girls pregnant with song. Though the dreamshifter was past caring about such things as babies and shared meals and wishing-wells, though her heart was dry and gritty as a sandstorm, the sound of children singing in the streets—singing Sajani Earth Dragon to sleep, as they had done every night for time out of mind—caused her breath to catch and her fingers to slow. Thus the timbre of her music shifted, its intent grew less dark, and it lifted the heart to light and life.

Akari Sun Dragon furled his wings at just that moment. He plummeted into the warm clear waters of Nar Bedayyan in search of his sleeping mate, plunging the world into a soft twilight and the scents of moonsrose and jasmine.

Hafsa Azeina's dreaming eyes opened wider to catch the last redgold rays, her nostrils flared in appreciation of the night-flowers' ardent celebration of life, and her intikallah unfurled, soft and scalding petals glowing white-hot with song for any echovete to see. She let the song take her where it would—when all paths lead to death, one might as well stop and watch a sunset.

The song carried her sa out the window and into the wide twilight. She spread herself thin upon the evening breeze and floated across the yard. Torches had been lit and they wrote their names in soot across the indigo sky. The light of the flames danced upon the oiled skin of a pair of massive wrestlers from the Black Isles as they stared at each other and roared like young bulls. But their violence was all lies and foolery, and she turned her mind back to the music.

The dreamshifter focused her dreaming eyes. She gathered herself in so that she was almost substantial and let herself drop like a stone, like a stooping hawk, down through the filtering starlight. She skimmed over a riotous mess of plant life, through the open window, and into a brilliantly lit room, and then she let herself go again to mist and memories and the faint smell of smoke. Her dreaming eyes did not see the world in the same light as her waking eyes, but Hafsa Azeina had been doing this for a long and bloody time.

She absorbed the bright songs, the loud blocks of color, the rich insistent pulse of life swirling about the floor like tide-pools seething with life. If she had been corporeal, she would have nodded in satisfaction.

I should have known he was involved, she thought. *The loremaster is drawn to stories like a mantid to flowers.*

Deep in Shehannam, she felt Khurra'an shift into wakefulness. He was irritated with her, and with his empty belly, and with the dark stone walls.

I should eat you, he grumbled. *It would solve many of my problems.*

She ignored that. *Look what I have found.*

He looked through her eyes, and gave a mental shrug. *You should have known... he is a liar, after all.*

That he is.

Loremaster Rothfaust sat as he often did, surrounded by an astonishing variety of flowers and an even more astonishing variety of children. His linen shirt was rolled up to reveal powerful forearms, and he had abandoned the robes of office for a gardener's tunic and vest heavily embroidered in green and gold and brown with a riot of red and blue flowers along the hem. His hands were black with dirt almost to his elbows, his beard was so littered with twigs and leaves and flower-petals that he looked like a bird's nest.

He was potting a young orchid, patting the bark and mosses gently into place about its roots, touching the pale leaves and talking to it as if it were one of the children who stared at him wide-eyed, waiting for him to finish settling the plant so that he might tell them a story.

"There you are," he said, as he gave the moss a final pat and lifted the red pot with both hands. "Pretty little thing." For a man his size he moved with surprising grace as he turned and set the little pot with its spray of tiny white and pink blossoms among a dozen or more of its kind.

"Here, Loremaster." One small boy held a bowl of water so full it sloshed over his dimpled hands and soaked the front of his grubby tunic. Rothfaust smiled and took the bowl, but set it aside and wiped his hands on a bit of cloth.

"It is rest she needs now, rest and time to get over the shock. Orchids do not like to move from place to place, even when their feet are cramped. Now, who wants a story?" He laughed at the enthusiastic response and walked over to sit on a low wooden bench. The children arranged themselves on the floor around him, and Loremaster Rothfaust smiled at them. "What would my little flowers like to hear tonight? A sad story? A funny story?" He tweaked the nose of the grubby child with the wet tunic. "A scary story? No?" He laughed as the boy shook his head vehemently. "Not a scary story, then."

"A love story!" giggled one of the middle-sized girls.

"A hero story!" one of the bigger boys countered. "And no kissing!"

"Hmmm. A heroic love story with no kissing. Hm." He stroked his beard, hiding a smile behind his hand. "I believe I know just the tale. Have you ever heard the story of Zula Din, and how she learned the name of the sun?" He stretched his large, sandaled feet out in front of him, crossed his arms over his chest, and leaned back with a smile.

"Everyone knows the name of the sun," complained the older boy. "It is Akari."

"Nobody knows the real name of the sun." This from one of the smallest children, a dark-skinned girl with the look of the Zeera about her almond-shaped eyes. "Our mouths are too small to speak his name."

"Just so, Annana, just so." Rothfaust nodded. "But Zula Din was a warrior and a storyteller, and she was a daughter of the First People besides—she was made of sterner stuff than you or I.

"It so happens that in the First Days, the world was a cold place and dark. Illindra had not yet hung the stars in her web, and the moons were young and shy, so the First People hid in the dark, cold and afraid..." His voice sank into the low singsong of a true storyteller, wrapping the children in a web of his own.

Excellent. This would make her work so much easier.

As the loremaster wove his tale of love and adventure, Hafsa Azeina breathed her own song into it. As she wove the music of the leg-bone flute into and through and around his story, the children began to fidget, and then to droop, and finally to slump one after the other, eyes glazing over and breath leaving their little bodies in long, reluctant sighs.

Rothfaust never ceased in the telling of his tale, never broke the line or the cadence of his words. He leaned forward and gathered the grubby child into his lap. He stroked the boy's drooping curls, and with gentle fingers, closed his dark eyes.

"And this is how Zula Din pinned Akari Sun Dragon to the sky using his true name, and how he came to love her. But there was no kissing." Rothfaust looked up from the child's face, his mouth a straight hard line and his eyes snapping with fury. He looked directly at her. "If you harm them…"

Hafsa Azeina was so startled that she almost dropped the tune. *I would never.*

"You would, if you thought you had to. You would. I am warning you now—if you bring harm to these children, I will hunt you as you have never been hunted in this life."

She allowed herself to take a more substantial form and floated down to hover near him, careful not to brush against the sleeping children.

I will not. His mind was hot to the touch, his thoughts the blue-white of a flame's heart, and they smelled of things that grew in the warm shade.

"What do you want?"

She saw no benefit in lying. *An ally.*

"Ah. And why would you seek an ally in me, Dreamshifter?"

The air shuddered at her laugh. *We have a history, you and I. We were friends, once.*

"You came to me then as a frightened little hare, desperate to save the life of her child. You return now as the hawk. Indeed, if the stories I hear hold any truth in them, you have become a monster. What need does a monster have of friends?"

I am a monster, she agreed, *though not the monster you imagine. And my daughter is no monster at all—she is innocent.*

"If by 'innocent' you mean 'ignorant,' I have to agree. You cannot protect your daughter by keeping her in the dark, Queen Consort."

The queen consort is dead. I killed her myself.

"Indeed?" He raised his eyebrows.

There is no escape from Atualon save through death. It was necessary.

"A pity, that. I would dearly have loved to have a long talk with her... a very long talk. There are things I cannot tell anyone else, and especially not to a barbarian dreamshifter who comes to me with blood on her tongue." He reached up to stroke his beard, and looked down at the child in his lap. "It occurs to me that the way out is often the way in, as well. If the dreamshifter were to die..."

Die again, live again. Scorn dripped from the words like venom. *Do you think it is so easy?*

"As easy as falling asleep and waking to the sun of a strange world. I risked much to help the queen consort, and I would do so again—but I cannot do as much for a foreign sorcerer, no matter how much she may look like an old friend. I am bound to serve the rulers of Atualon, and some rules even I will not break."

Are you not bound to protect my daughter, then? What if I were to tell you that the Nightmare Man is real, as we had suspected? That I believe he was involved in the Araids' attack on Sulema? I may be a monster, but I have my limits. I do not eat children.

His hand tightened spasmodically on the boy's tunic, but Loremaster Rothfaust shook his head, stubborn as ever.

"You have no power here, Dreamshifter. Such things as I might know, such things as I might say are for the ears of the queen consort." He looked straight at her then, and his eyes held a warning. "Or for the ne Atu, if they were to come asking. As I said, I am bound."

Bound by whom? she wondered, but there was no time to ask. The song trailed off into wind and memory, calling her back, carrying her home. Loremaster Rothfaust and his tender little flock faded from her vision as if they had never been.

As she sped back to her chambers on the wings of a dying song, Hafsa Azeina came upon her apprentice Daru sitting on the wide steps of the Queen's Tower, sitting cross-legged and playing a strange little tune on his bird-skull flute. His eyes were closed, a look of serenity lit his thin face, and his intikallah spat and glowed with sparks like a campfire made from too-green wood. The boy's knives lay to one side, and shadows thick as poisoned syrup gathered about him, so much like the children had gathered about Loremaster Rothfaust that she paused in her flight, though the song had grown dangerously quiet.

Daru, she sent softly so as not to startle him, *what are you doing?*

I'm playing for them, he answered in kind, never pausing in his playing. *They are hungry.*

Yes, but… why? That is very dangerous.

I am used to it. His music shrugged and took on an amused violet-green tint. *Better they follow me than the other children. Besides… if I play for the shadows, they let me throw my knives at them.*

She felt her dream-self flicker. *Throw your knives at them?*

Ashta says that a knife dancer practices even in his sleep, and they are the only things that come into my dreams besides you. They think it is funny.

Ashta said you should throw knives at shadows?

His music took a dark turn. *Ashta said I should throw my knives at birds… and small-cats. But she also said I should never throw my knives if I did not mean to kill. I like birds.* His whistle piped plaintively. *And cats… I do not think Khurra'an would like it if I started killing cats. Even the little ones.*

No, she agreed, *he would not. I suppose if the shadows do not mind, there is no real harm in it. Still… it is dangerous for you to spend so much time near them. You look like the piper in the old stories, the one who stole all the little children.*

The shadows whispered and hissed among themselves at this, with a sound like hot wind through dead leaves.

Daru played a sterner note, and the shadows subsided.

They are always with me, whether I play or no. He played the final notes of his odd little tune and let the music disperse among the shadows, swirling into nothingness like so many sparkling sand-dae. The shadows dispersed as well—most of them, anyway—and Daru sat still as death on the dark steps, hand holding the little flute in his lap. He did not open his eyes, and his intikallah still shot off bright-hot sparks in every direction.

"They used to try and steal me," he said, his voice ringing oddly in the empty dragonstone stairwell. "Sometimes they still do. Someday maybe they will succeed. They have stopped trying to steal Sulema… does that mean she is all better? She has come to the city and met her father, so will we be going home now?"

Not for a long time, no, she answered. *She still tires very easily. It may be some time before she regains her strength for such a journey.*

His smooth young brow furrowed like an old man's. "Ashta says she may never go back home. What does that mean? Sulema is Ja'Akari. She belongs to the people. How could she not go back? This is not her place."

Hafsa Azeina felt herself fading, and shored up her music. The boy deserved an answer.

There is no need for Sulema to hurry back to the Zeera, Daru. For now, it is enough to know that she will live. There are skilled healers in Atualon, and her father is here. It is right that she gets to know her father, and that he should spend time with her as well. He loves her. Her brother is here, and there are cousins… family is important. Blood is important. You know this.

"Blood is important," he agreed, "but her blood is the wrong color for Atualon. Her song is not here. Her song is in the Zeera." Deep in the corners, the shadows shifted and chuckled, a nasty sound. "Your blood is the wrong color, too. It is blue and green. Like the sea." He turned his bird-skull flute over in his hand, caressing it with his fingertips. "You are a long way from home. We all are. We should go home."

The absence from her body was beginning to burn as her song played itself out, but still the dreamshifter lingered.

Is this a foretelling?

Daru waited a long time, so long she could feel the mist of her substance tearing itself thin, so long that she wondered whether

341

he had fallen asleep. His intikallah dimmed and spluttered as if he were unsure of his answer.

"No," he said after long last. "I do not think so. It is probably just a dream."

Probably, she agreed, as the world ran red with pain and she fled back to her mortal shell. *It is probably just a dream.* But she was a dreamshifter, and he was a dreamshifter's apprentice. They both knew better.

The song had ended by the time Hafsa Azeina returned to her body. She could feel her heart and lungs screaming, could hear the silence in her blood vessels as the blood forgot which way it was supposed to go. There was no song to guide her, so she flew up the dead bone and into her own mouth like corpse-breath, foul and poisoned, and when ka and sa recombined, she stiffened and arched her back and fell over as if she had been struck on the side of the head by a hammer.

Khurra'an was roaring inside her head, but her blood roared even louder and she could not make out what he was saying. Certainly it was not complimentary.

By the time she pulled herself together and sat up, the vash'ai was gone. She could feel his disgust with her carelessness through their bond, and sent a wordless apology.

No, he rebuffed her. *No. Stupid cub, you. Get us all killed. I am going to go break something's neck and lap up its blood and pretend it is you.* Then she was alone in her thoughts.

But not alone in her room. Mattu Halfmask stood at a respectful distance, hands behind his back like a small child trying to conceal a forbidden treat.

Or like a grown man, she thought, scrambling to her feet, *concealing a knife.* Tonight he peered out from behind the gilded eyes of a white crane, framed all in feathers the color of soot and blood.

He stepped toward her as she swayed on her feet but stopped again when she threw her hands up between them. He pursed his eyes as he stared at the leg-bone flute.

"I had heard…" His smile was sardonic. "No one I knew, I hope."

Hafsa Azeina turned her back to him as she replaced the flute in her box. She clenched her fists, hard, and shook them out again to still the shaking.

Too close. She had cut it far too close.

Stupid cub...

She continued to ignore Mattu as she washed her face with chill water from an ewer and dried it on a soft cloth. Both the water and the cloth went pink with her blood. She scowled and rolled her shoulders free of stiffness before turning to face her uninvited guest.

"Yes?" she asked, folding her arms over her chest. She was still scowling.

Mattu Halfmask turned half away from her again, and looked out the wide window overlooking the palace yard.

"I love to watch my sister's troupe rehearse. She wrote this play herself, you know... it is about a young boy who mistakes a mymyc for a horse and tries to ride it. This spectacle will give her the audience she so desires, and she is quite beside herself with excitement."

His hands were empty, and still clasped behind his back. Hafsa Azeina stepped closer for a look. Down in the torchlit yard, a handful of fools were play-acting. Two of them, dressed head-to-foot in black, stood close to each other and pranced like a horse, while another waved a red halter and chased them around in a circle.

Several of the Ja'Akari stood in a knot, watching the rehearsal and laughing. Their vests hung open as if they had been sparring. The young Zeeranim were watched, in turn, by a group of young Atualonian men with short straight swords at their hips and fatuous looks on their faces. It was a lovely night, fragrant and warm, and the torches and the stars winked at each other playfully.

She could not remember the last time she had seen such a ridiculous display.

"I can see why they call it a spectacle," she said. "Whose idiot idea was this?"

"Oh, it was Leviathus's idea, a grand celebration of his sister's return, but Ka Atu was only too happy to oblige." Mattu grinned beneath his mask. "It *will* be a grand celebration—fools and wrestlers, fireworks and dancers. Some of your barbarian warriors have even agreed to a demonstration of their fighting skills. Of course there will be magic. I am surprised that Leviathus has not tried to talk you into a performance."

She snorted. "He knows better than to ask."

"Does he? I wonder. He does not always know when to keep that pretty mouth of his shut. Not two days ago, he asked me if I knew anything about the Nightmare Man."

The breath froze in her lungs.

"I told him nothing, of course. My dear cousin has so much on his mind these days, what with watching his father fade away, his sister nearly die, and his beloved stepmother almost kill herself with death-music. Now he has this spectacle to plan." He waved out into the night. "I figured I would save him a bit of worry, and come straight to you. You were bound to find out in any case, sooner or later, unless you *do* kill yourself.

"Tell me, Queen Consort—where would your ka fly off to, if it were separated from your body when you die?" He shuddered theatrically. "Somewhere dreadful, I assume. Stuck in Illindra's web, perhaps? Into the shadow-realm of Eth? Or would it simply fade away? I have always wondered."

Hafsa Azeina leaned her back against the window frame and looked out into the night, letting her eyes grow cold and distant, and running an idle hand over the sill.

"Did you come here to speak in riddles? I am tired, Mattu. Perhaps I will feel like playing your game another day."

White teeth flashed at her. "You were always my favorite, Hafsa Azeina. Sharp as that flayer's knife. Not like my sister's fools, or her foolish audience... who would ever be short-sighted enough to try and ride a mymyc? That idiot would surely have a short life."

"Idiots often have short lives," she replied. "Good night to you, Mattu."

"Oh, very well, if you will not play, I will simply say what I have come here to say and be done with it. I dug around in the musty old box of my memories and found a bit of something that may interest you. Do you remember my brother Pythos?"

"I remember the stories, though I never met him." The second-eldest son of Serpentus Ka Atu, Pythos had been killed when Wyvernus seized the Dragon Throne.

"It was rumored back then—I remember well, though I was not much higher than my mother's knee, and not expected to understand what the adults were whispering back and forth over my head—that Pythos had taken an interest in his twin siblings. An unhealthy interest. It was said that he had been seen visiting the herb-sellers' carts on market day... also that he had been to visit a certain child-seller in Eid Kalish."

"A child-seller?" She did not mask her surprise. "He could not have been much more than a child himself."

"Thirteen or fourteen at the most," Mattu agreed. "Fifteen when he died. It was rumored at the time that he was interested in selling off his competition, but before he could act on his plans Serpentus was deposed and killed—or killed and deposed, I am not clear on how that works—and my brother was tossed down the side of the mountain. Lucky for me, I suppose. His Draiksguard were all executed, of course, as was his secretary, but our old wet-nurse is still kicking around here somewhere, and Pythos's body double—and better yet, his favorite concubine. They were both very young at the time, and she was rumored to have been with child, but no child ever surfaced."

"Why was his body double spared, when the guards and servants were executed? That seems unusual."

"Ah, that is a curious story as well. The official version is that the lad was visiting sick relatives in the countryside when Atukos came under siege." He smiled, and his eyes lit in the torchlight. "Darker rumors would have it that this boy was a distant relative... some by-blow of a cousin of Serpentus, or some such."

"This is all very interesting, but I am not sure what it has to do with the Nightmare Man. Or with me."

"Intrigue, and rebellions, and plots against the king? And you are forced to return Sulema to Atualon just as the old king breathes his last. This is the very stuff of nightmares, or I am one of my sister's fools. I will leave it to you to sift through rumor and innuendo. As for myself, I believe *I* will head down to the yard and enjoy my sister's play, and the sight of your young barbarians. Their penchant for flaunting their tits is causing tongues to wag among our older citizens, you know. That is a spectacle in itself."

He stepped away from the window and sketched a mocking little bow.

Hafsa Azeina nodded to him, reluctantly. "I appreciate the information, Mattu. I may have misjudged you."

He laughed at that, and turned to stride from her rooms. "Oh, Hafsa Azeina," he shook his head. "I doubt that very much."

Once she had made up her mind to do a thing, Hafsa Azeina never hesitated.

The hairdresser she had summoned gathered up the dreamshifter's locks in both hands, tugging and twisting at the tangled mess, unable to hide the dismay in her voice. "It will all have to be cut away."

"Not cut," she replied, and scowled irritably at her own reflection. She hated mirrors. "Combed out. I wish to save as much hair as possible."

"But, Meissati…"

"You will address my mistress as 'Queen Consort,'" Daru corrected, as he had been instructed.

"Queen Consort, forgive me," the woman stammered, "I will need to fetch my apprentices. And oils. And…"

Hafsa Azeina raised her hand, forestalling any further protest. And smoothed the scowl from her face. Again.

"Make it so."

"Your command, Meissati." The woman bowed her way out of the rooms.

Hafsa Azeina smoothed the scowl from her face. Again.

Cool as rain, she reminded herself, *calm as a windless day.*

Timid as a tarbok, scoffed Khurra'an. *Why would you disguise yourself as prey?*

The better to lure them in, she replied.

Ah… an ambush predator, then. Like the mymyc.

Exactly so.

The Ja'Akari do not approve of liars. I do not think your Zeeranim would like this.

What of you? Do you approve?

I am a cat, he answered, which was no answer at all. *Enjoy your game, Dreamshifter. I am going to go find something to eat.* He sauntered from her rooms, tail-up and laughing.

Hafsa Azeina glanced at the mirror, and smoothed the scowl from her face. Again.

Serene as a mountain lake, she reminded herself, *confident as the stars, steady as the moons.*

There she saw it, at long last, peering out at her from her own eyes.

The face of a queen.

THIRTY-THREE

He sat deep in the saddle as Ehuani danced and arched her neck, ears swiveling this way and that as she listened to his request and thought about whether or not she might grant it this time. Finally the pert little ears pricked forward and she acquiesced, stepping lightly underneath herself, flowing from ears to tail into a lovely, light canter.

It was like riding a song, like riding the wind. Ismai let the approval flow through him and into her, and felt her respond with a burst of life.

Life.

Grief caught up with him once more. It poured through him like a hot summer rain and tore through his body like a sandstorm, scouring him bare and bloody. His mare pinned her ears and skittered sideways, going all stiff through her back again. He leaned forward in the saddle, pressed his face into her soft mane, and let the tears flow as they would. Ehuani curled her neck and bit him gently on the foot, forgiving his momentary lapse. She slowed to a sweet and ground-eating trot, and he let her go as she pleased, not much caring whether they rode toward the evening, or toward the dawn, or down the throat of a dragon.

His mother would have loved Ehuani, would have run her slender hands over the mare's silvery hide, would have admired the strength in her and the fire. Likely she would have started planning breedings as soon as she laid eyes on her, in her mind's eye a line of straight-legged and deep-chested foals trotting one after another. Much as she had done with his older sisters and his brother, he thought, much as she would have done with him.

The sword at his hip tapped lightly against his leg, reminding him that she had made him a gift with her own hands, with her own voice had declared him the son of her heart. She was so beautiful. No woman had ever been so beautiful as his mother, none had given so much of herself to her pride and her children.

They said the babe would live. Another sister, praise Atu. Doubtless they would hold a sharib for her naming. As she grew, every woman in Aish Kalumm would coo and dimple and exclaim that this child was growing up to be as beautiful as her mother.

His heart hurt. He let Ehuani go where she would, and at a pace of her own choosing, much as the Ja'Sajani had done with him since the day a rider brought this fell news from the City of Mothers. East, west, up, down, it did not much matter to him. His heart would not find what it needed most, not in any direction. She had gifted him the sword with her own hands. Her favorite son. He thought of Tammas, whose duties would surely keep him in Aish Kalumm now, he thought of Dennet and Neptara and especially little Rudya, who would be so lost without her *Amma*. He should go to them. They had said he should go to them, to grieve with his family. To welcome his new little sister into the pride.

His heart rejected the idea. He did not want to see them, any of them, not even little Rudya and certainly not the red and wrinkled bratling whose birth had killed their mother. He wanted… nothing. He wanted nothing. If Ehuani had not been with him, he would not have cared if the stinking bonelord rose from the sand and swallowed him. His heart felt already as if it had been eaten, and the rest of him had staggered on without realizing it was no longer whole.

Since he had given Ehuani her head, it was no real surprise that she took the path to comfort. She was an intelligent horse, even among the asil. For all his dark thinking about the bonelord, Ismai paid some small mind to the world around them, to the ground beneath his mare's hooves and Akari Sun Dragon high overhead—too high overhead, really. It was late in the day to be taking this path. But he did not turn back. He had Char's torch in his saddlebag, and tarbok-and-goat pemmican and waterskins enough to last him a handful of days. The blackthorn oasis would provide sufficient water and grass for Ehuani's comfort...

...and he wanted to see Char again. She was only a child, but she was the gentlest and wisest person Ismai had ever known. Certainly she was nothing like the women in his family, with their bright eyes and sharp tongues and quick strong hands, and neither was she like Sulema, fervid and noisy as a campfire at sharib. She was still and deep, like a secret pool of water sweet enough to soothe and nourish even the sun-baked heart of a lost boy.

Death stalked beside him. Ruh'ayya's mood had been as black as his own since the news had reached them. The messenger was Zeeravashani, and his sleek golden queen had taken Ruh'ayya away from the humans for a day and a half. When they returned, the other queen fairly shimmered with outrage, and she gave Ismai such a look of green-eyed hate that he had staggered back a few steps. Ruh'ayya had a torn ear, a torn face where claws had raked dangerously close to an eye, and deep gashes and puncture wounds from her muzzle to the tufted end of her tail.

Ismai had ignored his own hurts long enough to tend hers, and she was very stoic about having her wounds cleaned and medicated and stitched up, but when he asked what had happened she would say only that Paraja was angry with her. He did not press the matter.

Before long, Ehuani was pinning her ears and twisting her tail. By the time they arrived at the oasis, she was tucking her chin and threatening to throw him. She was not used to being ridden so far, and it was past her dinnertime. Akari Sun Dragon spread his wings over a wide and glorious day, but Ismai found that his vision was dark about the edges, as if he were peering out at the world from the bottom of a dim and stinking sack, and someone was drawing the top closed.

I will set my tent here, he sent to Ruh'ayya, *and let Ehuani graze. Would you please check to see whether there are any greater predators about?* Bonelord, he thought but did not say.

There are no predators here besides us. Stupid human, she thought but did not say. *I am going to go kill something.* With a flick of her tail, she was gone.

Ehuani pretended to be spooked by the cat's sudden movement and shied violently sideways, nearly unseating him. Ismai gritted his teeth and relaxed his hands, willing himself not to yank on the reins. He dismounted, careful not to kick his horse or to land in a patch of old dried thorns. Then he removed the saddlebags and his mare's tack, and let her go with a little pat on the rump. She snorted and tossed her head, but waited until he was out of range before kicking both hind legs out to show what she really thought.

He might have chased after her, as it was never a good idea to let a horse get away with such behavior. He might have shrugged it off and laughed. A spirited mare was treasure beyond rubies. Ismai did neither. He simply stood in the sand, a few strides from the oasis, saddlebags slung over one arm, tack in the other, and a shamsi he did not deserve hanging heavy at his side.

It seemed too much to ask, suddenly, that he should take those last strides, and pitch a tent. Drink some water. Eat some food. Check Ehuani's legs and hooves, brush her hide, scout for predators, try once more to talk to his stubborn hurting vash'ai… it was too much.

He dropped his burdens and stood swaying in the heat, blue robes whipping about him in the wind. He heard Ehuani nicker, and he felt Ruh'ayya's soft exclamation at the back of his mind, but he could not seem to care enough even to turn his head and see whose feet were whispering through the sand behind him. As if he could not guess. Still, he jumped a little when she laid her skinny little hand on his shoulder.

"Ismai." Her words were smoke and honey. Smoke from the funeral pyre, honey among the burnt offerings. "Ismai, I am so sorry."

Then he was able to let go. At the touch of her hand, the touch of her voice, and not a moment before, Ismai dropped to his knees like a puppet whose strings had been cut. She caught him as he fell, strong and tough as old roots, deep and sweet as the night sky.

He clutched at her tattered robes, his arms went about her middle and he pressed his face into her belly and he clung to her and he cried like a little boy. The sound of his own voice was so lost, so lost, so wracked with pain and longing that it dragged him over the edge of the well of sorrow and into an endless abyss.

Char stroked his hair, she held him like his mother had held him when he was young and hurt, she rocked back and forth crooning a lullaby, and it was the most beautiful thing in all the world.

Ismai wept until he was empty, until he was hollow, until his body was leaden and his mind as empty as the night sky. When his tears had run dry and been soaked up by the Zeera, he clung to his friend for a short while longer before staggering to his feet. He wiped his face on his sleeve as a child might, and pushed his touar back into place. He felt fragile and strangely light, as if he might float away with the moons' breeze.

"I am sorry," he told her.

"Sorry?" Char reached a thin brown hand toward his arm, but her fingertips did not quite brush his robes. "Why sorry?"

"I am sorry to bring my weakness here to your home." He looked up at the pale sky. Ismai had missed the first star of evening, and now they shone by the handful. "I only wanted to spend a few days alone. Do you mind if I camp here? I will not disturb you."

"Weakness?" From the corner of his eye, Ismai could see that she smiled. A child's smile, secret, fleeting. "So strange that you should name yourself weak, Ismai son of Nurati. The desert grieves your loss. The world grieves your loss. The stars grieve your loss." More softly, she added, "I grieve your loss. You are welcome to stay as long as you like, but I wonder..." She hesitated.

He waited. Delpha was half full, Didi her little sister shone gibbous. They hung in the air with a sense of expectation.

"Would you like to come down to the Valley?" she whispered. "It is very... peaceful. It is a good place to grieve. A healing place. I think you would be welcome."

Ismai hardly dared to breathe. He had come to the blackthorn oasis several times since their first meeting, but never had Char invited him to her valley. And he had heard the stories. The Valley of Death...

Why not? he thought. "I would like that very much." He picked up his horse's tack, and his saddlebags, and shook them free of sand.

It was a short walk, and the harsh winds of day made way for the softer breeze of the evening. Ismai still felt hollowed-out, spent, and so tired he could hardly keep his feet straight. Char reached for Ehuani's saddle, and after a slight hesitation Ismai handed it to her. His boots and her bare feet whispered *shushhhh-shushhhh* through the sand, and off to the south and west the dunes began to sing.

Their song filled some of the darker empty corners of his heart, as they had since he was very small, though his heart had never before had such vast empty spaces to fill.

What a beautiful night, he thought. It seemed wrong that there should be a beautiful night after the death of Umm Nurati. But the indigo sky was beautiful, and the torches that lit the path down into Eid Kalmut were merry and welcoming, and the best part was that he did not have to explain any of this to his companion. She walked next to him, and she walked with him, and he was less alone than he had ever been in his whole life.

Then the smell of burning flesh reached him, and Ismai remembered some of the worse stories of Eid Kalmut. He stopped dead in his tracks until Char tugged at his sleeve, urging him forward. "What," he asked, "is that?"

He thought she might have smiled. "Roast hare and potatoes."

"Oh." His heart started up again. "I smelled something burning and I thought..." A nasty suspicion came to him. "Wait... you did that on purpose?"

She laughed and skipped ahead, down the smooth stone path between the torches. The valley to either side of the path, he saw, was thick with grasses and fur-willow and low flowering shrubs. He followed, almost smiling himself.

Since he was a small child, the Mothers had been frightening him with tales of Eid Kalmut, the Valley of Death. Dead kings were buried in this place, it was said, kings and queens and sorcerers and criminals of the worst sort. Wraiths haunted the passages and pathways of Eid Kalmut, bloodmyst and Horned Hunters and worse, lusting for the taste of a young child's flesh.

The reality was an entirely different story.

The walls of Eid Kalmut were steep and verdant, striated rock in rainbow hues of pink and orange and red, even some greens and blues in the torchlight, festooned like a feast-tent with ribbons and streamers and garlands of living things. A cloud of tiny bats whirred from a crack in the rocks as he passed, circling his head twice as if unsure what to make of him before flittering off into the night in search of bloodsucking insects. Ismai wished them much luck.

As for kings and queens… the walls were riddled with hundreds of hundreds of arched doorways. As Ismai drew near, he could see that there was a person seated in each one, a person long since gone to dry bones and old leather, but dressed in cloaks and robes and furs finer and more elaborate than anything he could remember, even finer than those worn by the Atualonian prince.

Each alcove was sealed with a delicate filigree wall of some shining metal, and the dead people on their carven wood chairs did not look as if they had any intention of rising up and eating his brains, as in the old stories. Rather, they looked… serene. As if they had lived well and died well and were perfectly content with the way things had turned out.

"It is beautiful here," he whispered. "Who are these people? Are they really kings and queens?" They certainly seemed so, with their fine clothes and haughty bones, and the antlered crowns upon their heads.

"They are my charges," she answered. "It is my duty to watch over them, just as it is your duty to watch over your pride."

Ismai said nothing.

"Not your fault," she told him, stepping more briskly. "Your mother faced a terrible enemy, and she fell. There is nothing you could have done to save her."

"My mother died in childbirth," he corrected. "How did you know she had died?"

"You can sleep here, by the fire. Are you hungry?"

He was famished, and three fat rabbits sizzled and crackled over the flames. He set his bags and saddle down, and put his hands on his hips.

"How did you know? What do you mean, enemy? My mother had no enemies. She was beloved of all the prides."

"The prides are not the whole world, though, are they? Perhaps I spoke of Time, the enemy who defeats us all." She looked away. "Eat, if you like. I am not hungry, but they were an offering and I do not like to see life wasted."

"An offering? Whose offering?"

"Eat."

Ismai made a frustrated sound in his throat, but he sat down and ate. The rabbits were very fat, crisp and dripping with hot juices, and he ate them down to the bones. She pushed the roast potatoes toward him and he ate those too, wondering where she might have gotten such things, but tired of asking questions into the wind. He supposed it was better to simply savor her company, and swallow the mystery.

It occurred to him that his mother might have said such a thing, and another pang took his heart. No less was his grief than it had been, no cooler to touch, but somehow the food and the fire and the company made it more bearable.

And I have found a fat young tarbok, purred Ruh'ayya. *I have eaten my fill of his entrails, and tomorrow I will roll in what is left.*

You are so gross, he thought, and felt her soft laughter.

Char sat on her heels before the fire, and cocked her head to one side. "You are talking to the young queen?"

He nodded and dug around in his bag for a waterskin. "She has made a kill and is quite pleased with herself."

"She is very strong, to have survived her first challenge. If she lives, she will be most powerful."

"Her first challenge?" he asked.

"Oh," she said.

"You know," he mused, leaning back against his saddlebags. So comfortable. "Sometimes talking to you is like playing riddle games with a rock."

The shadows did not quite hide her smile. "You play the riddle game with rocks?"

"My mother said it was good practice, if I ever wanted to understand women."

"You will win the riddle game against a rock before you ever understand women."

"Sometimes you do not sound much like a child," he told her.

"Sometimes I do not feel much like a child," she agreed. "Ismai—how is it you can look at my face?" She turned and faced him fully for the first time.

He shifted uncomfortably. "What do you mean? Your face is your face. I could look away, if you like."

"No, that is not what I mean. No one has ever looked..." Her voice grew uncertain. "Not without staring, or turning away. Or..." She shook her head slowly. "When you see my face, you see me."

"Why do you not laugh when I trip over my own feet, or fall off my horse?" He shrugged. "I am sorry you were hurt, and I am very sorry if people hurt you now. But your face is your face."

"You are a very strange boy."

"So I have been told."

"Ismai... wait, no." She twisted her hands together in her lap. "Wait, yes, yes. Stay right here. You will not follow me?"

"Never," he told her gently.

She stood and ran off into the dark, a scared little rabbit with a burned-off face.

Ismai bundled up the rabbit bones and threw them into the fire. The greasy black smoke twisted up toward the sky. He thought a small prayer for the rabbits, that their bright little souls might find their way to a pleasant world. The bones crackled and spat at him in their pyre, angry that their lives had been cut short so that he could fill his belly. But such was the life of a rabbit.

The dead kings stared at him across the fire, their eyes empty and solemn.

Somewhere far away a bintshi wailed, and Ismai felt his blood stir in response. He wondered what had drawn it so far from the Seared Lands, and shivered again.

A cloud of the little bats flapped and fluttered overhead, blotting out the pale moons.

Ruh'ayya's presence was a warm comfort in the back of his mind. She had gorged and rolled in offal, and was well pleased with life.

It must be nice to be a cat, he thought, *living only for the present. What matters today, or days past, when one has bathed in the blood of a good kill?*

You know nothing, she thought at him, but the thought had no claws in it. He sent a wash of gratitude and affection toward her, to which she responded with quiet amusement.

He was so near sleep that when Char's face emerged from the gloom, he jumped half out of his skin and kicked a stone into the fire, sending up a shower of sparks. She had pulled a tattered hood up over her head, and in her arms she held a bundle.

"*Shssss,*" she chided. "He is sleeping."

Ismai scrambled to his feet, and met her halfway. "What...? What?" He hushed his voice at her sharp look. "You have a child? No—you are too young."

"I am not as young as I seem." Her voice was scarce a whisper, and amused. "He is not mine... not really. I had thought to keep him, but..." She looked down at the swaddled child. "This is a resting-place for the dead, not a growing-place for the living. Here, take him." She held out her burdened arms, though her eyes belied the gesture. "He is broken, but he is not worthless."

"Broken?" Ismai took the sleeping child. He was heavier than he looked, and warm. Only one fat cheek and a hint of long-lashed sleeping eyes peeked from beneath the coverlet.

Char lifted the blankets aside. This close, Ismai could see the raw flesh above her eyes, and the exposed bone at one temple where an ear should be. He wondered if it hurt—it must—and his heart ached for her pain. Then he looked down at the child.

The little boy was four or five moons old, he guessed, perhaps old enough to fuss over cut teeth and roll about, maybe old enough to scoot around a bit. Rudya had begun crawling when she was just a bit older than this. This child would not be crawling on all fours. The boy was missing an arm just below the elbow. It looked to be a defect of birth, and not the result of some injury.

"Where did you get him?" he whispered, pulling the blankets tight against the chill. The child slept on, blissfully unaware.

"He is not worthless." Char's eyes flashed in her ruined face. "He is healthy, and strong. He is one of yours. You should take him home to your people, and never let them hurt him."

"Hurt him?" Ismai frowned. "We do not hurt children. Only a monster would harm a child."

Char was silent for a long, long time. Finally she whispered, "Where I come from…"

She did not finish the thought.

Ismai shifted the boy's weight in his arms. "I will take him, if that is what you truly wish. He will be well looked after—the Mothers are always delighted to have another child to fuss and coo over—and so few boy babies are born to us. He will be welcome.

"So would you, Char. You should come with me, too. As you said, this is a resting-place for the dead, and no place for a child." He held his breath, fearing a harsh reply, but she only shook her head.

"You are sweet, Ismai. But this is my home now. These are my people. I look after them, and they look after me." She held up a hand when he would protest. "Please, Ismai. Take the child and go."

"May I at least spend the night?"

"Best not." She sighed. "I am glad that you will be taking the boy, really I am, but I am sad, too, and when I am unhappy—" her eyes glittered "—Eid Kalmut is not a safe place to be."

"The bonelord—"

"Arushdemma will not bother you. He has a belly full of slavers."

That startled him. "Slavers?"

"Bad men from the river. They were taking the boy to Eid

Kalish, to sell him." Her eyes were as dark as the realm of Eth, those dark places in the sky untouched by any star. "I do not like slavers, Ismai."

"As you wish," he agreed slowly. "Ehuani is going to have a fit, you know. And Ruh'ayya may never forgive me."

I am coming, brother. We need to leave this place. Ruh'ayya's voice sounded tense. *Now.*

Char's eyes glittered. "Please go, Ismai."

Ismai nodded, and then he did a thing that surprised himself— he stepped as close to Char as he dared, and put an arm about her shoulders, gently, so as not to startle or hurt her. "I hope you know I would never hurt you," he said in the softest voice. "I hope you know I am your friend."

"My friend." A single tear spilled from her eye and trembled down her ruined cheek. "Yes. Please, you should go now." She ducked from beneath his arm. "I will carry your bags... come on."

He followed her up the steep path, choosing his way carefully, wondering how under the moons he was going to make the ride back to camp with an infant in his arms. Ehuani was waiting for them at the mouth of the Valley, as was Ruh'ayya. Char saddled his horse, and fastened his bags in place, and held the child as he mounted. He was pleased to see that Ehuani seemed fresh and eager to go, not at all put out by the unexpected journey.

Ismai reached for the infant, and settled him into the crook of one arm. "He is a good sleeper."

"He is." Char smiled, tears flowing freely now. "He is a good boy. I will miss him." She reached up a maimed hand and brushed at the baby's soft cheek. "Goodbye, Sammai."

"Sammai?" Ismai was taken aback. "You named him after me?"

"I could hardly name him otherwise." A dark cloud passed before the moons. "Ismai... go. Do not look back, this time. It is ill luck for you."

"*Jai tu wai*, Char." He laid his leg against Ehuani's warm side, and his mare stepped out willingly.

Warning or no, as he rode away he looked back and she was

watching him. Shrouded in shadow, as always, but the moonslight kissed briefly upon her face. When she saw him watching, she raised her hand in a brief wave, and then she was swallowed by the night.

Ismai had often puzzled over the strange fact that the road home always seemed shorter than the way out. One could ride all day to get to a place, and then turn around, take three strides, and be back where he had started. This was not such a ride.

For one thing, the babe—though he slept so deeply Ismai began to worry that it was an unnatural sleep or that the boy was ill—was heavy as a bag of stones. Ismai cradled him in the crook of one arm so that he could hold the reins in his other hand, and no matter how he shifted the boy's weight, his arm alternated between icy cramps and burning knots of pain, and soon his lower back joined the red chorus. Fire blazed a path from shoulder to shoulder and flared brighter with every careful step Ehuani took. Nor did he dare to ask for a faster pace, so walk they did.

The stars and moons were generous with their light, and the night was soft and warm. Ismai knew the way, so the path did not pose a problem. Neither did predators, lesser or greater. He heard no more of the bintshi's deadly plaintive song, there was no roar or grunt or shriek in the night, and no tangles of refuse rose up from the desert with the fell laugh of a bonelord. Not even the sands sang.

And the Zeera was never silent.

So Ismai rode through the night with most of the muscles in his body on fire, and every sense strained to the point of pain as his ka searched the night sands for the source of disquiet. Every hair along his arms and on the back of his neck prickled with the cold breath of dread, and Ruh'ayya sang a low, whining song under her breath as they crept along. Ehuani, his skittish and hot-blooded horse, was the only thing in the Zeera that seemed untroubled by whatever it was. She stepped along at a sedate walk, flicking her ears occasionally in a lazy manner, and never once offering to pick up the pace.

It was not the worst ride of Ismai's life, but it certainly seemed the longest.

Akari Sun Dragon had begun his courtship of the eastern sky by the time the three of them dragged into camp, footsore and road-weary. The camp was already ringing with the songs of forge and fire and industry, and the raucous mess finally woke the child from his slumber. The boy scrunched his face and wailed, announcing his outrage to the world. He opened his eyes—they were a greenish-brown and fringed with the softest-looking lashes—took one look at Ismai, and screamed fit to bust a bintshi, showing a fine set of two miniature teeth as he howled.

Make it stop! Ruh'ayya winced and flattened her ears.

How do you propose I do that? Ismai had brought Ehuani to a halt, but was not sure how he would dismount without dropping the now-flailing child. But the cries of an infant brought the camp to dead silence—and then to noisy life as every man there dropped what he was doing and hurried to find its source.

How should I know what a human cub wants? Lick its nose. Lick its butt. Give it a teat… just make it stop. She crouched, showed her fangs in a hissing snarl, and with a lash of her tail she was gone. *And it stinks!*

Ismai found himself once more the center of unwelcome attention. Tannerman Jorah took Ehuani's reins and steadied Ismai as he threw a leg over his mare's back and slid gracelessly to the ground. Mastersmith Hadid put a beefy hand on his shoulder to steady him as he tottered over to sit on a large rock at the fire's edge. The smith shouted for food and water to be brought for Ismai, and a churra in milk for the child. The entire campful of men milled around for a few moments staring wide-eyed at the boy and the squalling child.

It might have been funny were Ismai not wearied to the bone. He swayed where he sat, but held fast to Sammai, who was in no way grateful.

Loreman Aaraf stepped forward and reached for the child. Ismai held the boy out, surprised at his own reluctance. He took a few swallows of water and a bite of flatbread as the healer unwrapped the furious infant and looked him over. He peered into the child's wide and wailing mouth, rubbed the small ear between his leathery old fingers, poked his squishy belly, squeezed the dimpled knees and elbows, and finally ran his hand over the chubby half-arm, smiling a little when the boy poked him in the eye with it.

"A fine Zeerani boy, though I have not heard tell of such a child being born among us," he declared at last, handing him back to Ismai as his apprentice arrived with a bowl of warm churra milk, yellow and thick with sweet fat. "Half an arm will hardly slow that one down, I am thinking. He wants feeding—" he wrinkled his nose as the other men chuckled "—and changing, but for all that he is as healthy a child as we could wish. What tree might you have plucked this fine, fat fruit from, Ismai Ja'Sajani? For I have never heard that such a tree grows in these parts."

Ismai dipped a corner of bread into the milk, and let some drip into the child's mouth. It did not take much coaxing for Sammai to latch onto it and cease his bawling. Indeed, the roundness of his belly was soon explained as he gummed and gobbled his way through Ismai's breakfast. "No tree, Loreman Aaraf. The boy was given to my care by a friend of mine. A girl."

Mastersmith Hadid lifted both brows at this. "Girl? What girl? Is the child hers, then?" He looked closely at Ismai. "Is he yours? You have not been here long enough to have fathered a child! And where is his mother?"

Boraz Ja'Sajani folded both arms across his chest and scowled fiercely at Ismai.

"Boy?"

Ismai sighed and shifted the child, who was making a happy mess of the last bit of milk-sopped bread and who indeed stank like a three-day-dead lionsnake. Perhaps worse.

"Her name is Char. She is young, and wounded, and very

shy. I had hoped to talk her into coming back with us to Aish Kalumm…" He broke off at their stares. "What?"

"Char? *Charon?*" Aaraf gaped open-mouthed at him, and took a half-step back. "Charon of Eid Kalmut?"

"She lives there, yes. She has no people… what?"

"You met the Guardian," Hadid whispered. The smith's eyes were wide and white as a spooked horse's. "The Guardian of Eid Kalmut."

Istaz Aadl took a half step forward, and drew his sword. "That is no infant… it is a fell spirit of death."

Ismai curled his body protectively about Sammai.

Ruh'ayya roared, not far away. *I come.* Another vash'ai roared an answer to her challenge, and a third.

"You will not harm this child." Ismai glared at the youthmaster, though he could scarce keep his eyes from the man's shamsi.

Istaz Aadl bared his teeth. "You insolent—"

Jasin stepped forward and stood between Ismai and the youthmaster. After a moment, Hadid did the same. Aadl shot them both a dark look, but lowered his sword.

"I was abandoned by my people and bought from the slavers' ships," Jasin said. He met Ismai's eyes, and nodded.

"Many of our children are found or boughten," the loreman agreed. "The Zeeranim do not harm children, Aadl."

"How do we know this is a child?" Istaz Aadl demanded. "No one has ever spoken to the Guardian and come away untouched. How do we know this is not some fell spirit come to kill us all in our sleep?"

Just then, the boy looked at Ismai, and smiled, and made the strangest face. The silence of the Zeera was split by a terrible noise, and a worse smell. The silence lasted a heartbeat more, and then the entire camp erupted in laughter.

"*Ai yeh*," Jasin groaned. "Not even an evil spirit could smell like that."

"*Za fik*," Ismai gasped. "*Za fik!*" He held the cooing, grinning, stinking infant as far away as his arms could reach.

Ruh'ayya bounded, teeth bared, into the circle, and then stopped and sneezed.

"Well, Aadl, I believe that answers your question." Hadid laughed and slapped the shorter man on his back. Aadl still scowled, but he sheathed his sword.

"I still say the child is ill luck."

"Time will tell," the big smith answered with a shrug, "but I believe we can agree that this is, indeed, a child. Also that young Ismai Ja'Sajani here may have the changing of it. After that, who knows?"

"I will take the babe to Aish Kalumm," the loremaster offered. "My apprentice and I need to gather river-herbs in any case, and we can take the milk-churra with us. Would you care to accompany us, Ismai Ja'Sajani? The boy was given into your care, after all. What say you?"

Ismai held the baby closer, ignoring the stink, and stroked his soft brown cheek. Sammai grabbed his finger in one fat hand and waved his stump triumphantly, screeching.

Nice fangs, Ruh'ayya laughed.

"Char said there were slavers," he said slowly. "Slavers in the Zeera, come to steal our children. I say… not on my watch."

"Slavers," Hadid growled. "Not on my watch."

"Not on my watch," agreed Jasin. His fingers were white where they gripped the hilt of his shamsi.

"I think the loremen should take Sammai to the Mothers, but I would like to stay and hunt for any remaining slavers." Ismai played with the infant's tiny, tender fingers. "I would see their blood upon the sand." He felt foolish even as he said the words, a boy playing at being a man, but it was what his mother would have wanted him to do.

More—it was what *he* wanted to do.

Makil Ja'Sajani, near the back of the group, raised his shamsi high, so that it flashed in the light of the Sun Dragon.

"*Ja'Sajani.*"

"Ja'Sajani!" One by one, the other wardens raised their swords in silent salute. Mastersmith Hadid folded his massive arms across his chest and nodded.

Istaz Aadl was last. He looked at Ismai for a long moment, his face unreadable, before pointing his sword first at Ismai and then toward the sun.

"We may make a warden of you yet," the youthmaster said, and then he grinned. "If we can keep you from falling off your horse."

THIRTY-FOUR

"I do not think this is the time or the place for this fool spectacle to be held. Atualon is on a knife's edge as it is—between rumors of the king's ill health, the threat of war from the east, and an influx of barbarians with barbaric ways, you could ladle tension from the air and eat it as a soup. Add a few dozen Ja'Akari to the mix—shortly after they have lost their First Mother, mind you—a few foreign sorcerers, and Matteira's rabble-rousers... the whole city may go up in flames." Hafsa Azeina pinched the bridge of her nose. "I say it is foolishness."

Loremaster Rothfaust spread his hands wide. Luli, his sunshell-colored mantid, peeked from beneath his beard, tilted her buggy little face at them, and chirruped. "Yet here we are, and here they are, and it is up to us to make sure the spectacle proceeds smoothly." He reached up and patted his little pet, and smiled around the room. "It is the will of Ka Atu."

"It is the will of Ka Atu that I speak on his behalf on such matters, that he may devote more of his time to ensuring the safety of us all." Indeed, she saw how exhausted he was at day's end, and wondered how the stubborn old goat had managed by himself for this long. "The Council needs to spend more time working to support his efforts, and less time worrying about song and dance. Have you forgotten the threats that face us even now? Do you think the Daemon Emperor and his generals spend their days frolicking and throwing flowers to a troupe of fools?"

"Would that he might," Loremaster Rothfaust muttered into his beard. "The world would be a better place if there were more fools and fewer kings."

The Third Circle was breaking fast together in the Sunrise Chamber. Hafsa Azeina, as queen consort, had commanded—not asked, commanded—that they attend her here before dawn, and tempers were sharp. She accepted a mug of coffee from a servant girl with a nod of thanks. Rothfaust took one as well, and winked at the girl over the top of the mug. The only patreon to decline the treat was Santorus, who made a point of sticking his nose in the air and making a snide comment about "foreign drink."

It was too early for this nonsense.

"This is wonderful stuff. Wonderful!" Ezio enthused. He inhaled the coffee's steam and rolled his eyes. "I have no idea how we ever managed without it. My reckoners thrive on the stuff. Marvelous! Have we worked out the trade agreements yet? I dare say this would smooth the edges even of the Daemon Emperor. What need for war, when one has coffee? And you say it is made from beans? Astonishing!"

"That explains it, then," laughed Mattu Halfmask. "Beans for the bean counters." Today he wore the face of a spike-horned stag with antlers in spring velvet.

Yes. Definitely too early.

"I, myself, was rather looking forward to the diversion." Aasah smiled as he spooned honey into his coffee. "We of Atualon should greet all others with open arms."

"And closed purses, eh, Ezio?" Mattu grinned at the older man's cross look. "I see that you take your coffee as you take your women, Shadowmancer. Speaking of dark and sweet, where is your little apprentice?"

Aasah set his mug down with a click. His face had gone dangerously blank.

"Yaela is none of your business."

Mattu opened his mouth again, but Hafsa Azeina cut him off with a short motion of her hand.

"Enough, Halfmask. If you want to die in pieces, may I suggest you sign up to fight one of the bear dancers? It would probably be an easier death."

His mismatched eyes crinkled. "I was hoping to die in my sleep."

Hafsa Azeina held out her empty mug, and the servant girl hurried to fill it. "You may yet."

"What exactly are we here for, might I ask?" Ezio smiled as a pair of young boys brought platters of fruits and goat's-stomach cheese. "Ah!"

"To discuss this spectacle, for the most part. I share the concerns of our beloved Issa." The loremaster smiled at Hafsa Azeina's nod—they had discussed this beforehand. "Much as I, too, have been looking forward to the entertainments, perhaps now is not the time. The daughter of Ka Atu is but recently returned. Perhaps a sober celebration in her honor would be more appropriate. We might wait on holding any celebration at all until she has fully healed from her wounds, and until our, ah, honored guests have departed. There have been incidents…"

"If those desert sluts would not walk around with their breasts bare—" Santorus began.

"*Desert sluts?*"

Every man in the room shot to his feet. Mattu Halfmask was the first, Hafsa Azeina noted, and Santorus last to rise. She remained seated and kept her face cool, though her heart leapt like a stag to see her daughter's face flushed with health and fury.

"Desert sluts?" Sulema asked again. She wore a gold circlet and the white-and-gold robes of the ne Atu, and the angry glare of a pissed-off female. She walked to stand beside her mother, feet planted shoulder-wide, fingers rubbing absently at her newly mended arm, wide mouth in a hard line. "Surely you are not referring to my people, Patreon… Santorus, is it?"

Leviathus followed his sister into the chamber, not bothering to hide his amusement. "Santorus has never approved of foreign women and their wicked ways."

"Or Atualonian women, with *their* wicked ways," Mattu agreed, and drained his cup. "Or women at all. Good morning, ne Atu, I trust you slept well?"

"The messenger was slow to tell us of this meeting." Leviathus stopped just behind Hafsa Azeina's chair, lending her his tacit support.

"He was *bribed*." Sulema's eyes fairly glowed with outrage.

"I trust you showed him the error of his ways?"

"I set him to cleaning churra pits." Sulema threw herself down on the bench beside Hafsa Azeina, and took a cup of coffee from the blushing servant boy. "What is that horrible smell?"

"Goat's-stomach cheese, ne Atu." Ezio smiled beatifically at her, and pushed the tray closer. "Try some… it thickens and cools the blood, eh, Master Santorus?"

The healer nodded, eyes still shifting away from the daughter of Wyvernus.

"It stinks!" She wrinkled her freckled nose.

"My sister has the sensibilities of a princess," Leviathus said. "She prefers to break her fast on spiders' eggs."

"Spiders' eggs!" exclaimed Rothfaust. "What a horrible thought!"

Sulema and her brother shared a grin, and Hafsa Azeina was surprised to feel jealousy stab her heart. She cleared her throat and waited for the men to turn their eyes back to her.

"We were discussing the spectacle," she tried again.

"It will be wonderful!" Sulema enthused, suddenly bright as the sunrise that had begun to flood the chamber. "Leviathus was telling me about it… it was his idea. There will be fighting, and races, and magic… and dancing bears! He says none of the Atualonians have ever seen Ja'Akari fight. The healers say my arm is fit enough for light sparring, and Saskia has agreed to dance with me—"

"What?" The smile was wiped clean from Leviathus's face. "Wait, no…"

"Ne Atu, fighting in the arena like a common slu— like a…" Santorus spluttered to a flummoxed halt. "It is not seemly. No!"

Loremaster Rothfaust sat back and stroked his beard, saying nothing, though his eyes were suspiciously bright. Luli peeked out at Sulema, waved her delicate antennae, and trilled sweetly.

Hafsa Azeina sighed and reminded herself that it was unqueenly to punch a man in the nose, even if he was an idiot.

"No?" Sulema stood, every inch of her radiating affronted pride. "No. You old men tell me I cannot do this thing. That it is not seemly. *I* am Sulema Ja'Akari. I will dance the swords if I choose, and I will wear what I choose to wear. I will fight *naked* if that is my desire. I will take a hayatani." The girl looked straight at Mattu Halfmask as she said this. "If one wagging old tongue dares touch my name, it will be wagging its way into the soup pot. Brother, would you care to walk in the gardens with a desert slut? I believe I have had my share of these windy old men and their stinky cheeses."

Leviathus bowed to the Third Circle, hiding his laugh with a cough, and the two of them exited in a swirl of white-and-gold arrogance.

"That went well," Ezio muttered, spreading a knife full of pungent cheese on a round of flat bread.

Hafsa Azeina pushed the cloud of short hair back from her face and glared at the men seated around her.

"You are all idiots," she informed them. "That settles it. Your spectacle will just have to wait for a better time. Were it to be held now, with tensions so high and common sense so sorely lacking, such a thing would be destined to degenerate into goatfuckery and bloodshed. I speak for Ka Atu in this, and I forbid it."

"I can see where the girl gets her shy nature," ventured Loremaster Rothfaust into the silence. Luli peeped and pulled her head back into his wild gray beard.

Hafsa Azeina found that she had lost her patience with stinky old men and their cheeses, as well. She rose, causing them all to scramble to their feet once more, and gave them the faintest nod of her head. "If there is nothing else." Her tone indicated that there had better not be. "Patreons."

As Hafsa Azeina stormed down the corridors, servants and courtiers alike scattered from her path. Her foul mood had not been improved by the morning's foolery. Her legs ached from walking on hard stone morning to night, the halls grew close and oppressive, and she could blame her malaise neither on a woman's moonsblood nor on her link to Khurra'an.

The vash'ai was in a fine mood, as the kitchen-girls had let him kill a young pig and even now were brushing his hair in the sunlight. She could feel him purring all the way across the palace.

You grow fat and lazy, she chided him, but her heart was not in it.

You should try it sometime. Maybe get that knot out of your tail, he responded.

She found herself wishing for the company of Ani. The youthmistress could always be counted on for a level-headed view of things, and was more observant than she seemed. If all else failed, they could share a bottle of usca and she could listen to the other woman's exploits.

Then again, her friend would have been wholeheartedly in favor of that fool spectacle.

Friend. She had not thought of the other woman as a friend for some time, and wondered whether it was still true. Can a monster have friends? Can the queen consort have a life of her own? She shrugged the thought away. This place and these people with their false smiles and clouds of perfume were getting to her. It would be nice to get on a horse and just ride with someone whose ambitions ran no deeper than hunting tarbok and occasionally hunting Askander Ja'Sajani.

Once in her chambers, she stripped off the gaudy robes of the queen consort and dressed in a Zeerani tunic, sheer and simple. She tied what was left of her hair back as best she could with a leather thong. She washed the powders and paints from her face, and scrubbed away the perfumes until she smelled more like herself and less like a whorehouse on a hot day. Then she drank half a pitcher of sweet water.

Ah, she thought, *human again.* Or as close as she would ever be.

A pounding on the door warned of Saskia, and Hafsa Azeina's lips twitched. The girl was likely to break a door down before she learned to knock like civilized folk. The dreamshifter rose even as the door banged open. Saskia stood framed in the doorway, all sullen scowl and affronted elbows. Had she been a lionsnake, her feathers would have been standing straight out around her head.

"Some outlander *bint* wishes to see you. I left her in the atrium," she said, and turned to stomp off.

"Saskia Ja'Akari." She made it a request, so as not to add further insult to the warrior's injured pride. "Please, stay."

The girl's scowl darkened, and she leaned against the door's frame. "Dreamshifter?"

"I would ask a favor of you. I need you to act as my private guard while we are in Atualon."

"What? Why?"

"It is customary for a member of the royal family to be accompanied by a private guard," she explained, "so no one will think twice if you are with me at all times. Well, they will think twice, because you are a barbarian, and pretty besides. But if you are known as my guard, the palace will be open to you. Would you agree to do this?"

"Why do you need a guard? You are a ruler of this land. You are in no danger."

"I am consort to the ruler, not a ruler in my own right. A disgraced consort, no less. Were it not for the king's desire to win over Sulema, my life would be forfeit." She smiled without a trace of humor. "Such a life as it is. You are Ja'Akari, Saskia. Think like a warrior. Does this place *feel* safe to you?"

"No. It feels like a trap."

"One that has been sprung, yes."

"If this is a trap, Dreamshifter, who is the intended prey?"

"An excellent question. Now you think like a Ja'Akari. I need you to be my eyes and ears. As a guard, you may walk unremarked where I cannot—the kitchens, the barracks, the inns. Keep your eyes open, and your ears, and your ka. Be wary of your dreams. There are traps in Shehannam as well."

Saskia snorted and pushed herself upright. "Well, this is

encouraging, Dreamshifter. Some of the others were worried that you had gone back to the outlanders' ways. I will be happy to correct them."

"Best you do not."

"You wish me to *lie*?" The girl sounded scandalized.

"Of course not. But I do trust you to be discreet."

The girl considered her words for a moment, then nodded.

"If I flush out our enemies, you will devour their hearts, that we may rest easier at night."

Hafsa Azeina inclined her head.

"Then I will do this thing, and when it is finished we will go home. This is good. *Ehuani*, when we go I may take a few of these Atualonian men home with me. The outlanders may not be suitable for hayatani, but," her grin was predatory, "I do like the kilts. I am beginning to think our men should show off more leg."

The girl was incorrigible. Hafsa Azeina remembered that there was a reason for this visit.

"I had best go see this visitor you spoke of. What does she look like?"

Saskia shrugged. "Like an outlander. Pale and weak."

Hafsa Azeina reached out to Khurra'an. The sire dozed in a sunlit corner of the kitchen courtyard. *Can you meet me in the atrium?*

Danger?

Always.

I come.

She left her quarters and Saskia fell in behind her, moving with the loose-hipped and arrogant walk of a warrior. The young woman eyed the Draiksguard openly, and men snapped to attention as they passed. Hafsa Azeina smiled grimly. She should have thought of such a ruse earlier. Next to this vibrant girl, she would be all but invisible.

The Queen's Atrium was at the bottom of the tower, and it had once been Hafsa Azeina's favorite place in all the world. A very feminine, very female retreat with high arches and panes of clear glass to let sunlight and air into the gardens, pink crushed stone pathways, a riot of verdant life and brilliant flowers. At its very center the Queen's Pool burbled and splashed merrily, crowded with stone turtles and whimsical fishes and birds and fantastical animals. Hafsa Azeina recognized a golden kirin peeking from between the fronds of a giant fern. She remembered the day Wyvernus had given it to her, and how she had kissed him.

In the center of the pool, a sculpture of Sajani Earth Dragon depicted in human form lay supine upon a giant lily-pad. So skillfully had she been wrought that her blue alabaster skin looked soft and warm. It seemed that she might wake with a smile at any moment. Coins of gold and silver, gems and jewels and pearls of every description, and even humble pewter slags littered the lily-pad and shone in the water all around her sleeping form. A true dragon's horde, wishes for wealth and health and happiness. And, of course, wishes for children.

How perilous of us, she thought, *to entrust all our hopes to a dragon.*

The Queen's Atrium had once hummed with life like a hive full of fat honey-bees. Now the queen's maids were gone, and with them the children, and their swarming attendants. A few gardeners grubbed in the dirt. One short woman in a plantmaster's smock was scolding a group of Draiksguard as they maneuvered the roots of a young tree into a hole, like a wren harassing an arrogance of dragons.

It was quiet now, but despite the warmth and promise of *saghaani*—and this, a young day late in the spring, was the very essence of beauty in youth—it felt like a dread quiet, the kind of sound one might experience in a sickroom or before an execution, or in the hours before a deadly storm.

A young woman sat on a white stone bench near the pool. She was wrapped neck-to-ankles in a gown cut in the Western style and meant to hide and suggest a woman's curves. Her glossy hair was bound in a net of spidersilk and jewels fashioned to look like tiny red roses, so realistic that dew on their miniature leaves glistened in the early light. Her face and lips were flushed with health, her dark eyes bright with mischief, and her fingertips and the soles of her bare feet glittered with gold dust. She was exquisite, a doll on a shelf, and though the skin of her face was naked to the sun, still it was no more her true face than her brother's masks were his.

Hafsa Azeina stopped near the woman, and she could hear Saskia's quiet breath at her back.

"Matteira." She inclined her head. "Good morning to you."

"It is, is it not?" The lovely young woman rose with exquisite grace and held out both hands so there was nothing for Hafsa Azeina to do but take them. They were surprisingly strong, and warm, and calloused. "I have not been to the atrium in so long—hardly ever, since Mother… I see the gardeners have tended her roses well."

"I should say Atualon has tended her roses well," Hafsa Azeina suggested, as Matteira bent to kiss her fingertips after the manner of the river folk. "You were beautiful as a child, but it is a scandal that any woman should be so lovely. Bashaba was a true friend to me when we were young. You favor her, you know."

"So I have been told. Oh, Zeina, we have missed you! You must promise never, never to go away again. Atualon is simply no fun without you. Look at you… dressed like a barbarian warrior-queen, and your skin spotted like a cat's. And your hair, your beautiful hair! Was Ka Atu furious?"

"Ka Atu can hardly complain about my hair, since he seems to have misplaced his own." A reluctant smile tugged at the corner of her mouth. Matteira had been as delightful a child as she was beautiful. "I hear you own a fools' troupe now?"

Matteira waved her hand. "Oh, yes. They needed a patroness and I needed something to spend my brother's money on besides clothes. Speaking of which, we need to get you to a real dressmaker. Zeina, oh. Oh!" Her eyes went wide and round. "Ohhhh, he's beautiful. Is he yours? I had heard the barbarians had great cats for pets, but oh, Zeina! Is he safe?"

Pets? Khurra'an huffed as he came up to stand beside her.

"Safe?" She laughed. "Of course he is not safe. Neither is he a pet, Matteira—you should know better. Khurra'an is foremost sire of the vash'ai. Khurra'an, beloved, forgive this impertinent cub. If you kill her for her insolence, please make it a clean death."

"A clean death is better than many would give the daughter of Serpentus."

The words hung in the air between them like an angry new ghost.

"Is this why you have come, Matteira? Your life and your brother's were secured long ago. Certainly my return does nothing to change this. Unless you or Mattu have suddenly become echovete, and wish to reclaim your father's throne."

"Not I," the girl said, with a sober look. *This* was the girl behind the mask. "Not Mattu."

"In that case, you are no threat to me and mine." *Are you?*

"A threat… no. A way out, perhaps. I know you have no wish to remain in Atualon. This is no place for you or your daughter."

"*Your blood is the wrong color,*" Daru had said. The hairs on Hafsa Azeina's nape prickled as Matteira fumbled at the purse on her hip. It had been long years since she had misjudged an enemy.

"Hands still," she growled. Khurra'an rumbled a low counterpart, and the girl froze.

"It is not… I am not… it is not what you think," she protested. Khurra'an padded closer, until his nose was a ghost's breath from the girl's collarbone. The girl held so still she was hardly there at all.

She is not afraid of me, the cat thought. *Or of you.*

She is shaking like a leaf.

Like a bird pretending at a broken wing. There is no smell of fear on this one. He sounded more amused than anything. *But she does not smell of a threat, either.*

Hafsa Azeina stared into the girl's eyes, and knew that her own were as cold and hard as drowned stones.

"Well? Let us see, then."

Matteira drew forth a book—a slender volume bound in dark leather, with leaves stamped in gold all along its spine. She held it out, hand trembling, and the dreamshifter stepped forward to take it.

"You can stop pretending to be afraid of me. I have lived too long among the barbarians—lies and games simply are not as much fun as they used to be."

Matteira relaxed, folded her arms across her chest, and gave Khurra'an an accusing glare. He bared his tusks in a cat's grin and threw himself on the ground between them.

Tell her to rub my belly.

Do you promise to keep your claws sheathed?

No.

Then I will not. She looked at the book, and then looked closer. *A Guide to the Herbs of Atualon, their Lore and Uses, Volume Nine.* She turned the slim and beautiful volume over. Her hands were shaking now, and it was no pretense. There, on the back cover, was stamped the name of the woman who had written and illustrated this book: *Bashaba.* She opened the book. Its spine was stiff, the pages white and crisp as new-flensed bones.

"Your mother wrote this." There was no mistaking that hand, the artist's eye.

"She did."

"I had thought there were only six volumes in this collection. When was this written?"

"She finished it this past Winterseve, just in time for my name-day."

Hafsa Azeina sank to the bench. The world about her seemed to shudder, as if she was in Shehannam and the Huntress had sounded her horn.

"Bashaba is *alive*?"

"Very much so, alive and locked away from the world. She has been held in Salar Merraj since my father was killed, sealed away from atulfah and held hostage against my good behavior and Mattu's. We exchange letters once a year, though I am not allowed to see her." Her voice broke on the last word, and she fell silent.

"I never knew." She slammed her mind's doors shut, lest Wyvernus feel her growing rage. "I was told she had been killed."

Matteira took the bench next to her, and plucked the book out of her nerveless fingers. "I know. That was one of the things we had to promise—never to tell anyone she was alive. If anyone found out, she would be killed."

"You were *children*."

Matteira's smile was devoid of all warmth. "Welcome to Atualon."

Her thoughts had scattered like a clutch of spiderlings, and Hafsa Azeina struggled to gather them in.

"What do you want from me, exactly? Why come to me now, and risk your mother's death after all these years?"

"My mother has grown tired of captivity. She wishes to be free."

"I can hardly help your mother to escape when I am trapped as well."

"You misunderstand me." Matteira replaced the book in its leather purse. "My mother does not wish to escape. She wishes to return to Atualon... as queen."

"That is not possible. She has been sealed."

"Anything is possible, once a woman sets her heart to it. My mother believes that she has found a way to dissolve her seal. She would be able to return to Atualon and take her place as Sa Atu, wielding power beside Ka Atu as she once did for my father. Perhaps in time she would bear another child, and that child might be echovete. The ruling families would be united once more, under the guidance of two great leaders. The Dragon would be kept peacefully at rest for another generation. I would have my mother back. And you—" her smile widened, like a cat that knows it has caught its prey "—you and your daughter would be free to leave."

It is as if I have been playing a game of Snakes and Stones, Hafsa Azeina thought, *only to find out my enemies have been playing Twenty Moons.* But she said only, "What do you wish me to do?"

"My brother and I have sent messengers out—discreet messengers, I assure you—to the *parens* of those families I believe might listen to reason. Several of the members of the First Circle have agreed to meet with us on neutral ground, a Mer family stronghold. If you would but speak to them with us, and join them to our cause, we might approach Ka Atu together and persuade him to see reason."

"We might approach Akari Sun Dragon and persuade him not to burn so brightly, while we are at it. Wyvernus would never agree to such a thing."

"Would he not? If he refuses us, he is left with his failing strength and one untrained girl. If he agrees, he will have a true queen and helpmeet. Would he give up a chance to hold onto the Dragon Throne, do you think, for this new-found daughter?"

"Everyone gets what they want," Hafsa Azeina mused. "How often in life does that happen?"

Never, when two-leggeds are involved, opined Khurra'an. *I have watched you play your human games. Not once have I seen a game end with all hunters and no prey.*

I have played deadlier games than this, and with deadlier opponents. Never have I been prey. "I will meet with these parens," she decided, "and I will hear what they have to say."

Bashaba was *alive*—Wyvernus had lied to her, for all those years he had lied to her. The thought was a thorn hooked deep into her flesh.

A thought that was not hers came to her then, seductive and dark.

When a thorn is sharp and wicked, Belzaleel suggested, *one needs a sharp and wicked blade to cut it free.*

THIRTY-FIVE

In the pastures below Atukos, Saskia and the other new Ja'Akari played a game of aklashi.

Sulema watched them from her seat on the balcony. They played with a ball, not a sheep's head, and Murya on her little silver bay darted in and around the others as if they stood still, whooping and flapping her elbows as she hit the ball for another point. For all her speed and agility, Murya was a ridiculously sloppy rider. She stuck to her horse like a burr and handled the club well, but Sulema thought she looked like a sack full of cats stuck atop a horse. Saskia intercepted the ball and they were off again, tearing across the pasture and shrieking like a bintshi.

It stung. She wanted to be down there with her pridemates, laughing and playing aklashi under the sun. She could see Atemi in a far pasture, head high and tail flagged, running back and forth and whinnying. She wanted to play, too. Sulema slapped an open palm upon her thigh. She hated the weakness that bound her here, the fever that would not abate, the soft pillows that propped her up, and the short dress they had given her to wear. She leaned back against the cushions and closed her eyes with a sigh, knowing that she was acting like a child, too frustrated to care.

"I am Ja'Akari," she muttered. "I am Ja'Akari."

Somewhere in her dreams, Jinchua laughed.

"You are Ja'Akari," a voice agreed. "So stop sulking like a child."

Sulema's eyes snapped open. "Istaza Ani!"

The older woman stepped forward and into the sunlight. "Sulema Ja'Akari."

"How did you get here?"

"I rode my horse—how do you think I got here?" She frowned. "You look pale. They eat too much bread and honey here, not enough meat. I brought this for you." She tossed a small bag, underhand. Sulema snatched it from the air without thinking, and opened it to peer inside.

Lionsnake jerky. She scowled, and then surprised herself by laughing. "I hate lionsnake!"

"I know that well. But you killed the damn thing, so you eat it. Feigning your own death will not excuse you."

Sulema brought a strip of the dried meat to her mouth and gnawed a piece off, grimacing at the taste.

"What were you thinking?" Ani asked. "Hunting a lionsnake that big by yourself was a foolish thing to do, even for you."

"I…" Sulema's voice trailed off. "I thought… it was supposed to be a small lionsnake."

"Oh?" Ani asked, her voice soft and dangerous. "Why did you think that?"

"I…" Sulema rubbed her aching temples. "I do not remember."

There was a long pause, and then Ani clucked her tongue. "It does not matter, I suppose. In any case, the skin and feathers have been saved, and we will give them to Hannei Ja'Akari. A warrior's first snake should be gifted to her sword-sister."

Sulema dropped the bag of pemmican and sat upright. "Hannei healed well?"

"Indeed she did, and better than you have."

"Oh. And, ah…" Sulema played with the strings that had held the bag of jerky closed. "And Tammas Ja'Sajani?"

Ani snorted. "I take it no outlander man has caught your eye?"

"Outlander men are all soft and pale as a fish's belly. Besides, they are afraid to so much as look at me. My father is the Dragon King, and my mother is a barbarian dreamshifter. I will *never* lose my blasted virginity."

Ani spluttered with laughter.

"As far as I know, no girl has yet sunk her claws into our handsome young warden." Her face softened, and Ani stepped forward and sat at the end of the stone bench. "He mourns his mother. They were very close."

"I wish I could go to him."

"You are not well enough to ride." Ani looked closely at her face. "Do you not like it here?"

"Oh, it is nice enough. Everything is very…" She waved her hand vaguely. "Very nice. And big. Everyone is so kind."

"And your father?" Ani asked. Sulema did not miss how her eyes sharpened. "How is it to know that you are the daughter of such a powerful man? He is, you know, one of the most powerful men in the world. Do you not enjoy these things?"

Sulema hesitated. *I am Ja'Akari,* she reminded herself, *and under the sun, we do not lie.*

"I like it," she whispered. "The servants, and the soft beds, and the wine—their beer is terrible, but their wine is better than ours— new clothes every day, and um…" She grinned. "Men everywhere. Have you seen how they dress? They have no shame."

Ani snorted.

"I like it very much," Sulema went on, more slowly now, "but it does not feel good, *ehuani.* Do you remember the time Hannei and I snuck into the kitchens when we were little, and ate an entire pan of honey cakes and drank a bottle of mead? It feels like that. Too sweet, and too much of it."

Ani smiled. "You are wiser than I thought, child."

"I am wiser than anyone thinks." Sulema grinned. "Please do not tell my mother." She leaned back and closed her eyes. "I am much improved since the healing, but I still tire so easily. Like an old woman."

Ani patted her knee. "It will pass. Oh, did anyone tell you? That lionsnake you killed had a clutch of eggs…"

She related to Sulema the story of how she and Hannei had gone off to hunt lionsnake whelps, and Sulema laughed at the image of Ani knocking the little beasties into the air for the vash'ai to chase.

"I have never heard of a wild vash'ai speaking with a human," she marveled. "Are you sure you are not Zeeravashani?"

"Very sure. Inna'hael assures me that we are not." Ani grimaced and rubbed at her arm, where only that morning he had bitten her.

"Daily." She changed the subject. "*I* have never heard of anyone as young as you walking Shehannam." She nodded at Sulema's fox-head staff, leaning in its accustomed place in the corner. "So, your kima'a is a fennec?"

Sulema smiled. "Her name is Jinchua. I have not found my way back to Shehannam since my father healed me, though I feel sometimes that I am close to it."

"Your mother will not teach you?"

"She says that it is too dangerous. When I return to Aish Kalumm, I will seek another. I know there is a dreamshifter from Uthrak…"

"Sulema." Ani lifted her hand. "Stop. You know you will not be going back to the Zeera."

Sulema's mouth dropped open. "Not return? But my father promised I could, if that was my choice. He promised! I am Ja'Akari…"

"You are Ja'Akari," Ani agreed, "and your heart will remain with the people, I know this. I know you. But I also know people, and I know a bit about politics, and power. You are the daughter of Ka Atu, Sulema, and you have proven that you are not surdus, you are not deaf to magic. This means you can learn to channel atulfah, and take your father's place. Do you know what they are calling you, in the streets below?"

"Sa Atu."

"Sa Atu," Ani agreed. "The Dragon's Legacy. Do you really believe they will let you go? Think, girl. You are a child no more… open your eyes."

"No," Sulema whispered. Her heart beat loud as a dancer's drums. "No, they will not." She looked away from Ani, away from the palace, down to where Murya rode her mare in a canter around the field, holding the ball over her head and whooping with victory. The game had come to an end. "It is not fair."

"Golden child," Ani said quietly, "what do you know of fair and unfair? Born into wealth and plenty, raised in a time without war, watched over day and night by the most powerful woman in the Zeera. *Unfair* is the annihilation of an entire people, to the point where they have to sell their last remaining girl-child into the Zeera in an attempt to save her life. Unfair is your mother having to flee from everything she knew, everything she loved, and become something she hates with all her heart. Unfair..." She shook her head. "Forgive me, child, this is none of your doing. But fair has nothing to do with life or death."

Sulema stared at her. She had never heard the youthmistress speak such words.

"My mother says 'life is pain.'"

"'Only death comes easy.' So you were listening."

"I was. I am. Tell me, please, what will happen now?"

"I am not a dreamshifter like your mother. I am not a leader of the people, nor even Ja'Akari. But I listen to the song of the world, Sulema. You should, too. You can hear it in the looks the vash'ai give their partners, when it seems no one is watching. You can hear it in the hunting cries of the greater predators stalking closer to the prides every year, not nearly as shy of us as they were in years past. You can hear it in the black sails of the slavers' ships, grown bold enough to snatch children from our very shores. Most assuredly you can hear it here, in the city of the Sleeping Dragon."

"Hear what?" she whispered, dreading the answer.

"The pounding of the drums of war, child. This city has been asleep for long years as Ka Atu grew old and resigned to the fact that he might die without an heir. Now a child of Ka Atu has returned, a child who may be able to control the pulse of sa and ka and inherit her father's throne. The Seared Lands to the west, that have been bound to Atualon for so long and had thought themselves nearly free, now face another lifetime of submission.

"The emperor in the east, who perhaps thought to take these lands as his own once Ka Atu died, may even now think he should strike before a new ruler rises to challenge him. Do you know what happened in these lands, Sulema, the last time such a thing came to pass?"

She could scarce force the words past her teeth. "The Sundering."

"The Sundering," Ani agreed. "Just the other side of living

memory, Sulema, nearly a thousand years ago, the leadership of Atualon was failing, much as it is now. Ka Atu had been wounded, or perhaps poisoned, and he had no heir. That particular ruler was not loved by anyone, but with his iron fist and his Baidun Daiel he had forced and held a generation's peace between the Three Powers: Quarabala in the west, Sindan in the east, and Atualon in between. There were grumblings and rumors about Ka Atu's abuse of atulfah, but none dared challenge him.

"So there was a lot of tension as everyone in the world waited to see whether Ka Atu would die, or name an heir, and if he did what manner of heir he might choose. On the very eve of his death, Ka Atu named as his heir a boy who was also heir to Salar Merraj, the tiny independent kingdom of salt merchants. For Ka Atu had loved their queen, and she had loved him in return, and of their love was born a single son. His name was Kal ne Mur. Ah, I see you remember."

"Kal ne Mur. The Daemon."

"Kal ne Mur was echovete, and very powerful, but dark rumors had begun at his birth and spread across the land. It is said that the ruling family of Salar Merraj is descended from an imperial princess who had been stolen from Khanbul. More, that this princess was herself daeborn. Whether these rumors were based in truth or spawned in a lie, it is known that children birthed so close to the Salt Lake are often born still, or malformed. Kal Ne Mur was a handsome young man, tall and well formed, but he was cursed with a deformity that would be unacceptable among any but the Salarians—a fine set of stag's antlers sprang from his brow.

"The Atualonians turned their backs on this new leader and would have cast him out but for the intervention of the Baidun Daiel. Kal ne Mur used them to force obedience upon the people of Atualon, though they loved him not.

"No one can say for sure how the Sundering began. Some say a fight in a tavern between the il Mer and the Atualonians. Some say there was an attempt made on the life of the new Ka Atu. Blame has been laid at the feet of the Quarabalese, the Sindanese, the Zeeranim. It has even been suggested that the vash'ai and some of the other greater predators conspired to foment a war that would eradicate humans from the face of the world. It does not really matter, in the end, who said the first words, threw the first punch, or fired the first arrow. What matters is what happened next.

"It was war, Sulema, war like we have never seen in our time. Quarabalese warriors with their black spears and deep sorceries massed in Min Yaarif with the intent of marching on Atualon, and they killed as they went, massacring whole villages of Zeeranim up and down the river. When the people tried to flee into the Zeera, we overstepped our borders with the vash'ai, and they declared all treaties null and void. Our dearest allies turned tooth and claw against us in our hour of need, and only a remnant of the people survived.

"The gentle Dzirani, my own people, fared even worse. Only two families that I know of survived. My father sold me into the Zeera, and though I have searched all my life, I have never found him or heard so much as a rumor of any other surviving Dzirani. I believe that I am the last, and I cannot bear children. My people's line ends with me.

"The Sindanese emperor called to his own allies in the east, and massed his Daechen princes with their foul magics, and they took to the Great Salt Road intending, I believe, to kill us all as we quarreled among ourselves: tens upon tens of thousands of his troops and sorcerers, every one of them trained to kill from their earliest days and knowing no love but for their emperor. They were the greatest power our world had ever seen, far greater than any power we know of today.

"Kal ne Mur, now king of Atualon and Salar Merraj, recalled all of his sorcerers, his ambassadors, even his merchants. Every citizen of Atualon was called home by sorcerous means, and set to guard the walls of their city. He raised an army to defend Atualon and destroy his enemies... an army of Baidun Daiel. Before this, the Baidun were ministers, lawmakers, keepers of the peace, and ambassadors. They were few in number and limited in what powers they could wield. But Kal ne Mur raised them by the hundreds, perhaps by the thousands. Where they came from no one seems to know, any more than we can agree on where they went when the red dust settled.

"What is known is that Ka Atu created them, armed them for war, and upon each face he set a golden mask with his own hands. He said it was so they might reflect the glory of Atualon upon the world. And they did that, though not perhaps in the manner he intended.

"The Baidun Daiel formed a shield all round the city, a sea of red and gold as far as the eye could see, so that it looked as if the city was set in a ring of fire. Kal ne Mur took the four most powerful of them with him, up into the Dragon's Tower—yes, in this very palace—and there, all accounts end. He and his sorcerers worked a magic so foul and so vast it cannot be contained in the human mind. Every magic-bearing creature, every sorcerer and dreamshifter and shadowmancer cried out in agony, and the lesser ones were swept away entirely as wave upon wave of power flowed into the city as if a great mouth were sucking the world dry.

"A great light grew in Atualon, it grew and swelled and pulsed so that any who turned their eyes toward it were struck blind, and many were killed. The city walls bubbled and ran, and every man, woman, and child in the city was struck senseless with pain and terror. Kal ne Mur, Ka Atu, held all the power in the world in his fist.

"And then he let it go.

"The very earth shuddered and split apart as he loosed his power upon her, and this is why people say that Ka Atu tried to wake the Dragon, to crack the world like a great egg and let all life spill free. Out of every ten people in Atualon, only three survived, and theirs was the most fortunate city by far. Whole prides disappeared, their stories, their songs gone forever. Many of the few survivors, human and beast alike, went mad and tore each other to bloody bits.

"Even now, so many years later that it seems we have peace, we dance upon the edge of a sword. Our women bear few young, and fewer still survive. The bond of the Zeeravashani, once strong as the desert's bones, is a brittle and unhappy song. The Quarabala, once a wonder of music and painting and dance, burned until no creature could live there. Even now the Seared Lands are so hot and unforgiving that only a handful of people survive deep in the earth near its very center. Even they may have perished. That man Aasah and his apprentice are the only Quarabalese I have ever seen. The emperor survived, but he withdrew to Khanbul, his daespawn army annihilated in that very first blast of magic. Such is the power of Ka Atu."

"Ka Atu," Sulema whispered. She tucked her hands together and shivered. Her heart was ice. "My father."

"Your father—and *you* will be Sa Atu, if these Atualonians have their way. I would spare you this knowledge if I could. I would spare you this path if I could, and see you ride with your pridemates, chasing men and breeding fine horses... or the other way around. Such power, alas, is not given to me."

"Why do you tell me these things?" Sulema fought the tightness in her throat. She would not look at the youthmistress, but neither did she wish to watch the Ja'Akari at their games, so she stared up at Akari Sun Dragon, and blamed her tears on him. "Do you hate me? They would have me become just like him, just as you say." A single tear rolled down her face, scalding her chill skin.

"Hate you?" Ani took Sulema's hands in both of hers, and kissed her fingertips. "Hate you? I could never hate you, *ehuani*. And as for turning you into your father..." She dropped Sulema's hands, and smiled through her unshed tears. "It would take a force more powerful than Ka Atu might wield, more powerful than all of the rulers and all of the sorcerers from the Three Powers combined, to turn you into something you do not wish to become. They do not know you as I do." She leaned forward and kissed Sulema's forehead. "You are a churra-headed brat."

Sulema leaned back into the pillows and rubbed at her head again, wishing she had not come outside into the bright sunlight. Ani patted her knee and rose.

"I am sorry I have tired you, though I am not sorry that I told you what others will not. I would not have you step into a pit of vipers with your eyes closed. I may not see you again before I go. Askander and I will be heading out with a shipment of salt-clay pots, a very generous gift from your brother. I quite like him, by the way."

"Askander? First Warden?" Sulema closed her eyes against the sun and laughed softly. "So, you are still chasing that one, are you?"

"Irreverent brat. Chasing and catching, if it is all the same to you."

"Tell him I said hello." Sulema yawned wide enough to crack her jaw. "And your Inna'hael. I would have liked to meet him…"

"*Jai tu wai.*" Ani's voice sounded very soft, and very far away. It sounded as if the youthmistress was weeping—but Istaza Ani never wept.

She cracked one eye open. "*Jai tu* wha'?"

"*Jai tu wai.* The cubs are saying that now, instead of 'goodbye.' It means 'until we see each other again.'"

"Ah. I like that." Sulema smiled again and let her eyes slip shut, just for a moment. "*Jai tu wai*, Istaza Ani."

If Ani replied, Sulema never heard it.

She floated down, light as a wish upon the wind.

Sulema slipped lightly into the Twilight Lands and ran along a river's edge. It was a wide, wise river, deep and swift, and her banks were littered with dead flowers. Sulema's feet sank into the cool, silty mud and she gazed to the east and wondered why it seemed there should be a city just beyond the slumbering hills. She turned upriver and followed the fennec's tracks once more.

They turned sharply toward the never-rising sun and disappeared into the tall green grass. She let her hands trail through the cool leaves, collecting dew, and stopped when she stumbled across an area where the ground had been trampled by some great and heedless beast. Here the fox's trail ended, and within its last print lay a gift for her—a round and shining stone the color of water at midnight.

It was as big as a plover's egg, smooth and heavy and cool as if she held a darkling moon in the palm of her hand. She rolled it between her thumb and forefinger, and when she saw that a hole had been drilled through she held it up to her face and looked…

…directly into the kohl-blacked eye of Mattu Halfmask. She screamed, dropped the stone, and…

…sat up so quickly she almost fell off the bench. It was dark. Her neck hurt, and one side of her face was wet, and the smell of the river clung to her clothes.

"I am sorry, ne Atu, I did not mean to wake you."

Sulema shook her head and ran her hand over her face. She was damp with cold sweat. Perhaps the fever that had plagued her since the lionsnake incident had broken at last. She cast about her blankets, feeling as if she had forgotten something, lost something precious…

"Are you all right? Would you like some water?" The man's voice was solicitous, but his eyes behind the lynx mask mocked her. "Mead, perhaps? I hear you have a particular fondness for barbarian drink."

"Barbarian?" She dropped her hands and scowled. "Perhaps you would like to taste a barbarian ass-kicking?"

"Spare me, youngling. If you tried to kick my ass right now, you would fall on your face and I would be forced to have the healer tuck you back in bed." He folded his arms across his chest, and Sulema scowled again when she realized she had been eyeing him. Men who strutted about in public with their legs bared were a distraction to which she had not yet become accustomed. "Or perhaps you would prefer I do it myself?"

Her head was spinning again. "Keep your hands off me."

"As you wish." He leaned back against the door frame. "I prefer my women somewhat wiser, in any case. Not to mention healthy.

And..." he sniffed the air delicately. "Freshly bathed. Another time, perhaps."

Sulema was awash in anger. Handsome or not, she was going to kick his skirt-wearing saucy ass so hard his...

Then he winked at her. Her mouth opened in shock, and a laugh spilled out. Once she started laughing she could not seem to stop. She laughed till her ribs hurt and her stomach ached and her bones had gone soft. Mattu Halfmask quirked his mouth at her, and that was all it took to send her off into hysterics again.

Eventually she was able to catch her runaway breath, and wiped tears from her face with the back of one hand.

"Oh you... you!" she half-laughed, half-hiccupped. "You are so rude!"

"I am absolutely rude. Rude, inappropriate, and inconveniently handsome, I know." Perfect teeth flashed in his dark face, and then he sobered. "I am also the only person here who has been honest with you, and it will only get worse. The game is far along, and you do not even realize yet that you are playing."

"Game?"

"Do not play stupid with me, Sulema. We both know better."

Sulema found herself appraising him from a new perspective.

"What is your game?"

"Oh now, it would not be any fun if I told you that, would it?" He winked again. "It would certainly not be in character. Let us just say that I may be of use to you, for now."

"I have been told not to trust you."

"A very good piece of advice, ne Atu. Let me be clear—you cannot trust anyone in Atualon. Least of all yourself. Guard your words, guard your face—that delightful lush mouth of yours is a dead giveaway, you know. See, that is what I am talking about— that *blush*! Now, stop trying to peek at my legs and attend. Guard your dreams especially, dear girl. Atukos is the City of Dreams, after all, and we have been predators here longer than you have been prey."

"Prey? You think so?" Sulema swung her legs over the edge of her seat. She was going to kick his ass. She was. Just as soon as the room stopped spinning.

"You see? This is what I mean." His voice was soft, and warm, and very close. "You wear your heart as if it were a hawk in jesses, for all the world to see." His hand was gentle as he turned her face to his, and his eyes were deep wells in the moonslight. He ran his fingers over the sensitive bare skin at her temple, and touched her braids. "The first time I saw you, you had a scowl on your face and fire in your eyes. Your hair… like the last sunrise. So beautiful. Your skin." He moved closer, just a breath closer, and ran a thumb along her collarbone. "Honey and a sprinkling of spice. You are a long drink of cool fire to a man like me, Sulema." His voice caressed her name, and his thumb caressed the skin at the base of her throat. Sulema felt the breath catch in her lungs, and saw his eyes deepen in response. His mouth parted… and then he stepped back. Not much, and not nearly enough. For the space of several heartbeats, only the sound of their ragged breathing could be heard.

A wyvern cried somewhere off in the mountains, a single, piercing, and terribly lonely sound.

Sulema tugged the edge of her robe up over her shoulder. "You should go," she said, not wishing any such thing at all.

He smiled, and held out both hands to her. His eyes were hungry, and angry, and kind. Sulema let him pull her to her feet, and stood swaying like a willow at the river's edge. Mattu Halfmask frowned.

"This is what I mean. If they see you like this, it will be all over. It is a wonder you have survived as long as you have. Has living among predators taught you nothing of hiding weakness?"

Sulema staggered and swooned against him, and as Mattu went to catch her, she took his wrist in her hand and twisted it around, up, and around again, till she had him in a lock and on his toes. When he laughed, she leaned in so close she could have kissed the edge of his painted leather mask.

And bit his ear. Hard.

"You were saying?"

"Peace!" He laughed again, and she twisted harder. "Ow… peace!

Peace! I yield!" She let him go, and he rubbed his arms and grinned at her, rolling his shoulder. "Does this mean I will not have to carry you? Thank the moons… I was afraid I might throw my back out. Here I thought all you barbarian women were little desert flowers. Remind me to kill the next poet who tells such a lie."

Sulema was torn between wanting to throw him out on his ear and wanting to drag him to her bedchamber.

"Did you come here to torment me?"

"No. Well, not *just* to torment you, anyway. I brought you something." He waved for her to follow, and ducked through the heavy curtains and into her rooms. Sulema followed him through the little room meant for dining, and across the wider round chamber with the fantastic dragon's-head fireplace and the dropped floor, and then stopped so quickly as he entered her bedchamber that she rocked back and forth on the balls of her feet. Heat and apprehension coiled around one another in the pit of her belly like wrestling snakes.

Surely not…

His head poked out from behind the curtain. "Oh, come now, sweetling. I am hardly going to take advantage of your weakened state." His eyes burned like dark coals behind the lynx's sober face. "Come on." With that, he ducked out of sight again.

Za fik. So be it. Sulema followed him into the room which was meant for sleeping, but which was larger by half than the quarters she had used to share with a whole fist of girls. Mattu stood at the edge of her curtained bed, looking altogether too well pleased with himself, mask or no. He held a finger to his lips, and winked. Then he brought his other hand out from behind his back and, with a flourish that made her jump, bowed and presented a small glass flask to her.

Sulema hesitated for a moment, and then took the bottle. It was a pretty thing, green and delicate, and filled with a thick reddish fluid that swirled and moved within the bottle as if it had a will of its own. Whatever it was, it looked disgusting. She wrinkled her nose, dreadfully certain that he was going to tell her she had to drink it.

"Drink this," he urged her. "Tonight, if you can. It is best if you drink it after a heavy meal, but no strong spirits, and—" he grinned wickedly "—when you are near a washroom."

"I hate medicines." Especially medicines that looked like something that lived at the bottom of a cistern and maybe had things living inside it.

"This will clear the rest of that venom from your system. You were bitten, you know. Do you remember nothing of what happened out there, when you hunted the lionsnake?"

Eyes. A snake's eyes, staring into hers, waiting for her to die. "What is this, exactly?"

His eyes searched hers. "It is, ah, a potion distilled from the venom of a lionsnake whelp. It is said to be effective against many types of—"

"You *made* this?"

"I bought it from Loremaster Rothfaust, and it cost me dearly. Do you trust me?"

She peered into the vial. "Not one bit. Do I *have* to take it with food, or can I drink this on an empty stomach?"

His mouth twitched. "You can take it on its own, but it is not advisable. Are you always this stubborn?"

"No, I am usually worse. This will take the weakness away? Do you swear it?"

"It will take several vials of the stuff over several moons' time, and the loremaster says it would be best if he has a sample of your blood to work with. But, yes, sweet warrior. I do swear it. I will taste it myself, if you wish."

"Why would you help me? It is not as if we were pridemates."

"Whoever tried to kill you may be trying to kill me—and my sister. There have been attempts." His merry eyes went cold and hard. "It is past time we discover who is behind the deaths of the ne Atu, and you may be our best hope of finding this viper in our midst. What are the words of your people? 'I fight against my sister, but I fight with my sister against my cousin…'"

"'…and I fight with my sister and my cousin against all

394

outlanders.' You are an outlander."

"Perhaps you might fight with an outlander against a common enemy. I would have you as an ally in this battle, Sulema Firehair."

Never step into a pit without first checking for vipers.

Sulema narrowed her eyes, considering the strange half-masked man who had come to her rooms. Then she unstoppered the bottle and raised it to her lips in a smooth motion, and knocked the stuff back as if it were a horn of usca.

"That is not so… *gah*. That is… *pfaugh!*" She shuddered, dropped the flask onto a cushioned chair, and rubbed at her mouth. "*Za fik*, what is in that? Churra piss and corpse fluids? *Gaaaaah!*"

"Churra piss and corpse fluids, for a start." He patted her shoulder. "It will get worse before it gets better, but I promise—it will get better. By this time tomorrow, you will be thanking me."

"*Gaaaah*. By this time tomorrow, if I live—*za fik*, that is nasty." She shuddered. "Remind me to thank you for your gift, once I have cleaned my teeth. *Gaaaah*."

Mattu laughed, mismatched eyes bright in the lynx's face. Sulema laced her fingers together, lest they give in to the sudden urge to snatch his mask away.

"Why do you wear a mask?" The words were out before she could stop them, and Sulema could feel her cheeks flush hot.

He just smiled.

"Everyone wears a mask." His voice had gone quiet. Soft. "I am simply more honest about mine."

"*I* do not."

He considered her for a long while. "No," he said at last, "I suppose you do not, at that. Maybe that is why…" His voice trailed off.

"Why what?"

"Why this." Then he was standing close, so close she could feel the heat of him. He cupped her face in both hands as a man dying of thirst might cup a handful of water, and leaned in, and he kissed her.

It was not an affectionate press of the lips against cheek or forehead, nor yet the quick slobbery awkward attempts at love between younglings hiding behind the tents. Mattu teased with his lips, his tongue, his teeth, he licked the inside of her mouth as if he might taste the answer to all his questions. Sulema found herself rising to meet his wordless plea, heat on heat, need on need, flesh on flesh. When he would have pulled back she refused, curling her hand against the back of his neck and holding him close. He laughed into her mouth and submitted to her demand for more.

Finally they parted, a hair's breadth only, and Sulema's body protested the loss. Her breath was ragged and caught in her throat.

"Why?" she asked again. But the question had changed, and her voice had changed. Her world had changed, and all for the kiss of a man in a mask.

"Because you are beautiful," he replied, "because the moons are full. Because we are young, and it is spring, and there is a song in the air. Mostly because I am a fool."

"I do not think you are a fool."

"Then you are a fool as well. This is likely to land us both in a great deal of trouble."

"It is only trouble if you get caught," Sulema told him in her woman's voice.

Then she kissed him again.

THIRTY-SIX

*O*ne thousand salt jars, thought Ani. Talieso pinned his
ears and shook his head at her, but moved closer to the
clattering wagons. *One thousand salt jars.*

"You look as if you fear they will jump off the wagons and run
away," Askander said. "Relax, pretty lady. Your little clay children
will be fine."

"A hundred salt jars for each pride," she told him, "and hundreds
more for the Mothers. Imagine what this means for us." They had
such a long road before them, a long road and treacherous.

"We are going to have to take cover before those rains hit."
Askander frowned up into the angry sky. "Much as I hate to say
it, we would be best off sheltering within the city until this bitch
blows over."

"Much as I hate to say it, you are right. Too close to the river, too
slow with these wagons, and we have too much to lose."

"Say that again? I have waited a lifetime to hear those words."
His mouth twitched in that way that made her want to kiss him.

"What? That we have too much to lose? I was not speaking of
you, *ehuani*. Middle-aged warders are as a plague of locusts upon
the earth. Only worse—the locusts, at least, are edible."

"If I am not edible, O beauteous one, why do you insist on
trying to bite pieces out of my hide? Anyway, that is not what I
meant. I wanted to hear you say 'you are right' again." He looked
at her face, and doubled over in his saddle laughing at her.

"Males are such a pain in my ass."

"You know you love us, Ani."

"Mmf." She turned to the horn-helmed young man who led
the salt merchants' caravan. "Bretan, we will be wanting to lodge
within walls until that storm blows over."

Bretan Mer was as handsome as his younger brother Soutan, but there the similarity ended. Where Soutan Mer was all mischief and sunlight dancing on the water, this one was as serious and staid a youth as she had ever met. He was built like a bull and wore a bull's horns upon his helm, and though his big brown eyes were thoughtful and quiet, they did not seem to miss much. Ani knew full well that he was the reason so many of the Ja'Akari had volunteered to return to the Zeera with her, and that he had rebuffed the attentions of at least two of them.

The poor boy did not stand a chance. Someone should probably explain Ayyam Binat to him, before it was too late.

On the other hand, she thought with a hidden grin, *let the girls have their fun.*

Thunder rumbled in the distance. She had not heard such a sound for many years—real thunder, the kind that presaged a cold, hard rain, and flash floods, and mudslides. She remembered, her father's eyes, his face creased with worry as he looked up into the angry sky—

Best get the horses in, he would have said. She could almost remember his face, his voice. But the memory was like a fistful of mud—if she tried to close her fingers, it was gone.

"Istaza Ani?" The young man regarded her with concern.

She raised her brows at him. *Impertinent brat.*

"Forgive me, Meissati. Have I overstepped my bounds?"

"The boy has already arranged lodgings for us in Bayyid Eidtein." Askander kept a straight face, but she would bite him later for laughing at her with his eyes.

"Yes, Meissati." He saluted in the odd manner of the salt folk, fist to shoulder. "The rains are often hard this time of year, and I had thought it best to be prudent. Have I erred, lady?" He seemed genuinely concerned.

"No, no, you did well. Thank you." She smiled at him encouragingly. These outlander males were so needy. "Will our salt jars be safe there?"

"Ah, yes, Meissati. We salt merchants are the Road's lifeblood.

Steal from us," and he smiled at last, "and you slit your own throat."

He is a bold one. Ani eyed the youth more closely. Nice, broad shoulders, good teeth. Big hands and feet… good breeding stock. Very well. She turned to Fairussa Ja'Akari, who rode to her right hand, and indicated the salt merchant with a jerk of her head. "I like this boy. He will do."

The girl's face brightened. "Very good, Youthmistress." She turned the full force of her smile on Bretan, who had the grace to blush.

"Will do?" He cleared his throat. "Will do what?"

"Whatever she says, poor boy," Askander told him, without a hint of sympathy. "Especially now that she has the permission of an elder. Has anyone explained Ayyam Binat to you yet?"

Ani stroked Talieso's soft neck. She could just see the low walls of the city, off in the distance. A roof over her head would be welcome tonight. As would one of those soft outlander beds—and the lean, warm body of the First Warden to warm it.

The churrim grumbled and spat, gnashing their flat little tusks and refusing to move faster than a slow shuffle. The clouds rumbled low and close to the ground, and by the time their party reached the low gates of Bayyid Eidtein Ani could feel the moisture beading cool upon her skin, and the sharp sting of lightning in the air. There was a time when she would have found the threat of being caught out in a storm exciting. Now she mostly wanted to get her jars and her horse away from danger and have a nice mug of dark ale.

Bretan led them through the gates, down a wide and well-tended cobbled street. He did not stop until they had reached the largest inn in the city, three stories tall and studded with windows of colored glass like a mother's jeweled skirts. She had passed this inn by when last they came through, not trusting any place so full of strangers, and now she pulled Talieso up short so that he snorted irritably.

"Are you sure this is a good idea?" She eyed the warm light that poured from the open doors. "I would hate to have to kill so many people at once. I am old, and need my rest."

"Old?" Bretan choked. "Oh, ah. Yes, Meissati. Mattu Halfmask owns the Grinning Mymyc, and our people run the place. It is as safe as any inn in the city, and safer than most. Your people will not be molested here." He eyed Fairussa as he said this, and she flashed her most charming smile at him. She had left her vest hanging open—many of the Ja'Akari had taken to dressing so, once they realized how entertaining the outlanders' reactions would be—and his eyes avoided her body as if one look at her tits would turn him to stone.

The poor boy should just give in and let the girl notch her belt.

Bretan disappeared into the inn and returned with a flock of women clad in the colorful long tunics favored by the salt folk. They made off with the churrim and wagons, and the outlanders' inferior horses, but had the sense not to touch the Zeerani asil. One of them, a tall young woman pale as an olive tree and with a wreath of flowers braided into her hair, bobbed a curtsy to Ani as if she were the mother of many children, and favored her with a sunny smile.

"Meissati, please allow me to show you to our best stable, if you please? We had it built just for asil, and I am so honored by your presence." Ani realized, with some humor, that the girl's most adoring smiles were aimed at Talieso. "Do you need your stallions kept separate? Oh, just look at you, you beautiful boy." She stepped closer, mindful not to touch, but so close to the stallion that she must be able to smell his sweet breath as he whuffled at her.

It was forbidden for outlanders to touch the blood horses, but there was no such restriction against the asil sniffing and nudging at a smitten girl and begging for treats.

"Talieso, mind your manners." She did not expect him to obey, and just as well. He had found a pocket full of sugar-treats and was making silly faces. "Shameless beast."

"He is so beautiful." The girl sighed in the soulful way known only to the horse-struck. "I have always wanted to see one of the asil up close. I am half-Zeerani." This last was said softly, and with a bit of a blush.

"Are you, now?"

"Yes, Meissati. My mother took a fancy to one of your men on her travels, and here I am. I suppose I inherited his love of the horse. My own boys are lovely, but yours! What is his name, if I might ask?"

"His name is Talieso. You do have the look of the Zeera about you."

"My mother says I favor my father." The girl bobbed another quick curtsy, and blushed when she saw so many eyes were upon her. "Oh, I am so sorry! I see a fine horse and forget all my manners. Please, let me show you to the stables."

"You know," Ani said, "the Zeeranim do not consider half-bloods to be corrupted, as you city folk do. If you wished to touch him, you may."

The girl reached to stroke the stallion's neck. When he whuffled at her fingers, seeking a treat, her eyes shone as if she had just been given the moons.

Ah, Ani thought, *to be young again, and in love.*

When the horses had been settled with an abundance of saltgrasses and water, and the girl—her name was Eleni—had pulled herself together, the Zeeranim were shown to the inn's common room. The storm raged outside, rattling the shutters and whistling beneath the doors, but it could not touch those inside the Grinning Mymyc.

It was an attractive establishment, with pale stone arches and long wooden tables, and a bread-hearth that took up almost an entire wall. Two slaves in clean smocks hurried to shutter the windows against the coming storm, and others to light beeswax candles, which lent a merry little light to the room as well as a pleasant herbal fragrance. Three little girls with their hair done in doll-like curls were spreading fresh rushes over the floor. Eleni was all smiles as she led them to a group of tables nearest the fire.

"Usually we would be busy on an evening such as this," she explained, "but Bretan said you might be coming with a large party, so we kept our rooms empty. We will be filled to bursting now, and your drovers may have to bed down in the loft above the churra-pens. But our lofts are roomy, and clean as any other inn's kitchens! So it is good that you came. My boys will have your belongings up in your rooms before you have finished supper.

"It is too bad, really, that you have come to us in such drear weather. Were it a pleasant evening, you might ride one of our dinner barges and dine on fish caught right before your eyes. I suppose they have none of that in your desert. You must come back and visit us again, when the lilies are in full bloom and the lesser serpents are singing! It is quite a treat, I can tell you that, and I have lived here my whole life."

Ani noticed that the girl had hay in her hair and horse slobber on her tunic. Also that her mindless chatter was a ruse. Even as she nattered on, Eleni coordinated a perfect dance of servants and slaves, and a host of well-dressed young women with the wild curly hair and laughing eyes of the salt-merchant families. Ani sat back, bemused, and watched the show.

This girl would make a fine mother.

A trio of handsome young men in short white vests and red silk pants danced and juggled and flirted their way across the common room, and took up a place near the fire. One of them played a set of birds'-bone pipes, one of them plucked a round-bellied stringed instrument with a voice like a whining girl, and the third began throwing pieces of fruit and bright scraps of colored silk into the air and juggling them between smiles and winks at the women. He even favored Ani with a saucy bow and a suggestive smirk.

"Wonder if he can juggle knives as well as he handles those pomegranates." Askander's face was dangerously blank.

"It is easy to juggle fruit that is not yet ripe," Ani suggested, and he relaxed with a little laugh.

Their party indeed filled the room to overflowing. Bretan came in after a bit and sat down at their table, across from Ani and Askander. He leaned over and addressed them in a low voice.

"Your jars are locked away safe and sound, with a fist of my best men among them," he assured her. "They will take their meals out there and sleep in shifts. No harm will come to your treasure, I swear it." He leaned back and nodded his thanks as a slip of a girl in a long yellow tunic brought him a big mug of dark ale. "*Hatanye*, Luenna. Look at you, growing like a river-willow. Next time I come through, I expect you will be taller than I am." The girl giggled and scampered off.

"Family?" Ani asked. Eleni bustled from the kitchens with an army of youths bearing platters and plates, jugs and bottles and mugs.

"Cousin." He smiled warmly at the approaching troops. "Most everyone here is a cousin of some sort—we of the Mer seem to be more fertile than most. My mother thinks it has something to do with the salt. Ah, Eleni, my sweet! You have outdone yourself again."

The Zeeranim, the salt merchants, and their guards were served first, but there was plenty and to spare for everyone in the inn: whole roast fowls with fruits and nuts and wild grains spilling from their steaming cavities, roast leg of something big and fat, a plate of eels, and an enormous red fish with buggy eyes and a suckling pig stuffed in its toothy maw, baked in a crust of salt. Askander sat forward and whistled through his teeth, and Bretan grinned at their reactions.

"I told you she would feed you well."

"So I shall," Eleni laughed. "I got to groom an asil stallion! I touched him with my own hands." Her smile was beatific. She held a stoppered bottle with two hands, and set it down on the table in front of Ani with a soft thud. "With my thanks, Meissati." She removed the glass stopper with a practiced twist of her hand.

Bretan frowned. "Eleni…"

"They are family," she sniffed, "or good as. Meissati Ani tells me that we are kin of sorts through my father, and that is good enough for me."

A seductive aroma misted from the lip of the ruby glass bottle. Eleni poured a small amount of liquid the color of blood and amber into a tiny glass, and handed it to Ani. She gave another to Askander, a third to Bretan, and took one for herself. Then she stoppered the bottle again in a manner that brooked no argument. She held up the little glass, and Bretan did the same. "*Dachu!*" They exclaimed in unison, and tossed the liquid into their mouths. Bretan grunted a little, and Eleni shook her head and snorted.

The room had gone quiet. Ani saw that the other patrons were all staring at them open-mouthed. She sniffed at the liquid suspiciously. It made her eyes water, and it made her throat ache with thirst. She hesitated, neither wanting to offend nor to die of poison. "What is it?"

"Dachu." Bretan coughed and blinked rapidly. "It is not commonly... *ach*... it is not often given to outsiders." He glared a bit at Eleni, who ignored him as if she had had long years of practice.

Ani shrugged and looked at Askander. They raised their glasses together, as the others had done. "It is a good day to die," she said.

"And a better day to live," he agreed. "Dachu!" They tossed back the liquor together.

It tasted like honey, and berries, and fire. Mostly fire. Ani held her mouth closed by sheer effort of will, but the tears streamed down her face. Askander looked a bit alarmed, and sniffed once or twice, but that was as much reaction as they got from him.

He would pay for that, later.

Then the glow took hold of her, and Ani took back every unkind thought she had ever held about these outlanders. Her heart was warm, warm as a summer rain, and it whispered through her veins like a promise. She felt as if she could ride for days... fourth circle of Yosh, she felt as if she could *run* for days, and faster than Talieso.

"Mmf." Askander pursed his lips and nodded. His eyes lit like coffee in the sunlight. "That is... ah. That is good. What is in this?"

"Trade secret." Eleni winked. She shook her head as he reached for the bottle, not smiling now. "Ah, ah. You do not want more of that, trust me. Dachu should not be taken more than once every two-moon. One small cup, thrice a year, will bring you health and long life. More than that..." She shook her head again.

"This is why we do not sell it." Bretan frowned at Eleni, as she

404

took the bottle up in both hands and sashayed away.

The glow was blossoming in Ani's midsection, spreading throughout her limbs. It did not make her feel an idiot, as too much mead or usca might, it just felt… good. More than good. She licked her lips and smiled at the burn on her tongue. It felt wonderful. She wondered if anything might induce the salt merchants to trade this drink of theirs.

She was still basking in the glow of Dachu when the door banged open. Two tall men stood in the doorway, dripping wet, their cloaks lashing about them in the rising winds like a wrathful bloodmyst. Lightning crashed behind them, and thunder roared an answer, and the light caught on the gold masks of the Baidun Daiel. When the lightning flashed again Ani could see that they were dragging a third man, naked and bloodied, between them.

Eleni came storming out of the kitchen, eyes flashing like the storm's light. "Close those doors! You goat-headed, pig-brained sacks of— Oh. Oh!" Her eyes went round and wide, and she dropped the glass she had been holding. It floated slowly down the long silence and then shattered against the flagstones, spraying sharp little fragments of glass that twinkled like tiny stars among the rushes. "Oh, oh, oh." She dropped into a curtsy so deep it seemed the floor would swallow her in one gulp.

"Rooms," rasped one of the gold-masks. "Two rooms. Food. Now." The blood-cloaked men began dragging their unfortunate companion toward the stairs, leaving the doors open to the storm. Ani had never heard any of the Baidun Daiel speak. There was something different about these two. Something about their masks was… not right.

As they dragged the man into the warm light of the fire and the beeswax candles, Ani stared in shock. His hair was dark and matted with blood, his face swollen almost beyond recognition. To any who had not been trained to notice a certain ripple of light, he would appear as a plain brown-haired man with features so average as to be nearly invisible.

But Hafsa Azeina had shown her how to see around such small

tricks, and Ani saw the red-haired man beneath the enchantment. Though the white-and-gold garments of the ne Atu had been stripped from him, and his features had been blurred with a spell of some sort, she recognized the brother of Sulema beyond any shadow of doubt.

Askander reached to stop her, but it was too late.

She rose to her full and unimpressive height, and gathered her ka in as Hafsa Azeina had taught her, long ago when they were friends. Let the power fill her, fill the center of her still glowing like a rose born in a bed of coals, and she heard the storm crackling in her voice when she spoke. She had not done this in a very long time, and the little power she could control was less than a spark to the dreamshifter's bright candle, but perhaps they would not be expecting a challenge.

"*Stop*," she growled.

They stopped.

Ani stepped around the table full of her companions and across a room so quiet she could hear the rushes tremble beneath her feet, could hear the glass crunch as it ground beneath her sandals. Dark eyes, empty eyes, glittered at her from behind the smooth gold masks. She could see fear in every other face in the room—cold fear, sick fear, a child's fear in the night. She could smell it… but the storm of fear washed around her heart, leaving her untouched.

"What do you do with this man?" She folded her arms across her chest. *It is a good day to die*, she thought. A beautiful day to die, with a song in the air and a storm tearing its way through her heart. Askander pulled out a dagger, the sound of bared steel grating in the tense silence, and began cleaning his fingernails with it.

Show-off.

The shorter gold-masked figure twitched his head back like a startled horse. "We found this man… in the storm." He had a voice like a box full of gravel.

"You found him like this? Beaten and naked in the streets? Attacked by bandits, no doubt."

"*Yessss.*" The taller of the two nodded fractionally. *His* voice was an iron nightmare. "Just so. Yes."

For a moment, the only sounds in the room were her own breath, and the drip, drip, drip of water from the men's scarlet cloaks onto the floor. In the firelight, the leather bindings of their armor looked like a serpent's wet scales, and droplets of rain hung motionless on their golden masks.

"Then I am in your debt." She smiled and relaxed her stance. Both of the Baidun Daiel stiffened. "This man is my property."

"Property?"

"I bought him at the slave-docks just this morning. I had sent him on an errand. No doubt he became lost in the storm, and your... *bandits* caught him unawares."

"You... *lie.*" The shorter man rasped, and his hand went to the hilt of the red sword at his waist.

The Zeeranim rose to their feet as one. Swords whispered *death, death.* Askander blew on his fingertips, unconcerned.

"*Mutaani,*" she smiled. "Ja'Akari do not lie." The same could not be said of Dziranim, but she saw no reason to explain the difference to these men.

"*Mutaani,*" the warriors echoed. Beauty in death.

The two men in their red cloaks and golden masks were still as a dead man's breath for a long moment, and then they dropped the third man to the ground.

"You say he is yours," one of the gold-masked men said to her. His eyes were odd, flat and intense at the same time.

"His blood is on your hands," said the other. They wheeled and strode into the storm. Eleni hurried to close and latch the door as the room exploded in shouts and frightened laughter.

Ani looked up and into the sober eyes of the bull-helmed youth.

"Guts and goatfuckery, what was in that drink?" she asked him. "Whatever it is, I could use another shot."

"Whatever it is, it does not seem to make a person smarter," Askander drawled. He sheathed his dagger and stood, glancing regretfully at the nearly untouched feast. "Looks like we will be heading out into the storm, after all."

"Yes," Bretan agreed. "Eleni! You and the girls need to close up and go. Now. We must leave, too, the sooner the better." He looked at Ani. "I hope this man of yours is worth all our blood."

She strode to the still and bloodied form of Leviathus ap Wyvernus ne Atu, brother of the daughter of her heart. She turned him over and gave a long sigh of relief when his chest rose and fell with life. The glamor still held, though it had begun to unravel a bit around the edges.

Best take him with us, she thought, *and send word to Hafsa Azeina that he is safe. I cannot tell snake from viper in this place.*

"I hope so, too," she said. "Fairussa, Gavria, dress and bind his wounds as best you can in a hurry. We leave now."

"Yes, Youthmistress." Fairussa bowed her head. "It is a very good day to die."

"*Mutaani.*" She smiled grimly. "But let us try to survive this one, shall we?"

THIRTY-SEVEN

Hannei rode as an equal with the First Warrior and a fist of seasoned warriors for the first time in her life. For years she had looked forward to her first sharib, to being honored and feasted along with the other Ja'Akari by the Ja'Sajani. Never had she imagined that her first sharib might come after a death—and that this death might be that of the First Mother was unthinkable. Unspeakable.

Khutlani.

The warm air caressed the oiled skin of her temples, and her new-braided hair pulled her face tight as the skin of a drum. Clad only in a warrior's short trousers, she felt as bare and free under the sun as a woman could wish. As if there was not a place in the world for shadows to hide. Beside her rode Sareta, resplendent in her warrior's garb. The black and green, gold and scarlet plumes of a lionsnake bull swept back from her head, and the long ceremonial belt of the pride's foremost warrior draped to one side of her saddle, gleaming in the sun with thread-of-gold. Tiny brass bells attached to her vest matched those on her mare's tack. The bells sang a merry tune with every step, and announced to the world that on this day the Ja'Akari rode in peace.

Beyond the walls of Aish Kalumm, on the shores of the river Dibris, stood the new First Mother with her hands spread wide in welcome. Akari Sun Dragon fanned his fiery wings and blessed the people, and the sharib spread before them spoke of hope, and life, and plenty. As the wind came down the river, the sands began their ululation, calling to her, welcoming her, singing Hannei home at last.

"Is it as good as your dreams?" asked the First Warrior as they unsaddled their mares and left them to graze under the watchful eyes of the younglings. Hannei nodded to a big-eyed girl, hardly as tall as her hip, who stared at them in mute worship.

"It is as I had dreamed," she agreed. "Though it feels wrong…" Hannei let the wind carry her words away.

"Life goes on, young warrior," Sareta answered. "No matter what."

She bowed her head.

As they took their places among the Ja'Akari, Neptara daughter of Nurati caught sight of them. She waved both arms as if shooing birds away from a crop, and then hiked her long skirts up to her knees and hurried to join them, a broad grin blossoming upon her beautiful face. Truly, it hurt to look at a daughter of Nurati and think that such a woman might never walk among them again. A world bereft of Umm Nurati was as unthinkable as the Zeera without sun, or sand, or horses.

"*Aue*, Hannei, look at you!" Neptara clasped Hannei's hands and kissed her cheeks. "You are so gorgeous! Our enemies will fall on their swords rather than fight you. And that mare of yours! Is she Uthraki? They *never* sell their good mares." Her grin was infectious. Hannei saw that she wore her mother's pearl-and-ebon torc at her throat. "You shine like a sword in the sunlight, *ehuani*. Yesterday we were running through the streets wearing nothing but mud, and stealing sweets from the kitchen. Look at us today! My mother would…" Her smile faltered, and tears filled her eyes. She dropped Hannei's hands and made as if to turn away. "Forgive me, cousin. This is your first sharib as Ja'Akari, and I did not mean… I did not mean to…"

Hannei put her arm around the taller girl's shoulders, and gave her a small squeeze. "Your mother was worth a river of tears, *ehuani*." She felt a little uncomfortable, speaking of one so newly dead, but she and Neptara had been children running naked in the streets just yesterday, after all. "She smiles upon you with the sun."

"*Khutlani*," the First Warrior warned, but her face was soft. "It is too soon to speak of such things. Under the sun I see you, Umm Neptara."

Neptara lowered her eyes. "Under the sun I see you, First Warrior."

"Umm Neptara?" Hannei squeaked in a very un-warriorlike voice. "*Umm* Neptara? When did this happen?"

Neptara—Umm Neptara—dashed the tears from her face with the back of her hand. Now Hannei noticed the thin copper bracelets of a mother-in-waiting. "Some four moons ago," she grinned. "I will not tell you exactly which night."

"Are you still with Zeevi?"

"None for me but my Zeevi," the other girl agreed with a blush.

"He is good to you, then?"

"He is. When I told him…" She glanced at the First Warrior and leaned in close to whisper, "He cried."

"Good, then I will not have to kill him. I am happy for you, *ehuani*. And so soon!" For the other girl had only taken her hayatani last year.

"Have you taken your hayatani yet?"

"Not yet. But the day is young!" The girls shared a laugh under the sun. It felt good.

First warrior was right—life does go on.

Sareta harrumphed, but her eyes were merry.

"*Za fik*, you two. Next you will start discussing the attributes of this stallion or that, and I am long past the days of rump-patting. I will see you at the feast this evening, Hannei Ja'Akari?"

Hannei bowed deeply, and her face felt sunburned from the inside. "You honor me, First Warrior."

"Yes, I do." The older woman winked. "Ah! Weaver Munwal! A moment of your time…" She was off in a swirl of white silk and bright feathers.

Neptara sighed after her. "When I was a little girl, I wanted nothing but to be First Warrior. To ride across the sands on my good war-trained mare, keep the prides safe, and grind our enemies beneath my heel."

"And now?" Hannei could not quite fathom giving up that dream. It was all she had ever wanted, as well.

The other girl shrugged easily. "Now I hope for a quieter life. I have been painting with Master Louwana and she says I have a fine hand for illustrating. I love it. I have the pride within me—" she touched her belly in that odd manner peculiar to expectant mothers "—and you, my friend, will be First Warrior and keep her safe."

Hannei shook her head at Neptara's serene expression. "You will paint pretty pictures and bear children, when you could be riding with the wind?"

"You would rather ride into danger than kiss your daughter's cheek?" Neptara laughed. "Every color has its place in the painting, *ehuani*. Peace, cousin. Who knows what tomorrow may bring? Perhaps I will ride into the face of death, and you will bear a half-dozen cubs."

"*Ai yeh*, Atu forbid! But I am happy for you, if this is your wish."

"We are both happy." A cheeky grin. "Let us go find Tammas Ja'Sajani, and see if we can increase your happiness! It is not mete that such a pretty girl as you is still a virgin." She clucked her tongue disapprovingly. "You will get your headdress tonight, and it is well time for you to claim your due as a warrior. You look so beautiful today, he can hardly refuse you."

Indeed, Hannei felt beautiful. Her oiled braids swayed and stroked at the skin of her back, and her breasts were bared to the sun as was proper for a newmade warrior. Istaza Ani had once laughed that for the first year of a warrior's adult life, no man would ever make eye contact with her, and she had been right. Uncomfortable as she found the heavy beaded girdle, she felt her heart swell with pride beneath all the admiring stares. One or two glances she might have been tempted to return—the Ja'Sajani always looked so handsome in their sky-blue touar—but Hannei had specific prey in mind.

The life of a Ja'Akari had only been half of her childhood dream, after all. The other half…

The crowd parted before her as if at the thought, and she saw the other half of her dream in all of his muscle-bound, dimpled glory.

"I was wondering how long it would take my brother to appear, once you arrived," Neptara teased. "You must have him, Hannei, the two of you would make beautiful children."

Indeed we would, Hannei thought. Tammas had his mother's fine bone structure, but in his face the features were strong rather than delicate. His eyes glowed with their own warm humor, and that curly hair, *ai yeh.* Those shoulders.

"This *is* my first sharib, after all. It is only fair…"

Tammas looked up just at that moment, and his eyes locked with hers. Hannei felt something warm and wild uncoiling in the pit of her belly, like Sajani Earth Dragon waking after her long sleep. There were fires lit within her, flames that both fed her desire and fed upon it, and she gasped as she saw, for the first time, an answering flame kindle deep within a man.

Tammas closed the distance between them in a few long strides.

He moves, she thought, *as if he owns the world.*

"Hannei Ja'Akari." His voice was like his eyes, warm and sweet and intoxicating. She had never expected to drown in the desert. "Hannei. Under the sun I see you and wish you a good sharib. As Ja'Sajani, I am honored to serve you today… if you wish."

"Tammas Ja'Sajani," she answered, and blushed at the sound of her own voice. "I would like that very much."

His laugh shivered across her bare skin, though his eyes never strayed from hers.

"If you want anything on this day, you need but ask," he purred. "You never can tell… I might just say no." Then he leaned forward and kissed her on the mouth.

Her heart stopped. Akari Sun Dragon stopped his long flight across the sky and his bright golden scales dimmed toward latesun. The music stopped, the laughter, the smells and sounds of sharib, everything in the world stopped as Tammas kissed Hannei for the first time. Her hand rose of its own volition and curled into a fist in his hair as she pressed herself into him, heedless of anything but the taste and touch, the smell and the warmth.

She could feel the sweat at the back of his neck beneath her fingertips. She could feel the muscles in his jaw flex as he opened his mouth and devoured hers. The ground beneath her feet shuddered as deeply as her own flesh as Sajani stirred in her sleep, roused from her dreams by their passion.

Eventually he pulled back, just a little, and the Dragon fell once more into dreaming. A hawk screamed overhead, and the sound of sharib broke upon them like sand in a storm. Someone laughed nearby, the sound as harsh and unwelcome as a carrion crow's mocking voice.

"...need to get a tent."

"Ssst!" Neptara hissed. "It is Ayyam Binat, and her right."

"Hannei Ja'Akari. Have you chosen this man as your hayatani?"

At the sound of the First Warrior's voice, Hannei was able to find her breath. She took a small step back from Tammas. He did the same... but she could still feel the heat of him.

"Yes," she said, and blushed again. "If he agrees."

"Ohhhh, yes." Tammas's voice was so deep and husky she could not help but sway close to him again.

"Here I thought this sharib was going to be dull." The First Warrior's voice was dry and crackled with good humor. "Well, it is a good match, in any case. Ah, *ah*! Not before dinner, children." Hands were on them, between them, pushing the two of them farther apart. "Hannei Ja'Akari, I think you had best stay with me until after the ceremonies. It would not do for you to miss your first sharib, now would it? Feast before dessert, girl."

This time the laughter was good-natured. Hannei sighed as a crowd of blue touar surrounded Tammas and led him away. His bonded vash'ai, magnificent Dairuz, padded over and regarded her with his yellow-and-green eyes. He pulled his lips back from his tusks and opened his mouth at her, curling his pink tongue as he tasted her scent, and then shook his head with a satisfied grunt.

You will do, he said to her directly. *A fine queen, a strong huntress for him. I approve.*

"Sire." She bowed her head. He stared at her a moment longer and then, catlike, turned away with no further word.

The First Warrior watched her closely. Her face gave nothing away, but Hannei thought she did not approve.

"First Warrior. I know I am supposed to ask his mother's permission first, but…"

"I can tell you that Nurati would have given her permission, Hannei Ja'Akari. She had you in mind for Tammas all along. *Ehuani*, it is too late now for regret."

Hannei regretted nothing.

Were Akari himself to forbid me this man, she thought, *I would disobey.*

Neptara poked her arm and grinned. "I thought the two of you were going to—"

"Here, girl." An older woman, short and sturdy and wearing bright robes of yellow and green, pressed a wineskin into Hannei's hand. "This will help. I went through the same thing, when I was your age. One day I could not stand the sight of my Hadid, and the next it was as if I had been struck by lightning."

Hannei lifted the wineskin to her lips, in part to block the image of middle-aged persons kissing one another, and shot a thin stream of jiinberry wine into her mouth. It was crisp, and sweet, and tasted of summer days on the river.

"My thanks, Craftmistress." She tried to hand the wineskin back, but the other woman stepped back, both hands high, a grin creasing her round features.

"Oh, you keep it, girl." She chuckled. "You are going to need all the help you can get. Well do I remember Ayyam Binat."

Hannei laughed and took another mouthful of wine. It was better, with Tammas away, but she could feel him pulling at her spirit as if he were a lodestone and she a handful of iron dust.

Or more accurately, iron lust.

The rest of the day trickled by like sand through an hourglass, every minute of it spent soaked in awareness of his presence.

The Ja'Sajani hosted this sharib, as the Ja'Akari would host one in autumn, the wardens would feast and gift the warriors profusely, placing the women in their debt until the harvest time. In this small way the people sought to maintain the balance of sa and ka.

415

The first order of business was the granting and passing on of honors and titles. Although Hannei usually dozed through this part—something she and Sulema had both learned to do with their eyes open—this year was different. This year, instead of Umm Nurati presenting them all with her newest babe, a new First Mother was presented to the people. Nurati, the Mother of Mothers, would never again bless them with her beauty and grace.

Hannei could scarce remember Nurati's predecessor, a dusky woman with white hair who had favored garlands of red and yellow flowers. She had certainly never expected to watch as Nurati's replacement stood to have the white sand-eagle headdress placed upon her brow, or the silver-and-lapis torc fastened about her neck. This new woman seemed an impostor, even to the child she held in her arms, the fussing, squalling infant daughter of Nurati.

Hannei craned her neck to see Tammas. Tears shone on his face, and she wished she were standing at his side.

After the naming of a new First Mother came the results of the Ja'Sajani census counts—live births, stillbirths, debts incurred and paid, and deaths. More had died this past year than had been born, as had been the norm since before Hannei's time, but this had been an especially bad year. Only two people—one of them Ismai—had been chosen Zeeravashani, and Paraja had elected to return to the wild vash'ai following the death of her kithren. A sore blow to the people.

She listened with only half a heart as the stallion rights for the year were announced. The beads she and Sulema had tied into the manes of those young Uthraki stallions had gone unnoticed, and they now had the right to breed their mares to Zeitan fleet-foot and Ruhho the brave-hearted black. Sulema should be with her on this day of all days—this was to have been their victory together, not hers alone. But at the next thought she smothered a grin.

When Sulema found out about Tammas, she was going to *kill* her.

Hannei wondered whether her sword-sister had found any of the outlander men suitable as hayatani, but thought not.

Several of the Ja'Sajani danced for them, a man's dance of high jumps and shouts and suggestive spear-thrusting. It was an exciting dance, meant to rouse the blood and catch the eyes of young women on the prowl. And it was quite effective. Hannei drank the last of the jiinberry wine and was glad Tammas had not been chosen for this year's dance. A warrior could only be expected resist so much, after all.

As if he heard her thought, Tammas turned his head just enough to catch her eye, and his dimples deepened in a way that made her think of him…

"Hannei Ja'Akari."

At the sound of the familiar voice, her head whipped forward with an audible snap. Neptara winced in sympathy. Sareta rose and made her way to the table where the other important women were seated. Ismai stood there, dressed all in Ja'Sajani blue and looking more like his older brother than ever. He held a large silk-draped bundle in his hands and a grin on his face. At his side stood his young vash'ai queen with the laughing eyes.

"Hannei!" he called again, though he looked straight at her. "Hannei Ja'Akari!"

Hannei stepped forward, pushing her way through a crowd that mostly outranked her, murmuring a thousand and one apologies as she did so. She stopped as she came before her younger cousin and bowed, and then started a little when she straightened and had to look up at his face. When had Ismai grown so tall? When had his shoulders grown so broad?

"I cannot reach your head from there."

"Ja'Sajani?" She stepped forward.

Ismai whisked the silk cover away with a flourish, and the crowd gasped its admiration. In his hands, he held a lionsnake headdress nearly the equal of Sareta's own. His grin widened and he held it high for all to see.

"Feather and flesh and bone of an enemy," he said, looking down at her with pride in his eyes. "Slain by your sword-sister's hand, to be worn by you with honor." He set the headdress upon

Hannei's brow, and fastened it into her hair.

Fashioned from the bright blue and green, indigo and violet and black plumes of the old she-bitch Sulema had killed, the headdress swept back from her temples and brushed the tops of her shoulders. Tiny silver bells and a teardrop of lapis lazuli as large as her thumb depended from a network of delicate silver chains draped across her forehead.

It was light as a breath, and lifted her heart for all to see. It was heavier than a mountain, weighted down as it was with her duty to the pride.

Next Ismai shook out a vest elaborately beaded with snake's teeth, lapis and bone. He reached around Hannei and fastened the clasps, blushing furiously as he did so. He took great care never to touch her skin, and she resisted the urge to tease him as if they were still children.

Hannei thought she must look like a daughter of Zula Din preparing to ride into battle. For the first time, she felt like a warrior. The magnificence of the moment swelled in her chest until it threatened to spill from her eyes.

"Ja'Akari," whispered Ismai, playmate of her youth, now in the blue touar of a man grown. "*Aue*, Hannei, truly you are Ja'Akari." Then he winked. "I told you so."

The First Warrior stood, stern-faced and proud as the Zeera herself, and thrust both fists high into the air in an age-old sign of defiance. "Ja'Akari!"

"Ja'Akari!" The crowd roared its approval. "Ja'Akari!"

Tammas raised his eyes to hers, and brushed his lips with his fingertips, and she could feel his kiss on her soul.

Hannei was not the only Ja'Akari honored by the Ja'Sajani that night. Many a new warrior found herself gifted with blade or bow or blooded mare, and more than one young woman looked upon the gift-giver with hungry eyes. *When one has fasted on stale water and pemmican*, Istaza Ani would have said, *every dish makes your mouth water.*

Still, Hannei felt herself set above her peers. Her beloved

Sulema had honored her with lionsnake plumes, and the Zeera had honored her with the gift of a virtuous man. She half expected one of her elders to snatch it all away from her at any moment, with cries of "*Khutlani! Khutlani!*" and a walking-stick rapped smartly on the top of her head.

Her dreams had been made flesh.

The moons were drunk on starlight by the time the last gifts had been given, exclaimed over, and tucked away into the heads of the elders as a debt to be paid off at harvest-time when the Ja'Akari would play host to their brothers. Then came the dancing, the feast, the usca and the mead, and then, of course, more dancing.

Hannei was seated between the First Warrior and Tammas, and she was so completely overwhelmed that she forgot to be hungry. She sampled the dishes set before her—to do otherwise would have been unthinkable—though her stomach ached just to see the sheer quantity of food laid out before them. Paya-root bread and guava mash, salted fish on a bed of bitter herbs, and bowls piled high with roast meats and eggs. This sharib was meant to coax the year to plenty, and, *ehuani*, the tables groaned under the weight of it.

Tammas was the most tempting dish of all.

He sat by her side in his sky-blue touar. His hair curling out from beneath the cloth in a way that made her long to reach up and brush it back. A sapphire winked at her from his earlobe every time he moved, and the scent of him drew her like a bee to honey. She watched as he held a roast egg between his long, strong fingers, cracked its delicate shell, and brought the tender flesh to his mouth…

Yeh Atu, this man would be the death of her. All he had to do was eat an egg, and she was a puddle of lust shivering at his feet.

His eyes met hers, and his mouth parted, and he licked his lips.

"Stop that," she hissed. "No fair."

He laughed, and she wanted to tear his clothes off. His hand touched hers as they both reached for the mead, and another wave of heat hit her with such force she felt drunk before the first sip.

"I cannot take this a moment longer." The First Warrior set her horn cup down with an irritated thunk. "I understand that you two cannot help it, but by Atu I am going to knock your heads together if I have to spend another moment in your presence."

Hannei felt her cheeks flush. "First Warrior…"

"No! Go! *Gaaah*, I do not want to hear it. I certainly do not want to see it." She waved them away with both hands. "The two of you are not going to make it through the men's dance, in any case, and I have no desire to watch a pair of cubs mating in the sand. Go. Go! Go find a tent, or a clump of grass, or something. Just go." She reached for the mead as if she would wash a sour taste from her mouth.

"I do not think she is joking," Tammas whispered. His eyes were as bright as the moons. "My tent is down by the river, just past the horses…"

Heat flushed through Hannei's body in a way that was entirely new to her, and frightening. "It is early."

"I am supposed to dance with the wardens this year."

"But…"

"Naked."

Hannei looked at Tammas, helpless and lost in a storm of her own making. When he stood and held his hands out to her, she let herself be led from the firelight, and out into the soft embrace of a Zeerani night. The moons had never hung so low, nor the stars shone so bright as they did then, and never had the sands sung so sweetly. Tammas held her hand, his touch warm and gentle and so filled with promise she did not know whether she wanted to run away with him, or run away from him, only that her legs begged her to *hurry, hurry, hurry*.

When they came to his dark blue tent, she froze like a doe before the vash'ai. Indeed, Dairuz brushed against her legs as he disappeared into the night, and she felt his touch against her mind.

Welcome, Little Sister.

A cool breeze picked up on the Dibris, born of rain and longing and the quickening of a world reborn. It caressed the bare skin of her temples, and teased through the feathers of her headdress, and set the small silver bells to singing as she shivered from a sudden fever. Tammas turned to her, and reached to take her other hand.

He opened his mouth, and she knew that he was going to tell her *do not be afraid* and *I will not hurt you* and *you are lovely* and all of those other silly things a man tells a woman when what he really means is *you are mine*. But Hannei found that she was not afraid, and that she wanted him even if there was to be pain, and she did not need his empty words half so much as she needed his touch upon her body. So she reached up, and unfastened the clasps of her vest, and let it fall away.

They never made it into the tent.

The moons and the stars bore witness as they came together under the desert sky, as they found delight in one another, as sa met ka and flesh met flesh and the desert sang them a song so sweet and so powerful they would have wept, had they been able to hear it over the cries and sighs and soft, soft sounds of their loving. Not till the moons were on the far side of the sky, and small Didi had begun to grow pale and weary, did they finally find their ease in a heavy and satisfied tangle.

Hannei felt the sweat of her lover drying upon her aching skin, and she could taste her own scent upon Tammas as she pressed her lips sleepily against his throat, and she wrapped her arms about her man and fell into the deepest, most heedless slumber of her life.

The sky in the east had just begun to pale in anticipation of Akari Sun Dragon's first kiss when Tammas stirred, and stretched, and kissed the top of her head. Hannei tightened her arms around his waist and smiled, not yet ready to open her eyes or wonder where her clothing had got to or worry whether anyone might see them. She felt his laugh more than heard it—he purred like a great cat—and pushed away, leaving half of her chilled and bereft. She frowned, and opened her eyes, and stretched... oh. Oh. *That* stung a little.

"Shhh." He leaned over and kissed her on the mouth, and his moons-shadow passed over her as he stood. "I have something for you."

As loath as she was to have him leave, Hannei had to admit that even in the near-dark it was a pleasure to watch him walk away. And duck into his tent. And reemerge, carrying a wide goblet carefully in both hands.

"Nothing looks good on you," she told him.

He looked startled. "What?"

She grinned, and rolled over to sit cross-legged in the sand. "Nothing looks *very* good on you."

"Ah." He laughed, and knelt before her. She rose on her knees to meet him, and her fingers twined with his around the loving cup. "Sassy girl."

She felt shy, she felt brazen, and soft. Her legs still had not decided whether they wanted to run with him or to him, but they trembled so that she would probably do well to crawl into his tent and fall back asleep... eventually.

"Your girl," she whispered, and her eyes felt full of the moons.

"My girl," he agreed, and touched the cup to her lips.

Her body had begun to ache, a deep, satisfying ache that sang in her belly and in her limbs and down in her womb. The cup was cool, and his fingers were strong and warm. Hannei drank deep of the sweet, sweet water, and smiled at him over the rim of the cup. She could see her forever in his eyes. "My man," she told him. "Mine."

"Yours," he agreed, and the moons cast a shadow over his face

—she remembered that, vividly, afterward. The moons cast a shadow over his face—

Together, they brought the cup to his mouth, and his lips parted, and the moons cast a shadow over his face.

The night spilled from his mouth to stain the water black.

He looked at her, and his eyes widened with puzzlement, and

his mouth moved as if he would ask her a question

—and the moons cast a shadow over his face—

Blood spilled from his mouth to stain the water black.

He was still looking at her, his eyes full of the question she could never, would never, could never answer

—and the moons cast a shadow over his face—

His fingers went slack, and the cup spilled from his hands to stain the desert with his blood, and his hands rose slowly up to his chest, as if he would tell her, again, what was in his heart.

A blade jutted from his chest, a hand's length of ugly metal gleamed red-black with his blood in the light of the grieving moons, and then it disappeared back into his torn flesh and blood spilled from his mouth, so much blood, his mouth formed a question and his eyes held all of the questions forever but blood was the only answer. He fell to the sand, and the shadows received him into their cold arms, as she had held him only moments before.

Hannei could not move.

A part of her—some cold, cold, wicked part of her—remarked that it was as if she had been turned to stone, to bone, to a pillar of sand, when the blade of the First Warrior pierced her lover's heart. That tall, spare woman she had loved as a mother, respected as a teacher, looked at her with eyes full of the cold night sky so full of sorrow and pain there was no room left for remorse.

"I am sorry, child," Her voice was low, and slow, as if it had traveled from beyond the stars to reach them.

The strength bled from Hannei, and she toppled sideways into the sand. She saw the dull gleam of Tammas's shamsi lying just beyond him and her hand twitched, but she could not… could not…

"I am sorry, child." Sareta insisted, and her voice was soft and warm and lifeless. "But the line of Zula Din has grown soft and wicked, and so must be ended. Best to cut the taint out now, than let it continue to poison the prides until there is nothing left of the people but old stories and bones in the sand."

Poison. Hannei trembled, and then shook, as pain wracked her body. She burned, she burned, a fire had been set into her flesh that nothing could soothe. Water, and blood, and poison… Sareta kicked the loving cup away almost casually.

On the far side of the moons, vash'ai raised their voices in a song of fire and fury.

We come, little sister. We come.

The First Warrior knelt beside her, face full of cold starlight and colder sorrow.

"You are Ja'Akari," she insisted, "you must understand. The pride comes first. That woman would have sold us to the Dragon King, would have trapped us in cities of stone and mud until our hearts grew soft and rotten. The line of Zula Din would have been the death of the people."

Hannei saw the flash of a blade and would have flinched away, or cried out, but her own body was no longer hers to command. Something burned into the palm of her hand. A knife, a fell thing, and her flesh cried out in horror at the touch.

We come…

But nobody was coming to save them, it was all in her head. When the First Warrior pressed the heavy torc of ebon and pearls into Hannei's other hand, she knew—she knew—that it was too late for any of them. The line of Zula Din was ended. Nurati, and Tammas, and Neptara… and the children? Had they killed Ismai as well, and the little children?

Hannei had strength enough for a single tear. It spilled from her eye, and across her face, and down her newly shorn temple, before it was finally swallowed by the desert. So many tears, so many tears to make a desert. So many tears.

Screams, screams in the dark, and the smell of smoke.

The First Warrior stood and turned away, looking out across the desert toward the tents, and the rising flames.

"Thus perishes the line of Zula Din," she said, more to herself than to the slain enemies at her feet. "In the end, she was right— love kills more swiftly than the sword."

She left them there without so much as a single backward glance.

Hannei blinked—she could do that, only just—blinked away that last tear, and the sand, and the salt of her lover's sweat, and perhaps his blood as well. She watched as his chest rose, and fell.

Rose, and fell. His eyes stared through her as his chest rose…

And fell. Rose, and fell.

Rose…

The moons roared. *We come, little sister.*

And fell. Rose…

And fell.

And fell.

And fell.

THIRTY-EIGHT

Sulema exploded up through her invisible opponent's defenses, arms arrowing up and out in Blackthorn Unfolds. The movement carried her up and over in a spin. She trapped an imaginary arm next to her side and ran her sword backwards through an imaginary midsection. Pivot and carry-through, and she stood in victory in a pile of her imaginary enemy's imaginary guts, real sweat pouring down between her breasts.

The stiffness in her fingers and the numb cold creeping up her arms—these things were real, too. This morning she had nearly dropped her cup of coffee, and Daru's eyes upon her had been much too sharp.

"*Trust no one in Atualon*," Mattu had said. "*Do not put your trust in the Halfmask*," her brother had insisted. Even young Daru had warned her… about shadows, of all things. "*The shadows here are not to be trusted*," he had said. All very good advice, she was sure.

Sulema had never had much talent for taking good advice.

She breathed as she ran through her forms, deep strong breaths as her father had been teaching her, trying to imagine herself drawing power from the ground. To see this power as a pulsing cord, or as a web, pulsing blue and gold. But it was much easier to picture herself covered in the blood of the man who had killed her Azra'hael and broken her warrior's body.

Nightmare Man, she promised, *I will find you.*

A tap sounded at her wooden door. Sulema swept her dead opponent's invisible guts out of the ring with her bare foot, and had begun Dance to the Moons before remembering that an outland guest would not enter her room without an invitation even if, as now, their presence was expected.

Her sword arm swept up, and Sulema imagined a vash'ai sitting back on his haunches to sing the moons down from the sky. A young vash'ai, mane scarce, eyes the color of a red-sun dawn and a voice like honey in her heart.

Azra'hael, she mourned, and turned to face the enemy that stalked her from behind. *He was Azra'hael, and he was mine.*

Her sword split the air, it split her enemy's skull, it split time itself so that she might reach through the rift and touch her kithren mind-to-mind. *He was mine, and I was his.*

"Enter," she called, but her voice was thick with unshed tears. Weak and tremulous, and that would not do. So she scowled and cleared her throat and tried again. "Enter!"

This time, it was a command.

This time, he obeyed.

The door swung open, and Mattu stood there wearing the face of a ram and a battle-kilt of studded leather short enough to make a blind woman stare.

"You sent for me, Meissati?"

Sulema flicked her wrist, underhand sweep parting the two halves of her enemy's throat, turning her face away from the spray of heart's-blood and flowing into a defensive stance, holding onto victory for a heartbeat and then bowing low to the moons, grateful that their light had shown her the way to victory as they had so many times before. Then she let it drop away—the moons, the soft desert night, the song of the vash'ai, the smell of death, everything—and stood in the middle of a white chalk hoti, dripping sweat onto the cool stone floor.

Mattu stepped forward, but she held up a hand to forestall him.

"*Ah-aat,*" she warned. "Wait." She erased part of the circle with a bare foot, and then smiled at him, wondering whether she had given offense. These outlanders, she had learned, had very sensitive skin. But he just smiled.

"I believe this is yours." He coaxed Sulema's little messenger from his shoulder onto his finger, and held the mantid out toward her mistress.

"Leilei! Good girl!" she called, and held out her own hand, whistling the little six-note tune as Loremaster Rothfaust had instructed. Leilei hopped onto her hand, clinging with her prickly little feet and combing her antennae between delicately serrated front legs, as she did when she was pleased. "I did not know if she would find your rooms. Usually she finds the kitchen. I suspect your hearthmothers have been giving her sweets." She lifted Leilei into her bamboo cage, where the pretty little insect began preening and crooning to herself. Mattu was still standing in the doorway. "Oh, you can come in now."

"May I?" he asked, with a sardonic twist to his mouth. His eyes lingered—outland men reacted strangely to the sight of a woman with her vest off—but he said nothing more as he stepped into the room, and closed the door behind him. "So this was not a simple mantid-training exercise? She did not come to my rooms, by the way. She found me at the training grounds. I expect you will be hearing about this from your brother and your father."

"Why would they care how Leilei found you?"

"If a mantid tracks to a person's room, she is following the scent of their orchid. If she follows them anywhere else, it can only mean they have followed the scent of that person's sweat. In order to do that…"

"She would have to know how you smelled." *I know how you smell,* she thought. "But why would my brother or father care about that?"

"Oh, they would care. A great deal, I should think. You are the daughter of Ka Atu…"

"I am Sulema Ja'Akari." *I belong to myself,* she wanted to say, but Ja'Akari do not lie. So she told him a partial truth instead. "The weakness is growing worse. See?" She held out her sword-arm, which trembled under the weight of her shamsi. "My fingers are going cold again, and my toes too, I think. I was hoping you might take me to this Rothfaust for another dose of his churra-piss medicine."

"I had thought that might be it. The loremaster and I have talked,

428

and agree it might be best if you do not come to him directly. Until we have revealed our enemies..."

"We should not reveal our allies." She nodded approval. "You would make a good warden, Mattu Halfmask."

"Please," he said. "Just Mattu." He took a leather pouch from the belt at his waist and handed it to her. "The loremaster said he is closer to finding the tune in your blood, so this should be more effective than the last dose. It still smells like a dead sea-beast, though."

She accepted the pouch with her off hand, noting how the fingers trembled. The last dose had kept the shadows at bay for nearly a full moon. Perhaps it would be enough.

It will have to be enough, she thought. Daru had spoken of shadows for as long as she could remember, but she had never *seen* them before. Now, when she stared into the dark places between the candles, the shadows stared back.

Leilei chirruped sleepily from the confines of her little bamboo cage. She sounded happy enough, but Sulema thought that she could never be truly content, shut off from her freedom.

No more than she. At the moment she wanted nothing more than to put this weakness, this magic, this city behind her for good, to seek out the Mah'zula and live as a warrior of old.

Ehuani, she amended as she looked at Mattu, *I might want a little more.*

"Was there something else you wanted, ne Atu?" His eyes were hot. *He knows,* she thought.

"As a matter of fact," she said, and dropped the leather pouch. Freedom could wait. This could not.

She used her free hand to loosen the bindings of her warrior's girdle, and let it fall to the floor, taking her trousers with it. She set her sword carefully down and then stepped out of the puddle of clothes, naked.

"What is this?" he asked. His eyes, his voice had gone all dark and deep, and Sulema found herself swaying toward him. Heat coiled low in her belly, dispelling the chill in her limbs, driving away the weakness. She was a woman, and she was powerful.

"This is Ayyam Binat," she told him. "When a girl becomes a warrior, she may ask any man of the pride to her bed, so long as his mother approves."

"His *mother*?"

"I had heard that your mother was gone, so I asked your sister. She has given you her permission." Sulema did not add that the older woman had laughed until tears rolled down her face.

"I have no choice in the matter?"

"Of course you have a choice," she snapped. It was chilly in her room, and she was nervous. *Stupid man.* "We may be barbarians, but we are not barbaric."

"Oh," he said, and looked at her clothes on the floor.

"Oh," he said again, and his eyes lingered on her body. When his gaze met hers, Sulema knew he was fighting to deny her.

She knew he would lose.

"Oh," he said a third time, as if he had finally figured out what Sulema had known all along. He sighed and stepped toward her, and the candle-light danced to the beating of her heart. "Well, then, to be fair…"

Mattu reached up to his face, and removed his mask.

He stood there, more naked than she, looking at her through eyes that held not the shadow of a lie.

Sulema stepped closer and raised a hand to his face. "Ahhh," she breathed, "what happened?"

"When I was very small, your father's forces attacked my father's castle. They killed my brother, and tossed me down the mountain." He stood still as she traced the scars with her fingertips. "I was very small, but I survived. When my mother begged for my life, your father saw fit to spare it."

"But this is not why you wear the mask," she decided.

"No," he smiled. "Clever girl."

"Your scars are not so bad. Askander Ja'Sajani has worse."

"Who is this Askander?" he asked. "Your lover? I will have to kill him."

"No," she told him. "You will be my first."

430

"Your first." His breathing grew ragged. "Oh, sweet girl, you are going to get me in so much trouble."

"It is only trouble if you get caught," she reminded him.

"Then I am indeed in trouble," he said, "because you have caught me."

He bent down to kiss her…

…and that night Sulema learned, much to her surprise, that there was something in the world better than horses, or hunting, or sleep.

THIRTY-NINE

The new-hatched mantid sat up on her hind legs, little hands folded primly across a narrow pearlescent abdomen, shook out her delicate wings with a prismatic flash, tipped her head to the side, and hissed.

"Oh, look at *you*," Daru breathed. "Lovely girl. Do you want to be my friend?"

Dainty, feather-fine antennae unfurled partway, and an iridescent sheen washed across her multifaceted eyes. The mantid's sweet little triangular head tipped to the other side, and she hissed again. Daru thought she was the loveliest thing he had ever seen.

Catching a wild mantid was no easy thing. His hands and knees were raw, his clothes torn and filthy, and his breathing was labored after the long walk down the ramp used by the rag-tag men. The air reeked of sulfur and human waste and a strange, yeasty, cinnamony smell that turned his stomach and sat heavy in his lungs, but Ashta had told him that if he wanted to have a mantid of his own, he would have to catch a wild hatchling and train her up himself.

"If you can talk shadows into letting you throw knives at them," she had teased, "surely you can catch a little bug."

Atukos was crawling with mantids. Big as crows and easily as intelligent, the insects had caught his fancy with their pretty colors and winning ways, and Loremaster Rothfaust himself had said he had a way with them. But the charming pets, specially trained to the hand and able to carry messages in the form of sweet little tunes, were a vanity only available to the wealthiest citizens of Atualon, and well beyond the reach of a dreamshifter's apprentice.

This is how Daru found himself outside the city walls on an especially hot day, stinking of poop and rotten vegetables, hoping to find a hatchling of his own before the bug-men scooped them all up in their little black nets. Earlier excursions had yielded nothing but hatched eggs, an interesting skull, and the husk of a dead soldier beetle, but this time he had ventured closer to the beetle-fields, and had been rewarded for his daring—or would be rewarded, if he could manage to catch the golden-pearl hatchling that lingered so close to the thin catch-loop just beyond his fingertips.

Ashta had shown him how to twist and weave the noose so that he might catch a tender infant without doing any harm, and how to soak the cord in the musk of a cat's-paw orchid, but his intended pet was not convinced. She sat up higher on her rear legs, mandibles working at the smell of sweet musk, and combed one antennae again and again through a forelimb.

She took a tentative step toward the noose, and stopped. A second step, swaying and bobbing and waving her antennae... a third step, and she was his. Daru pulled gently on his end of the cord and the noose flipped up and over the little stick he had set so carefully, so that it closed gently about the little bug, trapping wings and forelimbs against her body. The heat of the sun and the stink of refuse pressed him down onto the hard-packed path, his knives dug into his ribs and one hip, and sweat plastered the hair to his temples, but the thrill of his victory flushed through Daru in a wave, and he could feel a grin spreading across his face.

"Hello, sweetling," he crooned to her.

The mantid tucked her head down as if contemplating her predicament, and her mandibles parted so that her long tongue could uncurl and taste the cord. She chirruped, a tiny, soft noise, but made no effort to break free. Perhaps she did not know how to fight, he thought. Or perhaps she was afraid to try. He inched closer, urging her onto his outstretched hand, and then he stood and held his new mantid, marveling at her gentle beauty and his own audacity. He cupped his hands about her and stroked the tip of his finger along her back, crooning a wordless tune.

"Pakka," he told her, and grinned when she tipped her head

all the way to the side. "Pakka. Do you like that name? It means raindrops on the river." He had never seen raindrops on the river, but it must be beautiful.

What are you doing with that bug?

Daru froze and spun to face the vash'ai, drawing Pakka protectively close to his bony chest.

Are you going to eat that? I do not think it will help you grow. Why are you eating bugs? Have your litter-mates finally pushed you from the pride? The great golden eyes flashed and the smoke-and-gold sire took a lazy step closer. *It is past time for you to leave. Past time for you to run. You weaken the pride... you weaken her.* His mouth gaped open, and sunlight dazzled on the gold-cuffed tusks.

Khurra'an drew back his black lips and sneezed in disgust. Even out here, in the bright light of day, Daru could feel the shadows gathering, giggling like naughty and hungry children.

You are sick. You are weak. Would it weaken me, to eat you? I think... not. He crouched, thick tail lashing from side to side as he kneaded the ground in anticipation.

Daru's mouth went dry as old bones, and Pakka trilled a protest as he clutched her too close. His eyes darted about wildly, but there was nobody there to help him, not even a rag-tag man. He groped with his mind, but his rising panic made it impossible to find Shehannam, let alone his mistress. His little knives called to him, but they would be as nothing to the vash'ai.

Run, little mouse. Khurra'an drew his forepaws in, black claws scraping across rock, and his haunches wiggled. *Run.*

Listen for the silence between your heartbeats, Ashta had told him. *The stillness between shadows. Then make your move.*

Daru drew in a breath, as deeply as he could. His heart was a big skin drum beating in his ears. The shadows held their breaths, too.

As Khurra'an pounced, Daru ducked and scuttled to one side, into the stillness between shadows, slipping like a breath between heartbeats. One claw scored his shoulder, tearing fabric and burning like a brand down his back. He cried out and twisted away from the flash of pain, from the heavy heat and cat-stink, felt the brush of Khurra'an's mane against his flesh as he wriggled and ducked and ran.

There was an angry grunt and *thump* as the cat caught empty air, and then the scrabble and scrape of claws on the hard-packed earth behind him. Daru tucked himself into a ball midstride and rolled, curling his body protectively around Pakka, who whistled and shrieked in protest when Khurra'an's shadow swallowed them both. Even as the vash'ai overshot his mark and flew overhead, snarling with frustration, Daru was on his feet and running, running toward the little caves that pockmarked the pale cliffs below the city.

He darted and wove like a hare under the hawk, breath searing his lungs and mantid scrabbling for purchase against his skin. He imagined Khurra'an's mouth closing over the top of his head, the proud tusks punching through the top of his skull, and knew that the shadows had finally won. Over and over again he lived his own death, heard teeth scraping across his skull, felt the hot red blood spray, heard his own neck snap. Over and over again the shadows shrieked their triumph and tore hungrily at his soul.

Daru's legs pumped on, his feet smacked against the ground, and he darted and wove even as his little rabbit's heart gave out in terror. The voices of the shadows faded away behind him, and his heartbeat slowed, slowed, *slowwwwed sloooowwwwwed* until he had a lifetime between beats. An eternity. The cliffs loomed before him and Daru saw one of the round caves, smaller and lower than the rest, just above his head. Still clutching the mantid to him with one hand, and praying he had not crushed her, Daru scrambled up the steep rock and squeezed himself into the rock through a hole barely big enough for a full-grown hare, much less a terrified boy.

He was able to wriggle through the crack and down a short tunnel, though he left skin and hair and one sandal on the rock behind him. When he heard Khurra'an scrabbling and scraping at the entrance to the tunnel, and felt the hot wind of the cat's breath and outrage, he slumped against the rock wall and wept with relief.

Come out, little mouse. Come out and play.

Daru hung his head and took air in great gulps, as if it were water and he had been lost in the desert for days. His skin stung—he had left a great deal of himself on the rocks back there—one knee throbbed, his back burned and it felt like maybe he was bleeding, and his heart hurt. After all these years, could Khurra'an not simply let him be? Tears dripped down his face and onto his hands, cupped protectively against his chest. He loosed them slowly, carefully, and held his breath.

Was she alive? Had he crushed her?

Pakka thrust her little head from between his fingers, swiveled her head this way and that, and peeped like a baby chicken. Daru let his breath go in a long, shuddering sob. She was alive. He was alive.

For the moment, at least.

He huddled in the dark, stroking Pakka with his fingertips—she seemed to like it—and listening to the fading snarls as Khurra'an gave up the hunt. His eyes adjusted to the ruddy gloom soon enough, the thin bit of sunlight sparkling in the thin red dust he had dislodged in his flight. He was in a small chamber, a hole in the ground just big enough for a boy and a bug, with two exits. There was the small hole he had wriggled through once already—and, looking at it, Daru could not imagine how he had ever squeezed himself in there—and a low, dark passage to one side. A faint, warm breeze rose from that passage, and with it the smell of warm bread and cinnamon. Daru decided that he must be in one of the vents that brought fresh air into the kitchens.

He tucked his chin and looked at the baby mantid.

"What do you think, Pakka? Should we go that way? If we come out into the kitchens, the ladies will probably patch me up and feed us. If we go out the other way, Khurra'an will probably catch me up and eat us. I do not want to be eaten today, do you?"

Pakka tipped her head down and twerped at him. She unfolded her forelegs and stroked his wrist, an odd little gesture that made him smile.

"To the kitchens it is, then—but first, let me do something

about these shadows." For they had gathered about him like small children waiting for one of Loremaster Rothfaust's many stories… naughty children, hungry children, whose eyes glistened like drying blood in the thin light. Daru drew his bird's-skull flute forth, sighing with relief to find it uncrushed.

The shadows whispered and chittered amongst themselves as he brought the bone instrument to his lips and played. *Pip-pip piiiii, pip-pip-peeee-oh, pip tit-ta-ta-tit-pip pip pip,* he played. A silly song, a child's song, flowers and sunlight and little fishes jumping in the river. A song, a game, and then to bed. The shadows cavorted like darkling flames, hungry naughty mouths singing along to a song with no words, pressing in and pulling back again in time to the beating of his own heart.

Finally the music softened, slowed, and rocked them all to sleep. Shadows poured across the dirt floor. Yawning and blinking their bloody little bat-eyes, they flowed away and left him alone.

For the moment, at least.

When he took the flute from his lips, Pakka surprised him by reaching out and touching it with one slender forelimb.

Pip-pip piiiii, she trilled. Her voice was sweet as berries. *Pip-pip-peeeee-ohhhhh.* She flittered her wings, briefly, and then crawled up Daru's arm and nestled in the soft, warm place between his neck and his shoulder. *Pip-pip piiii,* she sang happily, and clung to his skin. Daru stood slowly, careful not to dislodge the sweet little thing from her perch.

He could hear no sound coming from the sunlit tunnel, but he had seen many cats watching mouse-holes and was not the least bit reassured.

"The kitchens it is, then," he whispered again, and pushed away from the wall.

It was dark, but Daru had spent much of his life peering through the shadows. He took a long, steadying breath, and another, imagining as he did so that he was feeding the inner flames of his intikallah higher, hotter. A thin column of indigo and rose flame twined like flowering vines up along his backbone, and when his heart's-eye kallah blushed and his face flushed with warmth, he opened his dreaming eyes just as Hafsa Azeina had taught him.

Opening the dreaming eyes while fully awake was never easy—he had only been able to do it one time out of every three—but this time his efforts met with success. When he opened his waking eyes again, it was as if the tunnels were lit with a dull reddish light.

He drew in a breath, gathered his courage, and walked through the low passage.

He stood before a maze of twisting little passages, all alike, and they were filled with the sticky cobwebs of dreams. The tattered ends of discarded wishes danced in a breeze that never touched his flesh, and the tunnels were thick with dreamshifting and sorcery, a trap for the unwary. The web was hung with globes like silvered pearls, each of them endlessly reflecting everything. Daru looked away from the sight of his own eyes watching him watching himself watching him. That path, he knew, led to madness, and he did not want to get caught in the web, trapped like a fly for Eth to feed on.

Which way to go? he wondered. He let his ka unfurl, but just a little bit, because none of the dreaming webs were familiar to him. Some were probably just the remnants of innocent dreams, and those would dissolve at a touch, but others might be anchored in nightmares, or laid down with sorcery, and none of them felt like Hafsa Azeina's work. The last thing he needed was to get caught up in someone else's nightmare, or to have his soul ripped to bits and gobbled up by an Arachnist.

Those passages that glowed a faint greenish color he dismissed out of hand. He did not know what the color meant, but it looked sickly and filled him with unease. That left three passages tall enough and wide enough for him to pass through easily. The middle path was widest and tallest, and seemed the easiest way. The left-hand path had a gentle upward slope, and this passage was the one that smelled most strongly of cinnamon and yeast. The right-hand path looked to be the oldest and least used of the three. It angled sharply downward and had a neglected feel to it.

His feet, especially the bare one, wanted him to take the easiest path. But he had heard enough children's tales to know that was a bad idea. Daru figured that if he were a soul-eating sorcerer, he would set his trap on such a path. An image came to him, unbidden, of Sulema with her hands full of honey-cakes, her golden eyes full of laughing mischief. "*If in doubt, Daru,*" she would have said, "*follow your nose.*" He took two hesitant steps toward the left-hand path, and his empty stomach roiled at the thought of fresh spice bread.

Pip piiiii, trilled Pakka, and her sharp little feet stung as she clutched at his skin. *Peeeee-oh.*

He stopped. "No?" he asked her. "Why not?"

Dream-Sulema mocked his indecision. *Are you afraid to face the hearthmothers, then, little boy?* She brought the spice-bread to her mouth and tore at the soft loaf. Honey spilled from the corner of her mouth to drip, drip, drip down her chin. Daru felt as if his stomach was trying to gnaw its way through his spine, and made a hungry little noise in the back of his throat as one foot dragged itself forward. *Hungry…*

PEEEEEEEE-OHHHHHHHH! Pakka shrieked and bit his ear, breaking the spell.

Sulema's face dissolved into a wretched mask with maggoty eyes and blood dripping down its chin, and then broke apart into a mass of shadows. *Hungry,* they reminded him. *Hungry.* One of them tried to smile at him, showing a mouth full of pointed cat's teeth. *Follow your nose. Hungry.*

Daru reached up and touched his stinging earlobe. His fingers came away wet, and the shadows hissed at the smell of his blood.

"Hungry?" he asked.

They waited, rustling in the darkness like a dead man's clothes.

Daru took off his remaining sandal and threw it at the shadows. "Eat my shoe!" he shouted at them. Disappointed, they melted from his sight. Thus emboldened, he turned and walked down the right-hand path, careful not to brush up against any of the tattered webs with his ka. He reached up and gently untangled Pakka from his hair.

439

"You bit me," he told her.

Tit-tit-titta-pip, she agreed.

He laughed, and his heart lifted as his steps took him down into a darkness too thick to see through even with his dreaming eyes. Bits of rock stung his feet. The air did smell cleaner in this tunnel, and he imagined that there was a little breeze. Surely it would come out somewhere in the fortress, and then he could ask the outlanders to help him find his way back. Surely a boy would not be lost forever in the...

...dark? He spun as a light bobbed next to his head. What trickery was this? The light spun with his movement, and as Pakka *skreeked* in protest, the rose-colored light flickered and dimmed.

"Pakka?"

The little light flickered again, and she peeped in his ear. She was glowing.

"Clever girl," he murmured, and stroked her gently, mindful of the delicate wings. It was just a little light, really not enough to see by, but it cheered him nonetheless and he stepped livelier. After a while the floor became smoother, to the relief of his feet. The broken tunnel took on a more tended look, and it grew wider, the roof arching farther and farther from his head until it seemed he was walking down a great hall. It no longer felt as if he were walking downward, either. Though he could not be sure, it felt as if he were turning always a little to the left, inward and inward as if he were inside a giant snake that was coiled in upon itself.

A snake—or a sleeping dragon.

Then the floor dropped out from under his feet, and he fell.

...and fell...

He tumbled headlong into the dark, rolling through the air like one of the acrobats in that fools' troupe he had so enjoyed watching. Pakka fell away from him without a sound, and her flame was extinguished. The top of his head cracked sharply against something as he tumbled boneless and breathless, and there was a hungry roar from below, a foul wash of carrion-eater's breath hot on his face. His outflung arm hit something, hard, and he heard a dull snap like Hafsa Azeina breaking a big piece of kindling.

He opened his mouth to scream, but the shadows swallowed him whole.

FORTY

Some of the more elegant citizens of Atualon had cultivated a new and peculiar fashion, that of worshiping divines.

These elevated beings were seen as intermediaries between the human realm and Atualon herself. If a citizen were devout enough, wore the correct clothes, said the correct words—and spent enough coin in the process—a divine might be persuaded to favor the supplicant's cause and present their wishes to the sleeping dragon in the form of a dream.

Divination was just another Atualonian fad, but after this day, Leviathus would be sore tempted to burn a candle of sage and burrberry to Snafu, patron divine of fuckups and lost causes.

The day began well enough, all things considered. He emerged from his borrowed tent wearing borrowed clothes. The billowing sky-blue robes and headdress were cumbersome and unfamiliar, and too short for his frame, though the Zeeranim were kind enough to hide their grins behind polite masks.

The short bow was unfamiliar to him as well, and riding a churra was a jarring experience in more ways than one. But he was young and fit, by Atualonian standards, and seemed to be healing well, though his face was still swollen and tender to the touch. He would have to trust that the Zeerani man had set his nose straight. The one time he had asked for a mirror, the barbarians had laughed hard enough to split ribs, and he had not asked again.

As he approached the churra pens a stiff breeze kicked up, sending a swirl of sand and blue silk into his mouth. He coughed and spat, and then winced at the pain in his face. His thoughts darkened, and he marked another debt toward whoever had done this to him.

"Our istaz used to say that if we made an ugly face, it would get

442

stuck like that for the rest of our lives," Askander remarked. "You have only to look at *my* face to know this is true."

Leviathus turned and smiled. That hurt, too. "How do you keep this... *pfffft*—" he spat "—out of your mouth?"

"For one thing, try not to get your nose broken, so you do not have to breathe through your mouth." The man reached up and touched his own long and somewhat crooked nose. "Where are you headed on this fine day? Back to Atualon?" His eyes were full of wry mischief.

"How far would I get, this time?" He would have snorted. "No, Ja'Sajani, I thought I might go hunting. I promise to play where Mama can see me."

"First Warden," the man corrected gently. "*Mama* has said I am to accompany you... for your protection, of course."

"Of course. It is good of you to explain such things to me. Otherwise I may begin to feel like a prisoner."

Askander said nothing to that. He simply nodded to the girl guarding the churrim, and held up two fingers. She scurried off to catch and tack up two of the ornery creatures.

Leviathus had never seen churrim before coming to the Zeera, though every child who had ever heard a night-time story about Zula Din and her troupe of merry fools would have recognized them at first glance: long-eared, long-legged beasts with enormous, thickly-lashed eyes, soft clawed feet that splayed flat upon the sands for traction. Half again as tall as the sleek desert horses and twice as powerful, churrim were nearly as important to the survival of the Zeeranim as salt and water.

Obnoxious to handle and uncomfortable to ride, they also bit, and spat, and kicked, and they bore a strong, vaguely cinnamony smell that was pleasant enough at first but permeated one's self and belongings before much time had passed. Small enough reason, he supposed, to be grateful for a broken nose.

The girl returned with two beasts, and handed over the reins with hardly a smile. It was rude to mock a guest for being so poorly mounted.

Leviathus sighed, for the thousandth time regretting the outlander status that made it... *khutlani* for him to touch one of their pure-blood horses, and death for him to steal one. He and his mount, the slant-eyed black-and-tan male he usually rode, eyed each other with growing antipathy. Leviathus stepped close and tapped its side, indicating that it should kneel and allow him to mount. The beast snaked its wedge-shaped head back toward him and snapped its tusks together, rumbling with threat and menace.

"*Sheta! Yeh ghabbi!*" Askander slapped the thing's bony rump, hard, and it grudgingly folded to its knees. His own churra, a cream-and-red doe with gentle eyes, knelt quietly as if she wished nothing more than to please her human master. Leviathus shot them all a sour look and clambered atop the colorful padded mat that served as a saddle. The churrim lurched to their feet—his own with a chorus of grunts and groans and angry whistles—and ambled off into the desert.

One of the Ja'Akari winked at him as they passed, but he pretended not to notice.

"Where to?" he asked his nanny-guard. He had planned on hunting near the river, but they had turned eastward, away from camp and water both. "Would there not be more game near the Dibris?"

Askander showed a full set of strong white teeth. "There would be fine hunting near the river, *ehuani*, but we would not be the hunters." As if on cue, a long, low bellow sounded from the west, and was answered from the south. "There are few vash'ai this far from the village... best to stay away from the Dibris unless you are with a strong group."

"So, how do you find enough water for your horses?"

"Oh, the water is there, waiting for us to find it." The older man shrugged. "You let your ka loose, and feel for the water. That is all."

The animal beneath him lurched front-to-back, side-to-side. Leviathus held tight to the pommel of his strange saddle with one hand, the thick leather reins with his other.

"I cannot," he said. "I am surdus."

Askander twisted in his saddle and frowned. "Surdus is… deaf? It means you cannot hear, am I right?"

"Exactly. I am deaf to atulfah."

"Ah. I see. But the ka, it is not magic. It is part of you, like breath and blood. Ka is the breath of your spirit, just as sa is the breath of your heart." He said this as matter-of-factly as he might have said that the sun is hot, or rain is wet.

"This is not what they teach in Atualon."

"Of course not. Your rulers would make a man beg for air to fill his lungs, if they could." His face as he said this was smooth as old wood, but his eyes were canny. Leviathus was not sure how he was meant to react: should he laugh at the insult? Ignore it? Perhaps he was expected to challenge the other man to a fight? Never mind Askander's absent vash'ai, the man himself was as sleek and quick as a cat.

He chose to shrug off the words. "What are we hunting, then?"

Askander grinned, and his eyes lit like a boy's. "Ridgebacks."

"Ridgebacks?"

"Yes, russet ridgebacks. They are about this big," he gestured with his hands, "a bit heavier than a large hare. I saw one earlier, and where there is one ridgeback, there are thousands. They live in warrens under the ground. Not bad eating, though it is the eggs you want."

Eggs? "I… see. What should I be looking out for, then?"

"There will be little mounds of sand scattered about, very hard to see at first. There is always a sentry on top of one of the mounds, watching for danger. From a distance, they look a little like a hare with its ears sticking up." Askander held two hands up above his head, like a rabbit's ears. "You want to shoot the colony's sentry as soon as you see it, before it sees you and sounds the alarm. Otherwise…" He shook his head.

"They are dangerous, then?"

"This is the Zeera, man. Everything is dangerous." He grinned, again like a boy full of mischief, and Leviathus could not help but return it, aching face or no. "You look this way," he swept his arm to the west, "I will keep my eyes toward the river. We should not have to go too far."

Some small irregularity in the sand caught Leviathus's attention, and then he saw it—a reddish shape hunched on top of a little sand hill, twisting its long ears back and forth. It was larger than a *very* large hare, but it did not seem to have noticed their presence.

He nocked an arrow from the quiver at his side, drew back and aimed with one smooth motion—not so easy from the back of a lurching beast—and let the missile fly. His arrow flew straight and true. There was a small, audible thump of impact, and then the ears toppled to one side and were still.

Leviathus whooped and kicked his mount. Were it a horse, the thing would have responded with a brisk trot. As it was, the wedge-shaped head whipped back and the thing bit his knee hard enough to make him yelp. Askander jogged past on his placid doe, grinning, and Leviathus flailed and cussed at his divines-cursed churra in a vain attempt to hurry it along.

They got there eventually. The stupid beast plodded to a stop beside the smaller doe and flopped down with a grunt, nearly unseating him.

Askander stood a bit to one side of the small hill and gestured magnanimously to Leviathus.

"Your kill," he insisted.

Had Leviathus known the Zeeranim better, he would have been more cautious. As it was he bounded to the top of the mound, wincing a little at the pain in his ribs and face. He bent to retrieve his arrow, which had pierced the little beastie right through its middle. It took a minute for his mind to register what his eyes were so desperately trying to tell him.

The thing that he held skewered like a kabob over a spit was no rabbit, not even close. What he had mistaken for long red ears were the thick and hairy forelegs of a spider the size of his head. When those legs gave a twitch and began to uncurl, Leviathus did what any proud soldier-trained son of a king would do.

He flung the fucking thing as far as he could, arrow and all, and screamed like a little girl.

A rumble grew in the belly of the Zeera. Faint at first, the slightest tickle beneath his sandals, it quickly grew to a roar, a hissing, growling, earth-shaking roar not unlike the sound of a waterfall after a hard rain. The churrim lurched to their feet, ears stiff and quivering, before turning to shuffle off, bleating and gnashing their tusks. Askander's eyes grew wide and he slung his bow over his shoulder.

"Now you have gone and done it!" he shouted. "No, do not run. Stay still, it is your only hope. For the love of Atu, do not move!" Then, contrary to his own words, he sprinted away, puffs of yellow sand kicking up in his wake.

The next few moments would haunt Leviathus for the rest of his life. A hundred mouths opened along the flesh of the Zeera, and those hundred mouths vomited out thousands—tens of thousands—of reddish-brown spiders. Some were no larger than the palm of his hand, while most, like the one he had impaled, had bodies roughly the size of his head. A few of them, red-striped giants with eyes as big as grapes, might have been as large as a small child. They poured from the earth like a felldae plague from the old stories, wave upon wave upon wave of the chittering, skittering, monstrous things, and Leviathus felt a shriek rising in his throat.

One of the larger ones climbed his leg and up his back before launching itself from his shoulder, and Leviathus felt the blood drain from his face. The only thing that kept him upright was the image of a hundred thousand legs crawling over his prone torso. Facing certain death was one thing—facing a million spiders was another.

Then, just like that, they were gone.

The last of them poured forth from the ground and they thinned out, an ever-widening circle that expanded and expanded, ever out and away from him, until only the faintest smudge of them was visible against a far horizon.

Askander, who had not gone far at all, began to laugh.

It was not a polite chuckle, either. The First Warden bent from the waist, tears streaming from his eyes, mouth open wide enough to swallow a damn horse as he howled with laughter. Leviathus stomped over toward the churrim, which had not gone very far. When Askander caught the look on his face, he only howled louder.

"Not dangerous, are they?" He thumped the side of his churra. When the thing turned to bite him again, he gave it a good knock between the eyes. It blinked at him for a moment, grinding its flat tusks together, and then grudgingly settled to the ground.

"Harmless, unless you are a mouse." Askander walked over to his own doe, wiping tears from his face. "Are you a mouse, outlander?"

Leviathus did not deign to answer, but readied to mount his stupid churra.

"As I was saying, ne Atu," Askander sketched a mocking little bow, and then turned to dig into his saddlebags, "russet ridgebacks are good eating, if you can get the little buggers. But they are so fast, it is almost impossible to get enough for a meal." He turned, and when Leviathus's eyes fastened onto the pair of shovels in his hand, his grin widened even further. "It is the eggs you want." He threw one of the shovels to Leviathus, who caught it almost without thinking.

"Eggs?"

"Eggs." Askander turned and strode toward the empty mounds.

Leviathus stared at the shovel in his hands for a long moment, and his stomach roiled. He had a sudden, wild desire to throw the shovel after the blue-robed figure and run screaming all the way back to Atualon. When he got there, he would light candles to Bohica, the patroness divine of soldiers. For surely he had offended one of the divines, to have gained such fell luck.

A thin plume of yellow sand marked Askander's digging. Leviathus sighed and trudged up the hill.

It did not take long to find the eggs, and they had each filled several of Askander's big leather bags with the sticky, yellowish, eyeball-sized eggs full of translucent spiderlings. Indeed, they probably would have collected more before the spiders returned, except that Leviathus had to stop more than once as his gorge rose. If only, he thought desperately, they did not wriggle so.

It did not help that Askander kept smacking his lips and describing the taste of spiders' eggs in great detail. Never again would he tease the old men of the Third Circle for their stinky cheeses.

They abandoned their efforts as the russet ridgebacks began to return. Leviathus had never been so happy to clamber up into the churra's saddle, and he noticed that the beast moved with some alacrity away from the nests and the growing, chittering flood of pissed-off spiders.

He shot Askander a sideways look, and got an innocent, blank stare in return.

"Harmless, are they?" he asked again.

The warden shrugged.

So much for the romantic notion of hunting in the Zeera, he thought. *Next time I will head to the Dibris and go fishing, river-beasts or no.*

As they neared camp, he saw one of the bare-chested Ja'Akari break away from the others and run toward them shouting and waving a scrap of black cloth. Leviathus turned to ask Askander what this meant, but stopped short.

All merriment had fled from the man's face, his mouth had flattened into a grim line, and his skin had flushed. Leviathus had not really noticed before now how scarred the old stallion's skin really was. Leviathus reached for his arrows, but Askander shook his head tightly, and brought his mount to a halt.

"No," he said. "Put your bow down. Hands on your knees. Now. Make no sudden moves."

"Askander?"

"First Warden," came the terse reply, "as you value your life." A host of unfamiliar warriors poured forth from the camp, much as the spiders had poured forth from the earth, silent and swift.

They wore no headdresses. Rather, their hair was chopped short, bleached and stiffened until they looked like vash'ai manes. They wore no bells on their clothing, and neither had they donned vests in order to spare the outlanders' sensibilities. Not a peaceable party, then. Faster than sunset, the two men were surrounded by a group of hard-faced women bristling with weapons.

His churra trumpeted, stood half on its hind legs, and bolted, but not before one of the warriors grabbed Leviathus by the ankle and hauled him unceremoniously to the ground. He fell hard, jarring half-healed wounds and sending splinters of red agony into his face. He licked his lips, tasted blood, and looked up to see the round-cheeked face of a lass of no more than thirteen or fourteen years smirking at him. Lass or no, her sword was sharp, and she held the blade of it against his throat.

"*Antualleh*," she urged him with a sweet smile and cold eyes. "Try it."

He held very still, even as Askander's churra lowered itself nervously to the ground near him, and Askander—*the First Warden*, he reminded himself—dismounted.

"Ja'Akari." Askander came to stand beside him, face-to-face with the sweet-faced girl. "Ja'Akari! This man is a guest. We have shared salt, and bread, and water with him. Would you dishonor the people?"

"First Warden." She spat to one side. "You dishonor our blood when you share salt with this… *shara'haram*. It is *khutlani*. *Khutlani!*" Her sword shook with her fury.

"Now, Valri, that is hardly the Way." A pair of long, shapely legs came into view, a loincloth swaying between them in the style of ancient warriors. A strikingly handsome woman smiled down at Leviathus, showing too many teeth for his comfort, and then she held out a hand to him. Her hair stood short and stiff about her face like a black-and-gold mane, and her dark eyes were ringed with kohl. "It is not mete that a son of Ka Atu should sprawl on the ground like a vanquished enemy, now, is it?"

Leviathus took her hand—she had a grip like a blacksmith's—

and allowed himself to be pulled to his feet. The younger Ja'Akari pulled back, mouth sullen, eyes promising retribution.

"You know me," he said to the woman. A quick glance at Askander's wooden face showed him nothing. "Yet you are unknown to me."

Her full lips quirked into a malicious smile.

"You shall know me hereafter," she assured him. "I am Mariza, daughter of Akari. Come with me, king's son, and let us discuss your possible futures. Or shall we say, the possibility of your future."

"He is a guest," Askander growled. "He is not to be harmed."

"Of course, First Warden." The woman purred, so close to Leviathus's ear that chillflesh raised along the backs of his arms, as well as... other places. "He is not to be... harmed." All around them, Ja'Akari laughed like a murder of crows.

"I have his churra, Mariza," called one of the other women. "Oh! They have russet eggs!"

Mariza drew him by the hand into the dubious shelter of the tents. "How nice," she said, and laughed. "They must have known we were coming. Tonight, we shall have a feast!"

Leviathus allowed himself to be led, not that he had much choice in the matter. *Sweet Bohica,* he prayed silently, *get me out of this in one piece and I promise never to mock the divines again.*

Their camp was swollen and overrun with warriors, and these women—Mah'zula, they called themselves—seemed to share neither Ani's rough humor nor even Askander's air of quiet authority. The air about them boiled with barely suppressed anger, dry and brittle as the grasslands just before a storm and as ready to burst into violent flames at the slightest spark. It boiled with activity, as well. The salt merchants and their guards were packing the carts with sullen haste, and the Ja'Akari who had so recently laughed and even flirted with him watched on with faces hard as flint.

The face of Youthmistress Ani was dark and thunderous as a coming storm. She swept from the tents and across the sands toward them, every movement expressing her intent to do harm. Jaw clenched, fists clenched, she marched a straight and furious line to Mariza and stopped with their faces a hand's width apart.

"What do you think you are doing?" Her voice was as close to a shout as Leviathus had heard from any of the Zeeranim. "These jars are my responsibility. This man is my guest! What kind of goatfuckery do you think to pull here, you titless cub? Under the sun, you cannot do this thing. It is a crime against the people."

"Under the sun, I commit no crime against the people." Mariza raised her empty hands, and Leviathus saw the youthmistress's sword hand twitch at the insult. "Song in the wind is that there are slavers and pirates between Eid Kalmut and the villages. These pots belong to the people, and it would be… *unfortunate* if they fell into the wrong hands. We Mah'zula will see them home safely, *ehuani*, where your outlanders cannot."

"You milk-faced spawn of a maggot-riddled snake, you dare…"

Askander shook his head, the barest gesture, and a flicker of uncertainty crossed Ani's face. She relaxed the grip on her sword. "By whose word? You are *Kha'Akari*, Mariza. Your words hold no song."

"Kha'Akari no more, Istaza. I ride with the Mah'zula now, a *true* daughter of Akari." The other woman smiled, and her smile held victory. "If I am committing a crime against the people, why do the vash'ai hold their silence?" She waved a hand toward Inna'hael and Duq'aan, who sat near the tents and watched the events unfold as if the humans' doings were of no account.

"There are no Kha'Akari here, only warriors and outlanders. You travel with these shara'haram, allowing them to bear their weapons in our lands, against all tradition. You share salt and water with a son of the ancient enemy—and ride with a wild vash'ai." She clucked her tongue, dark eyes mocking, daring. "On which side of the river do you pitch your tent, I wonder… Bonesinger?"

Strangely, Ani relaxed at the younger woman's words, and even smiled.

"You go too far, Mariza. I will feed those words to you, *ehuani*."

"As you will, Istaza. My duty is clear, and my warriors will see this treasure through Eid Kalmut to Aish Kalumm. You are welcome to accompany the salt jars, of course, you and First Warden both, as you please. Or if you would prefer, you may accompany us to Min Yaarif with this prisoner. Five of one, a fist of the other."

"Min Yaarif?" The youthmistress frowned. "Why would you take him to Min Yaarif?"

Mariza grinned. "Have you not heard? The old king is dying, and the buzzards are circling, ready to grab a mouthful of warm meat from his corpse. War is expensive. The son of a dying king is worth more than salt jars, would you not agree?"

Leviathus felt sick. "You mean to *sell* me?"

"Sell you, barter you, ransom your worthless hide back to the loving arms of your worthless father." She eyed him in a way that had his skin crawling. "Or perhaps the Sindanese emperor will buy you for his comfort houses. I hear his daeborn soldiers have exotic tastes."

"You cannot sell a guest as a slave." Ani's knuckles were white as she gripped the pommel of her sword. "It is *khutlani*!"

Mariza was taller than the older woman by a head, and her stiffened hair made her seem taller still. As they faced off, Leviathus thought that Ani seemed small, and weak, with her sand-colored tunic and gray in her hair. The younger woman knew it, too. She shook her head and clucked her tongue.

"*Khutlani?*" she mocked. "So easily you use the words of my people to further your own ends... Dzirani."

It cannot be, Leviathus thought. *The Dziranim are all dead.*

"Enough."

Askander never moved, nor did he raise his voice, but every eye turned to him. His face was smooth, his eyes troubled. "The Zeera will run red with the blood of the people, but not on this day. I will take the merchants and the salt jars to Aish Kalumm. We will take the road through Eid Kalmut. The price for traversing the Valley of Death will be steep, but it is a safer way and shorter than the river roads. Ani, you accompany Mariza to Min Yaarif, and negotiate this boy's return to Atualon." He faced Mariza directly. "You will ransom the boy back to his father. This is allowed. Any

453

other way is *khutlani*. Under the sun you know me, Mariza. Who am I?"

"You are First Warden." She bowed, but looked as if she had bitten into a pie and found maggots.

"Who is this?" He placed a hand on Ani's shoulder. She glared daggers at him.

"Istaza of the Shahadrim."

"You and I will have words over this. But not on this day." He turned as if to leave. "Bretan!"

Ani reached out and took Askander's arm. Leviathus hoped never to see such a dark look directed his way.

"I do not need you to fight my battles for me, First Warden."

"No," he agreed, with a slight smile. "But you should allow me to, just this once. It makes me feel like a young stallion, and not an old fool." He brought her hand to his lips, and kissed the warrior's fingertips.

"You will pay for this, Askander."

"I am counting on it, lovely girl."

He let her hand go. Their fingertips touched a moment longer, and then he walked away. One of the great cats rose and followed him.

Ani turned to face Leviathus. "Pray to your false gods that he does not die," she told him.

Leviathus frowned. "Of course. I like the man. But—"

"Because if he does," she continued as if he had not spoken, "I will gut you myself. Your life for his is a very poor trade. For Sulema's sake I will help you as I can, boy, but do not expect me to pull the moons from the sky and string them on a necklace for you."

That night, long after the dust of the departed wagons had settled but before the salted-glue taste and wriggling crunch of raw spiders' eggs had faded from his mouth, Leviathus was dragged into the circle of firelight by a pair of strapping young women.

He caught a brief glimpse of Ani seated with her vash'ai on

the far side of the fire. She was flanked by a fist of the Mah'zula, and kept her eyes averted. Hers was the only familiar face. They pushed him down onto his knees in front of Mariza. He heard himself grunt as pain flared in his mending ribs, and clenched his fists.

Do not fight.

Leviathus blinked, and Ani's vash'ai blinked its round golden eyes as well.

She says to tell you not to fight. That they will kill you. Then she will fight, and they will kill her as well. Inna'hael yawned, showing tusks as long as his forearm. *You may thank me for speaking to you now.*

Ani met his eyes, briefly, and nodded.

"Thank you," he whispered.

"Why, you are welcome, boy," laughed Mariza. "I am pleased to note that the Dragon King has taught you to respect your betters."

She smiled, and Leviathus felt as if the spiderlings had hatched in his belly and were trying to crawl back out.

"You have a pretty mouth, boy. And pretty hair." She reached out to stroke his head, and Leviathus could barely suppress a shudder as she looked at him. There was something very wrong with the woman's eyes. "Is the rest of you as pretty? Let us find out."

Istaza Ani shifted uncomfortably. "Mariza…"

"Shut your hole, Dzirani spawn." Mariza curled her lips back from her teeth. "We are many, and you are one."

Ani stood, and her sword flashed golden in the firelight as Inna'hael came to his feet. The vash'ai was growling, a sound so deep it was felt rather than heard. "I am not alone."

"Perhaps. Perhaps not." Mariza did not look worried. "But how many of us will you—my apologies, the *two* of you—take down before I slit this pretty boy's throat?" She shook her head and sighed. "His father will be so disappointed. Sit down, Dzirani, before I send this pretty thing back to Atualon in pretty pieces."

Ani sank to the ground, her face pale. Inna'hael sat as well, though his black-and-white mane stood stiff with outrage and

Leviathus could still feel the cat's rumbling through the ground as he knelt.

"Now then, pretty boy, tell me—are you going to fight? I love it when they fight." Mariza took a fist full of his hair, and snarled at the women who held him down. "Strip him."

Leviathus felt her hand twist in his hair and she yanked a handful out by the roots, surprising a yell of pain from him. He heard Ani shout something in Zeerani, but her voice was quickly muffled. Hands were on him, pushing, pulling, and he heard fabric rip as his clothing gave way.

He fought.

He lost.

FORTY-ONE

Hafsa Azeina had missed her meeting with the parens at the Grinning Mymyc in Bayyid Eidtein. She had sent youngsters with messages to Matteira and Mattu, but only one of those messages reached its destination. The second child had dawdled in a kitchen doorway, ensnared by the scent of cinnamon, and waiting for a reply had caused the dreamshifter to be late. But for the rumbling belly of a small child, events might have unfolded in a very different manner.

"I pulled some of the bodies out myself," Imperator General Davidian said as they looked at the row of corpses laid out before them. "Many of the dead appear to be parens, though what business they had here in Bayyid Eidtein is not clear. The rest of the victims were women. Children. Sweet little children." His voice broke, and he shifted the dragon's-head helm under one arm as he dashed tears from his begrimed face.

"Some of them were Mer, some may have been merchants, or travelers. Do I dump them into an unmarked grave far from their homes, and leave their families to wonder at their fate?" The soot had settled into the deep creases on either side of his mouth, painting his face into a mask of grief. The Imperator General had aged well—certainly he had kept more of his hair than Wyvernus had—but this day, he looked as if he was feeling his age.

The dawn sky was a pale, pearly gray, streaked with delicate pink and the last hazy trails of night; too gentle a canvas for such a stark scene as was laid out before them. A dozen bodies, men, women, and yes, little children, laid out in a row upon blankets, as if such things could be any comfort to them now. Their deaths had been hard, one could see it in the contorted limbs like charred wood, in the silent shrieks begging for a release from pain. One more image of horror forever burned into her dreams, layer upon layer of pain and grief.

Sometimes, not even death comes easy.

It had been a hard lesson for Saskia. The girl's face was as pale as an outlander's, and she had been noisily sick.

"Eleni was a sweet girl," Davidian went on, still staring at the bodies. "She loved horses. The men would laugh that if you wanted Eleni to dance with you, you had better show up with hay in your hair. I have a daughter the same age, and a grandson. Tell me, how am I to explain this to her mother?"

"We had best find a way." An imperator unfamiliar to Hafsa Azeina shook his head and frowned at the blackened bodies. "The Grinning Mymyc is a Mer family stronghold. *Was* a Mer family stronghold. When Ninianne finds out about this… The woman is fierce when it comes to her family, and her private army outnumbers the king's troops two to one."

"More like four to one."

They all turned to find a heavily tattooed man standing there. Despite his apparent youth, a hairless face and gangly body hinting that he had not yet grown into himself, something in his eyes and the stillness that gathered about him like a cape told Hafsa Azeina that this was no mere boy.

"Il Mer." The Imperator General bowed, and his dragon's helm caught fire in the sunlight. "We are very sorry for your family's loss."

"Are you really?" The boy's eyes were dark and terrible. "I think you do not comprehend my family's loss. You leave our dead out here on indecent display, as if they were nothing." He gave an odd little shudder, and the hairs on Hafsa Azeina's arms stood on end. Something about this son of salt was not quite right.

You two-leggeds are so slow, Khurra'an chuckled in the back of her mind. *And you smell like roast pork.*

Her stomach rumbled. *You stay out of this.*

As you wish. He laughed again and was gone.

"Baram, Naamak, shield our folk from the eyes of these…

people." The young man shut his own eyes, and visibly took hold of his emotions before opening them again and looking straight at her. "Dreamshifter. I find it passing strange that you arrive just as the flames are dying. Tell me, what business might the Queen Consort of Atualon have at the Grinning Mymyc? Are you come to drink with some old friends?" He kicked at the charred and twisted foot of a patreon.

Akari Sun Dragon spread his wings above the horizon, bathing them in inappropriate blessing.

"What do you say, il Mer?" Davidian demanded. "You do not think this was an accident?"

"Only as accidental as the deaths of the ne Atu, so many years ago."

She said nothing.

"Soutan! *Aiyyeh!*" One of the Salarians called out. "This one is not ours. She is... ah... she is Atualonian."

Khurra'an nudged Hafsa Azeina from behind and came to stand very close beside her.

How can he tell? His eyes mocked her with their secrets. *You all smell like roast pork.*

I told you to stay away. Leave the bodies alone.

Tell your grandmother to hunt mice. I ate a whole tarbok. These are hardly worth my time. But he licked his chops anyway, long pink tongue curling around the gold band on his tusk. Atualonian and Mer alike edged away from him.

Davidian stepped closer, and bent down to examine the body. "He is right. This woman was Atualonian, and known to me. I had forgotten she had rooms here in Bayyid Eidtein."

"Who was she?"

"An old wet-nurse for the ne Atu. She was a pensioner and chose to live away from the city, though some of the children used to visit her, before, ah..."

"Before they all died." Soutan Mer shuddered again, and Hafsa Azeina felt her intikallah shiver in response. "We will take care of her, Imperator, since you seem to have such trouble taking care of your own." The men began to drape the sad, charred bodies in lengths of white linen.

"Of course—as you wish. Of course." The Imperator General bowed his head, flinching as the salt merchants exclaimed softly over the smallest corpse, too obviously a child, her long ringlets singed and matted with blood and mud and soot. Someone, perhaps her mother, had dressed that child in a pretty yellow tunic with flowers all about the hem, had brushed those long curls and fed her and kissed her soft round face, never imagining that it would be her last dress, her last morning, her last everything.

No more than Hafsa Azeina might have imagined how her own day might end.

"What is this?" The Imperator General stooped like a hawk. When he stood, Hafsa Azeina saw in his hands two halves of a broken, bloodied mask. "What is this? It looks like…"

Matteira screamed.

"*Halfmask*," Imperator General Davidian said, his face gone grim. "But what is this symbol, here between the eyes?"

"I know that sign." Soutan Mer's eyes had gone strange, the pupils dilated so that hardly any whites showed around the edges. He sketched a symbol in the air—a circle bisected by a jagged line. "The Eye of Eth. Used by Arachnists…" He looked straight at Hafsa Azeina, and she could hear the faint notes of the Hunt. "Arachnists, and sorcerers. Your people call it the dreaming eye, do they not… Dream Eater?"

Behind her, Hafsa Azeina could hear the *hushh-shushhh* of shamsi being drawn from their sheaths as the Ja'Akari made ready to die.

They have my back, she thought. *They have always had my back.* Another realization come too late.

Matteira reached out toward the shattered mask with both hands, wailing as if her soul had been sundered.

"I ask you thrice, Dream Eater—why have you come here?" Soutan Mer drew himself up. Akari Sun Dragon peered over the youth's shoulder at her, and it seemed that the boy wore a crown of golden antlers, and that the white-robed soldiers behind him glowed like vengeful spirits.

The world stilled and settled.

Ehuani, she thought, *no more lies.*

No! Khurra'an roared. *Stupid human!*

"I have come to seek the release of Bashaba, and reinstate her as Sa Atu."

"Treason!" The Imperator holding Mattu's mask bared his teeth in disgust.

Khurra'an snarled in the back of her mind. *Get out!*

The Huntress sounded her horn as the trap snapped shut.

"Ware, Dreamshifter!" one of the Ja'Akari shouted.

"*Mutaani,*" she breathed, and a smile kissed her mouth. *Death has found me at last.* The problems of the world were no longer hers to solve. Still smiling, she drew her shamsi and wheeled her mare as the Ja'Akari formed a loose circle with their horses, haunches in, swords shining bright and eager beneath the sun. The air shivered and rang with the war-cry of the vash'ai as Khurra'an drew back onto his haunches, hackles up, growling low in his throat.

Hafsa Azeina turned to catch Saskia's eye. "Go!" she yelled. "Ride to Atualon, tell Ka Atu! Then you guard my daughter!"

"No! Dreamshifter…"

"Go!" she shouted. "Ja'Akari! Go!"

Saskia's face was a terror, but she sheathed her sword and gave her sleek mare the heel. The asil mare, daughter of the desert, fleetest of horses, gathered in her fine, bold heart and flew.

The streets were lined with white-robed Salarians, mounted men with catch-poles and halberds and spears, and beyond them a handful of men with heavy crossbows.

Saskia cut through them like a new sword through silk and then they were gone. Three of the men peeled away to give chase, but they stood no chance of catching the Ja'Akari on her swift red mare.

The remaining Ja'Akari drew their circle closed, but they were a handful against many, hemmed in on all sides. Hafsa Azeina sighed her regret into the wind, that it should end like this despite all she had done.

A poor sacrifice to your ambition, my love. My blood will buy you scant pleasure.

"Show me yours, cowards!" Fiery Talilla spat into the sand and jerked the thongs of her vest so that it hung open in a show of contempt. "Or have you nothing to show?" The Ja'Akari laughed, strong white teeth flashing in faces so smooth and untroubled that Hafsa Azeina wanted to weep.

"I will show you mine before you die, cunt!" one of the white-robed men called in reply. The others were silent. Grim-faced, they showed little eagerness for this task.

"It is a good day to die," Talilla laughed. "Pity we have to die in such ugly company."

Hafsa Azeina watched with a bitter taste in her mouth as the Imperators pulled back.

"Kill them," a white-robed officer called, drawing his own short sword. "Kill their horses, too."

"*Aieee!*" Lavanya Ja'Akari screamed. "Coward son of a maggot-riddled pig's ass, show me yours!"

Salarians closed in from both sides.

There was a commotion in the back, the snarl of a cat and a man's scream cut short and the shriek of a dying horse, and then a blur of dappled gold shot past her and into the closing ranks. Khurra'an sprang upon their enemies, a fury of claw and tusk stoking terror and chaos in their midst. His mind was a fog of musk and bloodlust, and closed to her.

One of their attacker's horses reared, screaming, throwing its own rider to die beneath thrashing hooves as the vash'ai rent its hide bloody. It would not be enough. Even as she watched, one of the men raised an iron-banded club and brought it down with a sickening crunch upon Khurra'an's head, and Hafsa Azeina threw her head back and shrieked in grief and in fury as he slipped from her mind.

She felt as much as heard the *krak-chunk* of a crossbow releasing its bolt and her head jerked back sharply as if someone had grabbed a fistful of her hair and yanked. The bolt passed before her face, and the doe-eyed Talilla from Uthrak fell from her horse as gracefully as she had once danced.

Lavanya raised her shamsi and charged the soldiers with a roar that would have made Khurra'an proud. She and her rangy dun mare were cut down before they had gone four strides, the mischief and beauty of youth churned to mud and blood beneath the feet of their enemies. Hafsa Azeina trained her eyes on the man who had called for their deaths, and wished she might meet him once more in Shehannam.

Call me, a voice sang in her ear. *Even now I can save you. Call me, Annubasta. I would walk again among Men, and your enemies will tremble at your feet as I drink their souls.*

I think not.

Die then, Belzaleel laughed, *it is all the same to me. Perhaps I will seek out your daughter, once your bones are gone to dust. I hear she is a lovely thing...*

Hafsa Azeina shut the Liar's voice from her mind. "To me!" She cried. "Ja'Akari, to me! *Mutaani!*" Her sword flashed bloodgold in the light of the dying sun as she charged, and the hoofbeats—so like the pounding of a living heart—were soon lost in the clash and clamor of a short, brutal battle. Hafsa Azeina clove the officer's head from his shoulders—*No more dreams for you,* she thought— and brought the hilt of her sword down on a gleaming helmet that crunched and crushed beneath her blow.

A hand grabbed for her leg and she severed that as well, and was blinded by a hot spray of blood in her face. She saw a tall girl dragged from her horse, screaming and cursing the men for cowards even as their swords fell upon her and rose again, stabbing and hacking long after her screams had fallen silent.

Her little mare, her lovely Keila, silver and soft as moonlight, lurched beneath her and they came crashing down in a tangle of flesh and weapons. Hafsa Azeina rolled away, closing her ears and her heart to the sounds of her horse shrieking in agony. She hit her head on something, hard enough that the shadows pulled in close from the corners of her vision.

Keila was still screaming. *Oh, sweet horse.*

She had lost her sword, and her right arm hung limp and useless at her side. She tried to raise her left hand to wipe the gore from her eyes, but a sudden pain blossomed in her palm, hot and bright as if she had reached out to pluck a coal from the fire. She looked down, confused, and saw that a crossbow bolt had pierced her hand and pinned it to her breast. Blood pumped from the wound in a crimson tide and mixed with the gentle rain.

"Oh," she said, and fell to her knees.

They were waiting for her in the shadows.

FORTY-TWO

The Gate of the Iron Fist was flanked by two giant warriors. The golden giant was helmeted and armed in the ancient style, and held one hand upraised as if in blessing, although the stern set of his stone mouth did not bode well for the red warrior who knelt bareheaded on the far side of Supplicants' Square, broken sword before him and jeweled tears sparkling on his face.

Jian could hardly begin to imagine the lives that had been spent to carve these giants from the living rock and bring them down the Kaapua from the mountains, bound with the souls of a thousand willing soldiers and set here for all time, a testament to the emperor's implacable might. The walls of the city gleamed silver in the early light, and the square before them was split in two by a road of cobbled bloodstone ringed all about with skulls.

A riff of birdsong tickled down from the mountains and across the Kaapua to dance upon the jewel-blue moat, and the air was thick with the scents of jasmine and sweet *puali'i*. Jian looked upon the Forbidden City, the heart of Khanbul. He felt himself moved to fear, and to something approaching love.

"Stay clear of the water," Xienpei warned. "We lost three Daechen to the *zhilla* last year, and the emperor was not pleased." The flag bearers changed course to set foot upon the wide red road, and the bloodstone rang a martial welcome beneath their booted feet.

Jian followed at the head of his squad, aware and wary of the position. Perri marched at his shield, and Naruteo beyond him, carrying Jian's bundle as well as his own. After the day by the river when Jian had defeated him so soundly, the boy's yendaeshi had abandoned him to Xienpei, and he had become little more than a servant. Naruteo walked alone, and ate alone, and though the two of them had not spoken since that day something in his eyes made Jian grateful that access to weapons was strictly controlled.

The other boys whispered that Naruteo was being punished for losing a fight before his yendaeshi, but Jian wondered. It felt to him as if they were pieces in some elaborate game, and the players were still pondering their opening moves.

"Where are the soldiers?" Jian asked as they crossed the broad square. "I thought this was the Wall of Swords?"

"Look," Perri breathed beside him. "Look."

Then he saw it. The wall that surrounded the heart of the Forbidden City, so high that a man could scarce hope to reach the top of it with a well-shot arrow, so broad that on a misty morning you could not see one side from the other, bristled and glittered with the swords of thousands of vanquished enemies. Tens of thousands, perhaps. He could see them as they neared. Daggers and scythe-swords and shamsi from the west, glaudrung and shikkar and needle-thin pigstickers from the east. A massive two-handed greatsword crusted with jewels thrust from the stone beneath a short, rusted dagger.

"Come peasant, come king," he whispered, "fall to your knees before me and despair."

Xienpei, resplendent before them in her robes of spidersilk, glanced over her shoulder and smiled. The gems in her teeth dazzled and mocked him.

Naruteo snorted. "Idiots and weaklings. They were fools to think they could stand against the emperor's armies."

"We are the emperor's armies now," Jian said. "I would not say such things, if I were you." He did not look at Naruteo, but the other boy subsided with a grunt and Xienpei's smile widened before she turned away.

"If we are his armies, when do we march?" Naruteo complained. "My belly is full to aching with stories of the Dragon King's magic and his search for an heir. I say we strike while he is weak, before there is another to take his place. Strike the head from the downed serpent," he made a chopping motion with his hand, "and take his lands for our own, just as we have taken the East."

Perri hopped a bit in order to catch up with the others. His shorter legs made marching in step a challenge for him. "We are not the emperor's armies yet," he reminded them. "First we must be presented to the seers."

"I do not doubt that I will pass my Inseeing, do you?" Jian could not see Naruteo's face, but there was a sneer in his voice. "Perhaps you will fail and become lashai. Perhaps you will go mad. That happens sometimes to the weak, or so I have heard."

"Arrogance is a fine quality in Daechen." Xienpei spoke without turning, "But do not presume to know anything. Not even I can guess who the seers may send on, who they fail… or who they will consume."

"I am no easy meat," Naruteo growled. "I will march with the emperor's armies, and our enemies will fall to my sword. You ladies may wash my smallclothes for me, if you wish."

"I hear that the barbarian prides have lady warriors." Perri laughed. "And that they slice off their own breasts so that they will not catch on their bowstrings."

"I hear that you are a lady warrior," a voice called from the rear of the formation, "and that you sliced off your own dick because it was too small to be of use."

The banter degenerated from that point, but Jian was not paying attention. Inseeing. He knew that each Daechen would have to stand before the emperor's seers, and pass some sort of test, but the nature of that test—and the consequences of failure—were little more than conjecture in the halls of the Yellow Palace. The Yellow Daechen knew nothing, and Xienpei's malicious smile had warned him not to ask.

As if summoned by the thought, she dropped back to walk beside him, and spoke in a voice pitched for his ears alone.

"Naruteo has learned nothing from your fight," she told him. "Were every sword upon the Wall in the fist of a soldier as strong as he, still we would not have sufficient might to knock the Dragon King from his accursed throne. The might of Ka Atu is not measured in soldiers, but in the magic of the land beneath his feet, and that magic answers to him alone. Three times an emperor has thrown his might against the fortress Atukos, and three times have our armies been crushed beneath the weight of fell sorcery. We are more powerful now than we have been at any point in our history, and it is not enough. We cannot defeat the Dragon King in battle by waging war in his land, and we cannot draw him forth."

"Why fight the Dragon King at all?" Jian flinched inwardly at the sound of his own words, but it was a question he had wanted to ask for some time. "Why not leave him where he is, and be content with the lands we hold? If we cannot expect to win…"

"Do not even ask that question in your own head," she warned him softly, "not unless you wish to lose it. The coin does not get a say in how it is spent, and our lives are no more than coins in the emperor's purse. Do not hope for more than that, Daechen Jian." She tapped her sword thoughtfully as they marched on. "The emperor cannot ignore the Dragon King, any more than you could ignore a rotting limb. The taint of Atualon's sorcery spreads outward like poisoned blood. If the corruption is not sliced from the body, it will eventually reach the heart of the empire. The Sundering will be remembered fondly if ever that day comes to pass.

"And it will come to pass, if we fail to stop it."

"But if the Dragon King cannot be defeated…"

"I did not say he could not be defeated," she corrected him, "only that he cannot be defeated by bringing war to him on his own terms and on his own lands. Even a coin in a purse may wish to be spent wisely, and I am afraid that our beloved emperor is being counseled to cast his pearls before the swine. Not that he has asked my opinion." Her laughter was self-mocking and bitter.

Jian recalled maps that he had studied. "What if we did not come to this king through his own lands? We could approach by sea…"

"And feed the sea-beasts with our flesh." She smiled and shook her head. "Oh, if we had a thousand of you Issuq. Or better yet, fifty thousand, perhaps we could persuade the serpents to our cause. But Karkash Dhwani whispers into the emperor's ear, and

Karkash Dhwani is afraid of the sea. It was foretold that his death would come from the sea, and he will never allow such a plan to be spoken of in the emperor's presence."

Jian lowered his voice to match hers, conscious of the press of bodies all around them. "What if..."

She cut her eyes at him as they marched on.

"What if Karkash Dhwani did not have the emperor's ear? What if someone else were to lead the emperor's armies? Would such a thing be possible?"

"What if, indeed," she breathed. "You should know that under the direction of His Valiance, the Issuq and the Skaana, the Arluq and the Keyet—every sea-kin child born to the empire—have been all but eradicated. It has taken me a score of years to get two of you, and to keep you alive for even this long."

"Two of us?"

"It is my belief," she continued as if he had not spoken, "that if we could find a way to lull the serpents and the sea-beasts, if we could tame the waters of Nar Bedayyan to our cause, if, if, if... it might be possible. If every woman in the empire were to sing praise the sea during the Moonstide, and birth for us a sea-kin prince come Nian-da... perhaps. Perhaps the moons will come down from their lofty seats to dance a jig for us at dinnertime."

"Do you think they might?" Jian smiled. "I would love to see that."

"If your tongue grows too sharp, Daechen Jian, I will cut it from your mouth."

He bowed his head. "Yes, Yendaeshi."

They came to the end of the Path of Righteousness, and passed through the Gate of the Iron Fist, and the newest Daechen princes set foot for the first time upon the hallowed grounds of the Forbidden City. Jian had walked the streets of the city in his dreams for as long as he could remember, but neither his daydreams nor his nightmares had prepared him for the real thing.

As immense as the Forbidden City had seemed from the outside, it seemed to expand and unfold before him as if by magic. The city was as limitless as the ocean, as beautiful and every bit as perilous. A thin jade serpent of a river writhed before them, spanned by five wide stone bridges. The centermost was the emperor's Way, and death to anyone else. The Bridges of Daechen were paved in yellow and red, black and white, and carved with symbols of fealty. Across the jade river stretched the wide expanse of Companions' Square, and he could see that it was crowded already. The Yellow Daechen, youngest and least likely to survive, were last to arrive.

Xienpei and the other yendaeshi led their charges across the yellow-paved bridge, past the cart-merchants hawking their wares, and onto the wide square beyond. Jian followed close at the head of his squad, and his eyes felt wide as an owl's as he peered at the wonders all about him. The wall, so wide and vast as one approached the city, disappeared from view in each direction, as if the city itself was bigger on the inside. He could just see the Gate of Perseverance on the far side of the square, and great halls and towers to either side of it, slender as sea-reeds and red as garnets in the sunlight.

Tiny pale oval faces peered at them from the windows, and the brightly clad senior Daechen and yendaeshi who were already crowded into the square turned to regard them as well. Jian felt like a small crab that had been spotted by a flock of hungry gulls. A tall man all in black, hair drawn back in an old-style queue and pointed beard gleaming with oil, threw his head back and laughed at them like a barking fox. Jian saw that his teeth were small and sharp and white as jagged bone.

Jian reached up and touched the pearls at his throat. *Have courage, my son.*

Beyond the pointed man in black, beyond a cluster of red-clad men playing some sort of kicking game, stood a man so brilliant, so apart, it seemed he must have been fashioned from the flesh of the moons. He was clad all in leather armor like the overlapping scales of some great serpent over billowing silk—silver and white and pearl. A pair of massive antlers sprung from his brow. A long, elegant sword hung at his hip, and his eyes were as clear and bright as stars at twilight. Those eyes met Jian's, and the pale soldier

470

favored him with a long, slow smile before nodding and turning to one of his companions. Jian saw that the man was flanked by pale shadows, soldiers whose arms and armor had been fashioned in imitation. Like… but less.

"Yendaeshi," he breathed. "Who is that?"

"That," Xienpei replied, "is a Sen-Baradam with his Dammati. His name is Mardoni, but that is unimportant."

The Yellow Daechen drew to a halt and waited, every bit as tense as that moment between breaths when it is not sure whether a person will live, or die.

"Dammati?"

"Companions. Bloodsworn. Dammati are sworn to their Sen-Baradam. Their lives are his to direct, to spend, even to end. They would flay the skin off their own backs, did he ask it of them. In return, the Sen-Baradam spreads his power and wealth over the heads of his Dammati even as the emperor shields us with his love." Xienpei leaned in so close that Jian could smell the mint and garlic of her breath as she hissed into his ear. "Here is the power of Khanbul, boy, and as much freedom as any of us could ever hope for in this lifetime."

"Freedom?" He held his breath. Did she speak heresy?

"Sen-Baradam belong to the emperor, Daechen Jian, but they belong to themselves as well. Any Daechen may rise on high in the Khanbul. Unlike Atualon, where the Dragon King sucks the world dry and people are born into their place, here Daechen may persevere and become more. You must learn to form alliances and dance the dance of blood and fire. Gain this, and you earn your place in the Forbidden City. Earn this, boy, and you earn your freedom." Her eyes were fever-bright as she leaned back. "Freedom for your family, as well. Your wives, you children… your mother, should you wish it."

"Freedom." As well tell a child that he might hold the moons in his hands. As well weave a net of starlight to catch a dragon.

The pale man turned and walked away without a backward glance.

471

"Tell me," he breathed, "how do I become Sen-Baradam?"

Her eyes took on an odd, pale look. "There is a price to pay for this knowledge, Daechen Jian. Are you willing to pay?"

He did not hesitate. "Anything."

"There is a ritual…"

She took his hands in hers, and her lacquered nails dug into his palms deep enough to draw blood, as she explained to him what he must do. It seemed simple.

It felt like a trap.

"How do I pay for this?" he asked, when she had finished. "I have no coin."

"All the coin you need is right here, Daechen." She tapped his chest, just over his heart, and laughed.

"Forgive me, Yendaeshi, I do not understand."

"You will, soon enough." She smiled and turned away.

"Xienpei," called a man Jian had never seen before, dressed as yendaeshi but all in leaf-bright green. "Well met, and well timed! We are commanded to the Hall of the Fallen with all haste to hear the Enlightened word…"

Only yendaeshi were allowed to hear the words of the emperor, Jian knew, and that only after they had passed through the mouths and quills of the Enlightened. Mere Daechen would have to rely on the wisdom of their betters to distill and disseminate the word as they would, and of these the Yellow Daechen were least, and last.

They would spend this evening in the western barracks, and return to the square for the Feast of the Companions on the morrow. Jian was not displeased. They would be allowed some small freedom of the marketplace, time to bathe and rest from the day's exertions, and, best of all, respite from the watchful eye of the yendaeshi.

Jian had no wish to come any closer to the emperor, not this day, not even so close as to hear the translated whisper of his least imaginings.

And he had work to do.

❖

After finding what he sought at the market, Jian returned to the barracks of the Yellow Daechen. It was cool and dim within. The walls were red lacquered wood and painted screens, the floors sweet sandalwood worn smooth and warm with the passing of a thousand thousand footsteps. The young men bathed in silence in deep copper tubs, attended as always by the ever-voiceless lashai. Jian slid beneath the surface of the water and remained for some time with his eyes closed, listening to the slow muted sounds of his companions and the water's memories of rain and river, sea and storm, and rain again.

Later, Jian caught one of the lashai alone and gestured for her to attend.

"I will host a select few of my yearmates tonight," he informed her. "We should eat well in the Imperial City. Dragonfish and cat-faced eel, so fresh it does not yet know it is dead. Yellow ling and stone crab, and a bucket of blue oysters if they are to be found. Rosewater rice and noodles, and such vegetables and fruits as are young and tender."

The lashai nodded, eyes opaque. "Are you prepared to pay the price?"

"I have paid thrice over."

"As you say."

"As you say, *Daechen*." He had paid dearly to become a prince of the Forbidden City, and these slaves would do well to start treating him like one.

"Yes, Daechen." This time she bowed, and hurried away to do his bidding.

It was a beginning.

❖

She brought to his quarters fragrant rice and rice noodles, crisp vegetables and soft fruit, and the firm, sweet flesh of fish from the Kaapua. Jian prepared the fish with his own hands as his mother had taught him, tucking flesh and rice and roe in tidy nests of seaweed and river-cabbage. As the lashai set out the feast, Jian laid out the gifts Xienpei had bidden him procure for his guests—daggers of bright empire steel with grips of ebon fashioned to look like hawks' heads, and wyvern-hide scabbards embossed with the yellow Rose of the West. He had paid a terrible price to obtain these things.

Three words. Three names. Three drops of Daechen blood. Xienpei had told him that this was the only way out, and he would take it.

Or die trying.

He was arranging the daggers in the middle of the low table when the boys wandered in, Naruteo at their head. His face was flushed and his eyes narrowed to slits as he regarded the table set before him with open contempt.

"You dare," he ground out between clenched teeth, "you dare summon us like slave-girls to your pleasure."

Jian stood before the table and crossed his arms over his chest to still the pounding of his heart. "Hardly slave-girls," he protested, keeping his voice steady as best he could. "I invited you as friends—"

"Friends!" Naruteo spat. "I know what you seek to do, *bai dan*. You think to buy our blood with shit and trinkets."

Jian gripped his forearms to keep from throttling the other boy. "If you wish to leave, *wang sao*," he replied with exaggerated politeness, "do not trip over my shadow on your way out."

Naruteo bared his teeth and lowered his head as if to charge. A long moment hung in the air, breathless and still. Then he pivoted on his heel and strode from the room, shoving others out of his way, and a handful of others left with him. One or two shot regretful or angry looks over their shoulders, but most just shuffled along in Naruteo's wake like fish trying to survive in rough waters.

"*Jai tu wai,*" Jian whispered. He could feel the coming storm in his bones.

None of the Daechen seemed surprised. The yendaeshi must have told them all about this ritual. Perri was the first to claim a knife. He used it to cut a shallow slice across the palm of his hand, and then stirred his blood into the waiting cup of mare's milk.

"Sen-Baradam," he said. He bowed to Jian and took his place at the table as if it were the most natural and inevitable thing in the world. One by one the other boys followed suit. Gai Khan and Bardu, Teppei and slight, dark Sunzi from the northern peaks, all mixed their blood into the milk and watched in dark silence as Jian lifted it to his lips and drank their allegiance.

"Dammati," he bowed to them, "well met." He took his place at the head of the table and reached for a piece of fish. The flesh was salty and sweet on his tongue, and tasted of blood and victory.

His mother's pearls weighed heavy about his neck as he watched his Dammati eat. It was a small thing, but not without power.

It was a beginning.

FORTY-THREE

A light rain pattered against the glass roof of the Queen's Atrium and streaked down the sides like tears. Sulema stood near the pool, leaning on her staff and watching the colorful fish dart this way and that.

The doors to the atrium were flung wide, and the sanctum was invaded by a horde of grim-faced soldiers armored and armed for the battlefield. Sulema paid no mind to them, nor to the healers who fluttered about like dark butterflies. She had eyes only for the pair of heavy litters in their midst. On the first lay her mother, pale as salted silk with a rose of blackened blood painted upon her breast. Behind her, seven men staggered beneath the weight of Khurra'an. Sulema sucked in a breath at the sight of them, and gagged as her mouth filled with the stink of cat and blood and death.

"To her rooms," she told them, "quickly, now!" She knew the words were needless, and useless, but she had to do something. They bore her mother up the stairs, the long and winding stairs that Sulema had dashed up just that morning, so proud that she could make it to the top and down again with no sign of weakness or pain. So proud, and so useless. Her mouth twisted as she followed them to the top of the tower, listening to the men's heavy breathing and the *tap*, *tap*, *tap* of her fox-head staff ringing against the dragonglass stairs, and the shroud of silence wound all about her mother's still form.

They laid her mother upon her bed, and Khurra'an beside the hearth. His pale tongue lolled between the great, gold-banded tusks as his head flopped upon the stones, leaving a thick smear of gore. Sulema hurried to her mother's side, dropping her staff upon the bed and scattering the healers.

Useless, she thought, *every one of them.* These healers were the reason they had come to Atualon. Them, and her own stupidity.

My fault. If she had not gone after the lionsnake they would have remained in the Zeera, her mother would not be dying. Mattu would not be… missing. Not dead. None of the charred bodies had been his, no matter what they said.

She did her fumbling best to make her mother comfortable. Hafsa Azeina favored the old blue pillow, she knew, though it was ragged at the corners and the embroidered butterflies were mostly worn away. She did not care for heavy blankets, as she was a hot and restless sleeper. Sulema drew a thin linen sheet up to her chest, just below the thick spidersilk bandages, stiff and stinking with blood. The bottom edge of the bandage fluttered and sighed, and Sulema let her own breath out in a long, shaky sigh. Her mother yet lived.

Hafsa Azeina was dying. Sulema was familiar with the sights and sounds and smells of death, and as beauty can only be found in truth, she would not lie to herself. Her mother was dying… but she was not dead yet. Sulema cradled her mother's hand in both of hers, wondering that she had never seen her mother as fragile, never realized she was mortal.

"Mother," she whispered. How many times had she called her Hafsa Azeina or Dreamshifter or even "that woman"? She mourned them now. "My mother. I am sorry. I am so, so sorry."

"It is I who should apologize, I who have failed—"

Sulema did not turn. "No, Saskia. No. I do not wish to hear you. Go away."

"I promised the dreamshifter that I would look after you."

"As you looked after her?" She bit into the words as if they were poisoned fruit. "You would have done better to die with her."

"Sulema—"

"No. I said go. Go! All of you, go. *Go away!*" She was shouting, but it did not matter. None of it mattered now. "Can you save my mother? Can you?" She glared at the healers who stopped to stare at her, open-mouthed, at the soldiers who stood stone-faced and dumb as statues. Where were they, with their fine armor and sharp weapons, when her mother was attacked by the salt folk? "Just go, Yosh take you all, and leave us in peace."

"*Leave us.*"

At the sound of her father's voice, every soldier, every healer in the room bowed low and hurried away. Sulema turned and almost dropped her mother's hand in surprise.

Ka Atu, her father, stood in the doorway to her mother's chambers. He was clad all in robes of gold and thread-of-gold, and upon his face he wore a brilliant mask, a dragon's face so cunningly wrought that for a moment it seemed Akari Sun Dragon himself stood before her bathed in his own magnificence. He crossed the room to stand at her side, flanked by a fist of Baidun Daiel. Their black armor seemed darker in his presence, as if it drank the light, but their golden masks reflected the glory of Ka Atu so that she could hardly bear to look at them.

He reached out his hands and cupped them around her own, and her mother's. His touch was hot. She could feel the warmth pouring into her, like mead from a sun-warmed pitcher. His bright eyes were infinitely loving, infinitely sad as they looked at her.

"Sulema, my daughter, my heart," he said, his voice echoing behind the golden mask, "I am so sorry."

Sulema wept. She brought their hands—hers, her mother's, her father's—all of them to her chest and clung to them like a child who had suffered an unimaginable hurt. It felt as if the ground at her feet would open up and swallow her whole. It felt as if the sun would never shine again, and all the world was lost in darkness. Her heart was broken. She was broken, and would never be whole again.

Wyvernus loosed one hand and pulled her close, and she cried into his golden robes until her eyes were dry and her throat was raw and her heart was empty and numb. He burned, he burned, but the heat was good even as it hurt.

"I love her," he said at last. Sulema sniffed and pulled away, embarrassed and drained.

"I have loved her from the moment I first laid eyes on her, when she stepped down from that ship. She came to me a stranger from strange lands, across the wide and deadly sea, and we knew nothing of each other but what we had been told…" She heard a smile in his voice. "I had expected her to be taller, for all the stories. Oh, but she was lovely, she was all that was gentle and lovely and good. She was precious to me from the moment she saw me and smiled, and she has been precious to me every moment since."

"Gentle, and lovely, and good?" Sulema dashed the tears from her face with the back of one hand, and shook her head. "Are you sure you are speaking of the same woman?"

"Even so." The mask turned toward Hafsa Azeina, and the eyes behind it lingered on her still, slack face. "Even now. The people loved her, more than they ever loved me. She was the Heart of Atualon, and we never really recovered when she left us."

Sulema could not reconcile the image of a sweet moonslight-haired princess with that of the woman she had always known, sharp and brittle and deadly as cold flint.

"What happened?" she whispered.

"I did this," he replied. "Someone was killing the ne Atu, someone was murdering my children." His voice broke. "My princess, my beloved, was the only one among us wise enough to see, and I was not smart enough, not man enough, not king enough to listen to her. I was consumed with my duties and brushed her concerns aside, and so she had no one to turn to. I was not there the night she fled Atualon, and we may never know what happened that night on the Great Salt Road. I believe that whoever was killing the ne Atu came for you and she fled, and turned to dark magic in order to save your life, because I was not there for her.

"As I was not there for you."

Sulema clutched her mother's hand, horrified. All those years, and she had not known. "She became this… for me?"

Sulema realized in that moment that truth could hold sorrow as well as beauty.

Wyvernus squeezed her hands in his. "Yes, child, I believe she gave up the life she had in order to save yours. Would that I could call back the sands of time and fix this. I would do anything—"

"Can you?" Sulema asked in a rush. "Do anything? Can you heal her?" She bit her lip.

Wyvernus turned his head, and the Dragon regarded her. "I cannot put her back the way she was," he answered. "All the magic in the world, all the power a king may hold in his hands, cannot do that. I may be able to spare her life, though it is possible that I may fail or, at best, buy us no more than a little time in which to say goodbye."

"There is hope?"

"There is hope. But, Sulema... the cost will be high, for both of us."

"For both of us? I do not understand."

"Atulfah can do great things, Sulema, but as with all such things it demands sacrifice. If I demand so much of atulfah, so shall much be demanded of me. This will leave me weakened, and we are at the brink of war with the Daemon Emperor. If I attempt a healing of this magnitude, I will need you to take your place as my heir and lend me your strength in the days to come. Are you willing to do this thing? To leave your Zeera, the people you love, and all you have worked to achieve?"

His eyes burned into her, demanding truth.

"I am." Sulema clutched her mother's hand, willing her to live. There was blood caked beneath the broken fingernails. She would want warm water, and soft cloths, to clean away the blood and filth. "She gave her life so that I might live, and I will do no less for her."

"This will not absolve her of any crimes she may have committed. There have been disturbing rumors."

Sulema had heard the whispers, as well, but she refused to believe them. "Shadows and lies," Sulema insisted. "My mother does not treat with traitors and assassins. If she wants someone dead, she kills them herself."

Her father turned to face her, and she could see that he smiled. "Such a daughter we have made, my love. Such an heir you have brought to me." He removed Hafsa Azeina's hand from hers, and gently pushed her away. "Do not stand any closer than this," he warned her. "You may get burned."

The Dragon King stood at the head of Hafsa Azeina's bed and raised his arms high, tipping his golden-horned head back. The Baidun Daiel formed a circle about them and raised their arms as well. With their blood-red cloaks billowing about them, they looked like carrion birds gathered for the feast. Their faces were fixed on Ka Atu, and when he clenched his upraised hands, they arched their backs and went stiff all over as if he were a puppet master with his fists full of strings.

Then Ka Atu began to sing.

The voice that bellowed forth from that mask could not have been torn from a human throat, not from a thousand human throats. The Song of the Sun Dragon swelled forth like the desert at high tide, it filled the room with bright sun and dark moons and the piercing stare of starlight.

The air became thick and sorrowful, full of the slow, soft, lonely notes of the Dragon's Song, and Sulema fought to breathe. A single gasp escaped her lips. Akari Sun Dragon whipped his head about, seeking her.

His burning eyes lit upon Sulema's face, and the song shattered into a million shards of colored glass as Akari Sun Dragon claimed Sulema for his own.

Mind, body, and soul.

Three days later, by the pale light of the sister moons, Wyvernus made Sulema his heir, and named her the Heart of Atualon. He placed the shining coronet of Sa Atu upon her brow, and kissed her on both cheeks as the crowd chanted:

"Sa Atu!

"*Sa Atu!*

"SA ATU!"

With the wash of voices came a pale shadow of memory, like the notes of a faded lullaby, the smell of a garden far away and long lost to the wild. There had been sorrow, there had been song, but now there was only the Dragon.

When Ka Atu knelt at her feet, the crowd erupted in cheers and laughter, and there was not a dry eye in the kingdom.

MIST AND SHADOW

I f she had known that the afterlife was so like Shehannam, Hafsa Azeina would not have bothered dying. The mist that swirled about her feet, the shadowed sky overhead, even the flat nothing-smell of the air was the same. She sighed, and set foot upon the path that appeared before her, shining softly in the—

She froze, and looked down at her feet.

Her *feet*.

Her feet were feet, and her hands were hands. She clutched the staff she had held in life, and her wizard-locked hair was heavy and warm against her back. No claws, no fur... she tested her teeth with the tip of her tongue... no fangs.

Well, *that* was interesting.

The path split before her. One way led down and to the left, a dark road and choked with blackthorn. The other rose up and to the right, a wide and shining path, gently sloped and neatly paved.

I know this story, she thought, *I know the way.*

Then she thought, *to Yosh with it. I am tired of pain. Life was hard. Let my death be easy.* So she turned right and strolled up the path, taking her time, breathing deeply out of habit if not need, and thinking that the air should smell of roses. Would it be so much to wish for roses? It was not as if planting them would harm anything here, and a hint of color would be welcome. She smiled at the thought.

She had been walking for hours, for days perhaps, or had she only taken a handful of steps? She could not have said for sure, and she did not particularly care. The road had ended, and she had come to a small hill with two doors set into the stone. One was twisted, misshapen, and looked as if it had warped in the heat of a hellish fire. The other was round and green, and looked as if it might lead somewhere pleasant.

I know this story, too, she thought.

But she was tired of fighting monsters, tired of trials and travails, and so she pushed against the green door and it swung easily before her. On the other side she could see a hall with a wooden floor, brightly lit and welcoming.

"I see you have grown wiser." The voice was near her feet. "It took you long enough."

Hafsa Azeina nearly dropped her staff. A small cat sat on the path between her and the door, sleek and black with enormous tufted ears set above a delicate face. Those eyes, more familiar to her than her own and more beloved, regarded her with bright and emerald amusement.

"No," she whispered. "No. I killed you."

"As a matter of fact, you killed yourself," the cat said, and lifted one tiny paw so that she could clean between her toes with a bright pink tongue. "But I forgive you."

"Basta—"

"You have chosen your path," the cat interrupted. "Best get on with it. He is waiting for you." Before Hafsa Azeina could ask any more questions, Basta faded away. The long green eyes were last to go and winked at her in the gloom like a pair of lost stars.

She had forgotten how annoying that could be.

I forgive you...

Hafsa Azeina shook her head, bemused, and stepped through the door. As she did so, she caught sight of her staff, and started so badly that she almost dropped it again. No longer black as charred bone, the wood had turned a soft gray-green with a silvery sheen, and in place of the hideous skull the carved and painted likeness of Basta's head winked at her with emerald-chip eyes.

If she had a heart, it would have broken. If she had tears, she would have wept. But she was dead, ash and dust, and had none of these things.

The door closed behind her as she walked down the hall, ducking her head and peering about for cobwebs. Her hand gripped the staff—not a source of shame, now, but of comfort. After she had been walking for some time the hall narrowed, the wooden floor gave way to cold, rough stone, and she found herself in a confusion of low tunnels.

Ah hah, she thought, *I knew that was too easy to be true.*

But she had chosen her path, and the way back was always shut in these stories, and besides, she was dead. So there was nothing for it but to push forward and make the best of things.

Down and down she went, deeper and deeper into the womb of the earth, or so it seemed to her, a lost and comforting place out of time, out of mind. The walls grew warm and close about her and she trailed her free hand over the rock, enjoying the feel of it, and she could not help but feel that she was loved in return.

Eventually the walls fell away and she stood at the mouth of a wide, round cavern. The walls were smooth and round as the inside of an egg, or a bubble trapped in glass for all time. The better part of it was filled with a lake, and this lake glowed with a million million lights, as if it held a distant sky turned upside down beneath the still water. Stepping-stones as wide as tables led to a small island.

There was a figure waiting for her there, or figures perhaps, but who or what they were, she could not have said.

I know this story, too, she thought. *This is the last trial before the end.*

It seemed to her that it would be good to get this over with, and to rest, so she lifted her staff and gathered up her robes and stepped upon the broad gray stones. They were good stepping-stones, too. They did not twist under her feet, or sink into the starlit waters, or reveal themselves to be the knobbed back of a sea-thing child or a row of skulls. They were stones, nothing more, and stayed just where they were.

As she set foot upon the island, the waiting figure turned and revealed itself to her, and Hafsa Azeina knew then where she was. She had come back to the beginning of things, after all.

"I know you," she whispered. "Nightmare Man."

"Do you?" A voice like rotting parchment growled at her. "Do you really? You know nothing, Princess of the Seven Isles." A dark light blazed from his robes, it crawled across his mask in a craze of black lightning, and filled his mouth with death. "And now you never will." He raised his great war hammer in both hands, and as he did so his robes slipped back along the ground and revealed everything.

The island's dull black rock had been broken away to expose an expanse of smooth scales the color of glass, of rainbows and waterfalls, the color of a hummingbird's wing. Blue and green beneath the surface, swirls and whorls of white tinged with seashell-pink, the heartbreaking beauty of a dragon could be mistaken for nothing else in any time or place.

Hafsa Azeina lunged forward and swung from the hips even as his dark hammer fell, even as her heart broke. Triumph burned in his face like bloody coals as the weapon arced down.

It met the swing of her new-souled staff.

And all was lost in a blinding light.

ACKNOWLEDGEMENTS

I would like to give a nod of thanks to…

My parents, who gave me life and then gave me a dog.

My first reader and best friend, Kristine Alden, without whom this book would not be here.

My awesome early readers, Martie and Bonnie, whose enthusiasm and encouragement were the fuel I needed to make it to THE END.

My rockstar agent, Mark Gottlieb of Trident Media, for taking a chance on an unknown author with a huge and rather weird story.

My Dark Editorial Overlord, Steve Saffel of Titan Books, Wielder of The Carrot and The Stick.

Nick Landau, Vivian Cheung, Paul Gill, Miranda Jewess, Ella Chappell, Lydia Gittins, Samantha Matthews, and Katharine Carroll of Titan Books, for believing in my story.

Alice Nightingale, for being my champion.

My high-school English teacher, Deane O'Dell, who against all odds kindled the love of literature in the heart of an ungrateful young barbarian.

ABOUT THE AUTHOR

Deborah A. Wolf was born in a barn and raised on wildlife refuges, which explains a lot. As a child, whether she was wandering down the beach of an otherwise deserted island or exploring the hidden secrets of bush Alaska with her faithful dog Sitka, she always had a book at hand. She opened the forbidden door, and set foot upon the tangled path, and never looked back.

She attended any college that couldn't outrun her and has accumulated a handful of degrees, the most recent of which is a Master of Science in Information Systems Management from Ferris State University. Among other gigs, she has worked as an underwater photographer, Arabic linguist, and grumbling wage slave. Throughout it all, Deborah has held onto one true and passionate love: the love of storytelling.

Deborah currently lives in northern Michigan with her kids (some of whom are grown and all of whom are exceptional), an assortment of dogs and horses, and one cat whom she suspects is possessed by a demon.

For more fantastic fiction, author events, competitions,
limited editions and more

VISIT OUR WEBSITE
titanbooks.com

LIKE US ON FACEBOOK
facebook.com/titanbooks

FOLLOW US ON TWITTER
@TitanBooks

EMAIL US
readerfeedback@titanemail.com